THE
HIDDEN
CHILD

BOOKS BY REBECCA GRIFFITHS

The Girl at My Door

Sweet Sacrifice

Cry Baby

A Place to Lie

The Primrose Path

THE
HIDDEN
CHILD

REBECCA GRIFFITHS

bookouture

Published by Bookouture in 2022

An imprint of Storyfire Ltd.
Carmelite House
50 Victoria Embankment
London EC4Y 0DZ

www.bookouture.com

ISBN: 978-1-80019-894-4
eBook ISBN: 978-1-80019-893-7

This book is a work of fiction. Whilst some characters and circumstances
portrayed by the author are based on real people and historical fact, references
to real people, events, establishments, organizations or locales are intended
only to provide a sense of authenticity and are used fictitiously. All other
characters and all incidents and dialogue are drawn from the author's
imagination and are not to be construed as real.

For Beverley Hale... wherever you may be.

AUTHOR'S NOTE

This book is a work of fiction, and while it refers to actual people, places and controversial events in history, the story and characters woven around them have been invented for the purpose of the narrative.

Hell is empty... all the devils are here.

Shakespeare, *The Tempest,* Act 1, Scene 2

HUNT FOR VICTIMS ON
SADDLEWORTH MOOR

Further murder victims are expected to be found buried on the desolate Pennine moors where the body of a young girl was discovered two days ago. Police chiefs are to re-examine their files on eight people – four of them children – who have disappeared from the Manchester area over the past three years.

Manchester Evening News, October 18, 1965

PROLOGUE

Friday, 18 July 1941

Black Fell Farm, Saddleworth Moor, West Riding of Yorkshire

It had gone midnight, and the oil lamp Ronald lit in the barn cast soft, leaping shadows against the walls. The farmhouse on the opposite side of the yard was in darkness. His mother had retired to bed some time before. The clanking of the cattle grid galvanised him into action, and he unlocked the gun cabinet and took out his father's prized Purdey. Stared at the cartridges in his hand. The same panic that had assaulted him when his mother's cancer was diagnosed assaulted him now, and he knew he would remember this moment for the rest of his life: the smell of the hay gathered in from the fields that morning; the tightening skin on his sunburnt cheeks; the shire horses breathing in the dark... the pair of black-and-white sheepdogs who did not move, even when they heard the dry crackle of tyres hit the grit in the yard. They feared his father, Jacob Cappleman, as much as he did.

. . .

Then his father was there. Drunk and swaying on the threshold. Lit by the moon and looking for trouble, he wiped his wet mouth with a meaty fist. Dressed in his usual garb for a night down the Bull, his tweed waistcoat stretched over his impressive girth, the gold links of his precious fob watch hanging like a mayoral chain. The watch, inscribed with his name and awarded to him by the Lancashire Farming Union for services to king and country during the Great War, was worth more to Jacob Cappleman than the lives of his wife and sons.

'Been drinking profits away as usual?' Ronald said, emboldened by the loaded shotgun he held behind his back.

'*What?* Who are you to criticise me? Carryin' on with the woman your brother's betrothed to.' His father, thumbs jammed into his waistcoat pockets, stood like a QC at the Old Bailey. 'You should've been the one to go to war, not Tommy. Wouldn't have lost no sleep about you bein' blasted to kingdom come.'

'He hates you; you do know that?'

'What you bletherin' about?' His father leant against the barn door to steady himself.

'Tom. He hates you. Ever since you sold his dog.'

'*Ach.* Give over, you big jessie.' A fierce shake of the head. But Ronald could tell he'd rattled him, that the claim was not easily dismissed, and this pleased him. 'You're talkin' rot. And if that's all you've got for me to keep me mouth shut, then you're wastin' your breath. If your mother's happy to keep your filthy secret then shame on her, but you'll not silence me.' He dispensed the threat with a slow, self-righteous grin. 'Our Tommy's comin' home on leave tomorrow, so rest assured I'll be fillin' him in on what you and that jezebel have bin up to while he's bin fightin' Germans.'

Ronald refused to respond. Half-hidden in shadow, the gun

at his back – if his father came for him, he'd have him. God help him, he would.

'What's up with you? Cat got your tongue?' His father stood as if at the end of a long tunnel, a tiny figure with arms outstretched. The breeze ruffling his thick grey hair.

'Nowt up with me.' It felt good to confuse this man. Jacob Cappleman, always the one in control, had been brutalising Ronald and his brother since they could crawl. It was a miracle they hadn't died at his hands as children.

'Then why so calm all of a sudden?' His father lurched towards him and grabbed the flesh of Ronald's sunburnt cheek. Close to the scar that resulted from a violent thrashing he'd given him when he was nine. 'Tell me, go on.' His father squeezed. 'What you cookin' up?'

'Nowt to tell.' Ronald shook him off, the gun still clasped behind him. 'I don't care no more. You can say what you bloody well want.'

'*Don't care?* You don't fool me.' A sneer. 'Anyway, I'm off to me bed,' he announced after a quick squint at his fob watch.

Ronald didn't know when he decided not to shoot him, that the mess it would make would be too much. But when he swung the Purdey by the barrel and hit him with the full force of the buttstock, his father let go of a groan and clutched his head, wobbled, but didn't fall. Ronald struck him again with desperation and boldness because he could not see his face. This time, Jacob Cappleman crumpled softly to his knees and fell forward, face-down into the darkness.

Ronald couldn't move, not even to lower his gun-holding arm. He felt the night air travel down from the moor and sweep over him, cooling his face. An upstairs lamp went on in the farmhouse. Shone out from its round window and spilled its feeble light into the moonlit yard. It brought him back to the present with a jolt. He would not have his mother involved in this. It didn't matter that he'd done this for her, too. The poor woman had suffered this man's cruelty all her married life. No one would argue that Jacob Cappleman was a brute. As a man with the strength of two, the knowledge of his potential to harm had spread its tendrils far into the community.

Once Ronald had returned the shotgun to its place of safety, he lifted Bramble's halter from its hook, slipped it on over her head and fastened the buckle.

'Come on, lass,' his whispered encouragement. Remembering in time to take a spade as he led the young mare out of the barn and into the yard.

Ronald couldn't believe how calm he was. Not a tremor betrayed him. Not even when he heaved his father's lifeless body up and onto the shire's back and set off under a pitiless seam of moonlight for the moor and the lightning tree. His thoughts full of those big black rocks above Hollin Brown Knoll and the grave he would dig there.

1

TWENTY-FOUR YEARS LATER

Saturday, 4 September 1965

Underwood Court, Hattersley, North-East Cheshire

The child sensed something was different about this Saturday morning, even before Fred arrived in his maroon Cortina. The flat smelled different. Of shampoo and nail polish. Her mother smelled different too; like the honeysuckle that grew by her gran's front door, except artificial. Radio Luxembourg was on and her mother was singing along with Elvis, who was telling the world he couldn't help falling in love. What the child would love would be to tell her to be quiet, but she wouldn't. If her mother was singing, it meant she was in a good mood, and good moods were rare.

Sunlight was something else that was rare. But there it was, falling in through the passageway window like a solid gold bar. She showed it to her Tiny Tears doll, then hopped over it and into the kitchen, glancing at Elvis' face in a poster fixed to the wall. He was usually the first to greet her, but not today. Today, along with her mother, there was someone else. A woman she'd been told to call Aunty Myra.

'Bloomin' 'eck!' The woman with the puffed-up white hair pulled on her cigarette. 'It looks like she's been dipped in blood.'

Flinching under the unwanted attention, the child peered down on herself. At her shabby red coat, red tights and scuffed shoes.

'Where've you been, Maggot?' Her mother had stopped singing. 'Fred'll be here soon.'

'My, she's grown, Connie.' Aunty Myra took another drag of her fag while her black-rimmed eyes roamed over the child. 'Quite the little lady.'

Her mouth went dry. Something in the woman's expression made her want to run and hide.

'How's me little buggerlugs?'

The child shrugged. She might have known Myra Hindley since her cradle, but it didn't mean she trusted her.

'Oi! Answer your Aunty Myra.' Her mother cuffed her around the head. 'Have some respect, you little sod.'

'Quiet, ain't she?' The observation, along with a string of smoke, was exhaled from the red-painted mouth.

'Oh, leave her be. Here—' Tea was poured from the pot with its blue wool cosy, the mad chinking of a spoon against china. 'I've done us a brew.'

The child looked past them to a box of cornflakes on the worktop and took a bowl from the rack on the drainer, her ear buzzing from the smack.

'That's it, Maggot. Get some cereal down your neck.' Her mother squinted at herself in the mirror. 'God knows when you'll be eating again.'

The statement, with its ominous ring, had the child wondering where Fred was taking them. But she didn't ask because it wouldn't be down the park for a go on the swings or to Belle Vue to see the new baby elephant or any of the fun places her gran used to take her. Her mother and Fred liked coffee bars and pubs, and she was just in the way. She put Tiny Tears down on the side with a clunk, arranged the frilly white bonnet and matching dress her gran had made to hide the doll's modesty, then tipped some cornflakes into the bowl. Since moving from her grandparents' house, there was never enough milk – never much of anything, really – and she needed to top her breakfast up from the tap.

'I know I've said, but I love your hair.'

'Ta, Connie.' Her mother's compliment triggered a satisfied wiggle from Aunty Myra, and the child watched her smooth the leopard-print dress over her broad hips. 'Ian likes it.' A smile that showed lipstick had come off on her teeth.

'D'you reckon I should bleach mine?' Her mother was brushing her long dark hair. Making it gleam like glass.

A shake of the blonde head as the cigarette was screwed out in the ashtray. 'It wouldn't suit, Connie.'

The child lifted a hand to the matted clump of curls she couldn't pull her fingers through and wondered why her hair never warranted the attention her mother gave her own. She supposed her mother's hair must be very special. Why else was Fred always burying his nose in it? Snuffling and grunting like Johnny Morris on *Animal Magic* when he was pretending to be a pig; only Fred wasn't pretending and wasn't the least funny. Fred did other things, too. Things that forced the child to clamp her hands over her ears when she lay in bed. Nights she could swear he was killing her mother from the pitch of her screams.

To rid herself of the unsettling thoughts, she looked out of the window that offered views of the estate beyond their fifth-floor tenement flat. The sky was a spooky cartoon blue. A colour that could have come straight out of her box of crayons. She smiled at this, but the smile vanished when she shifted her gaze to the purpose-built blocks, then down to where a gang of rough boys kicked a football between two parked cars. The child didn't like boys. She wasn't like her mother, who enjoyed the attention; enjoyed being whistled at.

'Can't you do owt quietly?' her mother snapped when the child scraped out what was left of her cereal. 'I always have to know you're there.'

Eyes downcast, she rinsed her empty bowl over the pile of dirty crockery. Then there was a movement beside her and with it, the whiff of a different perfume. Aunty Myra finished with her tea, placed her cup on the drainer. The child gawped at the blood-red lipstick left behind on its rim.

'Come here, buggerlugs.' The woman flung her arms out to her sides and wriggled her fingers. 'Give your Aunty Myra a cuddle.'

The hug was as unexpected as it was unwanted, and the child held her breath and waited for it to finish.

'How are you liking living here?'

The child didn't answer; the question wasn't for her.

'It's great.' Her mother was now applying lipstick. Digging it out with the handle of a teaspoon. 'Loads better away from Mam and Dad.'

'Bet you're missing having a babysitter on tap?'

'Well, yeah.' Her mother gave the child a black look. 'Can't pretend it's not a pain having to drag Maggot around with us.'

'Can't Fred run her over to Glossop?'

'No. Mam's a lot on, with Dad being so poorly.'

'Little buggerlugs would cheer her up. You'd like to see your gran, wouldn't you?'

The child responded with a vigorous nod.

'Leave it, Myra. Truth is, Mam and me had a bit of a falling-out. She were dead set against me moving here. I've not seen owt of them in ages.'

The child stared at the tide of grease on the sink. She missed her gran. Missed her cuddles and kindness. There was no kindness here. No one bothered with her unless it was to tell her off.

'Moby and Dave are moving here soon.' Aunty Myra bashed out another cigarette and lit up again.

'Maureen? Your sister? I thought they were coming to Wardle Brook to be near you.' Her mother was plucking her eyebrows: she was going to a lot of effort for Fred today.

'I tried sorting things, but nowt came of it. Ian's happy. He reckons it's bad enough sharing space with me gran.'

'How is Maureen? After what happened to the baby?' The radio was turned down, and the room went strangely quiet. Crowding with shadows.

'Oh, Connie, it's been hell. Poor wee mite.' Aunty Myra dabbed away sudden tears. 'Shit, me make-up's all smudged.' She fanned her face with her hand. 'You won't tell Ian?' The backcombed head drooped to rootle through her handbag for her compact. 'He hates any kind of emotion. Sees it as a weakness.'

'But Maureen's your sister; baby Angela were your niece?'

'Just don't let on. For me, yeah?' A glance at the clock. 'Is that the time? I'd better dash. Ian'll be waiting.'

'Off anywhere nice?'

'That'll be up to Neddy.'

'Who's he?'

'Ian. I meant, Ian.' A brittle laugh, the death of her baby niece forgotten. 'But hazarding a guess, I'd say the moors. He loves it up there.'

'Have fun.'

'We will,' Aunty Myra said as she flounced out in her tight dress and knee-high boots, lobbing her casual promise to 'Catch up again soon' over her shoulder like a bride's bouquet.

2

Saturday, 4 September 1965

Black Fell Farm, Saddleworth Moor, West Riding of Yorkshire

Ronald kicked off his boots and plunged headlong into the kitchen with its frying smells. His brother, Thomas, wrapped in an apron and standing at the stove, flicked his spatula at the tap, reminding him to wash his hands before he did anything else. This done, Ronald peered out through the leaded window. Saw birds rattle down from the hard blue sky. The glass was lumpy, distorting the view of the yard as he measured the tasks that lay ahead.

Slurping milky tea and feeling no need to engage with his brother who moved within a space he had barely stepped out of since returning from the war, Ronald looked around at the pair of deep shabby armchairs and the framed photographs of his prize-winning Herdwick sheep. The whorls in the wooden table that were as smooth as glass. The ironing board that was never put away. This was a setting that offered succour. The hub of the house. There to cater and comfort the robust family neither he nor Thomas had. And thinking this brought a scrape of longing in his heart.

A quick flick of hot fat over the eggs, and Thomas plated up. 'Here you go.' He pushed the breakfast, shiny with grease, over the table top towards him. 'Much on today?'

It was the same question he asked each morning, using a voice that only spoke of the mundane, of safe things. If their conversation did stray and pick at the hem of real life, it only panicked him. A quiet man, Thomas said little and demanded little. Aside from the grief of their mother, the brothers shared next to nothing, but they rubbed along well enough and Ronald couldn't blame Thomas for playing his cards close to his chest; as with so many men of their generation – and the previous one – his brother had parts of himself he didn't dare turn to the light.

'Aye.' Ronald answered in his usual way and pulled up a chair. Sat with his legs apart and ate the meal with no word of thanks. 'Aren't you having owt?'

'Maybe later.' Thomas buffed his reading glasses on a cotton handkerchief he had ironed into a square. 'Up with the lark, were you, Ron?'

'Aye,' he said, munching on a slice of toast.

'No rest for the wicked.'

Ronald had always done a tour of the land first thing, and checking all was well with his flock was as essential now as it ever was. Crook in hand and a sack of feed rattling on his back, it was an uphill climb for the first two miles. He followed the hedge of blowsy hawthorn that each May was heavy with blossom as white as his brother's hair. Too steep for the tractor and his last remaining shire horse, Ronald made the journey on foot. Other men his age couldn't do this. He congratulated himself, blood pumping, thigh muscles burning. It was all about conditioning. Memory was another muscle you could condition. Ronald had. He'd conditioned it to remember a version of events he had needed to tell the police to avoid the hangman's noose. Not that there was time to dwell on the past. At Black Fell Farm, he had five hundred acres and the bills to worry about; not things that happened twenty-four years ago and were best forgotten. Or best buried... deep.

What began as a sturdy track petered out into a path carved by generations of sheep in the blanket bog and, reaching the plateau, he squinted up at a sky made restless with swifts. By next week, these birds would have flown south of the Sahara, but for now, they were a pleasant sight, floating on the wind's silky threads, filling the air with their screams and dark-winged symmetry. As a boy, he used to think he could touch the clouds from up here and, surveying his dominion as a man of fifty-three, he needed no map or compass; what would be a feature-less expanse of moorland to most was as familiar to him as the lines on his palms.

He shielded his eyes from the sun as he appraised the tilt and pitch of the land that led down to the valley and the silver-skinned reservoir. Seeing his ewes grazing peacefully should have lifted his spirits, but it didn't. It made him uneasy. So much relied on the success of this year's lambs, but spring had been slow to show itself and the summer was almost over. Ronald picked his way through the reeds, his sheep blaring out behind him. He dropped the sack of feed and took out his broth-er's old army knife, slit the bag open. Within seconds his ewes had crowded around him, bleating and butting, the ripe smell of their lanolin-laced fleeces in his nostrils. As they fed, he moved among them. He only had his shepherd's crook today. No dogs. Bess and Meg, the Border collie pups kept back from Dilly's last litter, could still be too lively, and he was reluctant to ruffle the delicate balance of calm he'd nurtured in his flock.

Tricked by the bright sunshine, he'd left the house with only his tweed jacket on over his overalls. He should have known better because he could see, casting east to the clouds jostling the horizon, that rain was on its way again. He carried this rather gloomy thought as he strolled down to Shiny Brook, the finest of all the waterways that netted his land. Swelled by recent rain, it gathered the sunlight as it rushed over the rocks, and he crossed it without wetting his feet, passing alongside the lightning tree with the names he scored into its trunk all those years ago.

His and hers.

The memory of her blew through him like a December wind. How he asked her to sit with him and pass a little time. He never meant to touch her. But when she bent forward, her long dark hair parting like the pages of a book, he couldn't stop himself.

He left the stream behind and strode away in the opposite direction. Already, the slant of the sun had crossed the vast granite ridge of Hollin Brown Knoll and slid over the moor. His ewes had wandered off to graze again, and it was quiet enough for him to hear the flapping wings of a passing crow.

With a sudden urge to urinate, he tucked himself in behind a thatch of gorse, when out of nowhere came the startling sound of gunshot, splitting the silence like the blade of an axe. Around him, his ewes scattered. The panicky cries of the lambs, some of them almost as big as their mothers, quivered into the pearly light.

'What the blazes?' Rebuttoning his overalls, he pushed a nervous hand through his thick grey hair, making it stand up in tufts.

The moor fell away into silence again. The only sound was the wind through the reeds. Ronald, hesitant, doubted what he heard. But no, within seconds, another spurt of gunshot rang out. There was no mistaking it. With his jaw set in grim determination, he took off at speed in the direction he believed it to be coming from. Mounting the brow of another hillock, and using his hand as a visor, he looked into the distance, down to the winding A635 that wriggled over Saddleworth Moor. That turquoise Mini Traveller with its mock Tudor sides was there again. It was a car he'd seen parked in the layby on and off for some months. Then he was looking at them. The couple he had taken an instant dislike to, nestled within the remains of a drystone wall. Ronald had a gift for reading people and knew, the first time he laid eyes on them, they were a bad lot. He had named them Platinum and Sporran – her with her bleached-blonde hair and him with his Scottish accent – often stumbling across them or the rubbish they left behind around Hoe Grain or farther down, closer to the banks of Shiny Brook and his cherished lightning tree. Why, when they had the whole of the moor, did they choose to come here? They didn't deserve it and certainly didn't respect it. While he resented them using it as their play-ground, what concerned him was that their unwanted activity might inadvertently unearth his secret.

Usually, these two were stretched out on a picnic blanket with their dogs, guzzling booze and snapping out photographs of one another. But not today. Today, to his horror, instead of the usual Box Brownie slung around his neck, Sporran was wielding a revolver. Ronald ducked behind a large boulder before they could see him and watched the man, with his mean, weaselly face, and the woman, tall and mannish, swigging from beer bottles then lining the empties along what remained of a drystone wall. The pair were strangely overdressed. She in a tight animal-print dress with high leather boots, he in a suit and tie. Inappropriate clothes for a trip to the moor. These were no hikers.

'Good shot, Neddy!' the hard-faced blonde shouted. Brassy and butch, she wobbled around in her impractical footwear.

'Ye think so, do ye? I reckon you're to watch this, Hessy.' He glugged from a bottle of whisky.

The gun fired a further five shots before it was reloaded. Whenever the man hit his target, shattering a bottle, the woman shrieked in delight. They looked drunk and out of control, and they didn't belong here.

'Chop, chop, Hessy. Line 'em up.' Sporran, repeatedly shoving away the flap of brown hair that flopped into his eyes, slurred his words. 'Quick, I'm on a roll.'

The man shook off his jacket and handed it to his girlfriend. Folding back his shirtsleeves, he showed off a set of sinewy forearms. Veal-white and sun-starved. They were the arms of a man who spent his days working at a desk.

The revolver was fired again and bottles exploded into the air, scattering shards of brown glass that flashed in the sun. Fearing for his treasured livestock and the damage this could do, Ronald's anger bubbled in his throat... *blasted townies, coming here, wrecking my livelihood, tainting this beautiful place...* until he could no longer hold it in. He abandoned the relative safety of the boulder and marched up to them, brandishing his crook.

'Hey, you!' He propelled his voice ahead of himself. 'What the hell d'you think you're playing at?'

Sporran spun to face him in his shiny leather uppers. 'Is he talkin' to us, Hessy?'

The man had a lean and reckless look. A look that frightened Ronald.

'Suppose he must be.' Hands on hips and thrusting out her pelvis, the woman made a show of checking the empty moorland. 'What with there being no one else for miles.' A wicked gleam in her eye.

'Do ye have some kinda problem, Grandad?'

'I asked you what you're playing at?' Ronald took another step closer. 'There's livestock around here. My precious livestock. You can't be mucking around with firearms.'

'I wouldnae be threatening a man like me, if I were ye.'

The sun slid behind a mob of storm clouds and the sky darkened.

'You're frightening my ewes.' Ronald was wishing he'd stayed out of sight. Although gangly and pasty-faced, the man was wild-eyed and had a gun in his hand.

'Is that right?' Sporran edged closer. Ronald, helpless, his heart thrashing like a trapped bird behind his ribs, watched the handgun being raised and aimed at him. 'Down on ye knees, Grandad.'

'W-w-what?' Terrified, Ronald swung his head in panic. The blonde was right. There was no one around. He was on his own with this pair of maniacs. He was at their mercy. 'You can't go pointing guns at people. You could get arrested.'

'Do ye think I care? I said get down! On ye knees, pal. Now!'

Ronald stood quite still. Would he die quickly or slowly? That was a question for these two to decide. There was nothing he could do to influence it.

The man jabbed the barrel of the revolver into Ronald's stomach.

'Are ye deaf? I said, get down on ye fuckin' knees.'

The woman pushed Ronald's legs from behind and jerked him off his feet. 'Go on, Neddy. Put a hole in him.'

Strange he should fear her more. But when he looked up and into the pitiless void in those cruel eyes she had dug out of her face with thick black kohl, he knew he was done for.

'Go on, do it. Do it for me, Neddy. We could bury him on the moor. Who'd know?' She opened her mouth and cackled like a magpie.

'D'ye want me to? D'ye think I should, Hessy?'

With Sporran's breath on his cheek and his dark shape looming over him, Ronald, on his knees, stared at the man's belt buckle. The evil insignia of the SS at eye level.

Was this the last thing he was going to see on earth? His eyes rolled to the left as if by some miracle there might be someone to save him. But of course no one was.

Then the steel muzzle was rammed against Ronald's temple. He heard the click as the gun was cocked. With the man's finger poised on the trigger, he couldn't think past the whooshing in his ears. A sound that grew near to deafening as the moor seemed to spin and slow around him. Sweat broke out across his back, his forehead. A bead of sweat ran down his cheek. He scrubbed it away with a frantic fist.

Ronald closed his eyes.

Like this, he thought; he was going to die like this?

On the moor, where no one would find him.

Then, straggling thoughts of Thomas and how he might never see him again, another bead of sweat slid down his face and mixed with the rain that had begun to fall.

3

Waggon and Horses, Hyde Road, Gorton, Manchester

A rumpus of clouds had replaced the sun by the time they reached the pub and rain peppered the windscreen. Fred needed to drive his Cortina around the car park three times before he found a space. When he did, he nosed into it, turned off the windscreen wipers and cut the engine.

'What! You are joking?' He pointed at the turquoise Mini Traveller parked in the opposite bay. 'That's Myra's motor. You never said those two were gonna be here.'

'I didn't know. She told me they were going to the moor.'

'Don't lie, Con. You fixed this up, didn't you?' His accusation floated between them.

'I didn't. I swear. They've probably come here because the weather's turned nasty.' Connie, all wriggly and giggly in her short-belted raincoat, shoved her boyfriend's hands away. 'Stop it, Fred... not in front of Maggot,' she hissed, close to his sandy-coloured moustache. But because she didn't really mean it, his fingers wandered up and under the hem of her coat again.

'Let's shag off somewhere else before they see us. Last thing I want is to spend me afternoon off with that long-legged weirdo.'

'Come on, it'll be nice. I've been dying to meet Ian properly. Myra's so secretive about him.' A fleeting thought of the stand-offish Scot who turned up in Gorton out of nowhere four years ago.

'Pretentious bastard.' Fred pulled back his hand and snatched the keys from the ignition. 'I know all I wanna know about Mr Och-Aye.'

'Right then, Maggot. You're to stay here. Reckon you can manage that?' Connie reached into the back of the car and smacked her daughter's legs to get her attention. 'God in heaven, would it kill you to smile now and again?' She didn't know why her daughter had the power to enrage her the way she did. The kid barely spoke a word and mostly stayed out of her way. But something in that look: accusing, as if Connie had failed her expectations; it brought out the worst in her. 'You're not to go spoiling things for me and Fred, d'you hear, Maggot? We're going to enjoy today, if it kills us.'

'Don't call her that, Connie, love.' Fred, defending the child as usual, took a metal comb from his pocket to marshal his sandy hair into an immaculate quiff. 'She's not a bad kid.'

'I'll thank you to keep your nib out. She's nowt to do with you,' Connie warned him before applying a fresh coat of lippy.

'I'm just saying.' Fred looked hurt. 'She understands more than she lets on, don't you, kiddo?' He winked at the child in the slice of driving mirror. 'Understands her mam needs time to herself. We'll bring you lemonade and crisps in a bit.' His promise slid beneath the strata of cigarette smoke and into the back seats where the child sat hugging her doll. 'Get a shift on, Connie. I'm spittin' feathers here.' He pocketed the comb and grabbed his tobacco tin from the dashboard.

There was more giggling and touching before they pushed

out into the hammering rain. Connie, tottering through the puddles in her white stilettos, Fred in his drainpipe jeans and winkle-pickers, holding his jacket over their heads to shelter them. Neither turned to check the child was happy with the arrangement; they were too busy with themselves to care. And alone in the hush, breathing back the heady mix of cigarette smoke, perfume and aftershave, she slumped against the seats and pushed her doll's plastic face, framed in its frilly white bonnet, to the window for her to see the high black-and-white sides of the pub and the sky that had darkened like a stain.

Hip to hip, Connie and Fred stepped into the raucous sounds of laughter and the thick smell of ale and Woodbines.

'They're definitely here, then.' Fred groaned, a hand to his bootlace tie.

'And they've seen us.' Connie raised an arm to wave as she took in the pub's low-beamed ceiling and the roaring welcome of a log fire. 'We can't ignore them.'

'Can I at least get us a drink, first?'

'If you want. I'll see you over there.' Connie, ever careful not to upset her old school friend, crossed the carpet towards them.

'Twice in one day.' Myra's greeting sounded more like a reprimand. 'You never said you were coming here.'

'Hi, Ian.'

'How ye daein'?' Ian didn't look pleased to see her either.

'I didn't know 'til Fred told me. But, *erm*,' Connie giggled, sensitive to their conjoined hostility, 'I thought you were going to the moor?'

'We did.' Myra, done up to the nines, her lacquered hair an immaculate white cloud, swapped secret smiles with Ian. It gave Connie the impression they'd been up to no good. 'But it started to tip down, so we came here for a drink on our way home.'

A drink? They look half-sloshed.

When Myra crossed her legs, Connie noticed there was mud on her boots. Funny choice of footwear, never mind outfit, for a walk on the moor. Not that Myra needed an excuse to dress up. Having secured a secretarial post at Millward's, she was a woman who could afford to spend money on herself. Unlike Connie, with her part-time factory job that paid a pittance, she didn't have a seven-year-old kid dragging her down. Going by their different upbringings and starts in life, everyone had expected it to be Connie who would achieve more. But it was Myra who wore the smart clothes and had her hair done regularly and had found herself an older, more sophisticated man who seemed intellectually set apart from the average Gorton bloke.

'Sit here, Con.' Myra patted the settee and Connie, ignoring the look Fred doled out along with a glass of Cherry B, sat beside her friend.

'Dinnae stand there hovering, pal.' Ian Brady, wearing the kind of suit her father would wear, beckoned Fred over. 'Ye making the place look untidy.'

Fred pulled up an armchair and, after what looked like a fortifying pull on his pint, put the dimpled glass down on the table.

This was a handsome old coaching inn and, lost to the dark oak beams and the gleaming brasses, Connie's mind drifted from the talk that was led by Brady, who only seemed to warm up when he was spouting off about politics. Thin-lipped and mean-eyed, he took control of the conversation while nursing a beer, holding it in both hands as if it was too heavy to lift. It made him look wimpish. The talk about the injustices of the working classes and the uneven distribution of wealth wasn't a topic Connie felt able to join in with, so she observed Ian instead. How his spittle showered the table when he talked, his wet and rather sloppy mouth moving ten to the dozen. That self-assured way he had of stretching his long legs out in front of him made her skin prickle. Legs he didn't think to move even when Connie got up to visit the lavatory, making her struggle over them, which she thought was weird.

When she returned, Ian and Fred had gone to the bar that was still busy with drinkers.

'So,' she began as soon as she'd plonked down next to Myra. 'You two getting married soon, or what?'

'*Gerroff.* Live in excruciating moderation and boredom 'til death us do part?'

'You what?' Connie didn't recognise Myra's language; she certainly never used such fancy words before Ian Brady came along.

'Me and Ian have a very good understanding that's far superior to married couples'.'

Connie thought of what she knew of Myra's parents: the dreary domestic set-up, the violent rows; a relationship not unlike her own parents'.

'Ian's very cultured. He loves classical music and reads proper literature. He's expanding my mind with all sorts.' Myra delivered the insight with a small smile.

'I'm sure he is.' *A snooty-looking oddball, more like.*

Connie continued to sneak sidelong glances at her friend's figure-hugging dress that finished halfway down her thighs. She certainly knew how to make the best of what she had by accentuating her good points and camouflaging the bad: a beaked nose and broad bottom. Connie consoled herself that she was prettier than Myra, that Myra was too mannish to be called pretty. Not that her supposed looks had got her anywhere – apart from pregnant, with no husband – and it made her a little resentful.

'I love your boots.'

'Neddy calls them me Nazi boots.' Myra, all pleased with herself.

'Why d'you call him that?'

A shrug. 'He calls me Hessy.'

'Hessy?'

'It's a nickname. A German thing. Ian loves owt German.'

'You are joking? My dad fought to rid us of them.' Connie clocked the look on Myra's face and, with a sharp intake of breath, changed the subject. 'Anyway, you always look great,' she said brightly. 'Where d'you get your clothes? I can't find stuff like that in the shops I go to.'

'Ashton Market. Knockdown prices, if you know where to look. I'll show you if you like? Get you kitted out properly.'

'Would you?' Connie flicked her hair off her shoulders. She had thought, having made such a great effort with her appearance, she looked just right for today's excursion and it hurt that Myra didn't think so. 'I've never been there. Didn't that little kiddie go missing from there?'

'What kiddie?'

'Getting on for two years ago. I remember because it were round the time President Kennedy were shot. What were his name?' It was on the tip of her tongue. 'Yeah, that's right... Kilbride. Yeah, that's it. John Kilbride.'

'So what if it were? It's nowt to do with me.'

'I know, I were just saying.'

An awkward silence ensued and Connie was glad when Fred and Ian were back at the table with their drinks and their talk swerved to other things.

'I heard ye've a criminal record.' Ian's question, fired off into the room, startled Connie. But it wasn't for her. 'Why dinnae ye tell me about that?'

'Why d'you wanna know?' Fred spluttered into his beer. 'It's years ago.'

'Let's just say I'm interested. Been in a spot of bother with the law ma'self, if you catch my drift.' Ian winked at him.

'It weren't owt.' Fred blushed. 'I were caught nicking electrical goods. I were only fourteen. Had to do a month in Borstal.'

'Store-breaking, eh? Did a wee stint in Borstal ma'self. I look on it as a kinda criminal apprenticeship.'

Connie thought Ian's eyes looked as dead as those of the fish she'd seen at the fishmonger's and kept one ear on the men's conversation while chatting to Myra. A stiletto of smoke rose from the ashtray, and time passed and drinks were drunk. The tipsier Connie became, the harder it was to listen to Ian's exhaustive philosophising. The endless drone of his voice buzzed like a swarm of flies, making it difficult to concentrate on what Myra was saying.

'Cor, he likes to intellectualise, don't he?' Connie said, watching the rain sluicing the pub windows. She thought everything Ian said had menacing undertones, but supposed his harsh Glaswegian accent didn't help. 'Reckons he's a right cut above the rest of us.'

'He likes to provoke and shock. To challenge the status quo.' Myra calmly smoking a cigarette. 'Nowt wrong with shunning the norm, Connie. Might benefit you to go against the tide and push boundaries of common acceptance now and again.'

'Get you!' she sniggered. 'You sound as bad as him.'

'I'm sorry if it upsets you that I'm bettering meself.'

Fred cocked a thumb at the stumpy bar billiards table in the corner. 'Fancy a game, Ian?'

'Bloody hate games,' he sneered before twisting his attention to Connie. 'Myra tells me ye work in a factory? Dinnae ye ever wanna do more with yeself?' The look was expressionless.

Astounded by his rudeness, she almost choked on her Cherry B. 'I suppose I could have, if I hadn't saddled myself with a kid when I were fifteen... I wanted to be a singer. Someone said I looked a bit like that Sandie Shaw.'

'Shoulda kept ye legs together, then.' The look had mutated to something nasty. 'Anyway, where's that bonnie wee bairn of yours today?'

'In the car.'

'Not very nice for the poor wee soul.'

'She's all right. She's used to it.' Connie, sensing she was under attack, ducked beneath her fringe. 'She's got her dolly to play with.' She knew that to say this was ridiculous, even before Ian's burst of spiked laughter.

'Why don't you bring her inside?' Myra shifted beside her.

'Kids aren't allowed. It won't kill her for an hour or so.'

'Not much of a mother, are ye?' Ian leant forward over his bony knees to stub out his fag. His eyes fixed on Connie. 'I thought ma mother were shite, but ye take the bloody pish.'

'I have to have time to myself.'

'Ye talk like she's some kinda *incon-ven-ience*.' The word, stretched out, stung like a slap. 'Dinnae ye worry someone might take her?'

'You what?' She squirmed; his gaze skewering down to the guilty core of her. 'Why would anyone do that?'

'Aye, what if ye went back to the car, and she wasnae there?' At this, Ian seized the arms of the chair and staggered upright. Abrupt. It was as if he'd suddenly switched off. 'We're going, Hessy.' He whistled to Myra as if she was a dog.

'*Jawohl, liebling.*' Myra leapt to her feet and clicked her heels. 'We've to scoot off now, but I reckon you two should come over one night.' She smoothed her dress over her hips. 'What d'you say, Neddy?'

Not a flicker from Ian Brady's pinched, unsmiling face.

'You can show Fred some of your books. Educate him.' The pair exchanged sly glances. 'Right, ta-rah, buggerlugs.' Myra bent down to give Connie a peck on the cheek and Fred a look that could kill.

4

Black Fell Farm, Saddleworth Moor, West Riding of Yorkshire

A curtain of rain swept eastwards and settled over the moor like a damp grey blanket. It crackled against the rocks and cold droplets slid down inside his collar. Ronald was oblivious to it. He was too busy tracking the progress of the Mini Traveller's turquoise roof along the moorland road, not daring to believe he was safe until it disappeared from view. When it had, he suddenly grew weak, as if his body had been drained of blood. He stumbled backwards and flopped down, drunk with fatigue, onto a mound of stones. Only then did he become conscious of the rain that, steadily falling for some time, had soaked his tweed jacket through to the lining.

He was perspiring. Its chilliness prickled over his skin. With his backside numb against the stones and his limbs heavy, he sat with his head between his knees to quell the rise of nausea. But when he felt the hot spread of urine between his legs, he burst into tears. His mouth a wide hole as he howled through the rain that streamed over him. He could still feel the ghost of the gun's steel muzzle pressed to his temple. Like a cold tattoo, it was there when he closed his eyes, along with that monster's mad stare when he'd crouched to push his face into Ronald's, with his finger poised on the trigger. And swirling around with these terrifying images, was the remembered voice of that woman urging him to: 'Do it... Put a hole in him, Neddy.'

Ronald thought of how close he'd come to death, and how he'd never been so frightened. The looks on their faces, the pleasure it had given them. The glee. They were evil... real evil. It wasn't as if Ronald was unfamiliar with violence; his father had brought him up on it, albeit a more frenzied kind. What he'd just undergone was different. It was visceral. It had been practised and administered by people who seemed comfortable with killing.

'Breathe... just breathe,' he mumbled. 'You're safe.' His words, rumbling and low, skidded into one another as he tried to convince the part of him that feared they might have changed their minds and were coming back to finish him.

The minutes rolled by and his heart rate slowed. His fear and shock receded, replaced by the sweet scuttle of birdsong. He lifted his gaze and was thankful to see his sheep were contentedly grazing. Soothed by this, he reached for his crook, his wet hand sliding over the glassy patina that had worn into the handle. On his feet, his legs unsteady, Ronald turned his back to the melancholy heights of Hollin Brown Knoll that were barely distinguishable through the weather, and pushed against the wind that seemed to have a shape to it. Needles of rain stung his face as he pinpointed the curve of land that eventually dipped down to Shiny Brook. Gradually, his strides became fluid, and before long he found his rhythm. But at the sight of the lightning tree, his defences crumbled again and, dropping his crook, he pressed his palms against its charred trunk and fought back further tears while his fingers followed the grooves of each letter he had carved there. PAMELA + RONALD.

Thinking they had meant something to the world. It was as if time had stood still in this place, and even now, he had the sense that, were he to turn quickly, he would find her standing beside him, her long dark hair tugged off her face by the wind, her smile lighting him up inside. He pressed his chest to the bark of the tree, to the curl and swirl of her name in the same way he had once done to her. Her name that, as well as into the tree, was etched on his heart.

Was it his imagination or were the skies blue back then? Time with her had seemed like an endless summer until the news came that his brother was due home on leave and he had to give her up... give her back. He had to stop torturing himself. The past was a country that was lost to him, and he needed to pack it off to the land of missed opportunities. Because he hadn't wanted to die today. When that gun had been forced against his head, it proved to him that life was precious, even without her.

Ronald scrubbed a hand across his face. Felt his scar and imagined it purple with cold. The scar his father gave him to remember him by that ran down past his left eye to his cheek-bone. When he let his hand fall to his side, he bent to retrieve his crook and saw something the rain had given up to the surface of the peat. Pale and alien, it caught his attention. Curious, he let his troubles drop away and stooped to retrieve it.

Lighter than stone, he teased it free of its peaty cradle and brought it into the light. Scraped out the shale and earth that was wedged inside with his fingers.

'How strange.' His voice competed with the rushing rain. 'What's this doing out here in the middle of nowhere?'

5

Waggon and Horses, Hyde Road, Gorton, Manchester

The atmosphere shifted when Myra and Ian left, and Connie and Fred relaxed into it.

'Were it summat we said, d'you think?' Fred yawned into his fist.

'Something *he* said, more like. D'you hear him?' Connie finished her drink and banged the empty glass down on the table. 'What the hell were that about? Being all aggressive? I were only trying to be friendly. You could've stuck up for me.' She picked up Myra's tumbler, sipped at what had been left in her rush to get away.

'You handled him fine on your own.' Fred joined her in the dip of the settee. 'Hard work, though. I'm glad they've gone.'

'*Huh.* From where I were sitting, you were having a fine old time.'

'Don't be like that, Con.' He was nuzzling her hair. His breath on her skin gave her goosebumps. It was impossible to stay cross with him for long. 'I thought you wanted me to make an effort? And I suppose the bloke's interesting enough.'

Connie shoved him away and searched his face. 'You are joking? What about all that Nazi stuff, you can't have liked that?'

'What Nazi stuff?'

'You heard him. It's why he likes Myra – her blonde hair. Aryan race is superior, according to him.'

'But he ain't blond.'

'Neither were bloody Hitler, but it didn't stop him.'

Fred took out his tobacco tin and rolled a cigarette. 'You've got to give it to him. He's dead clever.'

'Manipulative, more like.'

'He's loads of books he wants to lend me.'

'Sounds like you've fallen right under his spell.'

'Hardly.' He smoked his roll-up. 'I still reckon he's a nerdy weirdo. D'you see that suit he had on? Bloke dresses like me old man.' Fred, inadvertently echoing what she'd already thought, reached for his pint and finished it in one gulp. 'Who wears trousers with bloody turn-ups?' They laughed. 'Want another round?'

'Yeah, go on.'

Fred carried their empties to the bar, returning minutes later with their drinks along with a bottle of lemonade and a bag of crisps. 'I'll just take these out to the kiddie.'

'No, stay here. We'll go in a minute. How often do we get to spend proper time together?' When he sat down again, she snuggled into him. 'This is nice. Gi's a kiss.'

'It's Myra I don't like,' Fred said when he pulled away. 'Hoity-toity bitch, who does she think she is? She's like a black cloud on a sunny day. I don't envy Dave marrying into that fuck-up of a family. D'you see the look she give me? And what's with the warpaint and clingy clothes?'

'She wants to take me to Ashton Market and get me kitted out.'

'No way, Con. She looks tarty.' Fred exhaled a tail of smoke. 'I'd hate you going about dressed like her. Blokes looking at you for all the wrong reasons.'

'You should've seen what Myra were like before she bleached her hair. You wouldn't have looked twice.' Connie recalled the shock of it: her lank-haired school friend, transformed into a slinky, candyfloss blonde. For the first time Myra had a glimpse of the power a sexually attractive woman could wield and she loved it. Much to Connie's chagrin. 'Mam said it made her look sluttish and if I ever pulled a stunt like that I'd be out on the street.'

'Good, 'cos you're lovely as you are.' Fred flicked ash off his trousers.

Secretly pleased, she kissed his cheek, the edges of his moustache tickling her. Her mother might have said Myra looked cheap, but men were appreciative and she was causing more of a stir than Connie these days.

'How did those two get together, anyway?' Fred stubbed out his fag. 'Don't seem to have owt in common. Apart from being up their own arses.'

'Daft about their dogs.'

'That ain't enough. Never once seen him put his arm round her.' Fred cuddled Connie and buried his nose in her hair again. 'He don't even speak to her with any affection.'

'It's obvious she dotes on Ian, but she's not dominated by him. She's a hell of a strong personality. I've seen how she is with her father. Once, when her dad hit her mother, Myra set about him with the poker. Beat him to a pulp. I can't imagine any bloke getting one over on her.'

'I heard she fights like a man.' Fred raised his eyebrows. 'I dunno why you're friends with her.'

'I've known her years. She were fun when we were kids.'

'I'll take your word for it.'

'We sort of lost touch when I got pregnant with Maggot. It's only over the last year we've got friendly again.'

Fred swallowed the last of his beer and put his baccy tin away. 'We'd better go and check on the kid.'

'Stop fussing. She'll be fine.'

'But it's been ages, Con. It's nearly three, they'll be chucking us out any minute.' He stood up, jangled his keys in his pocket. 'Call in the offie on the way back? Carry on drinking at the flat?'

The suggestion was enough to propel Connie into action and, buttoning her raincoat, she linked an arm through Fred's and they walked out into the rain to find the Cortina marooned in a near-empty car park.

'Quick, Fred. Open up.' She hopped from foot to foot. Hitting the fresh air, she realised how drunk she was. 'I'm getting drenched.'

'It is open. I couldn't lock the kid in, could I?'

Inside the car, giggling and kissing, absorbed in themselves, they leant in close to light each other's fags. Fred started the car to put the radio on and demist the windscreen.

'I love the Kinks,' Connie cooed, squirming around on the black vinyl seats. 'Turn it up... *all day, and all of the night...*' She knew she had a good voice and belted it out.

Fred put his fag down in the car's ashtray and thrust a hand under the hem of her dress. She purred and, flinging her head back, let his fingers probe the warm softness on the inside of her thighs. She took his other hand and guided it down inside her bra. They kissed, tongue on tongue and, writhing about, seats squeaking, Connie could barely contain herself.

'Shit, Con.' Fred, coming up for air. 'We can't do this. Not in front of the kiddie.'

'You started it.' She grinned, reaching across the gearstick to squeeze the bulge in his crotch.

'Fair enough.' He licked his lips and repositioned himself behind the wheel. 'But let's get back, yeah? Be nicer at yours.'

Connie bent down into the footwell to retrieve the bottle of pop and crisps from her handbag. 'Here you go, Maggot. Look what we got you. Don't you be making crumbs on Fred's nice seats.' She swivelled to pass them to her daughter as Fred pushed his foot to the accelerator. 'Shit! Oh, my God!' Her hand flew to her mouth. 'Oh, my God!'

'What?' Fred slammed on the brake. 'What's the matter?'

'Where is she? Oh, my God!' Connie shrieked through her fingers. 'Where's Maggot?'

'What?'

'She's gone, Fred... she's gone. Maggot's gone.'

6

Black Fell Farm, Saddleworth Moor, West Riding of Yorkshire

What a strange thing to find. How long had it been there? A year or two, he guessed. Ronald frowned and looked at the shoe that just about fit into his hand. This was a party shoe, the kind of thing a teenage girl would wear. Pamela had owned a pair like this to go dancing down the Plaza Ballroom. It unnerved him, the discovery so unexpected and incongruous to the terrain. He shivered. From the cold and wet? Maybe. Although the chill he felt was more like... what was that old saying? *Aye, that's it —someone walking over your grave.*

Lashed by the rain, he washed the shoe in the brook. Held it against the rush of water to clean the earth away. The pink leather was mostly rotted, but using his fingernail to lift the length of the strap and the rusted buckle, he could tell it was of good quality. Turning it over to inspect the sole, he saw the heel had worn down more on one side than the other and pushed his fingers inside to feel the shallow indentations the owner's toes had made. Intimate things, shoes. It was as if he was waking a ghost, trespassing on something hallowed and, repelled by the idea, he jerked his fingers away. He didn't know why, but now he'd found this small, delicate relic of an unknown person's life he couldn't discard it. And gently, with care, he pushed it deep inside his wet jacket pocket to carry home with him.

The rain had eased by the time he reached the timber gate that led onto the farm's land, and he was grateful to finally be on home ground. Ronald scooped a dewdrop from his nose and doubted he had ever been this cold; his feet felt like blocks of ice inside their damp socks and it was a relief to be within reach of the warm embrace of the farmhouse kitchen and the meal his brother would have prepared.

The thunder of hooves had him spinning on his heels.

'You got a gun held to your head, too, lass?' he quizzed Bramble, as she charged along the fence beside him. The mare skidded to an ungainly halt at the gate and stood cannon-deep in mud. Ronald stared down at her hoofs that, as large as dinner plates, never failed to amaze.

'Tom's the one with apples.' He stroked her head, the flat plate of bone between her eyes, and felt the trauma of his recent ordeal ebb a little. 'He's the one who spoils you.' Glad for the warm breath of his last surviving shire, he reached up and let his hand follow the deep dish of her spine while he remembered that night when her unquestioning compliance had saved him. 'Dear Bramble.' He kissed her muzzle. 'My loyal friend.'

What a terrible morning it had been. His experience at the hands of that evil pair had left him reeling. The humiliation had given way to a vengeful anger, and he was determined to have them back. There was no way he would ever be at their mercy again. From now on, he would take his father's old Purdey whenever he was out on the moor, and the thought restored some of his dignity.

It was his barking sheepdogs that tore him from his intro-
spection, yelping and cartwheeling, pulled up on their hind legs
by their leashes and signalling the arrival of a stranger. Ronald,
fiercely private, resented visitors. They upset the equilibrium of
his day – as if this day hadn't been upset enough already. Luck-
ily, the farm was too far off the beaten track and most people
had forgotten they were there. Apart from the occasional vet
and that salesman with his glossy brochures flogging his filthy
insecticides, no one had set foot on the farm for years. The only
regular visitor was the post van, and that only drove as far as the
mailbox on the cattle grid.

Carrying his crook, the shoe safely stowed in his pocket,
Ronald was suddenly fearful of who the visitors might be. Had
Platinum and Sporran followed him back here? Did they now
know where he lived? He made his way down the hill to the
yard as quickly as he could. Slipping on loose stones, nearly
turning an ankle, as curious as he was anxious to see who was
causing the fuss. But scanning the length of the dirt track that
led to the farm, its gateway flagged by a pair of substantial oaks,
there was no sign of a car.

'How peculiar.' His eyes widened in astonishment when he
saw who it was. 'However did you get here? You must've walked
miles.'

Ronald watched the visitor inch forward into the yard.
Tentative, crouching with palms extended, while his young
collies, now calm with tails drumming, pushed their snouts into
the hands that were being held out to them in some kind of
greeting.

7

Waggon and Horses, Hyde Road, Gorton, Manchester

'I'm going to try inside... she might have needed the toilet.'

Handbag banging, a panicky and suddenly sober Connie left Fred behind in the car. The pub's side door was locked, so she ran to the main entrance through the rain. The doors were stiff on their hinges and screeched when she opened them. A sound that settled into the unnerving silence.

'Sorry, love. We're closed 'til six,' the man who was polishing the beer pumps told her.

'I know that. I just wanted to ask if you've seen my daughter?'

The look was blank, his bald pate shining under the pendant lighting.

'She's about this tall.' Connie measured the space with her hand. 'Wearing a red coat.'

'No, love. Kids aren't allowed in here.'

Little point arguing. Connie had known it was a long shot, but she needed to start somewhere. But where? Returning to the street that was washed in a murky ochre light, the idea that something terrible had happened to her child made her heart thump in her chest. Then she saw a patch of scrubland opposite. Could she have gone wandering in there?

'Kathy?' She charged over the road and shouted into the frowsy trees. It was distressing to think this was probably the first time she'd used her child's name in years. 'Kathy? Are you there?'

To her disappointment, there was no sign of life and, serenaded by her heels, she set off along the Hyde Road. Moving as if through a nightmare she couldn't wake from, she slipped on the pavement and, pressing a hand to a wall to steady herself, watched a dying bird at her feet. Its flapping was upsetting until she realised it was nothing more than a paper bag caught on the wind. On the move again, her feet inside her stilettos chafing the skin on her heels, the idea she couldn't trust her senses rattled her further. Splashing through puddles, the rain slapping her face, everywhere was tarmac and concrete, fog and drizzle, but no sign of her child.

Connie buttonholed everyone she came across, her desperation mounting. 'Have you seen my daughter? *Please*, you must've seen her?' Some were people she half-recognised from living on Furnival Road with her parents, but most were strangers.

Gulping down air and tasting the coal smoke from the factory chimneys that loomed over the residential streets, she saw, through the thick grey smog, the hideous rise of Gorton's foundry where her father had worked as a foreman. She passed the entrance to Eastway's, the furniture manufacturers that employed her as a machinist three days a week, then a cream-fronted picture house, a row of pubs, a dance hall and a Radio Rentals. Things for the worker to amuse himself with when he wasn't slaving away at a factory. The park, with its assortment of swings, brought a memory of a happy day when her father, a man who was barely well enough to get out of bed nowadays, had pushed his granddaughter high into the uninterrupted blue. When did they stop having fun? When was the last time she heard Kathy laugh? Connie's face crumpled, preparing to cry. But there wasn't time for tears, she told herself, she had to find her child.

Dumping Kathy in the car because she wanted to go drinking with her boyfriend – what kind of mother did that? One with a poor track record. But, she tried to persuade herself, running, running, it would be all right; she would find her.

'Excuse me?' she accosted a queue of people waiting at a bus stop. 'Has anyone seen my Kathy?' She wrung her hands and tried not to shriek. 'She's seven, nearly eight. Dark curly hair... *No?* Are you sure?' Their bemused expressions terrified her. Did they even know who her child was?

A bus pulled into the kerb and sent up a spray of rainwater, drenching her already sopping tights. Through the hiss of brakes, she identified the sound of children singing. It seemed to be coming from Gorton's Community Hall and she dashed across the yard that was marked out for hopscotch and netball. This was where she and Myra had hung out after school. Yes, they'd been older than Kathy, but it was where kids came when they were looking for things to do.

'Hello! Is anyone there?'

She inched along the corridor, dripping rainwater onto the linoleum, until she was met by a set of doors. Testing the handles and finding them locked, she squinted through the safety glass into the abandoned rooms falling away into blackness, as panic, a butterfly caught in a jar, fluttered inside her.

'Is anyone here?' she pleaded, then held her breath for the answer that didn't come.

Hurrying back outside, she circled the empty playground, hunting the darkened spaces between a magnolia tree and boundary wall. The markings for hopscotch were a muddle of colour through her anguish.

'Kathy! Where are you?'

Veering off down the side of the building, she found a window and, on tiptoes, she saw a light leaking from somewhere deep inside.

'Hello!' Connie shouted, spotting a cleaner dragging a mop around. She rapped the glass and the woman looked over. But only for a moment. With a frown of annoyance, she returned to her mopping.

Connie drummed harder, keeping on until her knuckles hurt. It worked. The woman dropped her mop and swayed towards her. Threw open the window.

'I heard children singing. Is my daughter with you?'

The woman teased out a tissue from her sleeve and blew her nose. 'Sorry, lass. There's nowt here but me.'

'But I heard singing?'

'Must've been wireless, lass. Sorry.'

Connie dashed back into the street without saying goodbye. Mumbling to herself like a madwoman, she watched a dray pull up alongside a pub and men rolling barrels towards a hatch that had opened up in the pavement. Then something caught her attention and although her feet were killing her, she broke into a full-out run.

'Kathy! Wait... Wait! It's me.'

But this wasn't Kathy. This was another child with brown curls and a red coat walking hand-in-hand with what she supposed must be an older sibling. Connie gulped down her anxiety and slowed to a walk. She had run out of places to search and flung a look at the sky, where a thin sun claimed its space in what remained of the dun-coloured afternoon.

'Connie!'

Someone was calling her name and, following the direction of the sound, she saw Fred on the corner of Far Lane and Hyde

Road. He had his back to the Waggon and Horses' high black-and-white exterior, and was waving something through the air.

'Where've you been?' Fred was red in the face and panting. 'I've been looking everywhere for you.'

'Looking for me? You should've been looking for Kathy.' Her muffled entreaty as she moved past him and into the car park.

'I have, I've searched everywhere. But look, Con, I found this.'

Connie took the delicate, frilly bonnet that wasn't white anymore. 'This is from Kathy's doll. Mam made it for her.' She ironed it flat in her hands. The thing was wet and gritty, and there were black rubber marks where a car's tyres had run over it. 'Where d'you find it?'

'Over there.'

She followed the direction of his finger; saw the empty space opposite his Cortina.

'Where Myra were parked?'

He nodded.

'But I don't understand. What's happened to her, Fred?' An icy feeling of dread settled on her heart. 'Where's she gone... where's Kathy?'

8

Ashton-under-Lyne, Lancashire

What Ronald really wanted was a beer. Laden with shopping, he'd worked up quite a thirst. He passed the door of a pub, but instead of stepping inside, he took a detour past the air vents, pumping out their beery smell. Breathing in, he could visualise it. The barman holding the lip of the glass to the pump. The black stout left to settle on the bar. The dark falling away from the cream. The patience making its arrival all the more appreciated. But he didn't give in to temptation. His thoughts drifted to Thomas, and about how he never drank. Afraid what his loosened tongue could tell – because he never talked of the things he'd experienced during the war. Only once, the day they buried their mother when he drank to drown his grief, did he share a memory of seeing men, boys, their insides shot out, taking days to die, stumbling around holding their guts in their arms like dirty laundry.

Pubs had been his father's domain. And as if to spite the father no one had seen for years, Ronald left his money where it was and distanced himself from the building, fearing if he did start drinking after the day he'd had, he wouldn't be able to stop. He could still feel the cold press of that revolver against his head and although he was desperate to eradicate the memory, drinking wasn't the answer. He tried to clear his mind by focusing on other things, like how he wouldn't ordinarily have driven to town this late in the day. 'It'll do you good to get away from the place.' He replayed the conversation with his brother, who gave him a list of things he claimed he needed as a matter of urgency. 'Go on, Ron. If you put your foot down, you'll make it before the shops shut.'

Satisfied with his purchases, Ronald put the scrap of paper with his brother's handwriting into a pocket. The only thing still left to buy was the stewing steak for Thomas to make beef tea because along with a book that took his fancy in a shop window, the pharmacy had cough mixture, a hot water bottle, talcum powder and aspirin, even jars of honey. A scout around the market resulted in him purchasing a set of towels and a soft, wool dressing gown in daffodil-yellow he was sure Thomas would approve of. Ronald secretly liked to please his brother, something that running errands like this allowed him to do. What he hoped was that in some small way, if the day of reckoning ever came and he was forced to confess his rotten act of betrayal, his brother might find it in his heart to forgive him. Don't be ridiculous, he chided himself; how could anything atone for ruining Thomas's life by destroying his chances of marrying the girl of his dreams and raising a family with her?

He negotiated the string of streets, spun with bunting. Passed cafés and sniffed the bite of coffee, the pungency of cigarettes. Around him, a flutter of youngsters: girls in dresses that ended above the knee; men in sunglasses, leather jackets, and chrome-studded belts. Amazed by their strangeness, Ronald had to concede that things had passed him by, and he was out of touch. He visited the market often enough, but when was the last time he had come along the high street? Tarmac, concrete, crowds – give him the moor any day. He didn't belong on urban streets and, sidestepping the youngsters, he aimed for the striped awning of a butcher's shop. But when he reached it, the steel trays in the window were scrubbed and empty. Too late, he groaned. Thomas would not be pleased about that.

The sun was out and cast long shadows over the cobbles. Confident he had seen the last of the rain, for now, he tucked his cap into the pocket of the corduroy jacket Thomas had bought him last Christmas, claiming that, with its leather elbow patches, it made him look like a college professor. Chance would be a fine thing, he almost laughed, staring up at the alien yellow orb as if it wasn't to be trusted. When he turned a corner, church bells rang out and Ronald saw a bride and groom standing in the arch of the church doorway. The bride was a beauty, with shoulders as pale as her dress. While the breeze fought over his hair, Ronald's mind floated a memory of him and Pamela holidaying at a little guesthouse on Lake Windermere. Where, on their first night, over a meal followed by a glass of brandy, she told him about the letter she'd received from Thomas. That he was due home on leave, and if Ronald would not come clean and tell his brother about the two of them, then it was over. He recalled how they had stepped out into the night, stood on the shore under a hood of stars, while a brisk wind found the gaps between the buttons of their clothes. But they remained silent. Locked in the knowledge that nothing would ever be the same. And then Pamela was married. Not to Thomas. She left him standing at the altar, the sunny yellow carnation in his buttonhole adding to the insult. It was another man who led her away on her wedding night and took off her dress, unhooked her pearls.

———

It was still light when Ronald drove along the A635 through Stalybridge and Mossley towards Saddleworth Moor, his bag of shopping propped on the seat beside him like a passenger. The moor rose and fell on either side of the twisting strip of tarmac, and long expanses of water lay glinting in the heather-marled valleys. He had driven like a maniac to Ashton, fearing the shops were going to be shut. Now, on the return journey, he was taking his time. Enjoying the sense of freedom driving always gave him. He wished he could have told his brother about those despicable people and the terrible ordeal he suffered at their hands. But for the same reason he made up a story about having a problem with the crows when Thomas inquired why, after over two decades, he'd fetched the Purdey from the barn to give it a clean, he was fearful of frightening him.

The moor that echoed his existence in its mind-numbing monotony was dissolving into the blue shine of evening, and soon the town he'd left behind would only be distinguishable by its lights. He rolled down the window and pushed his foot to the accelerator, heard the engine strain when he shifted down a gear to accommodate the hill. Emerging into the glare from a low-hanging sun that momentarily blinded him, he snatched at the visor and yanked it down. It caused him to swerve, and the danger of the waterlogged verge bouncing beneath the truck's wheels made him pull his mouth wide in a silent scream.

He righted the truck just in time.

He missed it by inches.

The turquoise Mini Traveller parked in the layby for the second time that day.

A cold feeling scuttled up between his shoulder blades and across his back. The remembered chill of steel from the muzzle of the revolver found him again. Along with the glassy gleam in that bastard's eye. The badness that oozed from them; the badness that made him think they were going to blow his brains out.

He pressed his foot to the brake. Nothing too obvious, nothing to draw their attention. Skimming past, he glimpsed the woman's white-blonde head, not quite as primped as usual, when she pitched from the car. While Sporran, in goggles and helmet and a long black leather coat, dismounted the Triumph motorbike he had parked alongside. They must have arrived seconds earlier, Ronald thought as he overtook them. His eyes flitting between the driving mirror and the road ahead.

Curiosity, a hook through his gut, had him pull into the next available layby. Tucked in beside a knuckle of rock that had tumbled down from the moor, it was a good position: far enough away so as not to alert them, but close enough to see what they were doing. He wound up the window, switched off the side-lights and engine. Listened to it ticking down as it cooled. Although his work on the farm was endless, he was in no hurry to return. Not when he considered the turmoil that awaited him because of the second unexpected event of that day. There was nothing Ronald could do to help. He was a farmer, not a doctor. His relationship with his brother, whatever he liked to tell himself, was already strained, and he worried things between them were about to get a lot worse.

When Ronald looked in his driving mirror again, he saw the woman was wearing what looked like a man's overcoat. She stomped around to the rear of the car and opened its cabinet-like doors, while her boyfriend, going by his operatic hand gestures, appeared to be shouting orders. Ronald had no way of knowing what the orders were, but watching her move away from the car, it looked like she had a spade in her hand. Then the man delved into the boot himself, dragging out and tussling with the heft of an untidy bundle of carpet.

What the hell are they doing?

For a terrible moment, he thought they might be on to him, and he fumbled for the keys, about to turn the ignition. But no, they turned away to scale the steep slope of grass that flanked the roadside. And as their shapes dissolved into a cluster of boulders protruding like fangs from the moorland floor, a deep unease fluttered in Ronald's chest.

9

Waggon and Horses, Hyde Road, Gorton, Manchester

Stunned into sobriety and shivering inside their sodden clothes, Connie and Fred sat side-by-side in the Cortina.

'It'll warm up in a minute.' Fred promised as he started the engine and leant over the steering wheel to wipe a hole in the condensation.

'You don't think that Ian and Myra could have taken her to teach me a lesson?' Connie's wet hair trickled down her face and mixed with her tears as she clutched the grubby bonnet from Kathy's doll. 'Is that what this is all about?'

'*What?*' Fred turned his face to hers. 'You can't be serious?'

The smell of wet clothes and damp shoe leather plugged the tight metal void of the car.

'Thing is, she knows Myra. She's known her since she were a baby. She'd go with Myra, easy.' Connie sobbed and wiped her nose on the back of her wrist.

'Without telling you? Christ, Con. They'd have to be crazy to pull a stunt like that. D'you really think she would?'

'I don't know... I don't know.' She cried harder, bouncing her fists in her lap. 'She might if Ian wanted her to. You heard him. You heard what he said to me.' Rainwater dripped from her fringe.

'There's no way.' Fred shook his head. 'I can't see it, Con, I can't.'

'At least if she's with them it means she's safe.' The idea, floating towards her like a lifeline through her thickening anxiety.

A flicker of his eyebrows and he tucked the chamois leather away. 'She's not with them, Con. She can't be.'

'It's worth a try. I know you think I'm barmy—'

'But if the kid's not there, then what?' He cut her off. 'Wouldn't we be wasting valuable time? Come on, Connie, we've gotta go to the police.'

'Oh, God. Do we have to?' A fresh wave of panic slopped through her.

'I wish we didn't need to involve them. I hate the bastards, but I dunno what else to do.' Fred pushed the car into first, then second gear, and drove out of the car park. 'All I know is if we don't report her missing and something bad's happened, it's gonna come down hard on us... hard on me.'

'I just don't want Mam finding out.' Connie didn't need Fred to elaborate. She knew all about his brush with the law, his criminal record. 'Because they'll have to tell her, won't they?'

'And what's wrong with that?'

'Oh, Fred, she'll bloody kill me. She already thinks I'm incapable of looking after her.' Connie, still crying, tugged at her wet hair, hurting her scalp. Fred squeezed her thigh, trying to comfort her. But she didn't want it and pushed him away. 'Where is she? Oh, God, oh, God. What am I going to do?' She was in danger of losing it completely. 'I can't believe I left her in the car. I'm a useless mother. Just like Mam says... even Ian thinks it.' Shaking, she tried to get a hold of her escalating emotions, but the tears kept coming.

'Connie... *Con?*' Fred, stroking her knees. 'Calm down, *please*. You sound all funny, your breathing's all funny.'

'My chest hurts.' She clutched the sudden shooting pain in her arm.

'You've to stay calm. You're gonna give yourself a heart attack at this rate.'

'How can I stay calm?' she shrieked. 'I've lost her... I've bloody lost her. How can I have left her on her own? Why was I so stupid?'

'Come on. Everything's gonna be fine, you'll see.'

'You don't know that.' Frantic, she was way fiercer than she meant to be. 'Kathy could be dead in a ditch, and it's all my fault.'

'Connie, listen to me – she can't have gone far. Think – where could she have gone?' Fred pulled up at a set of traffic lights and turned to her.

'I don't know... I don't know.' A dreadful pause. 'We're going to have to go to the police, aren't we?' Connie bawled. 'The likes of me don't deserve children. This is punishment for getting pregnant by someone else's husband.' She blinked through mascara-muddy lashes. 'Don't tell me it's not, because it's punishment for something.' She heard the bitterness and self-loathing in her voice and knew her boyfriend heard it too.

The lights turned green, and they were on the move again. 'You're not a bad mother. You do the best you can.' Something in his tone made her doubt his sincerity but she couldn't see his face. 'You've to stop thinking the worst. The police will find her. Everything's gonna be okay.'

'I can't be trusted,' she winced; her chest felt painfully tight. 'I always screw up.'

As Fred drove, Connie pushed her face to the passenger

window. Then, winding it down, she leant out through a burst of late sunshine, holding her hair back off her face with one hand as she scanned the wet streets for her missing child.

10

Saddleworth Moor, West Riding of Yorkshire

Ronald was still parked in the layby as the dusk deepened around him. The sky, turning salmon-pink and gold as night folded itself into the darkening blue, cast gradients of shadow that rippled like the skin of the sea over the moor. This was a lonely spot with barely a vehicle passing in all the time he'd been there. What did he think he was doing? Supposing they came back and saw him? He consulted the clock on the dashboard and decided that, despite the cold that was sidling in like the mists that clung to the crags above the reservoir, he wanted to give Platinum and her boyfriend another half an hour.

Saturday nights used to mean something, he thought as he found a pair of forgotten gloves in the side pocket of the door and pulled them on. Pinpointing the time when this had stopped being true, his mind yielded a blaze of the ballroom and himself, tall and pencil-thin in high-waisted trousers and a tank top, laced inside his dancing shoes. Not that he'd done much dancing. That was Thomas's forte. Big Band music, alternate

Saturdays down the Plaza in Manchester. The blast of trumpets and trombones, the piano and double bass, Glenn Miller-style. 'In the Mood' and 'Moonlight Serenade' were his favourites.

It was on such a night that Thomas met Pamela. Ronald had seen her too. She had been the best of the bunch. The memory brought a smile until he remembered the ballroom's vast and conker-coloured floor spread around him like a battle-field he wasn't brave enough to cross. It made him question what he had been brave enough to do while his brother was away fighting for king and country – what was Ronald's war record? He had been feeding the nation by walking up and down the same patch of moorland. Unlike Thomas, Ronald had stayed right where he was and waged war with the weather instead. He still did. There was no peacetime for him. The only peace he'd ever known was when the sun dared to show itself, and the biting north wind gave over to a softer, southerly one.

Some would say he took advantage of his brother's absence, and perhaps he did. Because even though Thomas was away, it didn't stop Ronald from frequenting the fortnightly dances, hoping for a glimpse of Pamela. But she tested his resolve. Weeks and weeks went by, and he was on the brink of aban-doning his quest. When, one night, she was suddenly there. Taking his breath away and more beautiful than he remem-bered as he stood on the sidelines watching her dance with a uniformed officer. His hot jealousy, burning in his chest until she doused it by saying the soldier was her brother home on leave. She had been the one to come over and say hello, to ask if he would dance with her. But it was Ronald, as the band played the last tune, who asked if he could see her again. This girl with skin as flawless as a china cup that he had been too shy to even look at when Thomas brought her home for tea, announcing they were to be married as soon as his regiment granted him leave. How handsome his brother had looked in his uniform, his eyes shining for the love of a girl and eager for adventure. Thomas should have married her before he went away to war. Didn't their mother say as much? Their mother, with her gift for knowing things before they happened. But it wasn't she who threatened to spill the beans and crack his brother's heart wide open. That had been their father.

Beyond the truck, the sun had set, and it was almost dark. The little light still left in the sky had been reduced to a sliver of orange against the withers of the moor. Other than this, the world beyond the truck's windows was leached of colour. Ronald looked again at the clock. He had been parked in the layby for over an hour. Grateful for the warmth of his corduroy jacket and the cable-knit sweater his brother made for him, it was a gnawing concern mixed with a sick fascination that kept him there.

Looking in his wing mirror, he could see that a fat, round moon had nudged into position above the giant crest of Hollin Brown Knoll. That protruding rise of molar-like rocks, a permanent reminder of the thing he wished he could forget. He loved the moon and always made a point of following its phases. Spellbound by its orbicular stare, his mind curved to what he thought he had seen before the sun went down and tried to unravel its meaning. Had his eyes been playing tricks, or was that woman really carrying a spade, and her boyfriend struggling with the weight of a bundle wrapped in old carpet? It had certainly looked that way. An unwelcome idea slithered into his head. Were they digging a grave? Was that what the spade was for? Ronald knew all about what it took to dig a grave on the moor. The sheer effort of slicing into saturated peat, hitting rock after rock. Fearing you could never make it deep enough to keep the terrible thing you had done from being exhumed by foxes. Could that man have been carrying a body? No, it was too small... But not too small for a child's body? Ronald remembered the shoe he had found. The shoe he hid in the barn for reasons he didn't quite understand. Did it have something to do with this pair? 'You shouldn't judge people by your own actions.' His late mother's voice filtered through to him. Not that she'd been aware of his ghastly secret. But she had been right. Just because he had done it, it didn't follow that others carried bodies to the moor and buried them.

Sitting in the cold like this was ridiculous. He needed to get back; it was going to be tricky enough inventing reasons he'd taken so long. Hand on the keys, he was about to fire the ignition when the dark was abruptly exchanged for the glare of headlamps. They burst in on him: shocking, glaring; saturating the truck's interior. They were back. He could see them moving around. Something about them, the situation and the oddness of it: his instinct told him it was wrong. Backlit by the car's lights, the man was a tall, thin silhouette in his long coat. He looked like a Nazi. The parallel was an uncomfortable one and sent a shiver up his spine. It seemed as if the heavy bundle had gone and the spade was being returned to the boot of the car, swapped for a bottle of something. Ronald watched them take turns to swig from it, holding it aloft as if to toast some significant achievement. Smoking and giggling, it was clear the horrible pair were enjoying themselves.

The knot of anxiety he felt whenever he clapped eyes on these two, even before today, tightened its hold. He was alone, he reminded himself. No dogs, no shepherd's crook... no gun. So why was he still here; what did he think it was going to achieve? Had he learnt nothing from his clash with them that morning? Get on home, he told himself. Whatever they were up to, it had nothing to do with him. It wasn't a crime to visit the moor at sundown. Odd, but not a crime.

Deciding it was best to leave them to it, he fumbled for the keys in the ignition, his fingers clumsy inside his gloves. Then a bright white light appeared out of nowhere.

Torchlight. Shining in his eyes.

The sharp rapping of a be-ringed hand on the window.
Platinum.

Close enough to see her moving mouth. An opening and closing black hole on the other side of the glass.

11

Underwood Court, Hattersley, North-East Cheshire

Connie had no recollection of how she got home or how the electric fire came to be on, any more than she knew how she came to be sitting in front of it dressed in a dry set of clothes. All she could remember was the police station and the smell of it, and when she dared to let herself think of her missing seven-year-old, the stink of disinfectant and vomit came back to her. She gazed into the orange bars of the fire, then up at the tiled mantelpiece bookended by a pair of china dogs. Then further, up to the ceiling and the paper lampshade she let Kathy choose – about the only thing she'd let her choose when they moved here. It made her feel more wretched to remember this and, dropping her head again, she looked through the fluted-glass door that led into the kitchen. Let her thoughts travel back to the morning that already seemed like a lifetime away. How she'd shouted at Kathy for not answering Myra. Telling her to get some cornflakes down her neck because she didn't know when she'd be eating again. And how Kathy had stood there, forlorn and scruffy in her coat, the hole in the knee of her red tights.

'Are you all right?' Fred had reached for her hand, tugging her back to the present. 'Speak to me, you've gone all pale... *Connie?*'

She couldn't answer, and stubbed out her fag, that had burnt away to a turd of ash without her noticing.

'Drink this.' Fred handed her a glass she didn't bother to look at. She just brought it to her lips and drank.

Whisky. She screwed her eyes against the taste she didn't like. But she liked the feel of it tracking through her, numbing her, sliding into her veins.

'Better?' Fred's eyes drilled into her, looking for reassurances she couldn't give.

He was as guilty as she was. The accusation burst in her mouth and she held it there, bloody, like loose teeth. Not that it mattered. Everyone would blame her. She was Kathy's mother. Connie could tell the police officer they reported her disappearance to thought so. He might well have given Fred a grilling on account of his criminal record, but she was the one he held responsible.

'How did we get here?' She didn't mean the flat.

'I drove you.' A puzzled look.

'Where is she, Fred?' Inside her head was a black void, and she groped around for something to cling to but found it empty. 'Where's Kathy?'

Fred shook his head. He looked as lost and frightened as she was. 'I dunno, love. But the police will find her, you mustn't worry.'

She gawped at the toast he had made her.

'You should try to eat something, Con.'

'I can't.' To watch him chewing, clearing the plate – it made her want to scream.

'Come on, just a little.' He handed her a square he'd buttered.

'Stop bloody mitherin' me.' She batted him away and rose to her feet.

What was the matter with him? Why was he carrying on as if their lives hadn't capsized? Fearful of exploding, of saying things she would regret, she locked herself inside the bathroom. Sat on the lowered toilet seat, listening to the dripping tap.

Where's my child? What the hell's happened to her?

Her unanswerable questions turning on a carousel she couldn't get off.

'You okay in there? You've been ages.' Fred was tapping on the door; kept on until she opened it.

His lips were shiny from the butter, and he had toast crumbs on his moustache and down his front. She was about to lock the door on him again when he showed her the doll's bonnet.

'I've washed it. It's come up good as new.'

He passed it to her, slightly damp, but clean.

'Thanks, Fred.' Tears filled her eyes. 'Don't you need to be getting back?'

'I don't wanna leave you on your own. And I've been thinking...' he faltered. 'I could move in permanent, if you want?'

'Won't your mam mind?' Connie stared at the frilly white bonnet in her hand.

'She'll understand. I'll go and tell her tomorrow.'

Connie went to the kitchen to fetch a glass of water. She saw that Fred had tidied up. The sink was gleaming. The surfaces wiped. It made her ashamed. Not his intention, she was sure, but ashamed was what she felt.

'Why did you say it were safe to leave her?' Back in the living room with its electric fire and curtain of cigarette smoke, she thrust her accusation at Fred, who was standing on the balcony smoking a roll-up. 'Because you did. You said it'd be fine. This is your fault.' Still gripping the bonnet, she said what she had been dying to say to the officer who took their statements at Ashton police station.

'Shit, Con. How d'you work that out?' Fred stepped back into the room and slid the glass doors across.

'Because it were your idea to go. You know they don't let kids in pubs. What were I supposed to do?' She didn't want to blame him, but the words were out and couldn't be put away again.

'I know you're frightened, but you're not dumping this on me. You shoulda dropped her off at your mam's, like I said.'

'I can't keep running to her every five minutes.'

'You're hardly doing that, you've not seen owt of 'em for weeks.'

'That's not the point. I'm supposed to be managing on my own. It's what moving here were about.'

Fred poured another measure of whisky and encouraged her to drink it. 'This isn't my fault, any more than it's yours – you've got to live; you've got to have some fun.'

'Fun?' She tottered forward; teeth bared. 'You call this fun?'

Night had dropped over the estate and the darkness nuzzled against the flat's lighted windows. It was one o'clock in the morning, and Connie was in her nightdress and dressing gown. A sticky patch where she'd tipped drink over herself some hours before. She sank down on the settee and kicked off her slippers. The day's sick turmoil washed over her. Wave on wave of it. Fred seemed to be talking to her from a long way off. When she thought back on the last few hours, everything appeared to be in a sort of haze. Mostly down to too much booze. She looked over at Fred. All the things she wanted to say, the assurances and apologies she wanted to give, but when it came to it, she could only manage a queasy smile. She forced her eyes open to stop the room from spinning. Then closed them again. Let it spin. She groaned and, rolling over to lie face-down on the settee, she drew her knees up to her chin.

Let me just die. Here and now.

Her thoughts were depressing ones as Fred slid a hand under her head, then replaced it with a cushion and she slept.

Connie woke hours later to a violent hammering on the flat's front door. It tipped her out of a swirl of dreams about her daughter running through the park with the bounce of summer sunshine in her hair.

Kathy, is that you?

Connie was in bed but had no memory of how she came to be there. She sat up and fumbled for the alarm clock. Three a.m.

Whoever it was, banged the door again.

It's Kathy, she's come home...

Stuffing her arms into her dressing gown, she stumbled along the passageway and opened the door. But instead of her daughter, it was two uniformed police officers hogging her welcome mat.

'Miss Openshaw?' One of them required confirmation.

Connie didn't answer. *Where was Kathy, why wasn't she with them?* She tugged the cord of her dressing gown tight against the night air that curled up the stairwell.

'Miss Openshaw?' the officer tried again.

'Y-yes,' she stammered, looking down at his polished boots and realising how cold her toes were.

'Your boyfriend here? His mother said he were,' one of them asked. She wasn't sure which.

'Fred? What d'you want with him?'

They barged past her.

'But where's Kathy?' Connie, flicking on a light switch, trotted along behind. 'Why isn't she with you?'

'That's what we've to find out, lass.' The same voice punctured her confusion. 'Your boyfriend in the bedroom, is he?'

A lamp had gone on and Fred was scrabbling into his clothes. Gruff, the police officers barely gave him time to button his shirt before manhandling him into the passageway.

'What d'you want with me?' At the sight of Fred's stricken face, Connie began to cry.

'We've to take you down the station for questioning. Come on, lad. No buggering about.'

Fred was still pulling on his trousers and buckling his belt when they dragged him out of the flat. She ran along behind them, shouting, grabbing the sleeves of their uniforms.

'But I've not down owt,' he pleaded, and Connie could see the whites of his eyes.

'Save it, lad. You've got previous, so don't come the innocent with us. Your sort never change.'

'Why won't you listen?' Connie's incredulity wheeled about them. 'We told you everything when we came down the station...' Her voice echoed around the stairwell. 'How long are you going to keep him?'

'A night in the cells should do it. Reckon that'd loosen your tongue, lad?'

Forced to let them take Fred away, Connie dashed to the balcony window and watched the patrol car drive him off into the dark. Turning back to the room, she grabbed her handbag, swapped her dressing gown for her raincoat, and left the flat. Her feet too sore for her shoes, she left her slippers on. The stinking lift clunked into mechanical life and spat her out on the ground floor. Addled by booze and sadness, she ambled through the night-time estate with the almost futuristic hum from the overhead pylons in her ears. Aiming for the telephone box on the corner of Hare Hill Road, she saw the fluorescent light spill out from the newsagent's and the closed-up chippy. The flap of discarded chip paper and empty pop bottles rolling in the wind.

The phone box shone like a beacon through the dark. Breathing in its metallic money smell, she lifted the receiver and fed pennies into the holding slot. Then, with a deep breath, she dialled the number, her fingers tripping over themselves. Shaking, it took her three goes to get it right. She listened to it ring and ring.

'Glossop, five four six. Hello?' The word quivered like a question mark.

Connie pressed the A button, almost too choked to speak. 'M-mam?'

'Constance... is that you, love?'

'M-mam. Oh, Mam. She's gone.'

'Gone... Who's gone?'

'Kathy... my little Kathy. She's gone.'

12

Monday, 6 September 1965

Ashton Market, Ashton-under-Lyne, Lancashire

Ronald's trailer and truck took up two spaces in the customer car park behind the market, but there was more than enough room, he decided, getting out to check. He locked up, pocketed the keys in his overalls and lit his pipe, trailing the tobacco's vanilla smell behind him as he moved towards the main entrance.

As soon as he walked around the corner, he knew her. It gave Ronald a peculiar feeling. Years and years had passed, but not enough, it seemed, to change someone so that you don't recognise them. Just long enough to force you to look twice. The first thing he noticed was that she didn't seem so sure of herself; she no longer walked as if she had the world in her pocket. She was slower, wider, wearing a dark winter coat unbuttoned over a floral frock that didn't suit her. It was the kind of thing that got left behind at a church jumble sale. Poor Pamela, it was obvious she'd fallen on hard times. He could have given her a good life.

So why hadn't he? Why had he been so weak, to have never asked for what he wanted? Why did he let her get away?

It surprised him to be neither pleased nor sorry to see her but he supposed this was what shock did to a person – it stunted your reaction to the unexpected. Last he heard, Pamela Wilcox had married Kenneth Openshaw and was living to the west of Gorton. What was she doing in Ashton? His feelings confused him. He had never forgotten her but he hadn't seriously expected to lay eyes on her again. She had taken on a certain shape in his memory the longer time had gone on; a shape that had worn smooth as a pebble from his over-attention.

He watched her, apprehension building in his stomach. Saw she was handing out leaflets. One had been taped to the inside of a shop window. Another fixed to a telegraph pole. The word 'MISSING' heaved in the breeze. The child's brown curls and dimpled smile overseeing her search. It was a face Ronald recognised.

He stood still, unsure what to do next. Puffing on his pipe and suddenly ashamed of his appearance, his indecision fluttered in his chest. Stay or go? He watched Pamela fasten another leaflet to a waste bin at the market's entrance. Then it was she who saw him and before he had the chance to return to his car and drive away like the coward he was, she was striding towards him. She wasn't what he'd been imagining all these years and at first, he was disappointed. She looked sad until her face broke out in a smile and he was given a chink of the young Pamela: the girl he was still in love with. She was still as intensely pretty as she had always been, with her quick, dark eyes and those beautifully defined eyebrows.

'Hello, Ronnie. I thought it were you.' Her voice had the same musical lilt he remembered. 'How are you?'

'I'm f-fine. A-aye,' he stammered, blushing like a teenager as he rubbed a hand over his stubble, wishing he'd shaved that morning. He had worked her out in the few seconds that were available to him, but what did she see in front of her? A middle-aged man with a mop of steel-grey hair, side-parted in an earnest manner. Craggy and broad, like a fallen bough left out in all seasons, his weathered look coming from years of squinting in the sun, the rain in his face. A man burdened by a lifetime of secrets and regrets.

'It's been a long time, hasn't it?' Her face went blank.

It was the sort of empty question that didn't require answering, and Ronald was grateful. He was fearful he might let it slip that he knew the exact number of years, months and days since they were last in each other's company and that there had barely been a moment when he hadn't thought of her.

He tucked his pipe away into the top pocket of his tweed jacket, even though it was still hot. 'How are you, Pam? How're you keeping?' He talked to the thin creases around her mouth; the lines that, like the rings on a tree, marked the passing of years.

Pamela diverted her gaze in a way that suggested she was reluctant to look at him. She turned the gold wedding ring, loose behind the knuckle, rhythmically, hypnotically and Ronald wondered if her husband was the reason for her reticence. The fact she had a man at home who'd be none too happy to hear she'd been seen talking to Ronald Cappleman. Nervous, needing to do something with his hands, he took out his pipe again and filled it with tobacco. Lit it and gave a few puffs to get it going.

'I'm all right,' she eventually replied and, returning her gaze to his, he saw a sorrow behind her eyes that made him fearful this could somehow be his fault.

'What's all this, then?' He waved a vague hand over the leaflets.

As she straightened her hair with her fidgety fingers, Ronald saw it was grey at the roots. Time, he thought gloomily; it ravaged everything. And despite himself, he thought about how her hair had been when he last saw her: long and dark as a raven's wing. He hated himself for this. Who was he to judge? When he was as rough as the acres of moorland he farmed. No, it wasn't fair of him to compare the young Pamela with the woman who stood before him now.

'It's my granddaughter.' Pamela gulped back tears. 'She went missing on Saturday.'

The child on the leaflet was her granddaughter? That explained why she looked so washed-out. He unglued his tongue from the roof of his mouth. 'That's terrible. Does she live near here?'

'What?' Pamela looked perplexed and wiped away tears with the back of her hand. 'No... no. Hattersley.' She searched her pockets for a hankie. 'My daughter moved them into one of them council flats on that new estate.'

'Oh, Pam. I'm so sorry.' Ronald didn't know what else to say.

'I'm okay... I'm okay.'

Looking into her face, he felt ashamed but couldn't stop himself hunting it for the young woman she used to be. He found her for a moment and tried to hold her there, but she slipped away again. 'I suppose you've been to the police?'

'A fat lot of good they are.' She found a hankie and dabbed her eyes. 'Connie, my daughter – Constance,' she corrected herself. 'Kathy's mam. She's been badgering them but all they've done so far is hassle her boyfriend.'

'You got those sorted quickly.' He gestured to the leaflets, thinking how she had always been a dynamo. Pamela was never one to let the grass grow under her feet, and it was nice to see that hadn't changed. She would have been good for him, he'd always known that, and to think it brought an ache to his heart.

'Aye, I had them done first thing this morning. Friend of my husband's.' She sniffed and wiped her nose. 'Been handing them out to all and sundry. Got to do something, haven't you?'

Ronald had a powerful urge to gather her up in his arms and kiss her, but he didn't. He merely nodded and smoked his pipe. 'Aye, I suppose you have,' he told the sadness he'd identified in the folds above her eyes.

'Is that all you've got to say?' She looked at him properly for the first time. 'You were never one for showing emotion, were you, Ronnie?'

'No, I don't suppose I were, lass.' It was the only thing he was prepared to be honest about as he stepped aside for an elderly couple with rosy cheeks.

'Shame you weren't.' Her voice, flat. 'We might have had a life together, if you had been.'

Ronald sucked back his breath. Her bluntness had shocked him.

'Hit a nerve, have I, Ronnie?' A small smile. 'I weren't the only one who betrayed him, were I?' She tucked her hankie away.

Two young boys rushed past. Boisterous, energetic.

'Kids of today.' He noticed the way Pamela followed them with her eyes as he swapped his pipe to the other side of his mouth.

'Still smoking your pipe, I see.'

'Aye. I gave up the cigs when you were around. Don't you remember telling me that a man who smoked a pipe were far more distinguished?'

'Well, well.' A half-smile. 'Fancy you remembering a funny old thing like that.'

I remember everything you said to me. How I've missed you, Pam. How fast time's flown... can it really be twenty-four years?

'Look—' She rummaged through her coat pockets and found an old receipt. 'I'll give you my telephone number.' Her voice disappearing into her bag as she dug around for a biro. 'Ring me some time, Ronnie?' She scribbled down a string of numbers and handed it to him. 'It'd be nice to see each other again, wouldn't it?'

'Aye, it would.' He nodded and thought: must be doing all right if they had a phone wired in at home. It wasn't something they could afford at the farm. But looking again at her rather shabby coat and the dress beneath, it made him question the kind of man she married. One with a strange set of priorities, he decided. 'That'd be grand.'

'You always were a man of few words, Ronnie Cappleman.' She twisted away to press a leaflet into the hand of a passing man in a grubby raincoat. 'You haven't changed a bit.' She raised an eyebrow, and he felt a thrill ripple through him in the way it had all those years ago. She peeled off another leaflet. 'Put it somewhere, would you? Somewhere it can be seen.'

'Owt to help.' He puffed on his pipe and folded the face of the missing child in half, then half again. Tucked it, and the old receipt she'd given him, into the pocket of his jacket, quickly, as if the face of Pamela's granddaughter had burnt his fingers. 'And Pam?' He reached out with his hand to prevent her from turning away. 'I will ring you, I will.'

She eyed him coolly and clamped her lips together so firmly, he didn't think he was going to get an answer.

'I won't hold my breath, Ronnie.' And she turned to step out in front of a couple with a pram to thrust a leaflet into the young mother's hand.

13

Hyde Road, Gorton, Manchester

Connie was afraid to go home and threaded her way along the warren of Gorton's red-brick terraced streets, thinking about the flat's empty rooms and her daughter's bed unslept in. It had been a relief when Fred offered to move in with her. She could just about cope with the place when he was there, but he was working in the menswear department of C&A today, and wouldn't be home until teatime. For such a young bloke – she was a little embarrassed to admit that at nineteen, he was four years her junior – he was mature and conscientious. He was the one who ensured she was up that morning, persuading her to eat a little breakfast and insisting she go to work to tell them what had happened.

Mr Foster, the foreman at Eastway's, had been kind and put a fatherly arm around her, saying: 'She'll turn up soon enough, lass, you'll see. In meantime, you're not to fret about coming here. Dangerous machines, these, you need your wits about you. So, we'll say no more about it and see you when your kiddie's turned up safe and sound.'

Safe and sound.

How many times had people said that since Saturday afternoon? The hollow words were enough to turn her stomach, especially when she thought of that pair of beefy officers who, for no good reason, locked Fred in a cell on Saturday night and didn't release him until the following morning.

Thin puddles disrupted the rutted paving slabs, filmed with oily rings of pollution. She dodged them, reluctant for the filthy water to splash her legs. She planned to see Myra after she'd finished work, but Millward's didn't close until five, and there were hours to kill. Connie – leaving a note for Kathy on the flat's front door in case she came home, the same note she left there today – had called over to Wardle Brook Avenue twice yesterday when Fred was collecting his stuff from his mother's, but neither Myra nor Ian were there.

The breeze that did nothing to disperse the veil of smog that hung about the town harvested Gorton's flotsam and gathered it to her heels. She was kicking it away when a flap of starlings, their blue-green wings as iridescent as the puddles, made her look up to the stunted limbs of trees with barely a leaf between them. She cursed her woollen skirt that clung to the static on her tights and made it difficult to form proper strides. Where was she going? She didn't know. The stiff breeze whipped her hair into her eyes and, pushing it away with her hand, she remained on watch for her child. What began as a frantic hunt was fast becoming a habit. As she walked, she ferreted out from her pocket a mangled tube of Wine Gums she couldn't remember buying. She picked off bits of fluff and put a sweet in her mouth, the sugary fruitiness unexpectedly comforting. What she knew of Gorton life – the never-ending routine of the fish-and-chip tang of Friday and Saturday nights, *Housewives' Choice* blaring from tinny radios, stray dogs barking – depressed her further. She understood her parents' reasons for moving away, even though their old road, with its private houses and back gardens, had been a step up from the slum dwellings of these streets. She passed a corner shop with racks of newspapers and crates of milk bottles stacked out front. The whiff of Woodbines reminded her she'd run out of cigarettes and she dipped inside.

'Packet of Capstan, full strength, if you would.' Connie swallowed the wine gum. 'And a newspaper, please.' She took a copy of the *Gorton & Openshaw Reporter* from the pile on the counter.

'That'll be one and six, lass.'

Embarrassed, scratching around in her purse for coins. 'Oh, I'm sorry. I'm tuppence short if I'm to keep my bus fare back.'

'No matter. Give it me next time you're in.' The shopkeeper shut the drawer of the till with his fist.

'Thank you... *erm,*' she wavered, unsure how to begin. 'You don't happen to have seen a little girl? Brown curls? Red co—'

'You're Mr Openshaw's daughter, aren't you?' He cut her off with a friendly smile. 'I thought I recognised you.'

She nodded, worrying where this might be leading.

'I were that sad to hear about him being so poorly.' The smile disappeared. 'It's a sorry state to retire and have no time to enjoy it.'

'Yeah, it is.' Aware of the women in housecoats and curlers, who'd halted their chatter and turned their interest to her. 'Thing is, you see,' she began, eager to bring things back to her missing child. 'My Kathy, she's—'

'Aye, lass. Your mam's been in,' the shopkeeper interrupted her a second time. 'She were saying you lost her up at Waggon and Horses.'

'Mam's been in here?' She pocketed the fags and folded the newspaper into her bag.

'Aye. First thing.'

'Oh, I didn't know.'

'Well, we're doin' all we can, lass.' He pointed beyond the

shelves piled with everything from tinned baked beans to fire-
lighters to indicate the front of the shop. 'Your mam's given us a
poster. I hope your little one turns up soon, it must be an awful
worry for you.'

Connie left the shop. The way ahead was distorted by her
tears. Casting a sidelong glance at her daughter's face in the
leaflet that had been fixed to the shop window caused her to
step off the kerb without looking. A blur of black and chrome,
the loud thrum of an engine; the speeding motorbike missed her
by inches. She stood in the gutter in the stinging aftermath,
staring after it, dumbstruck; her sobs coming thick and fast.
Here she was, helpless to do anything, and it seemed her
mother, so much more adept at being a mother, was getting
leaflets printed and doing something constructive. All of which
made Connie feel utterly useless. What was the point? she
asked herself. She didn't deserve to live.

14

16, Wardle Brook Avenue, Hattersley, North-East Cheshire

Number sixteen didn't have a knocker, so Connie banged the brown door with her fist. Stepped back. Patted down her raincoat and tightened the belt. Muffled sounds of the television surged and eddied, voices talking. A light went on, and Ian opened the door.

'What do ye want?' The confusion on his face echoed the chaos in the harshly lit hall.

'Can I speak to Myra?' She looked past him to the heap of clothes at the foot of the stairs, the muddy footwear and empty wine bottles. Sniffed the unpleasant smell of charred meat.

'Ye cannae just turn up here.' Dressed in his shirt, the sleeves folded back to the elbows, Ian looked flustered, sweaty. 'It isnae convenient.' He pushed his hand up through his fringe, only for it to fall into his eyes again.

He blocked her way; Connie was not going to be invited inside. His jerky movements added to her anxiety and, fiddling with the strap on her handbag, she hurried through her explanation about how Kathy had gone missing from the pub car park and asked if they had seen anything suspicious.

'Why would we?' His annoyance – a crimson sunset – bled up and over his neck and face.

There was no doubting she had interrupted something. Impatiently, he tapped his fingers against the door, bellowing for Myra to come and sort her friend out. Connie stared at him. Her daughter had disappeared. Did the man have no compassion? What did Myra see in him?

'Who is it, Neddy?' Myra shouted from somewhere inside the house. 'Your programme's about to start.'

Ian stepped back and closed the door. Left on the doorstep in the dark, waiting, she listened to their voices but couldn't hear what they said.

When Myra eventually showed herself, Connie was struck by her dishevelled appearance. There was nothing of the smart secretary-look here.

'You can't call round like this, Con.' She tugged on a pair of scruffy tartan pumps. There was no smile, and her expression was cold. 'Ian don't like it.'

'But Kathy's missing, didn't he say?' Connie had started to cry. 'I thought you might know something.'

Myra glared at her. 'Why would we?'

'Because we left her in the car, and when we went back, she'd gone.'

'Oh, stop your blubbering.' The door of number sixteen swung shut and Myra, chivvying, seizing her by the elbow, steered her down the garden path. Connie noticed her friend's hands and nails were filthy. 'I hope you didn't let Ian see you in that state. He hates histrionics.'

'Does he have to be so bloody rude; what's the matter with him?'

'He just don't like people turning up. We were all set to watch *Richard III*, it's on the BBC.'

'Christ, Myra. My daughter's vanished,' she shouted
through her tears. 'I come to you, my best friend, and all you're
worried about is what he thinks. I called over twice yesterday,
but no one were home.'

'It's not a crime to be out.' Myra gave her a funny look and
Connie saw her eyeliner had smudged. She looked a proper
mess. What had they been doing? 'Come on, we'll go and sit in
the car.'

Myra vaulted the picket fence at the bottom of the garden,
but misjudging the drop, she caught the hem of her skirt on a
fence post and ripped the material.

'Look what you've done.' Connie wiped her eyes.

'It don't matter.' Myra pulled a face. 'I only wear it when
I'm digging.'

'Digging?'

'The garden.' She dropped her keys on the tarmac. Connie
stooped to pick them up and returned them to her, only for
Myra to drop them again. 'Oops, butterfingers.'

'God, Myra, you're in more of a state than I am. What's the
matter?'

'Nowt's the matter. Except you, calling round whenever the
mood takes you.'

'D'you think I want to come here telling you my child's
gone missing? Bloody hell, Myra, I thought you were my friend.'
Connie followed her. Taking her time; she couldn't afford to go
tearing her clothes.

Myra unlocked the car. 'Get in. It's brass bloody monkeys
out here.' Unlacquered, her white fringe dropped into her eyes.
'Got any ciggies?' She settled herself behind the steering wheel.

Connie, slipping into the passenger seat, opened her bag
and handed over her packet. Watched Myra bash out two
cigarettes and light up, passing one back to her. The street-
lamp above them washed the car's interior in a pinky glow
and Connie saw the rear seats had been pushed flat and the

boot space laid with a sheet of polythene. The interior smelled nasty, of disinfectant and something it hadn't quite masked. She grimaced and wound down her window an inch to let some air in. Another time, she would have asked why there was a spade in the back, but it didn't seem important. The only thing she wanted to talk about was her missing child.

'I thought you'd taken Kathy to teach me a lesson.'

'You did?' Myra's look gave nothing away.

'After what Ian said to me. You can't blame me for thinking it.' She flicked ash out of the window.

'So where's she now then, if we took her? God, Connie, your kid going missing's nowt to do with us.'

'I'm sorry, I didn't mean owt by it.' Connie could tell she'd offended her; but it was always easy to offend Myra. 'You saw her in the back of Fred's car when you left the pub, didn't you?'

'Far as I remember.'

'I'm desperate. Where the hell's she gone?'

'Stop frettin'. Police are bound to find her soon.'

'They're not doing much, apart from hassling Fred. They took him down the station for questioning on Saturday. Kept him in overnight.'

'They think he's got something to do with it?'

'Stupid, aren't they? He were with me. I've told them he wouldn't hurt Kathy; he's nicer to her than I am.'

'Wouldn't be difficult.' Myra, mumbling, dropping ash down her front.

'Oh, ta. That's just the kind of thing I want to hear with her missing.'

'I'm only saying the truth. Don't be getting all maternal now she's gone. You should have shown more of that when she were around.' Myra gave the opinion with a snake of smoke from the corner of her mouth. 'Anyway, police wouldn't come for Fred if they didn't think he'd done owt.'

'You've changed your tune; you always said police were idiots.'

'I'm just saying I'm not surprised they've got their eye on him. Bloke's a petty crook, Con.' Myra stifled a yawn. 'Oh, don't look like that, you know he is.' She made room in the stinking ashtray, extinguished her cigarette. 'And, if you've got form...'

'He got done for stealing electrical goods, not children.' Connie fed her friend a hopeless look.

'Just saying.'

'Well, don't.' Connie held onto her spent cigarette butt, hating the idea of making contact with the ashtray. 'Fred's put all that behind him. That stuff he did, he were only a kid.'

'If you say so.' Myra tugged her skirt down over her dirty knees. Why did Myra look such a mess? What did she say she'd been doing... digging the garden? Since when did she have any interest in gardening?

'What's your mam saying about it? Kathy were the apple of her eye.'

'She's been amazing. Really practical.' A little alarmed that her child was being referred to in the past tense. 'She got leaflets printed, been handing them out everywhere.'

'She'll turn up soon, Con. Kids don't just vanish.'

'That's what I keep telling myself.'

'D'you remember that time we ran off? Camping by the reservoir? That's probably what your Kathy's done. She just got bored waiting.'

'*What?* She's only bloody seven. We were fourteen.'

'Calm down, I were only trying to help. You never know with kids, never know what they get up to.' Myra placed a grubby hand on her arm and, feeling the ominous weight of it, Connie resisted the urge to shake it off.

'My Kathy wouldn't just go, she's a good girl. She wouldn't disobey me. If I tell her to do something, she does it.'

'Too afraid not to.' Myra took back her hand and yawned again.

'Am I keeping you up?' Connie could hear the irritation in her voice but didn't care; it was obvious that, like her horrible boyfriend, Myra didn't give a damn what had happened to Kathy.

'I were wanting to watch that programme with Ian.'

'Don't let me stop you. It's only my daughter we're talking about.' She looked up in time to see a tabby cat tear along the wall, tail quivering in the streetlight.

'You shouldn't have left her in the car, then. It's your fault if she's buggered off.'

Connie winced and, determined to wait for an apology, stared out on the rows of front gardens, their white picket fences glowing in the dark. Then further, to the high-rise tenements and up to the sizzling electricity pylons that speared the night sky. She wondered if it was Ian who had changed Myra. If he was the one who brought out the worst in her. But then she reminded herself of times in their past when Myra had shown her nasty side all on her own.

'Sorry, Con. I shouldn't have said that.'

'The old Myra never would have.'

'I've said I'm sorry. You should know me by now – calling a spade a spade.'

'Talking of spades.' Connie jabbed a thumb into the rear of the car. 'What d'you need that spade for?'

'Erm.... oh, gi's another fag, Con.'

'Yeah, okay. But what's with the spade?' Passing her a cigarette, she watched as Myra fumbled to get the car lighter to work.

'Oh, that. Yeah. It's for digging peat. Up on moor. Peat for the garden.' Still struggling with the lighter and growing increasingly frustrated. 'Ruddy thing. I think there's a box of matches in there.' Myra pointed to the glove box and Connie opened it, let the flap drop down on her knees.

'What's this?' She flicked her spent butt out of the window and used both hands to prise out the Tiny Tears doll that was squashed inside. She held it up and peered into its plastic face that was flushed a creepy pink in the streetlight. 'But...' She couldn't get the words out and, pushing back its pale hair, she stared into the sleepy blue eyes. 'This is Baby Flopsy. This is the dress Mam made for it.' Connie turned it over. Read: 'Made in England' stamped on the back of its neck. 'It's Kathy's doll. What the hell are you doing with it?'

15

Wednesday, 8 September 1965

Black Fell Farm, Saddleworth Moor, West Riding of Yorkshire

Under a thrilling sky, his dogs by his side and his father's old Purdey broken over his arm, Ronald trudged uphill to the hedge of hawthorn that was singing with birds. He felt a great deal safer carrying the shotgun; if he had the misfortune of seeing those two again, he'd be ready for them. Mounting the ridge and walking into the slam of the wind, he looked out over the moor. Although tired after another disrupted night's sleep, the recent turn of events back at the farm hadn't stopped him rising with the sun to stride up the hill, talking to himself like a madman. Thomas's obstinacy enraged Ronald. What they were doing was wrong, and yet his brother refused to see sense.

Eyes watched him. His ewes, calling the last of their lambs, sensed his approach. Accompanied by the thrum of a bumblebee left over from summer and zigzagging among the purple heather, he followed his shadow that, like the pointer on a sundial, marked the shortening days. When he paused for a breather, his dogs pressed their snouts into his hand. This was how these three communicated, in gestures and looks. It was all they had. All he wanted. Ronald unbuttoned his jacket and let the breeze blow through him. He had a mind to search the land around the layby. To see if that evil pair had left any clues about what they were up to on Saturday evening. That woman's sudden appearance at the truck's window had scared the life out of him. It was lucky he'd been able to drive off before there was any trouble. Hessy and Neddy. He rolled their names around in his head... if indeed those were their names.

It was the dogs who alerted him. Noses to the ground, smelling out things that had been left there in the dark. Then a mad black flap of crows taking off from the reeds, their screams filling the air.

Something was wrong.

Horribly wrong.

Then he found the smell. Like walking into a wall. The bloated corpse of a vast-fleeced ewe among the reeds. Bluebottles took off and landed; he batted them away, disgusted one could accidentally touch him. Capsized, her poker-stiff legs, outraged at death, stabbed the sky. He covered his mouth and nose with his hand, preferring the smell of dog saliva to a rotting carcass. Wanting to make sure, he stepped up close. Curious as the living always were for news of death. She was mangled and bled out, and he saw holes ringed in black clotted blood where eyes should be. The ewe had been shot, and none too cleanly. A handgun, he reckoned, parting the fleece and inspecting the damage with the toe of his boot. A gun like the one that had been shoved against his head a few days ago.

'No, Meg.' He booted the dog's side to stop her from taking something away as a keepsake.

Crows, their beaks shining with blood, bobbing and cawing. He bent to pick up a stone to lob at them. They flew to the trees where they sat and eyed him, flaring out their wings and waiting until the coast was clear.

'Shoo. Go on, clear off,' he hollered and waved his arms. But he knew this was futile, unless he was prepared to keep watch. With the buzzard and fox waiting in the wings, the crows wouldn't be alone for long. 'Get out of here.'

How had he missed this on his rounds? The sheep must have been dead for days. He had his dogs to thank for finding her and, scolding himself for not bringing them out before today, he wondered how long the lamb, born late into the season, had been without its mother. But where was the lamb? Ronald checked around, hunting the pockets of grass between the rocks. Then he heard its cries and took several paces forward.

What stopped him was the sight of another ewe.

Half-hidden by thickets of gorse, she was stumbling over loose boulders, the strings of her pink-and-grey intestines wrapped around her legs. The grass glistened red from the wound in her belly and her head had twisted at a strange angle, sensing his presence. He gawped at the carnage. Disbelieving it. His breath coming in short bursts.

He had to kill her.

The tortured bleating continued as he rummaged for his cartridges. The unearthly moaning was unbearable, and it was a struggle to think straight. He loaded the Purdey and snapped it into place, then reached down inside himself for the part that had been carved out years before, when forced into another kind of killing. A small, stony, callous part in a space beyond emotions and hysterics. He had no option. Only he could put the animal out of its misery.

The ewe was still staggering around, disorientated. In all his years of farming, never once had he needed to do such a thing. He didn't dare to think how long she'd been suffering as her mouth coughed open and a tongue curled up, rigid and grey, fiendishly long. He fumbled and pulled the trigger. The ewe slumped to the ground with a muffled thud.

The gun recoil sent a shudder through him. The smell of burnt metal hung in the frigid air.

The world seemed to spin, then settle. While overhead, an army of slow, fat indigo clouds slid over the moor.

Ronald stood in the shimmering aftershock. Dazed. Only dimly aware of the mournful bleating of lambs – for there were two orphans now.

The bright snap of a twig somewhere close by brought him to his senses. It sang out in the ringing silence. He shifted his gaze to the horizon tufted with reeds, then back down to his feet. Saw a collection of spent bullet casings, along with a recent ash pile and several empty wine bottles. Evidence of the picnickers.

Were they still here?

A chilly feeling coursed through him as he hunted the shadows and the dips in the land, holding his breath for any sign. A troubling memory of the woman's eyes, as hard and unyielding as the moor itself, rippled across his mind. He waited in the silence, with nothing but the revving of the wind through the cotton grass. There was no doubting who was responsible for this slaughter, but knowing it didn't make it easier to deal with. If he hadn't been prepared to report them before this horror, he certainly couldn't have the police poking around at the farm now.

16

Underwood Court, Hattersley, North-East Cheshire

Connie slept. An arm thrown out to the side, twitching. The room was chilly. The electricity meter she and Fred forgot to feed had run out. She opened her eyes to the ceiling and followed a crack from the light fitting to the window. Her dream had taken her back to the car park at the Waggon and Horses, where her daughter appeared as real to her as the morning leaching in through the bedroom curtains.

She was halfway through the week already, this was the fourth day without her child. A sideways look at the alarm clock told her it was six fifteen, and she pulled the covers over herself and listened to the muffled thuds from the flat above. The lavatory flushed. Then sounds of Fred padding along the landing. Was he woken by bad dreams too?

'Ouch!' She had rolled onto the solid lump that was her daughter's Tiny Tears; the doll she discovered in the glove box of Myra's car on Monday evening. She untangled it from the bedcovers. 'Did they really find you in the car park on Saturday?' She quizzed the pink plastic face with its lolling eyelids. 'Were she telling the truth when she said she didn't know who you belonged to? I don't think she were telling the truth about much that night. I've never seen her in such a state.'

'You talking to yourself again?' Fred appeared in the doorway, a towel wrapped around him, his chest bare.

'Just thinking aloud... Myra wouldn't have lied about not knowing this were Kathy's doll, would she?'

'*Lie?* Don't be daft.' Fred twiddled the thin gold chain around his neck. 'Why would she lie about something like that?'

'So there's no need for us to tell the police?'

'About those two finding it? Nah, I don't think so,' he dismissed her concern. 'I doubt it'd be much use to them.'

Connie answered him with a smile, stroking the doll's white cotton dress that she had washed and ironed with a care and attention unknown to her before Kathy disappeared.

'You don't have to get up. Have a lie-in. I could feel you tossing and turning most of the night. You'd like a cup of tea? Some toast? I'll go and feed the meter, just let me put some clothes on.'

'D'you want me to make it?'

'No, let me look after you.' He reached out to squeeze her hand as a shaft of sunlight fell over his shoulder. 'You stay there.'

She watched him dress, tying a knot in his bold, striped tie. Blew him a sleepy kiss as he backed out of the room, then lay back against the pillows, her hand floating over to his side of the bed, feeling where he had been. She stared at the shapes in the curtains, hunting the folds in the pattern, wanting it to mean something. Then she must have drifted back to sleep because waking hours later, she found the cup of tea Fred had left on the bedside cabinet had gone cold.

———

The bus to Glossop shuddered to a halt against the kerb. When a surly teenage boy with a face full of angry red spots barged past, Connie grabbed his arm.

'Do you mind? I was here first.'

She pushed ahead of the boy, gave the conductor the right coins and pocketed her ticket. As she moved to the rear of the bus, none of the passengers so much as raised their heads to her. Didn't they care about the pain she was in? Didn't they want to help? Settled in her seat and swamped by grief for her missing child, their indifference made her want to scream.

Inside the bus, gliding along unknown streets of endless cramped housing, the view was blurred by her tears. It wasn't long before the factory workers' homes, with their small back-yards competing for light and air, were exchanged for wide green patches of open countryside. Fidgety and anxious, she fiddled with the cotton bonnet of Kathy's doll, then put it away in her bag. The bus swept into Glossop with its grand town hall and houses of buttery-coloured stone, then trundled past the railings of a primary school. Children were playing in the yard, their joyous shrieks and laughter finding her through an open window. She searched among them, desperate for a glimpse of a little girl with dark curls and a red coat. Her mother had said that a red coat stood out, that it was something people would remember, but nobody had.

Her parents' house, a street or two away from where the bus dropped her, was nothing like the house in Furnival Road where she grew up. This one had a large front garden and pretty borders to turn the head of the passer-by. Her father's doing. Who tended it now, she didn't know. He never let her mother so much as pick up his secateurs. Conscious of the twitching net curtains of neighbours, she saw the gate swinging open on her approach and a car she assumed was the doctor's, accelerating away. She walked down the path to stand in the porch. A space crammed with potted geraniums with heads the size of saucers. Someone had recently mowed the lawn; she identified the zing of fresh-cut grass.

'Oh, Connie. You are in a bad way.' Her mother opened the door, her face communicating everything. 'Don't suppose you've heard owt? Police been in touch?'

Connie stared down at her feet and shook her head.

'Ah, you poor love. Look at you. You've done your buttons up all wrong.' Her mother, puffy with fatigue, undid Connie's raincoat. 'Sorry for mitherin' you, I know you're not a little girl anymore but you need looking after.'

You don't look so hot yourself. Her mother usually made an effort with her appearance, especially for the doctor; everyone dressed up when the doctor called round.

'Who's doing the garden?' Connie couldn't tell her mother to stop fussing. She didn't want them to argue as soon as she'd stepped over the threshold.

'I am. Don't look so horrified.' A gentle laugh. 'I am capable.'

'It's not that—' Connie made a face; she wouldn't fancy pulling that rusty old lawnmower up and down. 'I'm just surprised Dad lets you.'

'Not got a choice, has he? And anyway, I enjoy gardening. It weren't my fault he never let me have a look in.' Her mother gathered her in her arms and cuddled her. 'Come on, lass. I'll fix you something to eat. I bet you've not been bothering for yourself, have you?'

'Fred's been looking after me.' Connie followed her mother along the hall. 'He's great like that.'

Despite it being a sunny day, the living room was dim. Left alone, her mother busy in the kitchen, Connie opened the sideboard and spied an unopened bottle of whisky lurking at the back. She made room for it in her substantial handbag and sat down on the settee just as her mother returned with a tray of tea and sandwiches.

'Cor, that were quick.'

'I knew you were coming, so I made them earlier. Let's have these first. Your dad's sleeping at the minute.'

'Was that the doctor's car I saw driving off?' Connie sat down and propped her bag behind her ankles, careful not to clunk the bottle.

'He's just been. He says your dad probably won't last the month.'

Connie, shocked, fought back tears.

'You're to prepare yourself, love. Say your goodbyes, eh? Be brave for him. Not everyone gets the chance to say goodbye.'

'God, Mam, don't say that.' Her tears fell regardless.

'He's tired. Such a fight he's put up, but it's had him in the end. He knows it, there's no good pretending, but—' Her mother placed a hand on Connie's arm. 'When you see him, best not tell him about Kathy. I don't want him churned up. It's enough of a job getting him to settle as it is. He gets so fretful nowadays.'

'Don't worry, Mam, I won't say.' She watched her mother sit and pour out the tea. Connie thought she looked tired and ill herself; the strain of nursing her father had taken its toll.

She took the cup and saucer that was handed to her and turned away, reluctant to let her mother see her tears. She should have been here, she should have moved to this house with them – her mother needed her; her father needed her.

Neither spoke. It was quiet enough to hear the ticking of the carriage clock on the mantelpiece. The sigh of the armchair as her mother repositioned herself. The room smelled strange and sour, not like a home at all, but more like a hospital ward. Connie tilted her gaze to the sunlight that was sliding in through a gap in the curtains that hadn't been fully opened. Things didn't look as neat as they usually did, she thought as she stirred a spoonful of sugar into her tea. She sipped it and looked over at the flying duck ornaments on the wall. Her father's choice. They had featured throughout her childhood on Furnival Road. She knew her mother hated them and wondered whether they too would be gone soon.

'It's sad it's taken this with Kathy to bring us together again, Connie, love. But I'm so glad to see you.' Her mother brushed crumbs from her front. 'I've been worrying how you're coping with work and everything.'

'They've told me not to come back until Kathy's home.'

'Saving on wages, more like. I bet they're not paying you?'

Connie shook her head.

'I'll give you some money to tide you over. Your father needn't know.' Her mother fetched her purse from the sideboard and after a little resistance, Connie took the badly needed cash.

'I had leaflets printed. I used a nice photo I had of Kathy.' Her mother pointed to a stack of sheets on the dining table. 'I've been handing them out again this morning.'

'I've seen them. Thanks, Mam. You're brilliant. I've been feeling so useless.'

'Why don't we both go out tomorrow for a few hours? I'll ask Mrs Wilson from next door to come and sit with your dad. Make you feel better to be doing something. Have the police said owt, though?'

'Two came round the other morning. A man and a woman. I found a good photo of Kathy for them to give to the papers. It's not unlike the one you used for the leaflet. It were taken at school. She looks smart in it. But no, they're saying bugger all. All they've done is hassle Fred. They've had him down the station twice since Saturday and they called in on him at work.'

'Poor Fred.'

Connie lifted her gaze to her mother's, searching her face for the irony that wasn't there.

'I mean it.' Her mother was on to her. 'I know I said I didn't approve, he's too young for you, but I don't think he's a bad lad.'

'People on the estate are calling him all sorts.' She put down her empty cup and watched the honeysuckle outside the window throw disorganised patterns on the opposite wall. 'I shouldn't have moved there; I should've come here with you. If I had, I'd still have Kathy.'

Her mother bit her lip. 'She'll turn up soon, don't you fret.' The awkwardness between them was palpable. Connie could tell it took everything her mother had not to tell her what a fool she had been, and that she blamed her for Kathy's disappearance.

'But where is she, Mam? Who's got her?'

'Come on, have another of these.' Her mother dodged the question by offering the plate of sandwiches. 'You used to run off all the time. Once, you stayed out for two whole nights. You used to run me and your father ragged.'

'Yeah, and like I told Myra, we were fourteen, not seven.' Connie took a sandwich, but she couldn't eat it and put it on her knee.

'I heard you were back in touch with Myra Hindley.' Her mother fed her a look over the rim of her teacup.

'Got your spies out?'

'Don't be silly, Constance.'

'What've you got against her? She's always been nice to you.'

'I wouldn't know where to start, love. I don't know why you bother with her. You can't have forgotten how cruel she used to be when you were little. And as for that boyfriend of hers...' Her mother pulled a face. 'Creepy-looking bugger. Gives me shivers.'

'*Ugh*, I know. I don't know what Myra sees in him.'

'I think we look for in others what we see in ourselves.'

'Oh, I don't care about those two. All I can think about is getting Kathy back.'

'I know, love. I'm the same.' Her mother glanced at the clock. 'D'you want to see your dad? He's probably awake now. It'll cheer him up seeing your face.'

'D'you think?' Connie wasn't so sure.

'Of course, silly.'

'Yeah, okay. I need the loo anyway. I'll pop in and see him before I come back down.'

Connie returned the uneaten sandwich to the plate and left her bag, heavy with the stolen bottle of whisky, behind.

Inside the bathroom, she washed her hands and opened the medicine cabinet above the basin for a nose and found rows of little brown bottles, their necks plugged with pink cotton wool. Valium. The label on one of them jumping out at her. She picked it up, rattled it against her ear. It sounded full. Why was her mother being prescribed these? Perhaps Connie could ask her own doctor for some, but because she didn't want to wait, she unscrewed the cap and tipped one into her palm. She was about to return the bottle when she changed her mind and tucked it away in the button-down pocket of her skirt.

Out on the landing and facing the room where her father lay dying, Connie stared at the beige-glossed door. The smell she'd identified downstairs was stronger up here, and she wasn't sure she had the strength to go inside. But she must. She'd promised her mother she would say her goodbyes. Needing to steel herself, her fingers poised on the handle, she stopped and looked at the single pill she was still holding in her hand. Might it help to steady her? Deciding it would, she swallowed it.

Black Fell Farm, Saddleworth Moor, West Riding of Yorkshire

Midges danced in the orange rays of sunshine as Ronald worked through his rage by taking longer and longer strides. He tried to rid himself of the mood of menace and uncertainty that had lurked in the background these past few days. With his shins breaded in grit and his fringe bouncing in his eyes, he struggled with the unstable bulk of two lambs and the shotgun. Ronald would never have said he was a vengeful person, but the humiliation inflicted on him by that pair, and now this wanton slaughter of his ewes, had opened up something inside him that could not be closed again. Anyone else would have gone to the police by now. Having a gun held to your head and being threatened with your life was a serious crime. But unlike anyone else, the last thing Ronald wanted was the police poking around in his life because he had crimes of his own to hide.

'We'll need two trips with the wheelbarrow to fetch those ewes,' he talked to his dogs: wagging, eager, close to his side. 'Just get these little'uns settled first.'

After the unpleasantness of the day and the horror of what he'd just dealt with, there was some comfort in walking over the brow of the hill and seeing the lighted windows of the farm-house. The light that shone from its round window, a guiding yellow eye beckoning him home. The line of jackdaws along the roof; the blade of smoke rising from the chimney to the heavens. Not that he believed in heaven. He knew that beyond this world, there was nothing. God was an invention created by one man to keep another at bay. He stopped going to church the year his mother died and didn't care two figs what his neigh-bours thought. His neighbours, with their sprays and insecti-cides, doing wrong to the land. Nature was his god. Nature was the omnipotent one. The thing all mortals would have to answer to in the end.

Only another four years and the bank would give him back the deeds and Black Fell Farm would belong to him and Thomas. That it stood in a hollow, that the walls had sunk and sagged in parts, didn't matter. Now he'd reached his fifties, Ronald had become sentimental. Choosing not to recall how his mother had spent the latter part of her life in bed with the curtains drawn, or the nights when his father, who never had a tender word for him, would take off his belt and leather him, saying he would beat sense into him if no one else would, or the terrible thing he did the night before his brother came home from France, but simpler things, plain facts. Such as the pair of mighty oaks which guarded the gateway and cattle grid to the farm that he planted with his grandfather. The red-snouted David Brown tractor he restored to its former glory after decades of neglect. The fine Suffolk barn he and a few of his farming friends had built from scratch at the start of the war. Now, at an age when he believed that much of his life was over and that what was left was a downward slope to be lived within the constraints and choices made in his youth, he was neither happy nor unhappy about this. There was still much to be done and he wouldn't dwell on the question so many asked him when he took his lambs to the mart: 'What will happen to the farm after you?' He would be leaving it in a better state than when he took up the reins, the answer that was always ready on his lips. For as long as he was able, he would rise at first light to walk the moor. He would sort through the stones and repair the drystone walls that portioned up his land. He would take out his spade and plant more trees. These things that would endure long after he had ceased to.

It had been some time since he last ate, and his belly grumbled. Thinking of what his brother might have cooked him had him smile a small, grateful smile into the shafts of sunshine that cracked open the valley. Panting, his face clammy, he reached the set of gates to the yard and slumped against them, exhausted. The lambs, heavier than ever in his arms, were bleating, tugging on his heartstrings. All around him, the evidence of his father and his father's father. Equipment and tools, rusted with age that no one had bothered to throw away, fearing they might one day come in useful. Thomas was there, straddling his three-legged stool and milking Miss Sunny. Chatting to her in a soothing, lilting voice as he squeezed the warm frothing milk from her as she lazily swung her tail and nudged him with her huge, wet nose. She was the last remaining patch-eyed cow from the small dairy herd they used to have.

'Orphans. Oh, dear, what happened?' Thomas swivelled on his stool.

'Aye. A pair of little mites also needing our attention.' Ronald had decided to save what he suspected that woman and her vile specimen of a boyfriend had done until later. 'How's the other patient? Been any improvement?'

Thomas shook his head and rose from the stool, lifting the bucket of milk to one side before Miss Sunny could kick it over. 'Not yet, but let's hope so soon.' He wiped his hands down his apron. 'Come on, we'll get these little ones settled.'

Ronald, still holding the lambs, followed his brother into the farmhouse, kicked off his boots without bothering to unlace them and left them in the porch. Pushing through the plastic strands of the fly screen, he carried the lambs into the warm smells of baking and something else, like cauliflower cheese. Saliva gathered in his mouth while he watched his brother drag out the large crate, along with bottles with rubber teats and the box of milk replacer they would need to take turns to feed every few hours. Things Ronald kept on hand – not that these occasional orphans were normally the result of their mothers being shot.

'Dear me, Ron, you look shattered. Where's the ewe?' Thomas gestured to the lambs, who were now in the crate padded with fresh straw.

'*Ewes*.' Ronald coughed into his hand. 'There were two. They'd been shot, Tom. And none too cleanly, neither. I had to put one of them out of its misery.'

'What! Oh, that's awful.' Thomas's hand flew to his mouth and he glanced at the Purdey Ronald had propped behind the door. 'It were a good job you had the gun with you.'

Ronald saw the look his brother gave at the mention of the shotgun. It was clear that Thomas knew there was more to his sudden keenness to take it on his rounds than the story he'd given him about the crows. 'Thing is, I know who's responsible.'

'You do?' His brother pushed the words through his fingers.

'I've been seeing them on the moor. Regular, like. A man and a woman.'

'You never said.' Eyes widening in alarm.

'It makes my blood boil I can't report them; that they'll go unpunished.'

'But you've got to, Ronnie. They can't be allowed to get away with killing our sheep. If they're capable of shooting them, it could be us next.'

'You want me to go to the police?' Ronald searched his brother's face; he'd obviously forgotten.

'Well, aye. They're the only ones who can help. These people have to be stopped.'

'And you're sure you want them poking around here?'

His brother's face paled, realising his mistake. 'Oh, no. Of course, we can't.' His fingers still hovering around his mouth. 'I'm an idiot. I forgot. No, we can't have them here, can we?'

18

56, Ashdale Avenue, Glossop, Derbyshire

Connie eased open the door of the spare room where her father now slept, her fingers touching then withdrawing from the unpleasant tackiness of the gloss paint. Poised on the threshold, she wanted to wait for some sign to tell her it was safe to go inside. But nothing came. With the curtains drawn, it was too dim to see if her father's eyes were open. She inched forward to stand at the foot of the bed, the feel of the metal bedstead cold under her grip. Her father was sleeping. She tracked his shape beneath the weight of the blue counterpane and watched his ribcage rise and fall... just. A long-distance runner entering the final lap. There was no longer a need to be afraid of him; there was very little of him left. If her mother hadn't directed her up here, Connie doubted she would have recognised him. She stared at her father and thought: *this man used to thrash me for the smallest misdemeanour and now he doesn't look capable of lifting his arms.*

With her thoughts tripping over themselves, she looked at the bedside cabinet. Saw it was littered with bottles of antiemetics, steroids, a sticky-sided bottle with a plastic spoon, a box of Kleenex, a glass of squash with its curious striped straw. Accoutrements of the dying, she supposed. Things her father needed to make this last stage of life more comfortable. The rustle of bedsheets and a faint sigh from the mattress as Ken Openshaw shifted his non-existent weight. Cloud-soft, the covers released a puff of decay that Connie averted her nose to. Her mother's tabby cat, which had been sleeping on the bed, tore out of the room.

'Pammy?' Her father's voice, barely there, floated to her through the shadows.

'No Dad, it's me. It's Connie.'

'C-Constance... it's you.' A snatch of air punctuated each word, while a bony hand roped with veins patted the bedcovers. 'Is Kathy with you?'

'It's a school day, Dad. She's at school,' she lied, keeping the promise she made to her mother, along with the tremor from her voice.

A croak along with another feeble pat of the bed, and Connie sat beside him. The minutes passed and into it, the sound of her father's ravaged breathing. A skitter of voices in the street. The bark of a dog.

'Let me see you.' That reedy voice again. Connie bent close enough to share the intimate smell of her father's breath.

'I'm sorry I were a disappointment to you, Dad.' Her eyes had filled with tears – it seemed as if it was the time for some confessions. 'Getting involved with Brian and getting pregnant. I never meant to bring shame on you. Whatever you think, I did love him. It weren't my fault he were married. He lied to me. Tricked me. I thought I had a future with him.'

'I know, lass.' Her father's eyes, huge in their sunken sockets, had taken on the opaque glaze of opals and were gummy at their corners. They were the eyes of someone who couldn't stand to look at anything for long.

Another uneasy silence lasted so long that Connie feared he might have fallen asleep. She was about to get up when the same hand, greedy, urgent, seized her arm.

'I c-can't—' he wheezed, then ran out of puff.

'Can't what, Dad?' She tried not to recoil from the unpleasantness radiating from his pores.

'I can't d-do it no m-more, lass.' A single, fat tear rolled down his cheek. She couldn't remember ever seeing him cry and was unsure what to do.

'What is it, Dad?' She stared at the sagging skin of his neck showing above the top button on his pyjamas.

'I-I should've t-told you years ago.'

'Told me what?' She strained to hear him.

'I've g-got to tell you.'

He coughed and she tried not to wince under the surprising grip of her father's icy fingers. She gritted her teeth; she'd always hated it when he touched her.

'What's the matter, Dad? What've you got to tell me?'

'I w-wanted to tell you y-years ago... but y-your mam wouldn't let me.' The voice rasped like sandpaper against the dry, fetid atmosphere. 'I'm s-sorry, Constance, love.'

'Sorry? About what? Tell me, Dad, you're frightening me.'

'I'm not your father.'

Connie wasn't prepared for that. Snatching back her arm, she gawped at him. A man, who, after long years of silence, had suddenly become voluble.

'What d'you mean, you're not my father? What are you on about?'

He licked his dry lips. 'Your mam. She w-were pregnant when I married her.'

Connie wished she could shut him up. Close the lid over the truth she had never consciously sought. The room felt too small to think straight. She pictured his breath as a rancid, crawling thing, condensing to a cloud. All the while, her mother was moving around downstairs, oblivious to the bombshell her husband had just dropped. It made Connie want to yell. To call her upstairs to bear witness.

'Why are you bothering to tell me this now?' she asked when she found her voice.

'I... I thought y-you had a right to know.' He fought for air. 'But I-I loved you like my own. I really did. I l-loved you like my own.'

'*Love?*' She spat out the word and sprang to her feet. 'You loved me? I don't remember much love. You never had a nice word to say to me.'

'That's not t-true, lass.' He coughed.

'Yes, it is. You used to beat me any excuse you got. That was you showing me love, was it?'

'You were a troublesome child.' He coughed again. 'I were doing it for your own good.'

'But what you're telling me now is I weren't yours to do it to, were I?' Connie, glassy-eyed with shock, was talking to herself, to her missing daughter. 'I were only a little girl... A little girl! What harm could I do to you?' Turning to the man who wasn't her father, she felt only disgust for him. What did it matter if she was his or not? The only thing that mattered was the way he had treated her as a child: the beatings, the humiliation. Was his method of parenting why Connie had treated her own child so badly? Why she sometimes hit Kathy? Was that how it worked?

'Don't let's fall out, Constance.' She listened to the low rattle deep inside his chest. 'I haven't got long, lass.'

She didn't answer; she had nothing to say. She watched a circle of sunlight bounce across the room.

'Constance?'

She ignored his plea. She didn't want to hear anything more from this man, this stranger... what was he to her now? Whether the numbness spreading through her was because of his revelation or the Valium she'd taken, she didn't know, and didn't much care. All she knew was that she wanted to get out of the room. To detach herself from him.

'Everything all right, love?' Her mother's voice drifted up, her slippered foot poised on the first step of the stairs.

Connie breathed in the slightly fresher air on the landing. 'Yeah, Mam.' *Mam.* A word so small and so familiar, but spoken now brought her an unexpected comfort and sense of belonging. 'Everything's fine.' She leant over the banister. 'I think he's asleep. Best leave him to it.'

'You'll stay for your supper? Fetched nice sausages from Tomkin's today. Pork and leek. Your favourites.' Her mother sang her invitation.

'Thanks, Mam.' Connie did her best to smile as she descended into the theme tune of *Coronation Street* on the television.

19

Monday, 13 September 1965

Underwood Court, Hattersley, North-East Cheshire

Connie woke up on the settee. The room was dark, the fire out. She had the worst hangover of her life and it was a struggle to reach semi-consciousness. Head thumping and a rotten taste in her mouth, she opened one eye and looked at the coffee table with its smeary glasses, heaped ashtray and empty bottles. Wary of standing up – fearing if she moved, she would be sick – she slid her legs off the settee and stumbled into the bathroom, vomited, and doused her face with cold water. She opened the cabinet and eyed the bottle of Valium. Later, she told herself, when she could keep something down. She didn't want to waste them.

She wandered back to the darkened living room. The air smelled stale. Of cigarettes and the meal Fred had cooked them last night that she hadn't been able to eat. She opened the curtains. Stars were dropping out now. A couple of lights had

come on in the estate and Connie told herself there was little
point going to bed; she would never sleep. Fred would be up in
less than an hour, and she didn't think she could bear to lie
down next to him just to hear him wake up and steal his first
sigh of the day. Fred wasn't the type to need an alarm clock.
Wired to be early, he'd probably had it beaten into him at
Borstal. Up and dressed for work, catching the bus to Ashton,
every day the same. His need for routine was something else he
carried from those days in detention and anything deviating
from it, she swore, would make him panic. Connie looked at a
blur of birds through the balcony window. Or was it her reflection in the glass? Grey and tired, she judged, always harsh. She
turned the radio on low. Radio Luxembourg and Jimmy Savile
telling her how great the morning was.

Except great was the last thing it was. Thoughts scratched
at the margins of her mind. Life wasn't pretty. It was sordid and
full of contradictions. She had been wondering what else her
parents had hidden from her, what else they had worked hard
not to show, not to say. She ransacked her memories for
evidence of other things they might have buried. Talking things
through with Fred again last night – what she now thought of
as Ken Openshaw's deathbed confession – had reminded her
how she was constantly told off by him as a child. Told off for
yawning at the table, for sitting too close to the fire, for looking
at herself in mirrors. It had seemed, when she hit thirteen, she
was in trouble just for being a girl. That her developing body,
the changes she hadn't wanted or known what to do with,
seemed to anger him. It was why she tried to make herself
invisible by staying out of his way. But her silences and
absences only annoyed him more. And then, that dreadful and
terrifying day came when she had no choice but to go home
and face the music. When she could no longer hide the bump
growing under her school uniform that was to go onto become
Kathy. Her father was about to throw her out on the street,

calling her a whore... a marriage-wrecker. And it would have been her fate, had her mother not stepped in and threatened to divorce him.

Connie tipped her head back and yawned. A big, indulgent yawn that would not have been tolerated when she was a child. Then the floorboards in the room next door creaked under her boyfriend's weight.

'*Uch*,' she sighed, wasn't it always the way? If she went to bed now, she reckoned she would sleep like a baby.

Mid-morning and Connie, still lying on the settee, hadn't washed or dressed. A knock at the door spurred her into action and, on her feet, tightening the cord on her dressing gown, she hunted for somewhere to hide the whisky bottle.

'Miss Openshaw?' The man in the overcoat and trilby required verification.

A wary nod as she pushed her long black hair out of her eyes.

'I'm Detective Chief Inspector Mounsey.' He flashed his warrant card. 'May I come in?'

'If you're here to take Fred in again, I'll bloody kill myself.' Connie barred the way. 'D'you really think I'd have let him anywhere near my Kathy if I thought for one minute, he could hurt her?'

'I've not come to take anyone in, lass.' The kind face smiled at her.

'I'm at the end of my tether.' She wanted to believe what he said, but was afraid to trust him. 'If we'd been professionals... doctors or teachers, they'd have believed us, been sympathetic. If I'd been someone important and left my kid to go to some swanky cocktail party, they wouldn't be treating us like this.'

She watched the inspector's gaze wander over her, saw what he saw: no make-up, food stains down her front. And read his pity. Read his non-judgemental appraisal as he peered over her shoulder and into the flat she hadn't bothered to tidy.

'Three times you've had him in, I can't stand it. Fred wouldn't harm a hair on her head, he—'

'I believe you,' Mounsey cut her off, his voice gentle. 'Now, can I come in, lass?'

She stepped aside.

'Is Fred here?' The inspector progressed down the passageway and stood in the centre of the living room, where he removed his hat, holding it upturned in front of him like a begging bowl.

'No, he's at work. Not that he's going to have a job for much longer if you lot don't stop hounding him.'

'I know there's been some trouble, that some of the unit down at Ashton suspect your Fred of foul play so far as Kathy's concerned, but please be assured, I'm not one of them. He's an easy target because he's got previous, that's all. But I'm not here to bother him, Miss Openshaw... may I call you Connie?' He had warm eyes, fatherly – not that she knew what that was like, she reminded herself. 'I've taken over operations at Ashton. I'm the one in charge of your daughter's case.'

Hearing this assured Connie; she couldn't help but like him. 'Please, sit. I'm sorry the place is such a tip, and I'm such a mess.' She looked down on herself in her dressing gown and slippers. 'I'm not coping very well.' She watched him move her bundle of knitting to the arm of the settee carefully, respect-fully, before sitting down. 'It's a cardigan for Kathy. For when she comes home,' she said, thinking she needed to explain. 'I know the longer she's missing, the less chance there is of you finding her, but I've not given up hope, inspector. I know she's still alive. I can feel it.'

'Can you talk me through what happened the day Kathy disappeared?'

'I don't know where to start.' Connie dropped into the

armchair and lit up a cigarette. She offered the packet to Mounsey, but he declined.

'From the beginning?'

As Connie talked and smoked, Mounsey slipped to his feet
and wandered to the sideboard. Picked through the crop of
framed photographs. 'Is this your Kathy as a baby?' he asked
when she'd finished giving her account of that day.

'Yeah.'

'And the woman holding her?'

'Her godmother. My old school friend. Myra... Myra
Hindley.'

A stiff nod. 'Is she local, this Myra?'

'Lives in Wardle Brook Avenue. Number sixteen.'

'Just round the corner?'

'That's right.'

'The same Myra who found your daughter's doll?'

'Yeah. In the pub car park.'

'And yet she claimed not to know who it belonged to?'

She nodded.

'A help to you, is she, this Myra?' A quiver of his eyebrows.

Connie shrugged. 'She's not got much time for kids; I think
she prefers dogs.'

'And yet you chose her to be godmother?' He put the photograph down with a neat little click.

'I had Kathy when I were fifteen, inspector. All my other
friends scarpered. Myra's been good to me in her way.'

Mounsey rubbed his hands together as he crossed the carpet
to look out of the balcony window, down to the estate below. 'I
think Kathy's disappearance could be linked to the disappearances of other children in the Manchester area.'

'Other children? Like who?' She didn't like the sound of
this.

'Lesley Ann Downey.'

'What?' Connie gasped. 'The little girl who's been in all the papers? Christmas time, weren't it? She went missing last Christmas?'

A sombre nod. 'Do you remember John Kilbride and Keith Bennett?'

'I remember something about John Kilbride. He went missing round the time President Kennedy were shot, weren't it?'

'The day after. That's right.'

'But that's' – she counted on her fingers – 'getting on for two years ago?'

'Aye, and it's why I've opened up an investigation into his disappearance. I don't like loose ends, Connie. The idea of missing children on my patch is deeply unsettling. But I have to say,' he stared down at the orange rag rug in front of the fire, 'I'm about the only copper who seems to support this idea.'

'Are you?'

'Aye.' He fixed her with his gaze. 'There's something nasty simmering under the surface of normal life, and I'm usually right; I've a good nose for this kind of thing. Now, what I'm here to ask you, specifically—' he broke off, waited until he had her attention again. 'Do you remember the police doing a recon-struction for John Kilbride at Ashton Market?'

'Yeah, it were on the telly.' She bent forward and extin-guished her cigarette. 'Did it do owt?'

'It gave us a few leads. But it were busy down there, early evening and dark. Your Kathy went missing in the daytime. And the Waggon and Horses, it's on that busy Hyde Road. I'm thinking it might be worth doing a similar thing to jog people's memories about Kathy.'

'But I left her in Fred's car to go drinking. What kind of mother does that make me?' Tears blurred the room, blurred the inspector's face. 'I'll not get any sympathy; folk'll say I deserved this to happen.'

'I'm not here to pass judgement on you, lass. But if it means we get answers?' Mounsey reasoned. 'Don't you want to get your kiddie back?'

''Course I do. What kind of question's that?' She dabbed her eyes with the tail of her dressing gown. 'Do you have children, inspector?'

'I have, aye.'

'Then you'll have an idea what we're going through. Thing is—' she'd started blubbing again, 'I think Kathy might have run away.'

'What makes you say that?'

'Because I weren't always a good mother to her. I used to get frustrated. I can't say she were happy at home. I had her too young, see. I've done my best, but—' she heaved out a sigh, 'I were only a kid myself when I had her.'

'But you haven't been living here long, and you've your parents?'

'Yeah, and Kathy dotes on her gran.' Connie wandered over to the sideboard, stood with her back to the room. 'These other missing children, they've been missing a while.' She picked up the same photograph of Myra and Kathy the inspector had looked at. It was the only time she ever remembered Myra holding her daughter as a baby. 'Are you saying someone's taken them? Hurt them?' She put the photograph down again and when she turned, something in Mounsey's expression frightened her. 'Oh, no, inspector.' An unwanted thought had crawled into her head. 'You think whoever took those other children took my Kathy, don't you?'

20

Thursday, 16 September 1965

Black Fell Farm, Saddleworth Moor, West Riding of Yorkshire

The tension that fizzed around the house was like the electricity that dropped between lightning and thunder. If Ronald and his brother had a blazing row, it would clear the air, but as was typical whenever there were disagreements, Thomas closed in on himself and refused to communicate. His obsession with an idea he didn't realise the implications or the seriousness of had left Ronald, the more pragmatic of the two, frustrated at his inability to make his brother understand the trouble they would be in if they were found out.

Carrying the shotgun, he undid the knot of the yard gate and tilted his head to the clouds pulled over the blue. Ronald was glad to get out of the house. He couldn't stand looking into Thomas's face; the blame he was firing out through his gunmetal silence. As he walked, he scattered his brother's hens: the flap of tangerine feathers pecking the yard.

'No, you stay there. You lasses had a good run this morning.'
Ronald directed his sheepdogs back to their beds in the barn,
then led Bramble out to graze. He unclipped her halter and
watched her for a moment, this mare with whom he shared his
darkest secrets.

When Ronald reached the summit, he stopped to take in the
view. His eyes following a tusk of sunlight as it travelled a
faraway hillside that was every kind of brown and green, before
throwing it back into the shade. This low, tussocky spread that
stretched around him was a watercolourist's dream and hearing
a high piping call, he shielded his eyes from the glare to watch a
cluster of meadow pipits perform their fluttering parachute
displays. Moving through his flock, pleased to see all was well,
he found that despite the trouble back at the farm with his
brother, he was enjoying himself.

He was thirsty, and was reminded of the orange he'd
slipped into the pocket of his jacket before coming out. The
fruit was heavy and the rind didn't easily come away when he
pushed his thumbnail into it. There was orange oil on his fingers
and he knew he didn't like the taste, so wiped it on the seat of
his overalls and left thin trails drying to white. It was sweet and
bitter all at once, and he was swallowing the second segment
when the sound of a radio and a bright clap of laughter found
him. It was the laugh of a woman.

He put the orange away and, down on his hands and knees,
crawled up the slight incline, taking care to stay out of sight.
There they were. In a vale of cotton grass that sloped down to
Shiny Brook and the lightning tree. *They like this spot, don't
they?* He refused, even in his mind, to call them by the pet
names he'd once given them. Sprawled on a tartan rug, the two
reprobates from town were deep in conversation and swigging
from bottles. Wine or whisky? He wasn't sure, but what he was

sure of, stumbling across them again like this, was that it brought the trauma of what they did to him on that terrible day flooding back. The tunnelling mole of his hatred had not gone away. He had been letting it burrow deeper, down to the essence of him, and was determined to have his revenge.

Reassured by the loaded shotgun resting in the crook of his arm, Ronald watched the man roll onto his front to undo the woman's blouse and ram his hand up and under the hem of her skirt. Rough and sordid, there was no tenderness on his part, but the woman seemed to enjoy it. He was sure they were too busy with themselves to notice him, but just in case, he stayed out of their eye-line by sinking further into the reeds. He could remember a time when he had lain on the same spot with Pamela. How he had told her he would always love her even though she hadn't been his to make promises to.

When Ronald next looked over, he saw the man was on his feet, his Box Brownie slung around his neck. Tall and skinny with a headful of brown hair he kept pushing back from his forehead, he gazed over the moor, straddling the great slabs of rock that had spilled down from the Knoll. Self-assured in his long leather coat, he acted as if he owned the place. Ronald, his knees and elbows wet from the spongy ground, hated him for it. But he still didn't move, watching through the rustling grasses while music from their radio carried to him on the wind. Observing them like this, their wild abandonment, made his insides go cold. These two were bad people. Smoking and passing the bottle between them, the man directed the woman to certain boulders where he photographed her, becoming increasingly agitated with her giggling, her failure to take him or his wagging finger seriously. The man's accent, as spiked as the reeds, as he manhandled his girlfriend into position where she posed in her high leather boots; her eyes, grey as gritstone, staring from her sulky face, deep-set and cruel. The pair were as fascinating as they were repellent and Ronald stayed put, watching as the sun was sinking behind him. Bleeding red over the moor.

'Hey! Dirty bastard. Seen enough, have you?' Her voice was aggressive and attached to a pair of pointy boots that were suddenly close to his head. 'Like spying on us, don't you? Caught you in the layby watching 'n all. Right dirty old git. People like you should be locked up.'

'Fuckin' perve.' The man marched towards him, pale with fury and spitting his wrath. 'Ye stinking pile of pish.'

Ronald scrambled to his feet in time to see him pull a flick knife from the folds of his coat, and watched him toss it from hand to hand, the blade snaring the light of the dying sun.

'This is private land; you're not supposed to be on here.' He repositioned the Purdey, making sure they both saw it. 'Go on, get out of here.'

'Fuck you, Grandad. You don't scare us. And anyway, this ain't private land, anyone can come here.' The woman, cocky, swapping smirks with her boyfriend. Close up, there was something inhuman about her colouring: the stark white hair, her red-painted mouth.

'You shot two of my ewes.'

'Aye? Prove it, Grandad.' Mad-eyed and dangerous, fiddling with his knife, the man had the arrogant, unedited laughter of someone with nothing to lose. 'We can do what we want, ye cannae touch us.'

'Clear off.' Ronald raised the shotgun, aimed it in their direction. The change that washed over their faces pleased him. 'Go on, clear the hell off.' His cheeks were burning. 'And take your filthy rubbish with you.' He was tempted to fire his gun. Would have done had his sheep not been grazing nearby.

To Ronald's astonishment, instead of moving away, the man stepped forward, almost close enough to feel his breath. 'Go on then, Grandad. I dare ye.' He pushed his puny chest against the end of the barrel. 'Put a hole in me like I shoulda done to ye.' Then he spread his arms out to his sides, his coat-tails flapping in the wind.

Ronald stayed perfectly still and thought about doing exactly as he was asked. It would be easy; way easier to shoot this bastard than it had been to shoot his precious ewe.

'Nah, I thought not.' Another laugh and the man dropped his arms to his sides. 'Ye havenae the balls. Ye didnae scare us, do he, Hessy? Ye cannae touch us, we're the untouchables.'

Ronald moved his thumb and cocked both hammers, wanting the arrogant bastard to hear the mechanism click. 'You've no idea what I'm capable of, lad.' His voice was calm with the knowledge he had killed before, and could do it again. 'Now skedaddle. Before I blast the pair of you to kingdom come.'

It was with considerable satisfaction that he watched the man turn away to gather their things together. Haphazardly shoving what was left of their picnic into a canvas bag while she struggled into her coat. It felt good to have them afraid of him; in fear for their lives.

'Not so clever now, are you?' he shouted after them, confident he was the one in charge.

'Is that right, Grandad?' The man stopped and turned. Looked him squarely in the eye. 'Ye wanna watch ye mouth. He didnae ken who he's dealing with, do he, Hessy? We know where ye live, pal. We've seen that handsome barn of yours. Go up a treat.' He took out his lighter, ignited the flame. 'And I'd say ye are too far away for anyone to save ye.'

They knew where he lived? What did that mean? Were these maniacs threatening to hurt Thomas? Ronald's thoughts, snapping like dogs. This revelation brought terrible new anxieties.

'Aye. I'd say ye to sleep with one eye open from now on, Grandad.' The man's parting shot before the pair of them scurried over the bank and down to the layby where the Mini Traveller was parked. ''Cos otherwise ye'll nae see me coming.'

21

Saturday, 18 September 1965

The Church and Friary of St Francis, Gorton, Manchester

Somehow another week had crept up on her without her realising. Connie, walking through the drizzle to offer a novena for her missing child, scraped back the vast storm doors and stepped inside the church. She was relieved to find it empty; she didn't want to talk with anyone. Her clicking heels resonated through the hallowed hush of candlelight, and she sat down on a pew to gather up the days since Kathy disappeared. The swift passing of time shocked her. With no job at the factory to measure her days into bite-sized chunks, her lack of discipline meant she was in danger of misplacing time altogether.

The church's vast, barn-like interior smelled of damp stone, its breath cold from years of failed prayers and soul-searching. As a youngster, Connie thought this was where God hid from the world, and there was no reason to think differently now. She couldn't say she was a connoisseur of churches; this was the only one she'd known, but it had always reminded her of an elaborate ballroom seen on a school trip with Myra to a National Trust property. With its swirling rococo moulding and tapestry-cushioned pews, she could envisage an orchestra striking up and lords and ladies waltzing down the aisle.

Sensing eyes, she looked up at the spotlit serenity of the Virgin Mary, her thoughts, spinning again to her missing child. *Please bring her back to me,* Connie silently pleaded to the life-size plaster figure with its disproportionally large pink hands, permanently pressed in prayer. *Am I ever going to have the chance to make it up to her?*

No time for answers. Not from there. A swish of a cassock from the shadows. The slap of leather soles against the flag-stones. Father Theodore, who, sliding into view, chose to stand in an arrow shaft of unexpected sunshine, for the heavenly light to illuminate his personage. Clever Father Theodore.

'Ah, Constance. What an unforeseen honour. It's many years since you graced this house of God.'

Not exactly been welcome since I got pregnant by a married man. She eyed him, keeping her thoughts to herself.

'I've not seen your mother for a while either, but I suppose Mrs Openshaw's been busy caring for your father.' The priest swept a fleshy hand up through his slick, liquorice-dark hair. 'Ah, my dear girl.' He paused, a thought obviously occurring. 'I do hope you're not here to talk funerals?' He dispensed a suit-ably pious sigh.

'Oh, no.' She weighed up whether to tell him her father wasn't her father, then changed her mind. She hadn't even spoken to her mother about it yet. 'We're hoping Dad's going to pull through,' she lied – she couldn't stand the pitying look he was giving her.

'Ah, that is good news.' His chuckle was girlish, excessive; making his flab wobble.

The flash of a gold tooth made him appear rakish, a pirate

on the south Mediterranean seas; hardly proper for a man of the cloth, she considered, counting his moles and wondering how he shaved around them.

'A quiet morning to come and talk to our dear Lord.' He pressed his soft priest's hands together, eternally in prayer like the Virgin Mary, looming over them. 'Although, any minute...' Unrushed, he paused to breathe. 'There'll be the children from Peacock Street and you won't be able to hear yourself think.' He chuckled again, that tuneful, untouched-by-life chuckle, before gliding away to see everything was ready for the Sacrifice of the Mass he would administer later.

Connie thought of the little children. The crocodile line they walked in from the primary school around the corner. Their socks pulled up to knees scabby from playground scrapes. Shame they needed to grow up. She eyed the Virgin Mary, her thoughts veering off again. It was the primary school she and Myra attended before failing the eleven plus and being bundled off to Ryder Brow, where everything unravelled. Peacock Street was same school her mother enrolled Kathy. The uniform hadn't changed any more than their weekly visits here. Steered along the pavement by featureless teachers or a forgotten nun.

The world between childhood and adulthood felt the furthest away it had ever been and she watched the phantoms of herself and Myra, the spilled light of childhood in their eyes as they stood in their white dresses and veils at the altar to receive their first Holy Communion. Other memories unfurled: of playing in the summer lanes around Mellands Fields; of their shoes sitting side-by-side on the pebble bank of the disused reservoir, their socks tucked neatly inside. Connie fussing, taking longer than necessary to pull on her swimming costume. Myra, always the feisty one, grabbing her hand and squealing in eagerness to be racing with her into the water. The same reservoir, with its 'No Swimming' signs that was to feature on the local news when Michael Higgins, a boy from their school, drowned. Townspeople went out in droves, searching the spill-way, the outlet works. 14 June 1957. The day of the Whit parade and the city was in the middle of a heatwave. Connie had been six months pregnant and drifting apart from Myra, who was steadily replacing her with Michael. Her jealousy made her wish they never found him. Something she hid from Myra when they came here to light candles, tipping the tails of the wick into ones already alight. Kneeling on hassocks and praying for his safe return, Connie let Myra think they were in it together. The emergency services pulled his pale, bloated body from the water before the week was out. Connie thought about the lone fisherman who found him. Alerted, he told a local reporter, by the bump, bump against the legs of his waders. The worst catch of his life, the *Manchester Evening News* had claimed, making sure the man looked suitably sad for the camera and his flimsy hook at fame.

When Connie rose to her feet, something caught her eye. She reached down to pick it up. It was a discarded newspaper, and she gasped at the headline.

'Is everything all right, Constance?' Father Theodore's voice sliced through the polished wood smell and guttering candlelight.

'Yes, thank you, Father.' She hadn't realised he was there. How long had he been watching?

'If you're sure?' His glossy black head, haloed in the sputtering gloom, was suddenly close to hers. He had seen the photograph of Kathy printed beside that of Lesley Ann Downey and the banner: CAN YOU SOLVE THE RIDDLE OF MANCHESTER'S MISSING CHILDREN? She braced herself for the feather-light touch on her upper arm. 'Really, Constance, I'm here if ever you need to talk.'

A nod was all she could manage. With the uncontrollable crumpling of her lips, the quivering of her mouth, she was about to cry and turned her head away.

I can't come to you for absolution. Not with this. I am on my own.

The images of the times she had smacked her daughter or shouted at her for nothing burst like blisters against the thirty-three buttons meandering down the priest's stiff black soutane. As she watched him walk away, she churned the only conclusion she could make around in her mind: that she had never deserved Kathy, and now she was going to suffer for what remained of her life by never knowing what had happened to her.

Connie opened her handbag and, with a furtive look around to check Father Theodore wasn't watching, she unscrewed the cap on the bottle of Valium, tipped one out and gulped it from her palm.

22

TWO WEEKS BEFORE

Saturday, 4 September 1965

Waggon and Horses, Hyde Road, Gorton, Manchester

'Look, Flopsy.' The child shook her Tiny Tears to make its eyes open, her voice almost swallowed up by the rain hammering the roof of the Cortina. 'They're like the pictures in my Cinderella book.' Pressing her doll to the rain-mottled window, its head clunking against the glass, she wanted it to share in the wonder of the pub sign with its gold carriage and dainty horses.

The child liked horses. Liked feeding them carrots over the fence when she visited her gran in Glossop. She loved all animals and wished more than anything to have a cat like her gran did, but her mother said she couldn't stand the hairs. Despite the dismal weather, the car's interior was stuffy, and she was warm inside her red coat. Not that she would take it off. Ashamed of the tunic dress beneath with its brown scorch mark caused by her mother's careless ironing, she kept the coat buttoned and wound down the window instead.

Her gran had taught her to tell the time and, following the clock's hands on the dashboard, she knew that more than an hour had passed.

'Oops,' she answered her grumbly tummy. She really was very hungry.

Even though Fred had not kept his promise of lemonade and crisps, the child still liked him. Liked him because her mother was loads nicer when he was around. But the thought of his hands wandering all over her mother and the squeaking bedsprings in the room next to hers, sat like a dark thing inside her and to rid herself of it, she opened the car door and wandered out into the rain with her dolly to see Aunty Myra's car. She liked the colour. It was blue like the sky when the sun showed itself.

'Turquoise,' she informed her doll, sharing the word learnt from her Ladybird book with the pretty pictures. Turquoise was the colour of one of Cinderella's ballgowns. The child was definitely one for words, and it pleased her to make this link. She cupped a hand to the car's wet window. Saw how the back seats had been pushed flat and the boot space covered with a sheet of plastic. Where were the dogs? The dogs were the only thing she liked about Myra, and it was sad not to see Lassie and Puppet. Bored, the child dawdled back to Fred's car and was about to climb inside again when she heard the skittering of little hooves coming from the back of a long white van with mesh-covered windows.

'Hello. Who are you?' she answered the sorrowful bleating and moved closer, pressing against the muddy sides to peer in on the two pairs of eyes that glinted from its darkened interior.

'Are you fat lambs? They're lambs, Flopsy,' she babbled to her doll while delighting in the way these creatures twitched their noses through the wire mesh, hopeful of treats in the same way she was. 'Aren't they pretty, Flopsy?' She wormed a finger through the hexagonal netting to stroke their fleecy topknots.

Anxious creatures, she could identify with the fear shimmering behind their eyes and knew they lived on the tips of their nerves in the same way she did.

'Where's your mammy?' She moved to the back of the van. 'Doesn't she want you either?'

The child interpreted their little bleats as answers and, believing they wanted to make friends, she snapped back the bolt and clambered in beside them out of the rain. The lambs rushed to her, butting her knees, their urgent muzzles seeking her fingers, trying to suckle. She giggled, loving their clean, milky smell and strangely insistent heads. And sitting between them on the bed of straw, stroking them, feeling the thin bones beneath their woolly jumpers, she soon forgot about her mother and Fred and how she'd been instructed to stay in the car.

A movement from the front of the van. Then the slam of the driver's door and the engine was fired up. The van hawking into gear was a sound like her grandfather made when he cleared his throat. Within seconds, they left the pub and its painted sign behind. She risked a look through the smeary back panel and into the cabin. Saw the driver throw his cap on the passenger seat, roll down the window and smoke a cigarette. She ducked down with the smell of it and the lambs who snuggled in beside her. Keeping below the driver's eye-line, she looked out through the mesh of the rear window, up to a sky whipped by rain clouds. She listened to the tick, ticking of the indicator, as the driver waited for a gap in the traffic and noticed how, within a few miles, the topography had changed. Gone were the soot-filled streets of Gorton and the nettle-filled waste grounds, traded in for a series of narrow lanes that opened onto fields and crows balancing on the telegraph wires, until the lonely spread of moorland took over and the wires ended.

The child wondered what her mother and Fred were doing. If they had finished their drinks and returned to the car and found her gone? This did not distress her as much as she supposed it ought to. What she felt instead was a deep, rippling thrill at the chance of something better, and she smiled at the lambs she held against her sides. But her smile slid away again when she realised her doll had gone. That she must have dropped it in the car park. She wouldn't cry, even though the idea of Flopsy lying in the rain made her sad. It was too late to do anything, so she hugged the lambs tighter to compensate. Let them lick her fingers as she invented a life for the man who was driving, deciding he and his wife had lots of children, so one more wouldn't be a problem. She pictured his wife in an apron and slippers, asking in a kind voice what she would like for tea. A woman who wouldn't shout or hit her and enjoyed ironing her clothes and didn't cry out in the night like she was being murdered. The house she gave this new family of hers had a staircase leading to upstairs rooms like her grandparents', unlike the horrible flat her mother had moved them into that was all on one level. It had a clean bathroom and a pretty garden, too. She pictured the bedroom she would have. The brothers and sisters for her to play with. The toys and dolls and animals they would have there.

The lambs were quiet. The only sound was the wet whoosh of tyres and the thump of windscreen wipers. The moorland road they journeyed seemed never-ending. Her view, portioned up by the meshed grill, was of ceaseless grass and reeds. She saw a sign, but not what it said. They were travelling too fast for her to read it. Which was a shame because she was as good at reading as she was at telling the time, all her teachers said so. Reading was her favourite thing and with a mother who had no time for her, storybooks – and the times she could see her gran – were what made life worthwhile.

The engine slowed as the van turned onto an uneven track and the child, along with the lambs, felt every bounce. An unexpected thrill when the wheels rattled over a cattle grid. Then the crunch of gravel as the van squeezed to a stop, shunting the child and the lambs forward with a violent bump. The driver got out and there were harsh voices followed by the banging of a door. The sound of aggressive barking had her push her nose to the mesh to see a pair of big dogs, teeth bared and full stretch on chains. The voices belonged to two men, but she couldn't see them and held her breath to listen, unsure what to do.

Then another shout went up. A woman this time. The voice was sharp like a smack and it reminded her of her mother. No, the child didn't like it here and with a quick goodbye to the lambs, she dashed into the rain and across the pockmarked yard, trying not to breathe in the nasty sour smell oozing from the barn. On and on she ran, past broken-down farm machinery and crumbling buildings with trees sprouting where windows should be. Through the gateway and onto a lane crippled with potholes and flanked by tangled hedgerows, she followed the spine of grey-green grass. It was fun to slosh through the muddy puddles until she slipped and fell down on her knees, cutting them and her hands, and streaking her sopping coat in mud. It was raining so hard she could barely see the way ahead. She pushed her wet curls off her forehead, but the rainwater still trickled into her eyes. As she scrubbed it away; the rainwater mixed with her tears because she was crying now. At the end of her reserves, she did her best not to let a single thought dominate her mind. Until she looked down at her muddy shoes. Her mother would be cross. These were her best ones.

Where was she? Miles from where she was supposed to be. She was going to be in big trouble and thinking this pushed her on, her chin fixed and doing that determined thing she did with her mouth that her mother said drove her up the wall. It was a silly thing to say when it was plain to anyone that people couldn't climb walls, but her mother said lots of things that had no foundation in the truth. Not that the child could think of any examples right now. She was too cold and her teeth were chattering, and she was the hungriest she had ever been. It was all she could do to put one foot in front of the other.

The wind slapped her wet cheeks, and she skidded on the mud, nearly falling again. Then she realised it had stopped raining. There were flies dancing in rays of sunlight and she listened to the gentle coo of a woodpigeon in the branches. It was like it was saying words. The emptiness of this world she had accidentally stumbled upon made a pleasant change from the constant crowds of town, the estate, sharing a cramped flat with her mother and Fred on the nights he stayed over. At least with her gone, her mother would have more space. The space she was forever complaining she didn't have, along with the life she had robbed her of by being born.

Her tummy grumbled. An angry bear. Breakfast had been hours ago, and that hadn't been anything substantial. She staggered forward into the afternoon, narrowing her eyes against the sun that had stained the surrounding moorland a rosy pink. The lane twisted down between silvery walls of hefty stones heaped above eye level, and it was as she turned the last bend that she saw it: the long, low, stonewalled cottage tucked in a wooded valley that fell between a pair of bright green hills.

It looked tidy and cared for. It looked loved.

The child sneezed, then coughed a little. Even though she was shivering from the cold, she felt hot beneath her clothes and her skin was burning. She tiptoed over a cattle grid and was about to drop when two dogs loped towards her, barking, full-stretch on their leashes. She moved towards them and, crouching to say hello, she let them lick the grit from her hands.

23

Saturday, 4 September 1965

Black Fell Farm, Saddleworth Moor, West Riding of Yorkshire

Birds scattered. Their sudden movement startled Ronald who was already jumpy after what that contemptible pair had put him through. To rid himself of the awful memory of having a gun held to his head, he let his mind swing to the discovery of the dancing shoe in its peaty grave. It was such a peculiar thing to find on the moor and it unsettled him almost as much as the terrifying ordeal he'd just endured.

The rain had stopped by the time he opened the gate onto the farm's land. After the torrential downpour, it was good to see the sun again. Certain hours brought their charged, distinctive light, and he could tell the time from where it fell. He clambered over the stile and along the bank of hawthorn before dropping to the sheltered spot that led to the marshy patch between his meadows. Colder than he ever remembered being, it was a relief to be returning to the warm embrace of the kitchen.

From the crest of the hill, he looked down on the farmhouse with its fine timbered barn and stone outbuildings. Anchored, much as he was, to its grassy harbour, he saw the usual row of jackdaws lining the roof and imagined their squawking squabble as they jostled for the best position. Then came the familiar thunder of hooves and a rush of air. Bramble. Cantering along the fence. When she slid to a halt and pressed her muzzle into his hands, he kissed her head, her warm breath soothing him.

It was the wild barking of his sheepdogs that alerted Ronald. Yelping and pulled onto their hind legs by their leashes, they were signalling a stranger. Carrying his crook, the shoe stowed in his pocket, distorting the shape of his jacket and banging against his thigh, Ronald was frightened those bastards might have followed him home. But there was no sign of a vehicle. Whoever this was, they had come on foot.

'How peculiar.' His eyes widened in astonishment when he saw who it was. 'However did you get here? You must've walked miles.' Ronald squinted through the shards of sunlight, distrusting what his eyes were showing him. But he was not mistaken. There really was a little child in a red coat wandering the lane towards the farm.

Observing her progress over the cattle grid, the way she held her hands, palms upwards, as if to plead with the heavens, he could tell, even from this height, that she had been caught in the same cloudburst he had been. Bedraggled, her curls made darker by the rain and stamped to her head, the poor little thing looked half-frozen and ready to drop. Ronald, reading the situation in an instant and wanting to rush to her aid, began to jog down the steep incline. But skidding on the loose stones that flaked away and rolled down the hill ahead of him, he forced himself to slow. Descending at a steadier pace, he watched, powerless to help as the child wobbled forwards into the yard, apparently not the least fazed by his boisterous sheepdogs. Meg and Bess, still barking, were now leaping around her and Ronald gasped, praying they didn't knock her to the ground. Then she was crouching and his young collies, calmer, their tails drumming, pushed their snouts into the hands she held out to them.

What's a little girl doing all the way out here on her own? Where are her parents?

Ronald scanned the dirt track that led to the farm.

Nothing. No one.

Strange, wasn't it?

Hurrying down, sensing she was on the verge of collapse, he reached the last gate too late. It was his brother who saved the day. Ronald didn't think he'd ever seen Thomas move that quickly, swinging out of the farmhouse and down the garden path. Wrapped in his apron, he darted across the yard and scooped the child up in his floury hands and carried her inside.

24

Saturday, 4 September 1965

Waggon and Horses, Hyde Road, Gorton, Manchester

Connie and Fred had no choice but to relinquish their search of the car park and the surrounding streets. Unbeknown to them, they were being watched by the landlord through the pub windows, and they made a sorry-looking pair.

'She's nowhere, Fred. She's gone... gone.' Connie, clutching the grubby bonnet from her daughter's doll, sobbed through the rain that still hadn't let up.

Ashton police station was a squat, red-brick building positioned on the north side of the town. Despite the acre of car park being virtually deserted, Fred, as usual, took an age to choose a parking space. Connie, in no mood to argue, prayed he settled on somewhere before everyone went home for the day.

'You okay, Con?' He secured the handbrake.

'Okay? How is any of this okay?' She gripped the collar of her damp raincoat to her jaw.

'All right. I only asked. *Erm*, d'you wanna clean your face up a bit?'

'Why? D'you think it'll make the police find her sooner?'

Connie stood aside as Fred talked to the desk sergeant: a man with frightening eyes who towered over them.

'If you'd like to take a seat, sir.' He spoke to Fred and ignored her. 'Someone will be along in a minute.'

The station stank of vomit and something sweeter that had been used to mask it. Fred did as he was told, and Connie followed him. They sat side-by-side on plastic chairs. It couldn't be a less welcoming space. The peeling paintwork, the fading photo fits of wanted criminals. There was a poster of Pauline Reade, her pretty face overlapped by more current notices, so that only the left-hand side of her was visible.

Pauline Reade.

Connie and Myra used to babysit for her parents. How long had she been missing? More than two years. This shocked her. She could remember it like yesterday. Her disappearance had reverberated like a thunderclap around the streets of Gorton. Connie never believed the rumours that Pauline went off with some boyfriend she told no one about. Pauline wasn't that kind of girl. She wasn't bad, like her.

The clock above the reception desk was ten minutes slow. Connie thought about how her daughter learnt to tell the time before anyone else in her class. Not that she could take the credit. It was her mother who taught her to do this and to read and do basic sums. Her mother, who always had a smile and a cuddle for her granddaughter, who made room in her life the moment she was born. These bald facts made Connie ashamed. Why hadn't she let her parents have her when they moved from

Furnival Road to Glossop? What did Connie think was going to happen by moving into a flat where it was only her and her child? She picked up Fred's hand and squeezed so hard she heard him yelp in pain.

'Her name's Maggo—' Fred elbowed her and she corrected herself. 'Kathy. Her name's Kathy. She'll be eight next month.'

The police officer, who was around the same age as her father and wearing a fat gold wedding ring, asked her for a photo. And when she said she didn't have one on her, he gave her a look she didn't understand. She knew her mother carried a picture of Kathy in her purse, but she didn't – was this what the look was for?

'And how are things at home, Miss Openshaw?'

'What kind of question's that?' She could swear he'd made a point of accentuating the *Miss,* but ignored it.

'Just routine ones.'

'Things are fine at home.' Connie adjusted herself inside her damp clothes.

'So, there's no way your daughter could have run away?'

'What would she need to do that for?'

'Well, if she hasn't run away—' he eyed her coldly, 'then where is she?'

'If I knew that, I wouldn't be here, would I? What are you asking me stupid questions for? Shouldn't you be out there looking for her?' Connie couldn't believe she had to spell it out. Was the man stupid?

'I'm sorry to have to say, Miss Openshaw, but I wouldn't leave either of my boys unattended in a pub car park half the afternoon. Perhaps your kiddie got bored waiting and wandered off.' The look mutated to accusatory. As if she and Fred had cooked something up between them.

'She were safe. We weren't gone long, were we, Fred?' It was her turn to nudge him.

'Not long,' he echoed obediently.

'But long enough. Evidently.' The officer strung out the word like a piece of elastic. 'I know your father, don't I? Fine upstanding man, Kenneth Openshaw. I'd venture to suggest that you're a bit of an embarrassment so far as he's concerned. Nice family, nice upbringing. Your folks live in Furnival Road, don't they? Posh part of Gorton, that.'

Connie shrugged; she didn't tell him her parents had moved.

'I'd say, you going and getting yourself knocked up by a married man and having to drop out of school,' he picked up where he left off, 'bit of a disgrace, aren't you?'

'I haven't come here to be insulted; I came here because I need your help to find my daughter. It's none of your business what my parents think of me. You should just do your job.' She folded her arms over her chest and refused to cry. 'Are you going to help find my Kathy, or what?'

'You're not doing yourself any favours hanging around with this waster,' the police officer tutted and jotted something else down on his pad.

Connie nudged Fred in the ribs again. She wanted him to stick up for himself.

'Did he tell you he did a stint in Borstal?' He glowered at Fred.

'Yeah. Me and Fred don't have secrets.' Connie was pleased to have trumped him. 'Anyway, what's that got to do with owt?'

'Remember when Pauline Reade went missing?' A dark smile.

'Pauline Reade... yeah, what of it?'

'This Fred of yours tell you about him and Pauline?'

'Tell me what?'

'Ah.' It was the officer's turn to trump her. 'And there was you thinking you had no secrets. This one used to step out with her, isn't that right, lad?'

'Fred?' Connie gawped at him.

'That weren't me. That were Dave... Dave Smith. He lived next door to her. We went all through this when Pauline went missing.'

'Oh, aye, that's right. I forgot the two of you know one another.' A nasty gleam in the police officer's eye. 'I'd say you're to watch yourself, Miss Openshaw. This one keeps very dubious company; very dubious company indeed.'

'But Dave didn't do nuffin'.' Fred shifted from foot to foot. 'He had nowt to do with Pauline going missing. And neither did I.'

'So you say, lad. So you say.'

'Yeah, he does say, thank you very much,' Connie chipped in. 'And anyway, what's this got to do with my Kathy?'

'That's what we've to find out. Don't we, lad? So, if you could just help us by jotting down your place of work so we know where to find you. We know where you live, of course, we've got your mother's address on file.' He rubbed his broad hairy hands together. The man was obviously enjoying himself.

'Where I'm working? What d'you wanna know that for?'

'Just routine, lad.' The officer handed Fred his pencil, and Connie watched as he scribbled it down. 'Righty-o.' He snapped his notepad shut. 'You'd better not be up to your old tricks, eh, lad?'

'Old tricks?' Fred echoed.

'Aye. And suffice to say you're not to leave country or owt. 'Cos we'll be looking into this.' He drummed the pencil against the hardcover of his pad. 'We'll no doubt be talking to you again, lad.'

. . .

'You never said you and Pauline were an item?' Connie quizzed Fred on their walk back to the car.

'That's 'cos we weren't.'

'So what the hell were all that about?'

'How the bloody hell should I know?' His answer said one thing but his face, that had turned a deathly pale, said another.

25

Saturday, 4 September 1965

Black Fell Farm, Saddleworth Moor, West Riding of Yorkshire

Although he was keen to find out how the child was, as well as who she was and how she ended up here, Ronald needed to make a detour to the barn to hide the dance shoe and remove his sodden clothes. Concealed from the house by the deep shadows cast by the high timber doors, he kicked off his boots and, standing in his socks, gave his wet hair a rigorous rub with an old towel. Then he slipped off his jacket, made heavy with rain, and unbuttoned his overalls, stepped out of them and hung them up to dry. His trousers were another problem, but because there was no sign he had soiled himself, he would change into a fresh pair inside.

'Made friends with our little visitor?' he chatted to his sheepdogs as they bounced around him, licking his hands in the same way they did to the child. 'Aye, aye.' He envied their energy; he barely had the strength to tug on a dry pair of boots.

'Calm down, you two... I came in here for something else. What were it?' He looked at the farm equipment, the tools for shearing, for trimming hoofs. Things that dated back to his great-grandfather and further. 'Aye, that's it.' His eyes landed on the gun cabinet. 'I won't be going out on the moor without that from now on.'

He encouraged his sheepdogs back to their beds and located the key to the cabinet. Took out his father's old twelve-bore shotgun that had remained untouched for almost a quarter of a century. Apart from his gold fob watch, there had been nothing in life more precious to his father than his Purdey side-by-side. Ronald brushed away the sticky coating of cobwebs and weighed the heavily grained walnut in his hands. Inspecting the trigger and barrel, he decided it would be as good as new after a clean and a thorough oiling.

He exchanged his boots for the slippers he kept in the porch. These were Thomas's rules and because his brother looked after the domestic side of things and left the running of the farm to him, he was happy to abide by them. Ronald went inside, carrying his wet jacket and the shotgun. Saw the table laid with their best white cloth and set for three. A jam jar of wildflowers, their dangling heads hanging over the rim like seasick passengers. Ronald and Thomas usually made do with mugs and enamel plates and hadn't bothered with a tablecloth for years.

'What's all this in aid of? We got visitors?' Ronald pretended he didn't know as he sniffed the beetroot that was steaming in a pan and filling the kitchen with its earthy breath.

'I've a surprise for you.' Thomas was looking happier than he'd done in a long time.

The kitchen was warm and cosy, and Ronald was grateful for it. He hung his tweed jacket next to the small red coat that was drying above the stove. Listened to the dripping rainwater fizz against the hotplates.

'You're not the only one who got caught in that, Ronnie. This little love got drenched right through.'

Ronald nodded at the child his brother had wrapped in a blanket and seated at the table, but he couldn't bring himself to smile. He didn't like to imagine himself through her eyes – his unshaven chin, his clothes soiled from a morning toiling the land – and was saved from any awkwardness by the kettle letting off steam, because she turned to watch its steel lid flapping in the same way he did. It amazed him how at home she looked after such a short time and, watching Thomas, a bowl of warm water and a flannel, washing her flushed and dirty face, then gently bathing her knees and hands, picking out the grit, he realised something deeper than words had passed between these two, and it made him uneasy.

'She had a nasty fall, didn't you, sweetheart?' Thomas, talking slowly, explaining the things Ronald had already worked out for himself.

'What the hell's going on?' Ronald hissed at his brother, who was emptying the soiled bowl of water down the sink.

'I know, isn't it astonishing?' he grinned. 'She's such a sweet little girl.'

'*Sweet little girl?* Where's she come from? She don't belong here.'

'Well, it were meant to be, Ron... it were meant to be.' Thomas dried his hands then moved back to the child, fussing around her. 'Come on, little one. Come and sit here with me.'

The child looked small for her age. Not that Ronald knew her age. But hazarding a guess, he'd say she was around six or seven. He wondered if his brother knew. If this had been one of the first things they established, along with their names and how she came to be here. What had undoubtedly been established was that Thomas had decided this girl was a gift he would not be giving up lightly. The child glanced at the 'Home Sweet Home' tapestry hanging by the door in its rusty frame, something their mother had made in the years she was too sick to leave her bed. What would she have made of this situation? He wondered as he excused himself from the kitchen to climb the stairs to his room at the top of the house, where he changed into a set of clean clothes.

When Ronald returned to the kitchen, Thomas was telling the child about the shire horses, pointing out the heavy leather harness in the shape of a horseshoe, the brasses pinned to the beams. His wide lap, a safe island where the child now sat.

'Only Bramble now. And she's too old to pull owt nowadays. See those rosettes? Bramble won them all.'

'Can I see her?' The child slid down from Thomas's knees.

'Of course, you can, sweetheart. Ronnie can take you out when you've warmed up and had something to eat... can't you, Ron?'

Ronald nodded, reluctant to engage with this strange idea of domesticity. The talk of the farm's huge bay shires had brought a memory of his father lifting him onto the back of one when he was a boy. Laughing to see him frightened. This snapshot in time summed his father up. A cruel man. A bully.

Someone had propped the window open, and a soft breeze travelled the room. Thomas, slipping on his oven gloves and lifting a glistening-topped fruit cake from the oven, encouraged Ronald and the child to sit up at the table. They did as they were told and Thomas distributed the plates like a pack of cards, his fingers stained purple from peeling the beetroot. The cat, who never bothered with them, appeared to have taken root in the child's lap. Her small pale hand crept out from under the blanket, stroking it. Ronald hadn't realised how weary he was until he sat down and yawned into his fist.

He could tell Thomas was already much changed by this chance arrival. His eyes, despite the horror he must have seen in the war, were as bright and blue as they had been when he was a boy. It worried him how quickly his brother had attached himself to the child because she wasn't staying – they needed to notify her family; she had to go home.

'But you must know your name. Everyone has a name.'

Ronald watched her press her mouth tight shut and shake her head: an emphatic *no* to his brother's question.

'All right, so you don't want to tell us your name, but you must know how you came to be here?' Thomas tried again gently. 'Where do you live, little one?'

'I don't know. But wherever it is, I don't want to go back.'

There was leftover beef and hot beetroot for tea. A bowl of steaming potatoes, slippery with butter. When Ronald reached across the table for the salt, the girl flinched, as if fearing she was about to be hit. The brothers swapped looks, then continued to eat in patchy silence. The men never touched, their fingers leaving the butter knife and breadboard before the other's grip. Thomas made noises when he ate. Little whistles and sucks that made Ronald wonder if he did the same and if this was another example in a long list of petty irritants neither spoke of.

'Nice, is it?' His brother was looking for reassurance. The child nodded. Like Ronald, she was chasing a rogue potato around her plate with a fork. 'All fresh from the garden.'

Ronald squinted out of the window at the vegetable plot where things grew in rows, and propped his knife and fork up on their ends, half-anticipating a sharp rebuke from his brother, who was always on at him about his table manners. The child was too small for their man-sized cutlery. These tarnished silver objects with their cracked ivory handles yellowed with age had belonged to the grandparents whose ghosts lived alongside them in this house. Their mother had used this cutlery.

Laying a place for their father at the table each evening. Not because she wanted Jacob Cappleman home, but in case he turned up and gave her a beating because there was no setting for him.

'You've a hearty appetite, for a little lass. You'll be eating us out of house and home. What d'you reckon, Ron?'

The child, suddenly shy, stopped eating and stared at her plate, where the beetroot juice bled into the slices of beef.

'Aye.' Ronald gave in and picked up the potato with his fingers, his teeth snapping through the waxy skin to the sweetness beneath. He didn't think she was eating much, but couldn't be bothered to contradict his brother.

'You seem preoccupied, Ron. Is owt the matter?'

Apart from finding a strange child in the house? Ronald kept his thoughts about this and the other thing that had happened to him that day to himself. There would be time enough for talking later. 'Nowt the matter with me.' He swallowed his mouthful and reached for the salt again. Carefully, so as not to alarm the child.

A chunk of beetroot slid off the child's fork, off the plate, and dropped onto the immaculate white tablecloth, immediately staining it. She burst into tears when she saw what she had done. She was a shadow of a child, with her cowering and flinching. Her behaviour reminded him of how he had been as a boy. Thinking this brought a stark recollection of his father looming over his bed. Dragging him out from under the covers to beat him. His mother's thin cries of anguish from the sidelines. The terror of him. The buckle on his belt.

'There, there,' Thomas tried to soothe her. 'I'm a silly one. Fancy putting a white cloth on for beetroot! It were bound to happen.'

Unsure what to do, Ronald dispensed a nervous cough and straightened his knife and fork over the meal he hadn't finished. He knew how precious the cloth was, but experience told him the marks wouldn't wash out. The tablecloth, one of the last vestiges of their dead mother. Ruined.

'I don't feel very well.' Two fat tears rolled down the child's flushed face. Tears she didn't bother to wipe away. They plopped on her plate and mixed with the beetroot juice.

His brother took the child's hot little hand in his. 'Oh, dear, you're burning up.'

Ronald watched the way she stared at Thomas's hand as if it wasn't something to be trusted.

'I think she's running a fever, Ron.' He stroked her damp curls off her forehead. 'Come on, let's get you tucked up in bed.'

'Do you want me to do owt?' Ronald, helpless, hovered at the foot of the stairs.

'Aye, Ron. Can you go to town and fetch a few things for her? Go on.' Thomas added, sensing him waver. 'It'll do you good to get away from the place for an hour or two.'

'Isn't it too late? Everything'll be shut by the time I get there.'

'Not if you put your foot down.'

26

Wednesday, 15 September 1965

Underwood Court, Hattersley, North-East Cheshire

Dawn bled in from the east, its fingers, moving over the sky, pinched out landmarks from the gloom. Connie stood on the balcony, watching it. Chain-smoking and clutching her daughter's Tiny Tears to her chest. As she blew her spent smoke as far as she could over the estate and the cloud-covered city beyond, she was thinking again about Myra's strangeness when she'd found Kathy's doll in the glove box of her car.

Below her, the familiar clanking of a milk float as it trundled around the deserted tarmac, and she listened to the chink of bottles in their crates as a white-coated figure moved in and out of the shadowy doorways. Lights were going on as people rose to greet a new day. When she stepped back inside the flat and slid the glass doors shut, she stood amid the shadows and looked the truth in the eye and squinted. Her child had disappeared, and it was all her fault. She wandered to the open door of her bedroom and stared at the bed. At the rise and fall of Fred's body beneath the covers. How was it he could sleep? Her mind wouldn't let her go for long enough. As persistent as the wind, it offered a dizzying array of alternatives: if she hadn't done this or hadn't done that, her child would still be with her.

Connie tipped the mug of tea and round of buttered toast Fred had made her into the sink and sat down on a kitchen chair. Stared at the flypaper. A curling ochre strip speckled with the candied bodies of insects. With heavy thoughts and no radio to distract her, she poured the dregs of whisky from the bottle she had stolen from her parents.

'Aren't you going out?' Fred, dressed for work and sipping his tea, had seen what she was doing.

'No.' She hid under her fringe to avoid eye contact. 'What if Kathy turns up? I don't want her finding the place empty.' Initially fearful of the empty flat, she was now afraid to leave it.

'I thought you were handing out leaflets with your mam?'

'What's the point? No one's seen her.'

She watched his expression change. 'Might do you good to get out.'

'Stop bloody mitherin' me.' Connie rose from her seat. Unsteady. She knew the change in her frightened him, but she couldn't help it. She was drowning in memories of Kathy – how she learnt to swap her baby sounds for the vocabulary she gave her until they too became her words; how she walked, stumbling and colliding with the world she'd stared into shape from her crib. Connie bit down on her knuckles. 'I don't know what to do, Fred. I can't stand being inside my own head.' Welling up with hot, painful tears. 'I know I deserve to feel this bad, but supposing she never comes home?'

He gathered her in his arms and she resisted the urge to pull away; hating to be touched, hating anything that forced her to acknowledge she was here and her daughter wasn't. She gritted her teeth and listened to the breeze from an open window bubbling like a pan of hot water over Fred's shoulder.

'I'm worried about you.' He held onto her; forced her to listen to what he had to say. 'You're drinking too much.'

'Fine one talking.' She wriggled free.

'I'm just saying.' He lit one of his roll-ups, drew on it deeply. 'And you've taken more of them tablets. You promised me you'd stop.'

'I have stopped.'

'Don't lie, Con. Your eyes are all funny.'

'It were you who got me started on whisky.'

'I wondered when it was gonna be my fault. All I'm saying is, you'll be no use to Kathy in this state. It'll be all right, it will.'

'You don't know that.' She downed what was left of her drink and wandered into the living room. Flopped on the settee. Alcohol and Valium fogging her senses.

'Where did you get it from? Costs money, that does. You're always saying you've got nowt.'

'From Mam's.'

'She gave you that?'

'I took it.'

'Bloody hell, Connie. You took her tablets too.'

She picked up Tiny Tears, sat rocking it in her arms. Sniffed its weird plastic smell.

'Connie, please. You're worrying me.'

'Rumours are rife out there.' She jerked her head in the direction of the estate. 'It's not just the cops who think you're involved; people are saying you've killed her.'

'They're calling you names too,' he bit back. 'Saying you're a bad mother and Kathy ran away because she were unhappy at home.'

'Where is she, Fred? What have you done to her?' she screamed and hurled the doll at him. Missed. It landed with a thump on the carpet, severing its head from its body. 'What have you done to my daughter?'

'Christ, Connie. How can you say that? You're hardly mother of the year.'

'Get out! Get out!' She rushed over to pick up the doll's head and shook it at him.

'Don't worry, I'm going. There's no talking to you when you're like this.'

A banging on the flat's front door. Loud enough to rattle the windows in their frames.

Connie's insides flipped over.

Her child was back.

'Kathy?' she croaked: Kathy was always her first thought these days. 'Is that you?' She felt a swell of hope as she charged to answer it, carrying the doll's head by its hair.

But this wasn't her child. This was the same pair of burly police officers who had come the other night.

'Your Fred gone to work yet?' one of them smirked from beneath his helmet.

'You're not taking him again,' Connie screeched. 'Inspector Mounsey promised you were going to leave him alone.'

'Just let us inside, lass. We've to take him down the station. Got a few more questions for him.'

She had no choice and stepped aside to let them in. Heavy men in heavy boots. She heard the floorboards creak beneath them. 'Why can't you get it into your thick skulls? Fred were with me when Kathy went missing.' She shot her boyfriend a look; she was deeply sorry for the awful things she'd said. 'He's not done nowt wrong.'

''Eh up.' One of the officers stopped halfway down the passageway. 'Loose boards?' He bent down to investigate, peeling back the rug and testing the floor with the heel of his hand. 'What you hiding under here, then? I reckon we've to take these boards up. What d'you say, Reg?' he asked his colleague. 'See what they've buried under here.'

'What the hell d'you think this is? Rillington Place? We've nowt buried under there.'

'Aye, lass. That were what that Christie fella said before they took up his floorboards.'

'This is madness. I don't know how many more times I've to say it, but Kathy's going missing's nowt to do with us. You should be out there looking for her, not harassing us every five minutes.'

'We'll have less of your lip if you don't mind, lady.' He scowled at her from beneath the brim of his helmet. 'Right then, Reg. Once we get laddo down the station, we'll come back with a crowbar.'

'But my landlord will kill me.' Connie, pleading. 'If you wreck the flat, he'll kick me out.'

'Then perhaps you better start telling us what you've done with the kiddie, and then we won't have to, will we?'

27

Friday, 17 September 1965

Black Fell Farm, Saddleworth Moor, West Riding of Yorkshire

Ronald went inside the kitchen to fill the kettle and set it to boil. Meaty smells of whatever his brother had left to simmer made his stomach grumble, and he moved to the wood-fired stove: the engine of the house that was never allowed to go out. Lifting the lid of the pan and narrowing his eyes against the steam, he poked a fork into a chunk of potato. Was about to eat it when the scrape of furniture from the room above made him drop the lid again.

Tipping his head to the ceiling he was almost too tall for, Ronald listened to the distressing sound of the child's cough forking through the floorboards. His concern that her fever had worsened reared its head again. The sound reminded him of his mother's cough. Something that was to become her signature tune in the dying months of her life.

A creak of the stairs. The scuff of slippers on the rug. Then the rattle of the Suffolk latch and his brother was there, cuddling a tatty teddy bear with leather pads for paws.

'I've mended his eye, look.' Thomas, his own eyes shining, held up the toy they had shared as children. 'I thought the child might like him.'

'Been busy with that, too.' Ronald pointed at the pedal-operated sewing machine.

'Just altering a few things of Mam's for the little one to wear.'

'I don't remember her wearing that.'

Thomas put down the teddy in favour of a blue sailor dress he was stitching. 'Sweet, isn't it?'

The news that Thomas was making the child clothes unsettled him. It confirmed his fears: his brother had grown deeply attached to her. Ronald may blame himself for his brother's thwarted existence, that he lost the woman he loved and any chance of a family of his own, but this child wasn't theirs, she could never be theirs, and what they were doing by keeping her was wrong.

He watched Thomas make a pot of tea. Squeezing the goodness out of the teabags he still hadn't recovered from the invention of.

'I know I've said, but she loves the dressing gown you bought her.' His brother dried his hands on his apron. 'Yellow suits her perfect.'

'Dinner smells good.' Ronald moistened his lips and took the cup of tea his brother passed him; he didn't want to talk about the dressing gown any more than he wanted to hear how well the girl had settled in. He had things to say, and he was gearing himself up to say them.

'I've made a stew and those little suet dumplings you like.' Thomas beckoned him towards the stove. 'I'm hoping I might persuade the child to eat some.'

'Has she had owt today?'

'Only a little beef tea. Mam used to swear by it when we were poorly, do you remember, Ron?'

He nodded. 'That's a good sign if she's eating, isn't it?' A spark of hope: if the child was better, well enough to travel, he could insist they took her home.

'She only ate a little, Ron.' His hope snuffed out. 'Have a taste of this for me?' Thomas invited, cupping a hand under the spoon he'd dipped into the viscous-looking liquid bubbling on the hotplate.

'Mm, it's good.' He risked a smile.

'More pepper?'

'No, it's perfect.' Ronald wiped the back of his hand over his mouth.

'There's bread. If you're hungry?' Thomas was being especially attentive and it made him suspicious.

'I don't want to spoil my tea.'

'Fresh from the oven? Go on, I'll butter you some.'

Ronald listened to the serrated knife saw through the crusty top of a loaf, while he worked out what he needed to say. His brother held out a plate with a slice of bread, the butter melting in yellow pools. Ronald put down his cup.

'Do you want jam?' A jar sat waiting, ready with a spoon. ''Course you do. Out walking the moor all day. Here you go.' Dropping the bread knife, his brother leant forward and spread the jam languorously, his plump midriff above his apron, heaving against the buttons of his shirt.

Ronald had forgotten when he first noticed, but along with gaining the extra weight that had insulated him, Thomas had lost his spirit and confidence. Since returning from the war and the humiliation of being jilted at the altar, his brother had become as benign and mild-mannered as Miss Sunny. But since the arrival of the child, Thomas had reclaimed his youthful exuberance. Some people might think he had turned into someone new, but they would be wrong. You couldn't make yourself into someone you weren't; Ronald had tried hard enough. But you could revert to the person you once were. And Thomas, after all these years, seemed to have done precisely that.

'The lambs are thriving,' Ronald responded to their little bleats as he tucked into the slice of bread. He hadn't realised how hungry he was. 'How's that little one's cough? Didn't sound too clever when I first came in.'

'Not so good. Better, I'm hoping, when I've given her more of this.' Thomas picked up the near-empty bottle of cough mixture.

'Don't suppose she's told you where she lives?' Ronald frowned. He wanted his brother to listen to the things he'd been rehearsing out with his sheep. 'Or how she came to be here?'

'I can't pressure her, Ronnie. She'll tell me when she's good 'n ready. We've to be patient.'

'That's all very well, Tom, but what about her family? They must be going out of their minds.' A flash of Pamela's woebe-gone face outside Ashton Market.

'I'm not so sure.'

'What d'you mean? You said the kiddie's not said owt.'

'She don't have to. I've seen the neglect and there's bruises she didn't get from playing.'

'What bruises?'

'Here.' Thomas rubbed his upper arms. 'Poor little mite.' His eyes were moist with tears.

'She told you her name?'

'Aye. She says it's Maggot. *Maggot*, can you believe that?'

'Must be what they call her,' Ronald replied, chewing and swallowing.

'Well, aye.' Thomas looked at him as if he was stupid. 'But can you believe it? Giving a beautiful little girl a name like that?'

Ronald could believe it. Even if Thomas had forgotten, he

hadn't. Their father had names for them, filthy names...
anything other than Ronnie and Tom. If it hadn't been for their
mother, they might not have known what their names were
either. And as for bruises – don't get him started.

'I've been calling her Grace... Gracie. You don't mind?'

'Why should I?'

'I think Mam would have liked us giving the child her
name.'

Ronald grunted his reply and finished the last of the crust.
'We've to report what's happened to the police. Longer we leave
it, more trouble we'll be in.' He took a sip of tea. 'I don't want to
argue about it no more, Tom.'

'There's no way I'm sending that child back to that hellhole.
If anyone needs reporting, it's her parents.'

Thomas's emotions were running very close to the surface,
and Ronald needed to tread carefully. He dropped his cup into
the saucer with a deliberate clatter. It was how he sometimes
needed to communicate in this house. With bangs and thumps.
Words were a waste of time when his brother had made his
mind up about something.

'Why are you being like this?' Thomas ducked away to see
to something in the oven. 'You're so angry these days. Where
does all this anger come from?'

Ronald listened to his brother's voice, but not the words he
said. He refused to be diverted. 'Tom, for heaven's sake, we have
to. We have to give her back.'

'We? *You*, you mean.' Thomas turned to him. 'But let me
remind you of something, first. I've been keeping a bigger secret
for you nigh on twenty-four years.' A dark smile.

The look Thomas gave him was enough to make Ronald's
blood slow. *He knows... he knows... what does he know?*

'I'm not an idiot, Ronnie. You're not as clever as you think at
hiding things from me. I didn't buy it that our wastrel of a father
were involved in a pub brawl, then vanished off the face of the

earth. How did he get his truck back to the farm? Lucky for you, the police were too stupid to join the dots.'

'S-so, you know?' Ronald stammered. It shocked him to hear his brother speak about this so calmly. 'You knew it were me that done it?' His mouth had gone dry, and he lifted his cup to drink his tea. Saw the black peat filling with bog water as clearly now as when he had dug that grave under the light of the moon all those years ago. He blinked it away. 'What are you going to do?'

'Nowt. Good riddance. It were a relief to come home and find him gone.'

'Why didn't you say? I've been lugging that guilt around for years.' *Never mind the guilt I have about Pamela.* His brother knowing about their father was one thing, but what about Ronald's other secret? The guilt that burnt a hole in his heart and the reason they were in this mess, or so he thought. Because if Thomas had married Pamela and brought up a family of his own, he would not be latching on to this child now.

'I thought you knew.' A shrug. 'Anyway, I'm just saying, I've kept my mouth shut for you, now you can do the same for me.' Thomas was daring him with his eyes.

'It's hardly the same thing, Tom.'

'Same it is to me. Secrets have to be respected... kept in the family.'

'If I could have just talked to you...talked to anyone.' Ronald collapsed onto a chair.

'We're not talking about that monster; we're talking about the child.' Thomas threw the oven gloves down. 'We didn't kidnap her, Ronnie. By some miracle she came here, she found us. This is heaven-sent, can't you see?' Thomas softened, becoming his compliant brother again. 'Let's not fall out about it. Come and see her. She's been asking for you.'

. . .

Thomas led the way, carrying the teddy bear and a hot water bottle he had filled from the kettle. They left the kitchen and moved into a carpeted room with a large open fireplace stacked with peat and logs. Ronald followed behind up the stairs, his brother's revelation still ringing in his ears. The afternoon sun flooded the landing, but there was no natural light in the passageway. Only an overhead bulb that, as well as casting giant shadows, seemed to congeal the gloom rather than diffuse it. Upstairs, under the eaves, there were three rooms with beds draped in eiderdowns the colours of ice cream. They had given the child their mother's old bedroom. A room that smelled of the first crop of apples and pears that had been recently harvested from the orchard and stored in boxes under the bed. Laid out, not touching, on old newspaper. Ronald could barely look at the child. She frightened him. Her eyes were impossibly bright and reminiscent of his mother's in the closing days of her life.

Thomas bent forward over his comfortable middle and pushed the hot water bottle between the sheets he had taken from the warm innards of the airing cupboard. The best linen they saved for the visitors who never came. Not the old, patched sheets he and Ronald used, worn through by their callused soles and repeatedly darned. Nothing was too good for this child.

The cat, a large tortoiseshell and a demon mouser, who usually tiptoed around unseen, was curled in a ball at the bottom of the bed. It seemed the child and the cat, in the same way as the child and Thomas, had become inseparable and, despite his best efforts to harden his heart, Ronald could not help be moved by the connection between them – a connection it was going to be down to him to sever, making him the villain all over again.

Thomas guided the child's arms into the sleeves of the dressing gown. 'This keeps her lovely and warm, doesn't it, Ronnie?'

'Aye.' Ronald looked at the chair he had carried upstairs the day the girl arrived. Saw the pillows and blankets and suspected this was where his brother kept vigil through the nights.

'Is that all you've got to say?'

'Aye.' He looked around the sparsely furnished room, his gaze resting on the painting of buttercups he and Thomas had given their mother a long time ago.

'Dear Lord.' His brother talked over the child's periodic coughing. 'Didn't I say it, Gracie? A man of few words, our Ronnie.'

Thomas perched on the edge of the bed and stroked where sweat had gathered under her curls. Her eyelids, fluttering and closing. The little thing looked exhausted. Ronald watched his brother cradle her clammy head in his hand and spoon in the cough mixture; tending the child in much the same way he had tended their dying mother. Poor Thomas, his years passed with the futility of running an empty house, struck him sore. The pointlessness of bed-making, doing the laundry... even drawing the curtains. His brother should have filled this house with his children. Ronald knew he was to blame, but letting the child stay didn't tip the balance; it didn't right his wrongs.

'I'm worried about her, Tom. I thought she were getting better,' Ronald whispered to his brother when he joined him in the passageway.

'It's a nasty cough, for sure.' Thomas pulled a face as he squeezed the bedroom door shut. 'The little love's still running quite a high fever.'

'We're going to have to fetch the doctor.' Ronald saw this as a way to return the child to her rightful place. 'If we don't get her proper medical help, she might die.'

'But I don't want people coming here... *interfering*.'

'They won't be interfering; they could save her life. Trust me, Tom, you don't want a death on your conscience. It's a heavy weight to carry, I can tell you.'

'Oh, give her another couple of days. Please?' His brother pressed his hands together. 'She'll get better. I know she will.'

'I'm sorry, Tom. We can't risk it; supposing she needs to go to hospital? No, I'm fetching the doctor.'

Ronald charged downstairs to the kitchen, got as far as pulling on his jacket. Then he hesitated. What was wrong with him? He should just go. This was his chance. The child had just turned up here; they'd done nothing wrong. But then he listened to them telling the police what had happened. Saw them reading the situation. How it would look through their eyes: two men, unmarried, childless, alone with a little girl.

She just walked into the yard; I tell you. She came out of nowhere.

Really?

He could read their scepticism from here. They would never believe he and Thomas were innocent. They would say they had abducted her. A little girl turning up at the farm? What were the chances of that and, if so, why hadn't they reported it immediately? The police would say they were taking advantage. They would make it sound sordid, and then they would become suspicious and start digging around in their past. Reopening the unresolved case of their missing father. They would dig up the moor and find that brute's bones by the tree with the names Ronald had carved into it. His life would be over. The shadow of the rope he'd been living under would become his reality.

Ronald tugged at the collar of his shirt and took a few paces backwards, glad for the warmth of the stove. He needed to think of a way out of this, but the room, the house, seemed to close in on him, and he carried his uncertainty back upstairs.

'All right, Tom. We'll give things a couple more days. But it's going to be down to you to nurse her back to health. It'll be down to you to keep her alive.'

At that moment the sheepdogs barked, and over them, the

growl of an engine. The brothers charged to the window and peered down on the yard in time to see a slim black motorbike speeding off towards the cattle grid. The shape of the rider, his black leather coat flapping.

'Who was that?' Thomas, his nose to the glass.

'I haven't got a clue. But I'd better see everything's all right.' Ronald trailed his lie back down the stairs. He knew who this was. The bastard's threat had been swirling around in his head since yesterday.

The light of the evening had washed the yard in a strange curd-yellow. No one was there. The bike had gone. But not the burn of exhaust that hung in the air. Turning into it, he was about to head back inside when he saw the damage. The gut-churning sight of the word PERVE scratched in giant letters on the side of the truck stopped him in his tracks.

Now what?

The brazen bastard had crossed the line; this was criminal damage, this was provable. How dared he turn up here, bold as brass? They'd called themselves the untouchables, hadn't they? Ronald supposed they were because he couldn't risk reporting them to the police. But what did this mean? What else were they going to damage? Was it going to be him and Thomas next... or worse, the child? The idea that pair of devils knew where he lived, that they could turn up at any time of day or night, pressed an icy finger of dread against his heart.

28

Saturday, 18 September 1965

Underwood Court, Hattersley, North-East Cheshire

The door of the flat opened, then closed again. Fred was home from work and came to find her in Kathy's room.

'You been out today?' He kissed her forehead.

'Yeah, I went to St Francis. Lit a candle for Kathy.'

He gave her a funny look but didn't ask her to elaborate. 'Well, don't go falling asleep in here again, will you? I miss you; I want the old Connie back. You're different with me these days.'

'What d'you expect?' She looked at Kathy's school coat hanging on the back of the door. It still held the shape of her. 'My child's missing. I might never see her again. 'Course I'm bloody different.'

'You're not the only one who's suffering. They're calling me all kinds of shit at work. Not to my face, but I hear them behind my back. *Whispering.*'

'About Kathy?'

A sombre nod.

'But that's not fair. What are they saying?' Her fingers, with a mind of their own, travelled the ridges on the candlewick bedspread that was as pink as the walls Fred had painted for Kathy. It wasn't comfortable to admit that her boyfriend had shown more kindness towards her child in the short time he'd been part of her life than Connie ever had.

'It don't matter.'

'It does.' She drew her knees up to her chest. 'What are they saying?'

'Leave it, Con.' He turned away. 'I'll get tea on.'

She followed Fred into the kitchen, which was always tidy since he'd moved in. She sat down at the oilcloth-covered table amid clothes that were drying on a wooden airer. As well as a packet of streaky bacon, a pint of milk, and a few bottles of stout from the pub, Fred had brought home a copy of the *Gorton & Openshaw Reporter*. The local press had taken a great interest in Kathy's disappearance and the shock of her daughter's photograph under the banner: MASS HUNT FOR MISSING GIRL; made her gasp. Loud enough for Fred to stop what he was doing to check on her.

'Are you okay?'

It was a stupid question and she couldn't answer it. All she could think about was how formal her daughter looked in the photograph. Too solemn for a seven-year-old. Did Kathy ever smile? *Not much to smile about*, said the other voice in her head that did nothing to balm her misgivings. It hadn't occurred to her to give the police one of her parents' family snaps, with Kathy looking cheery, the sun on her face. But thinking about it, she'd been right; it wouldn't have been appropriate. Mad, that – the thought bounced towards her like a ball she had no chance of catching – there might be such a thing as an appropriate picture of your missing child to hand over for printing and spreading nationwide.

'Mrs Bishop from round the corner were asking after Kathy.' Fred forked over the bacon.

'Why would she care? Her kids are safe. All people bother about is how they're going to pay the gas bill and what'll happen in the next episode of *Coronation Street*.'

'I know, but it were nice of her to ask. Not everyone's been so nice.'

Connie closed her ears to Fred. She knew she was right. It was beyond the scope of most people's understanding, beyond the comprehension of the workaday neighbours. Unless you were Pauline Reade's mother or John Kilbride's... or the mothers of those other missing children. Respectable married mothers, not like her.

She returned to the article while the space filled with the smell of frying bacon. Snatching at the print: *tracker dogs join in massive hunt for lost girl... canals dragged... attics searched... sheds... areas of waste ground... door-to-door... school torn apart and scores of people questioned by police...*

The words settled inside her, strange and dark. Where was Kathy? Where had she gone? Pain: a peeled onion bumped beneath her breastbone, and Connie wiped away fresh tears and read on. The report echoed all that Mounsey had said the police were doing to find her child. But seeing the black type against the white gave it a horrid truth, a reality, something that was no longer in the abstract.

'Here you go. I've done you a nice bacon butty with all the drippin'.'

'Oh, Fred. Really, I couldn't.' Connie picked up the fag that was smouldering in the ashtray and took a couple of puffs.

'Go on. I bet you've had nowt all day.'

While she was happy to have Fred living here – he was

useful around the place and more domesticated than she was – his fussing got on her nerves.

'At least have a cuppa.' He turned off the grill and filled the teapot. Buttoned it inside its cosy and set it down with the pint of milk. 'Might be a bit on strong side, but there's water in the kettle.'

'Shall I pour?' As she smoked, her eyes chased the light as it shifted against the wall: gold then blue, blue then gold, as the sun was covered, then uncovered by milky cloud.

'You stop right where you are. Let me look after you.'

'Give over. I can pour a flamin' cup of tea.'

Connie held her cup close to her face and breathed out against the steam. Fred pulled up a wooden chair and, licking his lips, undid the cap of the HP Sauce. Smacked the bottom of the bottle. The action inadvertently reminded her of the times she'd smacked Kathy. The clunk of her teacup against her saucer and she thrust herself back from the table, making the milk bottle topple on its side.

'Why d'you stay with me, Fred?' She mopped the spilled milk with a dishcloth, her eyes gritty behind their lids.

'Someone's gotta look after you.' He was up on his feet, too, trying to fold her in his arms.

'Don't touch me.' Connie stepped aside and rinsed out the cloth. 'I could've done a lot worse for her. I could've cleared off years ago; a lot of mothers do. What's so bad about having a bit of pleasure?' She began to cry. 'Why am I being punished? Oh, Fred, I can't stand not knowing. It's agony.'

After eating next to nothing, Connie joined Fred in the living room. She sat beside him on the settee and thought about reaching for his hand but didn't. Reluctant to give him the wrong idea. She wasn't interested in sex; she couldn't clear her mind for long enough. They drank the bottles of stout and sat smoking in silence.

'Want me to put some music on?'

She shook her head.

'Might help?' he offered and she could tell he was trying.

Connie shook her head again and stared out through the balcony window to the jagged city skyline. It would be dark soon, and she imagined Kathy lost and cold out there somewhere. She reached for the stout bottle again. Eyes closed, drinking deeply, befuddled by sorrow. Fred undid the buckle on his belt and leant back into the cushions. There was no sound apart from the ticking of the clock above the kitchen door.

'Fancy going to the pub?' he suggested as he drained the last of the stout.

'Make your mind up. You were on at me for drinking too much the other day.'

'We don't have to get blotto. I'm only talking one or two.'

'I'm a mess, Fred. I can't be seen out like this.'

'You look beautiful to me.'

Connie didn't believe him. She felt stale, and no matter how many times she brushed her teeth, her mouth still felt alien. She tested her breath in her hand, worried she might stink of booze.

'Come on, it's a nice evening. Help take your mind off it.'

'*It?*' she yelled at him.

'I meant Kathy. You know I meant Kathy.'

'Supposing I don't want my mind taken off it?'

'There's nowt you can do, Con. It'll do you good. Few drinks. Dave said him and Maureen might be there.'

She tied a scarf over her hair and Fred buckled his belt and put on his jacket. Holding hands, they left the flat with its note for Kathy still pinned to the door, and set off in the direction of the New Inn – the only pub within walking distance of Underwood

Court. The surprisingly balmy temperatures had drawn people outside. Connie and Fred walked past the rows of flat-faced council houses with the sound of radios coming from open windows. With no chimneys and only metal flues, she thought these dwellings looked like identical boxes with their wooden-slatted fronts and mean front gardens. Gangs of kids were playing in the street. Kicking footballs, games with skipping ropes and hoops. Freedom until their mothers called them in for tea.

An elderly woman with a blue rinse leant on her gate and called to them, 'Any luck with finding your Kathy?'

'No. No luck,' Connie replied. She knew that fear and confusion pulsed through the estate in response to one of their own going missing. Her daughter's disappearance made people nervous.

'She has to be somewhere,' the woman added. 'Children don't vanish, lass.'

'That's what we're hoping.' Fred did the talking; Connie was afraid of bursting into tears.

'She'll turn up, you'll see.' Another kindly neighbour pushed past with her pram.

'But the police have looked everywhere, ain't they?' A voice from somewhere behind them. Harsher, not half so kind.

'Aye. And it weren't like she were happy at home.' Someone else with a cigarette drooping from their lips. 'People are saying you used to hit her.'

'I did not.' Connie's protest sounded feeble to her ears and she noticed people were edging forward, each bolstered by the other. It wasn't long before a small throng had rounded on them.

'There were a lot of noise from your flat. A lot of shouting.' A man wearing National Health glasses jostled forward. 'You've done summat to her, haven't you?'

The awful thing was that Connie knew these people were

right to be suspicious. She was a rotten mother. Kathy was an inconvenience, as Ian said, and an unhappy child because of it. But it bothered her that people kept saying children didn't vanish. She wanted to remind them about Pauline Reade, John Kilbride and Keith Bennett. As well as that other little girl, Lesley Ann Downey. They had vanished. Police had looked everywhere for them, too, but there was no sign of them either.

'I love my daughter.' Connie couldn't stop herself from crying. 'How can you say such terrible things?'

'Huh, stop your snivelling. You only care 'cos she's gone,' another piped up, emboldened by the others.

'Crying over spilled milk. I don't believe 'em.' A nicotine-stained finger was wagged close to Connie's teary face. 'I reckon they're hiding summat.'

'If that's all you've to say then I suggest you shut up.' By now, a considerable crowd had gathered and Connie was more than a little frightened.

'Police are on to you, though, aren't they, lad? They're not buying it that the kiddie ran away.'

'Come on, Con. Let's get outta here.' Fred seized her arm and steered her forward.

'Folks are sayin' you killed her.' Someone else with eyes as dark and sour as apple seeds.

'What?' Fred bared his teeth. 'I never touched her.'

'Not what cops are sayin'.'

'They reckon that's why you took up with her mam. Could get close to the kiddie then, couldn't you?' A fat, toothless woman rushed up to them spouting foul things, filthy things. Things Connie was frightened to hear because she didn't want them in her head. She didn't want them to be true.

Hand in hand, trailing the jeers and taunts behind them, Connie and Fred eventually broke away and ducked down into a brick-walled ginnel that flanked the backyards of the terraced houses.

'Bloody hell. What were all that about?'

'I told you,' Fred said, panting.

'But we've not down owt. How can they say such horrible things? With my little girl going missing... why do people want to make that worse by accusing us?'

The voices faded and she and Fred relaxed a little.

But not for long.

A high timber gate suddenly swung wide. Trapping them.

''Eh up. Not so bloody fast.' The man blocking their way was as large as a wardrobe. 'You killed her, you bastard.' He was intimidating; the sleeves of his shirt rolled to the elbows showed off a hefty set of forearms that were decorated with blue tattoos. The word 'mother', curved around a heart, stood out accusingly.

'Shit. Now what?' Fred flinched.

'I've had enough of this.' Connie, indignant, thrust out her chest. 'Just clear off and leave us alone.'

'Aye, you'd like that. You'd like to get away with it. Murdering scum like you's gotta be cleaned off the street. Our kiddies aren't safe with the likes of you around.'

With no warning, Fred was seized by the neck and slammed against the wall. Connie screamed and wrestled to get the man off him, but she wasn't strong enough.

'Filth like you should have life screwed out of you.' The brute tightened his hold, choking Fred, who was turning purple.

'Get off. Get off him,' she shrieked and pummelled the man's broad, fat back.

Fred was let go, and he crumpled to the ground, clutching his neck, coughing and gasping. Connie rushed to comfort him as he sat, legs splayed, between the dandelions that pushed up through the cobbles.

'Fred's done nowt wrong, you bloody bully,' she screamed at his aggressor. 'Look what you've done.' She pointed to his bleeding nose and the cut above his eye. 'You've really hurt him.'

'Hurt him? I should string the bastard up. You'll swing for this, you fucker. But if you don't, there's people round here that'll make sure you get what's coming.' The man dragged a finger across his throat before disappearing behind his garden gate.

29

Sunday, 19 September 1965

Black Fell Farm, Saddleworth Moor, West Riding of Yorkshire

Ronald put down the axe and with a hand pressed to the small of his back, he tentatively uncurved his spine. He cast a satisfied look at the wood that, chopped and stacked and filling the woodshed, made living in such an exposed spot, at the mercy of the weather, possible. When he felt able to move again, he loaded the wheelbarrow in readiness for his daily pilgrimage to the house.

From the woodshed window, he watched his brother scraping the breadboard for the birds he'd encouraged to feed from his bird tables. Ronald's stomach growled from beneath his layers of knitwear, telling him it must be close to teatime. Shutting the door to the shed behind him, he gripped the handles of the wheelbarrow and trundled towards the house. It surprised him how suddenly the afternoon had become evening and the sun, dropping over the hills, had stained the yard in the pink glow of rosehips.

'See to the fire for the child, would you, Ron? It gets chilly up there,' Thomas murmured, elbow-deep in flour. 'I'll be up in a while.'

Ronald stacked the firewood beside the stove, then carried an armful of kindling and logs up to the room where the child slept. He pushed a poker into the fire. A fire so low it was nearly out. He placed the wood over the embers and watched the flames lick until it was ablaze. Life with the child had fallen into a kind of routine and Ronald liked the way his time with her bookended his working day. Not that he would let himself get used to it, used to her; the moment she was well enough to travel, she was going home.

He stood up from the fire and brushed his knees. It was dusky in here; the turn of her head made him jump. He hadn't realised she was awake.

'I've brought you an orange.'

He put the fruit on the bedside cabinet. The movement woke the cat, and it bolted from the room. When he flicked on the lamp, he saw how the ordeal of her fever had left its mark. Waxy and corpse-like, her face frightened him and to hide his fear, he crossed to the window to peek around the curtains. The light of the day was still in the yard, but he kept the curtains closed.

'Ronnie.' His name found him through the gloom. 'Will you read me *Winnie-the-Pooh*?' Her hand, petal-light, rested on the book he bought on a whim on his trip into town the day she arrived.

Ronald sat on the edge of the bed and turned the pages. 'Where do you want me to start?'

'From the beginning?' She shuffled upright, her thin arms

cradling the teddy bear that had belonged first to Ronald, then to Thomas.

'I'm not sure I've the time to read it all, lass.'

'Please, Ronnie. Please.' Her big brown eyes from beneath long dark lashes, working their magic. She knew what she was doing, and it made him chuckle. 'Why are you laughing?' she giggled a little, showing off her milk teeth.

'Because you're funny.' He stroked the page as if to clear the way and read out loud, embarrassed at the sound of his voice until he became as engrossed in the story as she was.

'You're like Eeyore,' she said, her voice overlapping his.

'Am I? How so?'

'Because he's a bit grumpy.' She pushed her little hand inside his; soft against his calluses. 'But Eeyore doesn't mean it, it's just the way he is. I love him best of all. I love him as much as I love this cat.' The tortoiseshell their mother had found as a kitten sauntered back into the room and reclaimed its position on the bed.

'She's rather fond of you, too.'

'Sweet pussy. My gran's got a cat.'

Ronald swallowed. This was the first time as far as he knew that she'd mentioned anyone from her family. 'Has she?'

The child coughed and flopped back on her pillows. Her gaze roaming the wallpaper. The peacock pattern repeated over and over.

'Do you want to tell me about your gran?' Ronald looked at her matted curls that framed her flushed little face.

'I miss her,' the child croaked, mucus rattling in her chest. 'It used to be nice living with her and Grandad, but Mam didn't want to live with them no more.'

'Why ever not?' *When your mother's plainly incapable of looking after you on her own.*

'Because Gran's busy nursing Grandad. He's really poorly.'

'Poorly, is he? Oh, that's sad to hear.' Ronald cast his mind back to Pamela and how drained she'd looked. *So, as well as the worry about her missing granddaughter, she had a sick husband to look after.* This situation was becoming impossible. Bad enough they were keeping the child here, but Ronald knew who her grandmother was and the pain she was in. 'You must miss your mam too?'

The child shook her head. Vigorously enough to make her cough. 'I only miss Gran and Flopsy.'

'Flopsy? Who's she?' He thought it must be her sister. It was a strange name, but people were calling their kids all sorts nowadays.

'My dolly.' She coughed again. Ronald could tell the air hurt her chest to breathe. 'I dropped her in the car park. I didn't mean to. Can we go back and look for her?'

'Where was the car park?'

'Not sure. A big pub on a big road.'

'How did you get there?'

'Mam's boyfriend took us in his car.'

'Well, you lost your dolly and you want to find her. Wouldn't your mam want to find you?'

Another shake of her head.

'Why?'

'Because I love my dolly but Mam don't love me.'

'Don't be silly, of course she does.'

'She don't.'

The stark declaration floored Ronald, and he was unsure how to respond. He listened to the grandfather clock in the hall downstairs, and gathered up the chimes while the cat moved to a more comfortable position. Ronald watched it through the half-light. The fluid weight of its paws, kneading and moulding the covers, making a nest. The child, the light of the fire reflecting in her eyes, removed her hand from his and stroked the cat.

Something shifted on the edge of his vision. It was Thomas. He was carrying a basin of steaming water and a bar of soap.

'Ready for your wash, little one?' Thomas opened the curtains and set about administering a blanket bath. Taking care to keep the rest of her wrapped up and warm, he soaped one arm, then the other. The child tugged the sleeves of her nightdress down to hide the tops of her arms, but Ronald had already noticed the fading bruises she hadn't wanted him to see. His brother tried to comb the knots from her hair. 'I'm not sure I can do this.' His eyes sorrowful. 'I don't want to hurt you, Gracie. Best if I cut the nasty parts out and then they can grow again.'

When Thomas disappeared, the child slumped against the pillows, her eyes fluttering, then closing. She was exhausted. But her appetite had improved, and she perked up when his brother returned with a tray of goodies.

'You're far too thin, little one.' Thomas shot Ronald a look. But he didn't want it, and turned away to watch the flickering firelight. 'Eat this up, poppet,' his brother continued, speaking loud enough to ensure Ronald heard what he said. 'I don't want a crumb left. Get you nice and strong.'

The brothers finished their meal and retired to the living room, where a splendid fire in the hearth threw out its heat. Ronald sat in his favourite armchair, smoking his pipe and watching the burning logs, their red cinders collapsing in the grate. There was a surprising reservation about Thomas's eyes this evening. Eyes that reminded Ronald of their mother's. Deep and blue and so large they should make ambiguity impossible. The room was still. The only sound was the occasional crackle of a page being turned. Ronald could tell his brother was pretending to read, that he had something on his mind and was moulding it in readiness of sharing.

'I'm worried you're getting too attached to her, Tom.' Ronald thought he might as well get what he had to say in first. 'That you'll not keep your promise.'

Thomas refused to meet his gaze; he was looking at the framed photograph of himself in his army uniform on the mantelpiece.

'You can't keep her. She's not some stray dog that wandered into the yard. She's got a mother... a family.' Ronald appreciated he was feeling this more acutely. That his chance meeting with her grandmother – a woman he'd never stopped loving – made this situation a hundred times worse for him. It was a shame he couldn't share this with his brother; it might make him understand.

'Keep who?' Thomas sighed dreamily.

He's in this mood, is he? A mood for games. But this is no game. 'You know damn well who.' Ronald scowled at him.

'If she were a boy, you'd let her stay.' Thomas was on his feet, placing logs onto the flames and jostling them into position with the poker. 'You'd say a boy would be useful about the place.'

'Did you hear me? I said you can't keep her. It wouldn't matter if she'd been a boy or a girl.'

His brother returned to his chair and the book he wasn't reading. Picked at the threads on its leather binding.

'Tom? We need to talk about this.'

'Fire away. I'm all ears.' He gave Ronald one of his infuriatingly affable smiles and removed his reading glasses.

'I know you don't want to hear this; I know how fond you've grown of her—'

'I've said, as soon as she's better,' Thomas interrupted him. 'She's still too poorly to travel, Ron, be reasonable.'

Ronald fed his pipe with more tobacco and relit it. He didn't believe Thomas would stick to their agreement, but rather than call him a liar, he came at things from another angle.

'Her family must be going out of their minds. Don't you care about them?'

'She hasn't got a family. Not one that deserves her.'

'You don't know that.' *Her grandmother deserves her.* 'The child's barely told us owt.'

'The fact she don't tell us her name, only that horrible nickname, tells me all I need to know about her mother.'

'Maybe it's a term of endearment.'

'Don't give me that.'

'You just don't want to see it, do you?'

'I've seen the neglect... the marks on her body, her knotty hair. That's proof enough for me.'

'But she could have got them playing.' Ronald didn't believe this, but he refused to validate his brother's reasons for not returning the child to where she belonged. 'Remember the scrapes we'd get into when we were nippers?'

'Our father's fists, you mean?' Thomas glared at him. 'I saw what I saw, Ronnie.'

'You saw what you wanted to see.'

'Is that so? Well, it's served you well enough in the past.'

'That's a bit below the belt, Tom.' Ronald was tuned into the subtext; the thinly veiled threat.

'I'm not giving her up. I've given up enough in my life. She came here. It's like she fell from the sky. It's meant to be, Ronnie, don't you see?'

'No, I bloody don't. You're being ridiculous. You can't keep her. She's not yours.'

'You talk as if I abducted her. She found us, Ronnie, can't you understand?'

'Do you seriously think you can hide her away for the rest of her life? What about school?'

'I'm going to teach her. I'm serious,' Thomas responded to the look Ronald gave him. 'And anyway, since when did you

become such a big advocate of school? You hated it; you barely
went.'

'All I know is, if we get caught... if someone twigs we've a
kiddie living here, then look out.' He bit down on his pipe.

'Just let her stay a couple more days. Let me look after her,
Ronnie. Feed her up a bit, spoil her a little.'

'And then what?' His tone was harsher than he meant it to
be. Harsh enough for the cat who, up to then, had been happily
licking itself in front of the fire, to scarper upstairs again.

'We'll call the authorities.'

'And say what? That she turned up a fortnight ago and we've
only just got around to telling them? That's worse than saying nowt.'

'All right, then let's say nowt.'

'Oh, I give up,' Ronald yawned, stretching into it and giving
himself over to it with a judder. 'I'm feeling peckish.'

'Again? You've only just had your supper.'

'I can't help it. Fresh air and exercise makes me hungry.'

'But I've tidied the kitchen.'

'I won't make a mess. I'll make myself a cold beef sandwich.
There's some over, isn't there?' He was up on his feet, muttering
something about butter on one side, mustard on the other, when
Thomas pushed past him into the kitchen.

'I'll do it, sit down.' This was said with a flap of his plump,
freckly hand. 'You'll only make a mess.' His brother disappeared
inside the larder, still grumbling. 'I wouldn't mind, but you
never put an ounce of weight on.'

'Men like me don't. Hey, Tom, stick the kettle on. We'll
have a brew.'

'But you've just had the best part of a pot.' Thomas tied his
apron around his middle.

'Oh, stop your mitherin'. Tea's not on ration, last time I
looked.' Ronald crouched beside the crate with the sleeping
orphaned lambs who were growing fatter by the day. 'Need to

heat a feed for these two, anyway. While you're doing that, I'll go see to the dogs. Won't be a jiffy.'

It was lovely to be outside. To leave the awkwardness in the house behind. The wind had died, and the air was still, not the merest shuffle from the leaves of the trees that huddled around the farmstead. Ronald was aiming for the barn and whistling to his dogs, when something stopped him dead.

Hang on a minute.

What were those grooves on the verge outside the farmhouse? They looked like tyre tracks made by a single wheel. Too fat for a bicycle, he decided, walking over to inspect them. A motorbike... *that* motorbike?

He could swear the tyre marks hadn't been there when he came back from his rounds. But they must have been. Otherwise, the dogs would have barked, and he'd have heard the engine.

Ronald scanned the yard, the driveway, as far as he could see beyond the cattle grid. All he saw was the David Brown tractor and his truck, scored with the insult he'd concealed from his brother with several layers of metallic paint.

Nothing else.

Nothing human.

Only the cold caw of a crow; its black shape flung against the evening sky. He shivered from the crawling unease that had slithered under his clothes. Had that bastard been to the farm again? Could he still be here – hiding somewhere, waiting to pounce, to damage?

Living on the fringes of this wilderness without so much as a telephone, it never occurred to him before that the isolation could be a problem. But cut off from the rest of the world, no one would know they were in trouble. There was no way of calling for help. The realisation of this left him feeling horribly exposed.

But he was being stupid, he told himself. Paranoid.

Really? Then why was the gate swinging onto the yard? He swore he hadn't left it like that.

I'd say ye to sleep with one eye open from now on, Grandad. He listened to the man's threat play out in his head: the menacing intent that made him afraid. *'Cos otherwise ye'll nae see me coming.*

Ronald recalled the dreadful press of the gun's muzzle against his temple. It was as clear as the image of that fiend's mean rat face and the sound of her cackling laugh.

What did they want with him? Why did they keep coming here? His unanswerable questions churned to a darkened sludge as he felt the pinch of danger.

30

Friday, 24 September 1965

16, Wardle Brook Avenue, Hattersley, North-East Cheshire

Dressed in black and looking for solace, Connie searched her bag for the bottle of Valium as she walked down streets with innocuous names like Sundial Close, Pudding Lane, Field Farm Walk. When she found the tablets, she untwisted the cap and tipped one into her palm, was swallowing it when she turned the corner into Wardle Brook Avenue. Things on the estate may have gone quiet, but she could sense the hostility towards her and Fred hadn't gone away; that it was still out there, simmering behind people's net curtains.

When she next looked up, she saw Myra's blonde head bobbing about in number sixteen's front garden. What was she doing? A question that was answered in a few quick steps.

'Myra! Stop it!' Connie grabbed her arm.

'Get off me. I'm killing it.' Myra was kicking a pigeon and

making enough noise to bring her neighbour out to see what the fuss was.

'For God's sake, stop it!' This was senseless and cruel. 'I thought you said you loved animals.'

'Not this. Fuckin' vermin. Die, you fucker,' Myra shouted as she administered a final kick.

'Hello.' An embarrassed Connie looked over at Mr Braithwaite, who had raised a hand in greeting.

'Don't bloody talk to him.' Myra, deliberately loud for her neighbour to hear, picked up the dead pigeon and hurled it into the road. 'Family's filth.'

'You don't mean that.' Connie gave the man an anguished look of apology. 'They seem nice.' She wanted to add that the Braithwaites were about the only ones who hadn't joined in with the abuse she and Fred were subjected to the other evening.

'Don't tell me what I mean. It's disgusting decent folk like us have to live next door to the likes of them.'

Too addled to argue, Connie followed Myra inside. 'Is Ian around?' Although his Triumph Tiger Cub wasn't parked out front, she wanted to make sure.

'Neddy? Nah. Probably gone to Manchester. People-watching down Central Station.' Myra's lip curled out a smile. 'He likes seeing them shirtlifters crawling about, says he finds them fascinating.'

'Shirtlifters?' Connie, wandering into the living room behind her, didn't understand.

'Yeah, you know – *queers*.'

'What's he got against them? They're not doing any harm. Live and let live, I'd say.'

'Oh, not doing any harm, eh?' Myra, snidey. 'So why's being homosexual against the law then?'

'I'm shocked at you. I know Ian doesn't have a nice word to say about anyone, but I thought you were more broad-minded.'

Connie pulled a face and wished she hadn't asked after him; she'd rather not know what the weirdo got up to in his spare time. 'I weren't really expecting you to be home this early.' She grabbed the back of an armchair to steady herself. Her head was swimming after one too many at her father's wake, and after seeing Myra kicking that poor pigeon, she feared she might be sick.

'Skived off.'

'Don't they mind?'

'Nah. I just tell 'em I've got me monthlies.'

'Hello,' Connie greeted Myra's grandmother, a woman everyone called Granny Maybury, who was feeding titbits to her caged budgerigar.

The old woman gave her a generous smile. 'I were sorry to hear about your dad. Dearie me, you do look worn out. Come and sit down, love.' A hand roped in blue-green veins beckoned her to the settee. 'Ah, don't cry, love.'

'I don't mean to get upset.' She was afraid Myra was going to tell her to pull herself together.

'There, there. You've had a rough time, what with your Kathy going missing. I take it you've heard nowt?'

Connie shook her head and tried to stop the tears, but they fell, regardless. She'd hoped the Valium would have kicked in by now. Longing for the numbing effect that let her forget the mess of her life for an hour or two. Perhaps, as she'd been fearing, they were losing their potency.

'Sorry I didn't come today, Con. You know I hate funerals.' Myra pulled a face. Some of her customary red lipstick had rubbed off on her teeth and it made her look ghoulish. 'Who fancies a cuppa?' She clapped her hands, then disappeared.

Granny Maybury fed the last scrap to her budgie, then joined Connie on the settee. 'You mustn't fret, lass. Nowt bad's happened to your little one, she'll be home before you know it.'

Platitudes. Connie was sick of hearing them and changed

the subject. 'How's things with Ian living here?' She lit a cigarette, hoping the nicotine would settle her stomach.

'He never speaks to me. Myra's never any money, what with them gadding off here, there and everywhere. Had to pay rent for her again this week.' The dogs had settled at their ankles, and Connie absent-mindedly stroked their ears.

'You're good to Myra.'

'Spoil her, you mean?' A thin smile from the wrinkled face. 'Not that she appreciates me. They pack me off to bed at seven every night to get me out of the way.'

'Myra's changed a lot since Ian.'

'Beats me why you still bother with her.'

'It's because we go way back. Not that I like coming here when Ian's home.'

'Don't blame you, lass. Don't like it much meself.' The woman wriggled on her cushion. 'Anyway, tell me, how's your mam? Fine woman, your mam. Not that she had owt time for our Myra.' A dry chuckle.

'Bit of an understatement.' A final pull on her cigarette and Connie made room for it in the crowded ashtray. 'Yeah, she's okay. It's been tough for her but she's been great about Kathy. You know how practical she is?' She waited for Granny Maybury's nod. 'She got leaflets printed. Been handing them out everywhere.'

'Pamela's a good sort. Her and your dad, well, it weren't much of a marriage. He used to slap her about, I heard. Oh, sorry, love. I shouldn't speak ill of the dead.'

'He told me he weren't me dad, last time I saw him. Not that it were much of a surprise. I think I always knew. He were always dead strict with me, Mam says it's why I went off the rails.'

'Well, I never.'

'I don't care. Honest, I don't,' Connie assured her. 'What with Kathy, I've hardly thought about it.'

'What are you two witches plotting?' Myra strode back into the room and handed them each a cup of tea.

'Any chance of a biscuit?' Granny Maybury looked hopeful.

'Biscuits?' Myra's black pencilled-in eyebrows met beneath her white-blonde bouffant. 'You'll be going to bed soon. Ian won't be happy if you're still up when he gets home.'

'But this is her house,' Connie blurted, looking around the light-filled space with its vase of plastic chrysanthemums, the oval mirror on its chain and the glazed horse and foal figurines on the mantelpiece.

'I'll thank you to keep your nib out.'

Connie shrank under the dark look Myra gave her, and the three of them drank their tea in silence.

'Right then, who's for another drink?' The clatter of teacup on saucer and Myra was on her feet.

'Tea. If you're putting the kettle on again,' Granny Maybury piped up.

'Tea? Nah.' Myra, all smiles. 'I'd say wine is called for.'

'You drink too much... I don't like it when she drinks.' The old woman twisted to Connie. 'She gets awful aggressive.'

'Well, you don't have to stay around to watch, Gran. You can always go up to your room.'

'Aye. I think I just might.'

'Good. I'll bring you up another tea in a bit.'

Connie wished Granny Maybury goodnight, then pointed to a pair of fireside chairs she liked the look of. 'They're nice. Where d'you get them?'

'Ashton... oh, shut the fuck up, Joey.' Myra shouted at the budgie and slung a cloth over the cage.

'The colour of walls is nice, too.'

'Dave and Ian painted them.' Myra reached into the side-board for a bottle of wine. 'It used to be just me and Ian, but now he's round here all the time.'

'Fred's missing him.'

'Who – Ian?' Myra looked horrified.

'No, silly, Dave. He's hardly set eyes on him since baby Angela died.'

They drank wine from long-stemmed glasses Myra said she bought with Green Shield Stamps. Bottles of Liebfraumilch Myra called 'Ian's wine', saying they'd better hide the empties otherwise there'd be 'trouble'. They sat smoking cigarettes and drinking, Elvis warbling from the red-and-cream Dansette. Beer had suddenly become too common in this house. Ian's influence again, Connie supposed, sipping her wine and finding she quite liked it. Liked the effect it was having on her, anyway.

The sound of a motorbike outside strangled the conversation in their throats. Then the scratch of a key in the lock, and Ian was home, striding into the living room in his helmet and goggles and long leather coat. The atmosphere changed. It was as if something dark and heavy had filled the space, pressing down on her, and Connie looked up at the ceiling, half expecting to see it.

'I didnae give ye permission to drink my wine.' He removed his goggles and bent to stroke the two boisterous collies who had bounded over, wagging and welcoming him home.

'Oh, shut up, Neddy. Poor Connie's just buried her dad. Where've you been, anyway?' Myra sipped from her glass. 'Watching them queers again?'

'Nah, didnae bother tonight.' Ian dropped his keys on the coffee table. 'Went up to that farm again instead.'

'The one on the moor?'

'Aye.' He darted a sly look at Myra. 'Great fun putting the frighteners on that old fucker.'

'Why; what did you do?' There was a liveliness in Myra's voice that Connie hadn't heard before.

'That'd be tellin'. But I've got big plans for him. I'll be having my revenge when the time's right. Ye dinnae see if I don't.'

'I'd have come with you, if you'd said.'

'We dinnae need to do a'thing together, Hessy. A man needs his secrets.' The muscles in Ian's jaw tightened. 'What ye playin' this pish for?' He barged over to the Dansette and changed the record to Alma Cogan, 'The Tennessee Waltz', and sang along to it in a tuneless way.

It surprised Connie that Myra allowed him to get away with such blatant discourtesy; she couldn't imagine her letting anyone else treat her with such disrespect. Still singing along, Ian hung up his motorbike gear in the hall, then moved to stand with his back to the doorway, scratching himself and staring at Connie through his mud-coloured eyes.

'Good funeral?' he sniffed. 'People do love a funeral. Death's such a magnet, wouldnae ye agree, Constance? A real crowd-puller, for want of a better word.' *Someone who claims to be so fond of words should look for better ones*, she thought as she brushed away a plucky fly he must have brought inside with him. 'Any news on that wee bairn of yours?'

Connie squirmed under his unwanted interest. He always made her feel uncomfortable. 'Not yet. The police aren't getting anywhere.'

'And the longer times goes on, the less chance of them finding her. Am I right?' Ian's lips were shiny from his own spit. 'They still got their sights on Fred?'

Connie nodded. Tears streaming down her face.

'*Uch*. Pull yeself together, woman. They're only on to him 'cos he's got previous. Hessy were sayin' he got set on in the street. Nasty.' The ghost of a smile. 'Ye wanna hope your kiddie turns up soon otherwise folks round here might lynch him.'

'But Fred's done nowt wrong.' Connie wiped away her tears. 'What happened to innocent until proven guilty?'

'Nae such thing, lassie.' Ian rubbed his hands together. 'Anyways, ye moping around with a face like a wet weekend, ye'll be losing him 'n all. I dinnae why ye whinin', ye were

always on about how the wee bairn stopped ye daeing stuff –
well, nothing stoppin' ye now, is there?'

Flabbergasted at his rudeness, Connie stared at him in
disbelief.

'Ian's right. That kid were a millstone round your neck.'
Myra, puffing on her cigarette, squinted against the smoke. 'You
never should've had her.' Connie must have communicated
something in her face because her friend backtracked a little.
'Sorry, Con. I shouldn't have said that.'

'I'm not sorry.' Ian again. ''Bout time there was some
straight-talkin'. Ye got what ye wanted, and the way the world's
going, the bairn's better off out of it.'

Connie didn't have to put up with this and got to her feet. 'I
need to get going. Fred'll be wondering where I am.'

'Off ye jolly well pop.' Ian swayed on the threshold in his
socks. His eyes were cold and callous. 'Ye turnin' up here whenever the mood takes ye, it's really not acceptable. Myra's busy
with me. I'm her life now.'

On her way to the door, Connie tripped over one of the
dogs, making it yelp.

'Hey, watch it.' Myra, immediately got down on her hands
and knees to comfort it. 'There, there, Puppet.'

Connie gawped at the back of Myra's head. Hating her for
joining in with Ian, she'd love to wipe the smug look off their
faces. 'Soppy about those dogs, aren't you? I'd like to see what
you'd do if one of them went missing.'

Ian whirled away, cursing. 'I'm away to me darkroom.
Where I'm not to be disturbed.' He wagged a finger of warning
before stomping upstairs.

'Don't go home yet, Con. We'll have another glass of
wine, eh?'

They listened to Ian crashing about for a minute. Then all
went quiet and Connie excused herself, claiming she needed
the lavatory. A welcome novelty for Myra to have a plumbed-in

bathroom upstairs. Not Connie, who grew up on Furnival Road and had always had an inside bathroom.

She pushed against a door that opened onto an interior flooded in a red light. She had just glimpsed numerous photographs hanging on lines of string, when a bloodcurdling scream rang out.

'Fuckin' get out, ye stupid bitch. Get fuckin' out! Shut the fuckin' door or I'll fuckin' kill ye.'

She closed the door, her heart beating like a trip hammer. Too frightened by Ian's violence to explain she had made a mistake, that she was sorry.

'What happened up there?' Myra asked when Connie, still shaking, re-joined her in the living room.

'It were Ian. He nearly tore my bloody head off. I thought it were the bathroom.'

'Ooo.' A half-smile. 'He's dead secretive about his darkroom. Even I'm not allowed in there.'

'Yeah, all right. But there were no need to scream at me.'

'Take no notice of him. That's just Ian being Ian. He speaks to me like that sometimes... I quite like it, gets me going,' Myra smirked, reaching behind her for another wine bottle. 'Right. How's about another drink?'

Connie held her glass out for a top-up and instead of sitting on the settee with Myra, she chose an armchair. It gave her a different view of the room and she saw, tucked away in the corner, what looked like a reel-to-reel tape-recorder.

She pointed to it. 'Wow. That must've cost a few bob.'

Myra glanced over her shoulder. 'I bought it for Ian last Christmas. He loves it, records all sorts. Sometimes I don't know it, but he's recording me.' A girly giggle.

'He better not be recording us.'

'Who knows?' Myra was giving her a wink when Ian began shrieking down to them from the landing.

'Hessy? Ye've gotta come. Quick!'

'Bloody hell. What's the matter with him now?' Myra groaned.

His shrieking, although more out of fear than anger this time, was something Connie found equally disturbing.

'There's a spider in the darkroom. It's huge. Ye gotta come and get it out... Hessy! Where are ye?'

'Bloody hell, you're such a baby.' Myra dashed away to sort it.

Connie thought about leaving. Of walking out without saying goodbye. But as she was making her mind up, she spotted a copy of the *Manchester Evening News*. Saw the grainy photographed face of a young girl under the banner: CAN YOU SOLVE THE RIDDLE OF MISSING LESLEY ANN DOWNEY?

'What you reading that for?' Myra asked her when she reappeared.

Connie shrugged. 'Says her parents are offering a reward.'

'You thought about offering one for Kathy?' She exhaled smoke in two grey tusks as she poured out more wine.

'What with?'

'You could tap your mam? She's plenty of money.' Myra had taken up her place on the settee again.

'Not much point. Whoever's got this little girl hasn't come forward to claim it, have they? Her parents must be going off their heads... bit like me.'

'Shouldn't have let her go off on her own at night then.' Myra rested her wrist on the arm of the settee. Curled and uncurled her fingers: a cat testing its claws.

Connie frowned. 'Bit harsh. Blaming her parents?'

'I'd say it served 'em right. Letting a ten-year-old go to the funfair on her own. I don't think they'll be seeing her again.'

'I sometimes see Mrs Reade.' Connie took a sip from her glass.

'What you talking about her for?' A pursing of the mouth

and Myra, pulling the newspaper into her lap, wet a finger and flicked through the pages.

'Only that it's sad seeing her roaming the streets looking for Pauline. Honestly, it could break your heart.' She thought about this for a second. 'Is that what it's going to be like for me? I'll go stark raving mad.'

'Nah, everyone's saying she ran off with some bloke. Your Kathy's too young to have done that.'

'I don't believe she did. Pauline didn't seem that kind of lass to me.'

'How d'you know? You hardly knew her.'

'No. But you did.'

Myra didn't answer. Instead, she stubbed out her cigarette and folded the newspaper in half. Turning sweet little Lesley Ann face-down on the table top.

31

Saturday, 25 September 1965

Black Fell Farm, Saddleworth Moor, West Riding of Yorkshire

When Ronald slipped the halter over Bramble's head and led her into the yard for the child to see, he knew he would not be doing this again. She was finally better. He had stopped waking in the night to the sound of her cough filtering through the walls. Thomas didn't want to believe it. He was still wrapping her in the yellow dressing gown and claiming her convalescence had many days to run.

Ronald raised a hand and waved at the bedroom window. It seemed the child had stopped waiting for something to happen and learnt that life on the farm meant there was no punishment, no slapping, nothing to be frightened of. She and Thomas had been having their elevenses together while he swept the yard. A mug of hot milk for her, a mug of tea for his brother. With each day much like the one before, the three of them had settled into a peaceful routine. Despite the guilt he had about Pamela, these past weeks had been the happiest he'd enjoyed for a long time. But unlike his brother, he knew it had to end. She was going home today, not that Thomas was going to make it easy.

Hours later, returning from the moor, his dogs by his side, Ronald found his brother sunning himself on the bench he touched up with red gloss paint each year. The child was seated beside him on an old milk churn. The tail end of their conversation carried to him on the breeze...

'Do I really have to go back home?'

'When you're well.'

'I'm still very sick.' She forced a cough that was barely there.

'You're much better.'

'No, I'm not.'

'Even if you don't go home, you'll want to do things around the farm?'

'But I've nowt to wear.'

'I've already thought of that...'

Ronald, finding himself the accidental eavesdropper yet again, was aware that Thomas had been busy altering their mother's old clothes into pinafore dresses and skirts for this little one. He'd heard the rattle of the old treadle sewing machine going late into the night.

'You look happy.' Thomas glanced up when he saw him.

The observation would have sounded benign to the untrained ear, but Ronald was tuned into the nuance. He wanted to challenge his brother, to ask why he wasn't keeping his side of the bargain by insisting the child was going home today. But he didn't. Instead, he waved a hand in the general direction of his brother's cup and inquired if there was any tea in the pot.

'Aye. And help yourself to a scone. Gracie and me have been baking, haven't we, sweetheart?'

'You packed her things? I got Mam's old vanity case from the top of wardrobe. That'll be big enough; she's not got much.' Ronald was determined to stick to his plan. 'I'm ready to drive to town as soon as you are.' The sky was as blue as the ribbon Thomas had tied into the girl's hair: a sky that was already melting into a pinkish horizon.

'Into town?' A blank look.

'I'm buggered if I'm going to spell it out, Tom.' He flicked his gaze to the child. 'You know what I'm saying.'

Thomas, deliberately obtuse, shrugged inside a purple V-neck he'd knitted for himself.

'Oh, I give up.' Ronald moved away, and was about to step inside the house when his brother intercepted him.

'Excuse me. Boots off, if you don't mind. I don't want you dragging sheep's doings all through my kitchen.'

The child giggled. Melodic as a wind chime. Despite its sweetness, it evoked a memory of their angry-fisted father ripping his mother's wind chimes down from the porch and stamping on them in his big black boots. Ronald carried the upsetting images into the cool, dark kitchen with its sweet smells of baking. He ignored the scones and poured some creosote-coloured tea from the pot. Scooping a handful of biscuits from the barrel, he ate them, standing up at the sink, looking out over his land. Finished, he put his empty teacup on the draining board and went back outside. Found Thomas perched on his stool under his cow. The child was still sitting on the churn, his brother's enormous book of clouds open in her lap.

'Well, Tom, you can't deny she's stronger than ever now.' He moved to stand beside him. Watched the steady streams of frothy milk bounce into the pail. Miss Sunny swinging her tail. 'We've to take her back. It's what we agreed.'

His brother began to whistle one of the show tunes he often set to play on the gramophone.

Anger spurted inside him. 'Tom? Are you listening to me?'

'I bet you're hungry?' Thomas swung his three-legged stool out from under him and got to his feet. Let Miss Sunny back into her field. 'I've roasted a chicken. I don't think Gracie's—'

'Stop!' Ronald cut him off. 'You can ignore me all you want, but it's happening. I'm taking her to the police station in Ashton. I'm sorry, Tom, but whatever this is...' He glanced at the child. 'It's over.'

'Over?' His brother looked on the verge of tears.

'Whatever you think's going on, it isn't real. You're living in cloud cuckoo land.' He tried not to shout for the sake of the girl.

'But... but—' Thomas spluttered in protest.

'Am I the only one who can see how wrong this is?' Exasperated, he threw his hands into the air. 'Stop looking at me like that. I'm not the baddie, I'm trying to put this right. We could go to prison. Don't you get it? Go with her and help her pack, Tom. You know it makes sense.'

'Come on, sweetheart. We best do what Ronnie says.' Thomas beckoned to the child. She looked up from the book and, setting it down on the bench, followed him inside; compliant as a lamb.

Ronald went in after them. Listened for the familiar creak of the stairs while he wondered what living here was going to be like after she'd gone. He didn't get very far.

'We'll have our tea first?' Thomas called down from the landing, his face flushed. 'One last meal together?'

The request hovered between them until Ronald nodded his agreement, deciding it wouldn't do any harm. As he waited in the tarnished light of the hall, he checked the pocket of his trousers for coins and the old receipt with Pamela's number on. He intended to make a call from a telephone box once he'd dropped the child at the police station. To hopefully explain what had gone on. Although he doubted it could be explained. It wasn't something he could fully understand himself.

When the girl reappeared at the foot of the stairs, she was wearing the sailor dress Thomas had made for her.

'My, that looks grand, lass. And Tommy's polished your shoes up. They look good as new.' He swallowed hard, feeling a twinge of pain he couldn't identify the origin of. 'Give me a little twirl?'

She obliged him. Her face as full of woe as Thomas's. But turning once, then twice again, she wobbled and fell forward, banged her hip against the newel post and stifled a cry.

Thomas served their meal as though nothing had happened. Roast chicken with roast potatoes and fruit salad. Ronald, thinking his brother had mixed things up in the misery of it all, questioned whether they should set the fruit salad aside for afters.

'No,' Thomas told him sternly. 'It's for now.'

Ronald watched the child stare dumbfounded at the vase of roses she had harvested from his brother's garden for yesterday's meal. The petals dropping like tears. Yesterday, already feeling like a foreign country.

They ate in silence, fixed on the flowers. Mournfully forking in mouthfuls none of them wanted. What should have been delicious turned to ash in their mouths. A sizeable moth alighted on a lamp that was needed to plug the unexpected gloom. Someone must have left a window open. No one spoke, but three pairs of eyes watched its flapping distress against the pleated shade. Its dark shadow flickering against the wall. When it paused, it allowed them to look at the beauty held in its patterned wings.

'That's a gypsy moth,' Ronald informed them, pointing to it with the tip of his knife. 'You know those little furry caterpillars, the ones that look like eyebrows? Well, that's what they turn into.'

Thomas and the child nodded obediently, and Ronald sensed their eyes as he scooped the moth in his hands to tip it outside.

'A portent,' Thomas said darkly. 'Except, it seems the worst has already happened.'

Ronald sat back down and dabbed his mouth with his napkin. It smelled of their cupboards: musty, damp. Turning from the clatter of crockery to look at the girl's hands, at the fork she couldn't quite manage, he didn't need to see her face to know she was crying; he read it in the set of her shoulders. In the haphazard way she shoved food around her plate. He nearly cried, too. Thinking of how the dynamics of their lives had changed. Of the grief that had pervaded this house before the child came and filled it with joy. And without her, things would revert to the way they had been before.

He followed a beam of sunlight as it vaulted from wall to sideboard, reflecting off the vase of weeping flowers. Gulped down its dazzle, as if this was to be the last of it. And it was. The light they sat in changed. Everything was cast into a strange yellow hue. He looked out at the hunchbacked clouds beyond the potted fern on the windowsill. To the sky that had blackened to a bruise above the darkening moor.

'It's going to tip down.' Thomas, echoing Ronald's thoughts, switched on another lamp. And they watched in sorrowful silence as more suicidal moths, drawn inside by the burning bulb, came to have their wings singed.

'I suppose the land could do with it.' It was all Ronald was prepared to say before scraping back his chair and leaving the table. He knew he forgot to be grateful. Eating all Thomas gave him without so much as a thank-you. If he and his brother had been a married couple, Thomas would have left him by now. He stared out of the window at the yard. 'I know you don't think I feel owt, Tom, but I don't want to do this either.' He rubbed an agitated hand over his stubble, listened to the rasp. 'But we've no choice. She's got to go home.'

'This is her home.'

He turned and fed his brother a look. 'We both know that's not true. And anyway, it's what we agreed. Get her well, get some flesh on her bones. It's what you said.'

Thomas was on his feet and crying so hard his stomach wobbled. Ronald sighed and wiped his large farmer's hands over his hair, down his cheek, feeling his scar.

'I always wanted a daughter, Ronnie.' His brother's eyes were full of tears. 'Please don't take her away from me.'

'Come on, little one.' Ronald lifted the truck's keys from the hook and jangled them in his hand. 'Let's get going.'

'But I don't want to go.' The child heaved in air then burst into tears. 'I want to stay here with you and Tom.'

Such a reasonable request, but Ronald needed to stay strong. 'It don't have to be forever, lass. When you're back with your mam, you can come and visit.'

The child was really sobbing now. Breathless, her narrow frame juddering. Thomas gathered her in his arms and tossed him a desperate look.

'We have to do this,' Ronald persisted, gritting his teeth. This was the hardest thing he'd ever had to do. 'Tommy and me, we could get into serious trouble if we keep you. You don't want that to happen, do you?'

The girl shook her head as tears rolled down her face.

'Right then, you say ta-ra to our Tommy. There's a good lass.'

Thomas was still sobbing. Ronald hadn't seen him cry like this since they buried their mother. He steeled himself against it, turning away when his brother and the child exchanged their farewells.

'Can I say bye-bye to Bramble first?' she hiccupped through her tears.

'Of course, you can.' Ronald took the vanity case Thomas had brought down from upstairs. The heartbreaking plea nearly crumbled the fragment of resolve he was clinging onto, but with a heavy sigh, he steered her out into what remained of the day.

'Ron?' Thomas untied his apron and folded it over the back of a chair. Stood staring down at the toes of his slippers. 'Ronnie?' His voice was choked. Ronald had to turn his back to him. Frightened he wouldn't be able to go through with it. Thomas wasn't the only one hurting, but he couldn't tell him this. 'Don't take her away from me. Please don't. I can't bear it.' Thomas pressed his hand to his chest. 'I think it'll kill me.'

'I've got to, Tom. I haven't got a choice.'

'I'll go to the police, Ron. I will. I'll tell them what you did.'

'I don't care. You'd be doing me a favour. I'm sick of dragging the guilt of it around.'

Outside, it smelled like it did when rain was on the way. Ronald tilted his nose to sniff the air, and as he did so, a loud bang rang out through the air. It was swiftly followed by several more.

Gunshot.

Close to the farmhouse.

He reached into the kitchen to retrieve the Purdey from behind its flap of curtain. Pulled on his jacket, patted the pockets to check for cartridges.

'What's going on, Ronnie?' Thomas's eyes communicated the same fretful look as the child's.

'I don't know. But you two are to stay here. Stay inside where it's safe.'

Then came the noise of an engine backfiring and what he thought from the snarling sounds was a motorbike revving just beyond the ridge above the farm.

Further gunshots split the silence.

'Are they fireworks?' The girl was beside him. Her teary eyes with their long, wet lashes questioning his.

'Out here? No, lass.' He propelled her back inside. 'Tom!' he yelled to the brother he couldn't see. 'Keep her with you. Keep her safe. I'll go and find out what's happening.'

The dogs barked, adding to the tension. It wasn't safe to take them with him, so he ordered them to stay in the barn. Pointing the barrel of the shotgun at the tumbling sky, he strode off in the direction he believed the gunshot was coming from as the crisp evening air sharpened to a spike in his throat.

32

Monday, 27 September 1965

56, Ashdale Avenue, Glossop, Derbyshire

Her mother was polishing the downstairs windows with vinegar and old newspapers when Connie arrived.

'What you doing, Mam? You're supposed to be putting your feet up.'

'I can't sit still, love. Any news on Kathy?' Her mother's eyebrows shot up.

Connie shook her head. Sick of the same question, of giving the same answer. 'How are you?'

'I'm fine so long as I keep busy.'

Her mother did look fine. Despite having buried her husband three days ago and the anxiety for her missing grand-daughter, it looked as if someone had lifted a load from her shoulders.

'Do you want a hand?'

'No. All done.' The newspaper was scrunched into a ball and dropped in the dustbin. 'It's a darn sight easier keeping them clean living here than it were in Gorton.' She wiped her hands down her front, and Connie noticed she wasn't wearing her wedding ring. 'It were hard keeping anything clean with them flamin' factories pumping out that filth. It's a dream here; your dad's rosebushes are loving the fresh air. Come in, lass. No need to stand on ceremony with me.'

Connie noticed the difference immediately. Her mother had thrown open the French doors onto the garden and the house looked brighter. When she went upstairs to use the bathroom, she saw that someone had cleared the sick room out. There was no sign of her father anywhere. Even the wardrobe was empty.

'How are you, you poor love?' Her mother put her arms around her when she joined her in the kitchen. It was lovely to feel the warm press of her, to be the little girl again. 'Any word from the police?'

'No, nowt.'

'It's the not knowing, isn't it? It's killing me, too.' Her mother pulled away, dabbing her eyes. 'Oh, dear, I'm sorry. I swore I weren't going to get upset in front of you.'

'It's all right, Mam. I'm worn out with it all. I don't know what to do and I've been thinking about stuff. Driving myself up the wall with the what-ifs and maybes.'

'Thinking what?' her mother sniffed.

'That I should've let Kathy live here with you. I should've listened... I couldn't cope with her on my own.'

'Hush, love. You've to stop tormenting yourself. But, oh, God—' her mother turned away, pretending to busy herself at the sink. 'Forgive me for saying this, Connie.' Rinsing and squeezing out her dishcloth, she began wiping things at random. 'But I wish you hadn't left her in that car. What in heaven's name were you thinking?'

A painful silence dropped between them and as Connie's impassive gaze followed the dishcloth as it left its snail-like trails over the Formica surfaces, all she could think was how right her mother was. What she'd done was beyond stupid. She hadn't cared enough about her child, and that was the awful truth. Connie didn't deserve a daughter as beautiful as Kathy; she deserved nothing.

'We'd never have done that with you, love.' She could tell her mother was being as gentle as she could, but there were things she needed to get off her chest. 'I'm sorry. I won't say no more because I know you're punishing yourself enough. You're still drinking, are you? I know you're suffering but it's no answer.'

'No, Mam.'

'Don't lie, Connie.' Her mother chucked her cloth into the sink. 'I could smell it on you as soon as you walked in.'

'Leave it, Mam, please.'

The kettle was filled and set to boil. Connie watched her mother scoop loose tea leaves from the caddy into the pot. She would rather a tot of something from the sideboard but wouldn't dare ask.

'You could always move in here and let me look after you.'

Keep an eye on me, you mean. 'With Fred?'

'Why not? Be nice to have the company.'

'I can't, Mam. Supposing Kathy came back and I weren't there?' Connie stared at her mother: had she undergone a personality transplant as well as a makeover?

'I know, love. Silly idea. But you're always welcome.'

'Thanks, Mam.' She looked around her. Her mother had been busy. The place was gleaming. 'You've a new washing machine.'

'Had it delivered this morning. I were pestering your father for months.' She stroked the top of the smart new twin-tub. 'You can bring your washing here if you want? Save using the launderette?'

'Thanks, but it sort of gives me something to do.'

'I wish you'd let me look after you. I hate the thought of you living on that horrible estate, 'specially after what happened to Fred. It's not safe. Go on, come here. It's not like I haven't bags of room. I'm rattling around in this place on my own.'

'I'll talk to Fred,' Connie said, knowing she wouldn't. There was no way her mother would tolerate her drinking or the strange hours she kept nowadays. 'Oh, look at that,' she gasped when they returned to the living room. 'You've taken his duck ornaments down.'

'Horrible bloody things. First thing I did,' her mother complained, following along behind with the tray.

'You're really not sorry he's gone, are you?' Connie surprised herself with her question.

'He weren't never the easiest of men, love. You know that.' A heavy sigh. 'Kept me on a very tight leash. I can understand why you wanted to get away from him, I wanted to 'n all.'

'You had a tough life with him.' Connie hadn't needed Granny Maybury to tell her, she'd witnessed it herself. 'I'm sorry I couldn't do owt.'

'Dear me, child. It's not for you to be sorry. I'm the one at fault, I should never have married him. I think he knew I never loved him, not properly, and that were his trouble.'

'So why did you?' Connie thought she knew the answer to this, but wanted her mother's side of things.

'Convenience.'

'How d'you mean?'

Her mother gave her a funny look. 'He lied, you know.'

'Lied?'

'Aye. That stupid deathbed confession, saying he weren't your dad. He told me about it.'

'What?' Connie had been coming to terms with the fact Ken Openshaw wasn't her father and growing to rather like the idea. 'Why would he lie about that?'

'Perhaps saying he lied were a bit strong. What I mean is, I think it must've been the morphine speaking. Poor sod thought I were his mother half the time.'

'I don't care either way, Mam. Honestly, it don't matter.' Connie flapped away her mother's concern. 'I've not had the chance to think about owt else because of Kathy.' She sat down on the settee, her gaze wandering out through the French doors, into the garden. 'And anyway, I'd rather he weren't my dad, if you want the truth.'

Her mother made a small noise and busied herself with the tea things. 'I did try to stop him going for you, Connie. But I weren't no match for him.'

Another silence settled over them. Connie was glad. Reluctant to dredge up more painful memories, she was sad enough about life as it was.

'*Corrie*'s starting.' She glanced at the clock and forced a smile. 'Want to watch it together?'

They sat in front of the black-and-white television with its slightly flickering screen and drank their tea. Elsie Tanner and Ena Sharples were at each other's throats. Connie and her mother had been avid fans of *Coronation Street* since it first aired five years ago, and it was good to hand herself over to a drama she wasn't part of. When the adverts kicked in, she observed her mother. A woman she had always thought had the glamour of Pat Phoenix until Ken Openshaw was diagnosed with cancer and she'd worn herself out nursing him. But she was getting herself back together again now, wasn't she? Pencil skirts, heels, her hair freshly styled. She looked rather too dressed up to be at home.

'You look different, Mam. Has something happened? Have you met someone?'

'I might have.' A coy smile.

'Really?'

'You don't mind?' The look was unsure, waiting for Connie's approval.

'I'd say it were about time you had some fun.'

'I feel bad, you know, what with Kathy still missing and that. But, well.' She crossed, then uncrossed her legs, seeming nervous. 'We'd not clapped eyes on each other for nigh on twenty-four years.'

'Wow, Mam. So, you knew him before you got married? Was he like your first boyfriend?'

Her mother shifted around in her chair. 'It weren't quite as simple as that, but aye, I suppose in a way he was.'

'So, what; you just bumped into one another?'

'At Ashton Market. I were handing out leaflets for Kathy. He's the loveliest man, Connie.' Her mother's eyes were misty with memories. 'I feel awful admitting it, but he's the man I should've always been with.'

The ring of the telephone cut between them.

'I'd better get that? It might be him.' She sprang to her feet, the girliest and most giggly Connie had ever known her. 'He rang me on Saturday and said he'd try to call again tonight.'

While her mother was talking to whoever it was, Connie took advantage and nipped upstairs to the bathroom with the plan of taking another bottle of Valium. Which she did. Shaking it to check it was full, she dropped it in her handbag. But when she shut the mirror-fronted cabinet, she saw her mother standing behind her, cuddling her cat. And she didn't look happy.

'Connie? What are you doing?'

33

Tuesday, 28 September 1965

Black Fell Farm, Saddleworth Moor, West Riding of Yorkshire

Sunlight prised his eyelids apart like a tin opener. Ronald had slept badly again and woke in a sweat and a tangle of sheets. His recurring nightmare of finding his father's skull picked clean by crows and gleaming white among the cotton grass had mutated into the trauma of having a gun held to his head... and the cackling laugh of that woman morphing into the cackling of magpies on the other side of his window tugged him into consciousness.

His fear of his father's bones being scattered was one thing. But that gold fob watch was something else. He knew he'd been stupid to bury it with the body because if his remains were ever discovered, he would be instantly identifiable. Ronald might as well have carved a tombstone and placed it on the grave. He sighed and, squeezing shut his eyes again, read the inscription he knew to be etched on the inside lid of the casing:

To Jacob Cappleman
for services to King and country in times of
conflict
Lancashire Farming Union

He unravelled his legs and pushed them out from under the covers. The floorboards were chilly beneath his bare feet. Stiff-limbed, he wandered to the window and drew the curtains on a pair of magpies. They were close enough to see the sheen on their wings wasn't black at all but shimmering blues and greens. He clapped his hands, and they flapped away. The morning made peaceful again. It was going to be a fine day and yet fine was the last thing he felt when he thought of the little visitor who was still with them.

Downstairs, the bolt rattled and the kitchen door opened onto the day Ronald should have been up to greet hours before. He yawned and ran through his recent telephone conversations with Pamela. How pleased she was to hear from him. His plan to return the child may have been thwarted on Saturday – to his frustration, by the time he reached the brow of the hill the motorbike had disappeared over the moor at a surprising speed – but he'd been determined to drive to the nearest phone box and call her. And again, yesterday, to firm up arrangements. Thomas was none the wiser.

Naked to the waist, he stood up at the washstand in his long johns and lathered and shaved, careful with the blade around his scar. He mopped his face on a towel and dressed in his clothes from the day before. He ran a hand through his hair and went downstairs, moving through the darkened house and into the kitchen where his brother and the child sat eating soft-boiled eggs and toast cut into soldiers.

'You're late starting,' Thomas accused, barely looking up.

'Rotten night.'

'There's tea in the pot. I'll do you toast?'

'Later. I'll take some bread and butter with me. I'd better make a start.'

'Suit yourself.'

The child watched him. Was she afraid of him now? Afraid he was going to rip her away from Thomas and return her to the place she didn't want to be returned to?

'You've fed these two?' Ronald pointed at the lambs who had almost outgrown the crate.

'Gracie's seen to them. They've become great pals.'

'They're not pets, Tom. I warned you not to get attached.' He was speaking about the child more than the lambs.

'I know that.' His brother dispensed an audible sigh.

Ronald stood with his back to them and sliced a couple of rounds of bread, applied a smear of butter. He tucked the crude sandwich into the pocket of his jacket, then poured himself a tea, blowing on it so he could drink it as quickly as possible. Over his shoulder, Thomas was showing the child a game he'd played since boyhood of turning the empty eggshell upside-down in his egg cup. The child smiled a smile that had nothing to do with Ronald. Lonely, on the margins of their pairing, he listened to them laugh in a way that made him think he'd joined in too late. That he'd missed the beginning of something. It troubled him more than he already was.

He wasn't imagining it. An air of blame hung about the house like a foul smell. No open window with the breeze blowing through would dispel it. Ronald finished his tea and without another word, moved to the porch where he pulled on his boots, slung the Purdey over his arm and strolled out across the dappled dampness of the yard under the clatter of rooks, trailing the news from the wireless behind him.

'... *more retaliatory air-strikes began against North Vietnam... after operation Rolling Thunder US combat forces arrived in February... escalation of force level continues...*'

Hadn't there been enough death and destruction in the

world? Ronald carried the dismal thoughts the report furnished him with over to the barn and opened the doors. Since that Scottish bastard made his threat, he had been meaning to buy a padlock but still hadn't got around to it. Whistling to his sheep-dogs, he was glad he had not confronted Thomas to clear the air – he didn't have the time or the energy for more arguments – and hooked the trailer to the tractor and set off to gather the last of the hay bales in readiness for winter. Keeping busy may help to take his mind off the problem, but it would not resolve the problem. Time was marching on and he still hadn't worked out a way to return the child to her people, to Pamela.

The land tilted down to the valley, then up again. Bumping along, his backside aching, the tractor's engine toiling, he reached the top meadows and looked out over the moor. He thought of those endless days spent destoning these fields with his back bent under a lowering sky filled with rooks. The black swirl of wings and their screaming cries, much as they were today. Turning his collar to the rising wind, he took off his cap and raked a hand through his hair that, in his youth, had been as black as the clouds that were gathering strength to the west. Haymaking brought images of his mother striding out to the fields with flasks and sandwiches wrapped in greaseproof paper, her skirts whipped by the wind. He blinked the memory away and was surprised by the tears in his eyes.

It had started to rain and Ronald, relieved to have collected the bales, sat in the barn, putting the finishing touches to a pair of rose arches he was making for Thomas. The child appeared. The two orphan lambs, who barely left her side, trotted along behind. Drowned in one of his mother's old cardigans, the cuffs dangling, she skipped to the doorway and stood watching him from the shadows, her head almost level with the workbench.

'I know you think I've got to go home, but I don't want to.

Not ever.' Her eyes were brimming with tears. 'I want to stay here with you and Tommy.'

Ronald said nothing; emotion trapped in his throat.

'Why can't I stay and live with you?'

He pursed his lips and shook his head. Such a dear little thing. He wanted to reach out and roll back the cuffs of the cardigan, but was afraid to move. 'Because they wouldn't let us, child.'

'Why not? Mam don't want me.'

'That's not true.' He picked up a curl of wood shaving, then put it down again. 'She's been making appeals on the wireless. Didn't Tommy tell you?'

The child shrugged and stroked the lambs, who were baaing and butting her legs for attention. 'I've never been as happy as this. I love it here.'

Ronald drew the child towards him. She stood against his knee. 'You've got to go home. Me and Tom, we could be in serious trouble.'

'But a little girl lived here once. Why can't I?'

'What do you mean?' Ronald frowned.

'There's a picture of her in my room.'

The sun made a sudden appearance through a break in the rain; a shaft of honey light, spearing in through the door and cutting the barn in half. Ronald thought of the painting. The girl with auburn ringlets under a broad-brimmed hat.

'Who is she?' the child wanted to know.

'Our mother.'

'Mother? But she's little. Little like me.'

'She grew up and married my father. She were very young. Had me before she were twenty. Thomas three years later.'

'What was her name?'

'Grace. Her name were Gracie.'

'That's my name.' She tapped her chest.

'Well, aye. It's the name we gave you because you won't tell us yours.' The lambs had wandered off to nibble the grass verges around the farm. It was time to put them out to pasture. 'But we've heard what your name is; it were on the radio.'

'That's not my name. My name's Gracie, now.' She moved her tongue between the gaps in her milk teeth. 'Did your mam sleep in my room?'

'She did, aye.'

'No one ever comes here. Not even the postman. I don't see why I can't stay.'

Ronald ran his hand over her dark curls. The curls his brother brushed each morning. How glossy they were now. 'They wouldn't let us, love.'

'But no one would know. I wouldn't tell.'

'What about school? Your gran?' The questions hovered in the air while he recalled the forlorn look on Pamela's face.

The child glanced at the floor. 'I do miss Gran.'

'And you can be sure she misses you. It don't mean you can't come and visit.'

'But I don't want to visit. I don't want to go to school, neither. Tom's teaching me. It's loads better. Please, Ronnie, I want to stay. With you and Tom and the lambs and Bramble.'

'It's a nice idea, lass,' Ronald said, his eyes prickling with tears. 'But it wouldn't do.' The child stifled a sob. 'Come on, let's go and see what Tom's made for our tea, shall we?'

———

Ronald shaved for the second time that day. Lathered up his flannel and washed under his arms. Cut his toenails. Rootling the wardrobe, he took an age to decide which of his three shirts he should wear, or even if he should wear a suit. It would have to be his funeral suit if he did. It was the only one he owned. He pulled it out of the wardrobe, held it up. It felt like another man had stepped into the room. He considered it for a moment before slotting it away. Too much, he decided, imagining the questions from Thomas if he went downstairs wearing that. There had been enough questions already. Tonight, he was glad of the child and the distraction she brought because his brother's focus was elsewhere. Not that Thomas hadn't been curious, but he'd seemed to accept that Ronald was off to a function at the Farmers' Union without the need for specifics.

'By 'eck, your hair's grown.' His brother's greeting found him above the hiss and press of the iron, the billowing steam. 'I'd have given it a trim if you'd asked.'

Ronald listened to the bump, bump of the iron on ironing board as Thomas worked his way through a pile of laundry collected from the line.

'I don't mind it.' He shrugged on his corduroy jacket and, pocketing the truck's keys, his pipe and a pouch of tobacco, he remembered to check he had enough money.

'It's rather louche, Ronnie. But it's up to you.' He watched his brother's fingers worrying the callused patch on his palm that his years of ironing had given him. 'So, you're off out again, are you?'

'Aye. No law against it, last I heard.'

Reluctant to lie to his brother about who he was meeting, it was without another word that Ronald slid the bolt on the kitchen door and stepped out into the windy yard and what was left of the daylight.

34

Waggon and Horses, Hyde Road, Gorton, Manchester

Ronald talked nonsense to the barman while he waited for Pamela to arrive. Things were quiet enough to hear the clicking of billiard balls. Nervous, his gaze flicking to the clock above the bar, the longer time went on, the more convinced he was that he had the wrong day. Or worse, she had changed her mind. Gradually, the pub filled up around him and, perched on a bar stool, working steadily through a pint of ale, he listened to the hum of the conversations he wasn't part of and looked at his hands. Brown to the wrist, the skin leathery, the knuckles cracked. Shepherd's hands. When did he get so old? Middle age had crept up on him without him noticing.

Then Pamela was there.

Brushing against his thigh and leaning in to kiss his cheek, stroking his hand. The suddenness of her perfume, her soft femininity, made his heart beat faster.

'I always loved the smell of your pipe.' She kissed him again.

'S-shall I-I get the beers in?' Self-conscious, Ronald slid

from his bar stool. 'I mean—' he faltered. 'If y-you still drink beer?'

'I do, and yes please.' She smiled, putting him at ease. 'I'll go and nab that table over there before someone else does.'

Ronald watched her walk away before turning back to the bar. Could it be happening? Was she really here? He grinned as he paid one and six for two pints of pale ale.

'Cheers.' They chinked glasses. 'Ken would never let me drink pints. He said it weren't ladylike.' Pamela took a hearty gulp and Ronald, pulling up a chair, couldn't help but laugh, tapping his top lip to indicate the blob of froth she had on hers. 'There were lots my Ken wouldn't let me do, come to think of it.' She stroked the sides of the glass, the pads of her fingers no doubt journeying her back to some unexpected place. Somewhere that unsettled her. She frowned. 'You've never married, have you, Ron?'

'Married to the farm, I suppose.'

Pamela's turn to laugh: a spoon tinkling against a jam jar. How could he have forgotten the sweetness of it? 'And to that moor. D'you remember the lightning tree?'

'The one I carved our names on? Aye. It's still there.'

She seemed to like this idea, her eyes shining as she unbuttoned her coat. But because she didn't take it off, he feared she didn't intend to stay long.

'I know I said on the phone,' he began, then hesitated, choosing his words carefully. 'But I were sorry to hear about your husband.'

'Thanks, Ron.' Her smile faded. 'It's been a tough time, what with him being so ill and then all this worry about my granddaughter.' She bunched her lips together, and he identified a quiver in her voice. 'That's why it's so nice to come out tonight. Helps take my mind off things I can't do owt about.'

'Nice for me, too.' He sucked on his pipe to get it going again. He needed to steer their conversation away from her granddaughter. The agony of knowing he could put an end to Pamela's misery in an instant tore at his heart. 'I were thinking you'd changed your mind about tonight.'

'You always were a worrier, Ronnie. We could have gone to the Bull if you'd rathered?' Pamela looked around the busy pub, taking in the low-beamed ceiling, the walls of shiny brasses. 'Less of a drive for you.' She seemed as nervous as him, her fingers fiddling with the buttons of her coat. 'I weren't sure I could face coming here.'

'Don't you like it? You should have said.'

'No, it's not that. It's because this was where our Kathy disappeared. Well, the car park.'

'Oh, that's terrible.' *How on earth did that little child walk to the farm from here? It must be a journey of at least fifteen miles.* 'The Bull never came to mind. It were my father's old haunt.'

'That's right, it were.' Pamela smacked the table. Made the pint glasses wobble. 'D'you remember the night he showed up? Me and you huddling in a corner waiting for him to go?'

'I remember.'

'Did he see us, d'you think?'

'He never said owt,' Ronald lied. Told himself he had good reason. The last thing he wanted was to open that can of worms.

'And he never told your Tommy about you and me?'

'No. Tom never knew.'

A small nod. 'Your father were a brute. He used to frighten the life out of me when I came up to the farm. I felt sorry for your mam. He died around the time Tommy came home on leave and we had to stop seeing one another, weren't it?' It was Ronald's turn to nod. 'Staggered off after some pub brawl... fell into a bog?' The question swung above them, sharp as a dagger.

He took a mouthful of beer before doling out the same version of events he had given the police, and as he talked, he lifted an involuntary hand to the scar on his face.

'Left you with an everlasting souvenir, didn't he?' Pamela

reached over the table and, with a fingertip, tenderly traced the journey of the scar from his eye and down his cheek. 'He were a horrible man.'

'Aye, he were.' Usually awkward whenever he was away from the farm, it surprised him how comfortable he felt in Pamela's company now that his initial nerves had ebbed away. The years that had fallen between them hadn't made the slightest difference. They seemed to have picked up where they'd left off. Don't relax too much, he warned himself, fearful he might inadvertently let something slip about the child. He hated lying to Pamela. It made him feel sick. But he would sort it, he promised himself; he would put things right. And soon. 'Are the police any closer to finding what's happened to your granddaughter?' he forced himself to ask.

'No. Despite the appeals Connie did for the paper and radio.'

As Pamela talked about her granddaughter, Ronald observed her: her black mascara, the pale blue eyeshadow, the odd grey hair, silvery among the dark. Pamela looked beautiful, and he wanted to tell her, but couldn't find a way without fearing he would be coming on too strong. Those dark rings she had under her eyes had gone. She looked brighter, happier. She looked like the Pamela he had known all those years ago.

'I don't know what to say to my Connie. She blames herself but insists she only left Kathy in the car for an hour or so.' Pamela rolled her eyes. 'It's a wonder the police don't charge her for neglect. She were never much of a mother.'

Ronald's mind curved to how the child was when she first arrived at the farm: her fear-filled eyes, the bruises on her arms, her pallid complexion. And how, after a relatively short time, with attention and love, she had bloomed like the snowdrops after a long, hard winter. Listening to Pamela's anguish, he wished he could tell her the child was safe and put her mind at ease. But each time he came close to doing so, an image of his brother's sorrowful face dropped behind his eyelids and stopped him.

'I feel bad saying those things about Connie, but I know you and me can be honest with each other.' Her declaration made him feel especially wretched. 'I'd have brought Kathy up. I wanted Connie to finish school, go to college... she's got a good brain if only she'd apply herself.' She took another mouthful of beer. 'I blame that Myra Hindley girl. Connie's never been able to shake her off. Bone bloody idle, that one, and such a bad influence... *ugh*, best not get me started on her, Ron.'

'You don't like this Myra, I take it?' Ronald undid the top button of his shirt and puffed on his pipe.

'Like her?' Pamela wrapped her arms around herself and shivered. 'No, I don't. And neither would you if you met her.' She sucked in air through her teeth. 'Thinks far too much of herself. And as for that bloke of hers. Ooo—' another shiver. 'He gives me the creeps. Not that I can understand half of what he says. Scottish, he is,' Pamela added, as if this explained everything. 'Riding round on that motorbike of his in his leather coat. *Ugh*, the pair deserve one another.'

A sudden chill swept across Ronald's back. 'This Myra girl, is she... erm...' He tiptoed up to his question, feigning a casual interest. 'What I mean is, you say she thinks a lot of herself... nice-looking, is she?'

'Reckons she is. Tries too hard, if you ask me. Lots of fancy clothes, but that hairstyle of hers... the girl thinks she's Marilyn Monroe.'

'Why's that then?'

'She bleaches it white. It's like a Belisha beacon. You can see her a mile off. But I suppose that's the whole idea.'

The chill had engulfed his body. Pamela's description had confirmed who these two were. And with it, the fear of something worse. If they were friends of Connie, they would know her daughter – the child he and Thomas were hiding back at the farm that this pair had taken it upon themselves to visit. Uninvited.

'Are you all right, Ron? You look like you've seen a ghost.'

'Aye. I'm fine,' he nodded, trying to hold it together.

'Anyway, enough about that horrible pair.' Pamela picked up her pint. 'Only to say,' she drank a little then smacked her lips together. 'Myra were always bad for my Connie, and I think she's got her drinking... Connie came round other night, stinking of booze. And I caught her pinching a bottle of Valium.'

'What d'you need those for?'

'Doctor prescribed them when I were nursing Ken, and having trouble sleeping.' She had another go at her beer. 'Life weren't much fun with him. Everything just so and in its place.' She laughed a laugh that didn't reach her eyes. 'Me and Connie, we didn't really come up to scratch. We always, well... disappointed him. It's why I didn't want children with him.'

'After you had Connie, you mean?'

'Connie weren't his, Ron.' Pamela raised her eyes to his for a second, then dropped them again. 'I were four months gone when I met Ken. You know, after I couldn't go through with marrying Tommy, Ken made an honest woman of me. I had a lot to be grateful to him for.'

'So, Connie weren't Ken's?' He shook his head, confused.

'No, Ron. Connie weren't Ken's.' She gave him a long look that was followed by a burst of laughter. 'Dear God, Ronnie. You always were slow on the uptake.'

'What d'you mean?'

'She's yours, Ron. Connie's yours.'

———

Inside the Gents' Ronald stood at the mirror and tried to unravel what he'd been told. Seeing, again, the look Pamela gave him when he had asked her why she'd never told him, saying he could have done something.

'You couldn't even tell your brother about you and me. What d'you mean, you could have done something? I couldn't wait around for you for ever, Ronnie. I gave you an ultimatum, don't you remember?'

The memory had smacked him between the eyes. On the last day of their trip to the Lakes, they had gone to the fairground in Ambleside. 'You've still not said what we're going to do about Tommy coming home?' Her question had hung in mid-air. Ronald had hesitated, forever fearful of sharing what was in his heart, and with the light of the fair behind her, he couldn't see her face; he couldn't make her out. All he could see was the whirling merry-go-round, and a group of children at a van reaching up for candyfloss as the crowd thinned out around them, their time together coming to an end.

'You stupid idiot,' he scolded his reflection. 'You could've had a whole different life if you'd been braver, asked for what you wanted. You've a daughter... *a daughter!*'

He raised his eyebrows. What did having a daughter even mean? He had no idea; he could only think of it hypothetically. Probably because he didn't know who Connie was; he'd never even laid eyes on her.

'But I know who *her* daughter is...' he continued to talk to himself in the mirror. 'She's my granddaughter.'

As well as marvelling at the astonishing fluke that the child had chanced upon their farm at all, to then learn she was his grandchild was too much of a coincidence to believe. Maybe Thomas was right when he said she'd been heaven-sent? Not that Ronald believed in heaven any more than he believed in coincidences, but even he had to concede that something miraculous had occurred.

He stared at his reflection and frowned, hunting the creases on his forehead for a way out of this mess. He was going to have to come clean right now. He would go back out there and tell Pamela where her grandchild was... where *his* grandchild was. Ronald tried to steady his breathing and compose himself and, rehearsing what he was going to say, he ran the conversation over in his mind, listening to how it would go. Then he listened to her imagined response: 'You knew she was my Connie's child, and you waited all this time to tell me? What kind of man are you?'

This was one almighty mess. Ronald couldn't believe it. He was back where he was twenty-four years ago – torn between his brother and Pamela.

Still wrestling with his dilemma, Ronald stepped back into the bar and was heading for the table where Pamela sat, when a voice he recognised brought him back with a bump.

'Hello, Mrs Openshaw. I thought it were you.' The woman – he now knew her to be Myra – was respectful while sounding condescending.

'Don't you *Mrs Openshaw* me, young lady.' Pamela's vehemence surprised him, and he liked the way she stood up for herself. 'I don't know why you've gone and taken a sudden interest in my Constance again, but you're to stay away from her, d'you hear? She's got enough trouble without you adding to it.'

Ronald took advantage of a pillar and, staying out of sight, reluctant to have any kind of confrontation in front of Pamela, decided he would only intervene if necessary.

'Or what?' The boyfriend barged between the women: menacing. It was strange to have been talking about these two, and then for them to appear. 'Ye old witch.' He thrust his face close to Pamela's. 'Ye wanna watch ye mouth. Hessy's told me what ye were like with her when she was a kid. Looking down ye nose. Ye wanna be careful, ye might end up getting hurt.'

'You!' Ronald strode out from behind the pillar. 'Who d'you think you're talking to, laddie? Just like you to intimidate a woman. You're not man enough for owt else, are you? Unless you've a gun in your hand. Care to prove me wrong on that count?'

'Looky here, it's Mr Farmer. This ye piece of skirt?'

Ronald, fist raised, took a step closer. Close enough to feel the bastard's hot breath.

'It's all right, Ronnie.' Pamela placed a restraining hand on his arm. 'These two were just leaving, weren't you?'

'Ye dinnae get to say whether we stay or go.'

Ronald, pushing aside Pamela's arm, moved in on the weasel-faced boyfriend who, sensing something in his expression, stepped away.

'All right, Grandad. We're going. But like I were saying to ye fancy woman – ye wanna be careful how ye go.' The black-edged threat was fired off through his fingers: a pretend gun. 'Wouldnae like either of ye to meet with some kinda *accident*.' And to the accompaniment of Myra's cackling laugh, he winked at them. 'Be seeing ye.'

35

Wednesday, 29 September 1965

Saddleworth Moor, West Riding of Yorkshire

Ian led the way in his smart stock clerk shoes. Striding ahead with a sense of purpose with Myra wobbling along behind on her heels, he navigated the moorland without a care while Connie and the others trudged in single file, carrying bags clanking with booze.

'I can't believe we let Myra talk us into this. What were wrong with celebrating Maureen and Dave's news down the pub like normal people?' Connie complained to Fred when he stopped to wait for her to catch up. 'It's bloody freezing.' She shivered and buttoned her raincoat as high as it would go. 'That wind cuts through everything.'

'Here—' Fred put his cigarette between his lips and shook himself out of his leather jacket. 'You have this.'

'Oh, no. You'll be cold then.'

'Nah, I'm all right.' He guided her arms into the sleeves.

'What is it about them and this place?' The jacket was still warm from his body. Connie snuggled into it and scanned the acres of bleak landscape that stretched as far as the eye could see. 'Myra says they come up here at night and stay 'til dawn. Can you believe that?' She'd already decided the moor wasn't somewhere she'd choose at any time. It was too crowded with ghosts for her liking.

'Maybe you've gotta be a flamin' Scot to appreciate it.'

'It's not just him; Myra loves it too. Calls it their "special place".'

'Bloody welcome to it.'

They stumbled along a rough path that meandered through the reeds and swaying grass, Fred in his Cuban heels, Connie in a pair of pumps. Whenever one of them lost their footing, Ian swore at them to pick their feet up. On and on they went until the path petered out, consumed by the dense swathes of heather that covered the moor like a giant purple counterpane. There was a burst of flapping and all heads turned to watch the streak of stripes and white underbelly of a bird as it rocketed away.

Connie noticed how Ian stopped every now and again to glance down across the vast valley to the reservoir, pale and shining, far below. She sensed he was searching for a certain spot.

'It's this way.' An assertive hand was raised for them all to follow.

'All looks the same to me. I don't think I could find my way back to the car.'

'Me neither.' Fred put an affectionate arm around her to jolly her along. 'But it can't be much farther.'

It was a relief when the land dipped down to a mossy clearing flanked by enormous boulders and a gushing stream.

'We always come here, don't we, Neddy?' Myra kicked away sheep droppings and showed her sister, Maureen, where to lay the blankets.

'Aye, we do. Nice and private. Safe from prying eyes.'

He was right. The birds and sheep were the only spectators, Connie thought as she stared at a hulking range of black rocks in the distance. She couldn't decide if the idea that they had been there since the beginning of time and would be there long after her was a comfort or not.

They sat around in a circle. Myra, in charge of the picnic, divvied out the rations. Ian, meanwhile, took out his transistor radio, and Motown poured out. The ground was damp, and Connie found herself a log. As large as a pew at St Francis's, it was stippled on its wetter underside with unidentifiable mushrooms she knew not to touch. She returned Fred's jacket to him and, wrapped in a blanket, she sat down on the log. A rolling ball of birds snatched her attention, bunching then unravelling along the horizon.

There was wine and whisky and warm beer in bottles that Fred and Dave cracked open with their teeth. Ian drank white German wine from a tumbler, supplemented by the odd swig from a bottle of Bell's, Myra copying him. Dressed to kill as usual, the outfit she had chosen for today's outing was more than a little risqué: high boots, short skirt, crimson lipstick. Hair coiffured to perfection. Her eyes done up like Dusty Springfield's. She certainly knew how to make the most of herself. But for a picnic on the moor? Only those hiker types, or the mad, would volunteer to come up here. Connie thought Ian looked mad; breathless and grinning, pacing around, hands in pockets.

'I live for this place.' His voice was thick with drink as he clambered aboard a great slab of rock. 'It owns my soul.' He stood up and spread his arms out to the side, his hair flapping in the wind.

'I don't like Ian much,' Connie whispered to Maureen, who joined her on the log. 'I know Myra's not an idiot. He must have something going for him, but I can't see it.'

'He bosses her about terrible.'

'I'd have thought that were impossible.'

'Still moping around about your little bastard?' Ian, necking whisky, had deigned to notice Connie.

Myra laughed as if Ian's unpleasantness was the most hilarious joke.

'Ian!' Maureen shot him a reproachful look.

'What?' He shrugged inside his grey three-piece suit. Even though he'd taken the day off, the man was still turned out for his desk at Millward's. 'She is. She's a little bastard. Nothing to be ashamed of; I'm a bastard too.'

Myra laughed again, and Connie resisted the urge to run over to them and smash their heads together.

'Take no notice, Con. He can be a real callous fucker,' Dave whispered, offering up a greaseproof parcel of goodies. Clad in tight black jeans and winkle-pickers, Dave Smith wasn't someone she'd ever had much time for. 'You should've seen him at Angela's funeral. He ain't one to spare your feelings. Wouldn't even come to the house or give his condolences.' He twirled a finger at his temple. 'Weird.' The word dropped between them like a hand grenade.

His show of solidarity touched her. 'I were so sorry to hear about baby Angela.' She took a pork pie and the bottle of beer Fred handed her.

Dave pursed his lips, his eyes shiny with emotion. 'Won't deny it's been rough few months. But there's you, you're going through it... any news on your kiddie?'

Connie shook her head. She supposed that for Maureen and Dave, as for her, time wasn't easily measured in separate days, that it flowed into one mass event, or non-event. 'But it's lovely you've got something to celebrate. Congratulations, both of you. A new baby on the way... it's wonderful.' She lifted her bottle and made a clumsy toast.

'Babies? I don't get it,' Myra sneered. 'Give me a puppy any day.' She laughed her cackle of a laugh.

'Myra's not happy about me being pregnant,' Maureen

confided when her sister had moved out of earshot. 'She hated the whole nappies and feeding thing with Angela.'

'Same when I had Kathy. She's not maternal at all.'

'Mothers *him*, though. You noticed?' Maureen kept her voice down. 'It's *Ian this, Ian that*.'

'She's started talking all posh 'n all.'

Maureen shot a nervous glance at Ian. 'That's his influence.'

'Bloody cheek.' Connie nearly choked on her beer. 'You need a flamin' translator when he gets going.'

Maureen stared down at her lap, her eyes suddenly sad. 'They seem to fit, though. Like two pieces in a jigsaw puzzle. I'm pleased for Myra, if she's happy. It's you what could do with cheering up, I heard.'

'Is that what Fred told you?' She looked over at her boyfriend, who was pulling a comb from his shirt pocket to slick back his hair. Waste of time in this wind, she wanted to tell him.

'You seem to be coping well. How come?'

'Probably the Valium. It helps numb everything.'

'Doctor prescribed me that when baby Angela died. Difficult to wean yourself off. Take care, Connie. It won't do no good in the long term.'

'It's strange because it doesn't seem so serious that Kathy's gone. I don't feel like crying and I know I should. Perhaps, if I didn't take them, I would cry. But I don't want to cry, so I take them. Oh, I don't know.' She was too befuddled to make sense of what she was saying, never mind thinking.

'How long's Kathy been missing?'

'Three and a half weeks.' Connie sipped her beer. She'd given up trying to light her cigarette, the wind kept blowing it out.

'God, you poor thing. No wonder you're on tranquillizers. I were reading about Keith Bennett in the paper. His mam's frantic; her boy's been missing since June last year.'

Myra grunted, she had moved to stand opposite them. 'I blame the parents. They wanna take better care of their kids.'

Connie gawped at her, aghast. This Mrs Bennett had lost her child, like she had lost Kathy. Where was Myra's compassion, what was wrong with her? But Connie didn't challenge her. Frightened she and Ian would gang up on her again, she removed the band from her ponytail and shook out her hair, tying it away under a headscarf.

'Mounsey, the detective who came to see us about Kathy, he reckons there might be a connection,' Fred said, straightening his bootlace tie.

'A connection?' Myra's blonde head jerked up.

'Dinnae talk pish. He doesnae know pish.' Ian, earwigging and glugging more whisky from the bottle. Connie watched the bob of his Adam's apple in his skinny neck, was repulsed by it. By him.

'I like Mounsey. He's one of the good guys. Got some sense, you know? He sorted it for me to do that radio appeal,' Connie told them. 'He's trying to sort a reconstruction. You know, like they did for John Kilbride who went missing from Ashton Market?'

'Yeah. It were on telly,' Maureen nodded. 'I thought it were a good way to jog people's memories.'

'Not done owt though, has it?' Myra joined in, her back straight, her arms crossed, the wind barely ruffling her lacquered hair.

'You've got to admit it's weird.' Fred, again. 'These kiddies going missing... I reckon this copper might be onto something. Supposing Kathy's disappearance were connected to them other ones?'

'But it can't be. Those other kids, they've been missing ages,' Connie shouted at him. 'My Kathy's going to come back. I know she is.'

'Stop lathering her up, man,' Ian told Fred off. 'Always

making a drama out of a'thing. I dinnae know how ye stand her. It's what I love most about Myra. She nae gets in a flap.'

'I don't know what you're griping about, Con,' Myra spoke again. 'You've got your life back, haven't you?'

'Call this a life?' Connie blinked through her tears. 'I can barely function.'

'Funny, 'cos when ye had the bairn, ye were craving a life of freedom. And now ye got ye freedom... Ach, there's nae pleasing ye.' Ian pushed a hand up through his floppy fringe.

'Yeah, stop your snivelling and buy yourself a dog.' Myra twisted away, her nose in the air.

'What the flamin' hell? Where did he get that from?' Maureen jabbed an urgent finger at Ian who was now wielding a revolver. 'Stop him!' she shrieked. 'Someone stop him!'

'I'm gonna shoot the fucker.' He took a long drink from the bottle Myra passed him, then lifted the firearm and aimed it at a pair of fleecy ewes that had wandered down to the stream to drink.

'For God's sake. No... *No!*' Connie screeched and slipped down from the log. She charged over to him, arms outstretched, hands splayed, and shunted him sideways.

The gun fired.

Screams filled the air. The sheep scattered.

'What's the matter with her? Ye wanna learn to control your woman.' Ian directed his complaint to Fred.

'Don't bloody maul me.' Connie thrust her boyfriend away. 'Christ! He were going to shoot them. What the hell's the matter with you?'

'He weren't really gonna shoot them, Con.'

'I fuckin' was,' Ian slurred and licked his lips. He removed his jacket and rolled up his shirt sleeves. Showed off his scrawny milk-white forearms. 'Hessy knows it. I've shot sheep out here before.'

'You what?' Connie was horrified. 'You're disgusting. You're a flamin' animal.'

'For God's sake, Con, lighten up, will you? Getting all hysterical. They're only for the knacker's yard. Who gives a shit?' Myra was at her side.

'That's it, Hessy. You stand up to her. Pile of sentimental pish, the lot of them.' Ian slid his cold-eyed gaze over them.

Connie thought again how Ian and Myra seemed to be bound tightly together. Reading it in their surreptitious glances, their private whisperings; it was as if no one else existed beyond them. And if they did, they were nothing. Trivial. Mere distractions.

She would give anything to go home. She no more liked the great outdoors – as Ian kept calling it, telling everyone how great it was – than she liked him. She was miserable and cold. No one had told her it would be this cold. She worried, too, that like Dave, her Fred might have fallen under Ian's spell. Because, like Dave, Fred was still just a lad, and this Ian Brady, with all his talk and confidence, was so much older. They were bound to want to impress him.

'Seen your mam in the Waggon and Horses last night. She were drinking pints with some fella.'

Although Connie hadn't met the man Myra was talking about, she knew her mother was meeting someone, but she let her friend think this was news. 'Oh, yeah? What were he like?'

'Some old farmer bloke. We know him, don't we, Neddy?'

'Aye. Right old fucker. Surprised me, seeing her out like that, when ye old man's barely gone cold. Anyway, get on and line up the empties, Hessy.' Ian whistled to Myra as if she was a dog. 'I wanna play shoot the bottle, as that barmy cow went and scared the sheep away.' He reloaded his revolver with bullets.

'See the way he bosses me about?' Myra trotted over to her boyfriend and curled her arms around his waist.

'Ach, stop ye bellyaching.' He threw her off him. 'Line 'em up.'

'*Jawohl, liebling*,' Myra replied, puffing on her cigarette.

Ian buffed the barrel of his gun on the front of his shirt. 'Who's for a game?'

'Aye, why not?'

'Fred?' Connie shook her head. 'Please don't. It's not safe. We've all had too much to drink.'

'It'll be all right.' Fred kissed her. He smelled of beer and aftershave. She put a hand to his face, to what remained of his black eye and the cut on his nose. He kissed her again. A strange, deliberate kiss, as if he was saying goodbye.

'Ach, give over. I cannae stand ye two mauling each other all the time.' Connie had noticed before today how Ian hated any show of affection. 'Where's Dave? He's nae a big sissy.'

Dave had wandered off. Probably to have a pee, Connie supposed, thinking she could do with one herself. But it was easier for the men; they could go anywhere.

''Eh up. What's this?' Dave kicked something with the toe of his shoe, loosening it from the peaty ground. 'Flamin' hell.' He crouched to lift it free. 'Look, everyone.' He held it high in the air. 'It's a flamin' skull.'

Connie watched Myra and Ian swap panicky looks, their faces horror-stricken.

'Put it down, Dave. It's horrible,' Maureen called to him.

Ian strode over for a closer look. 'Ach, ye twat. It's a bloody sheep's skull.' It was as if he'd thought it was something else entirely and, prising it from Dave's fingers, he slung it into the reeds. 'Right.' He wiped his hands off on his suit trousers. 'If none of you wants to play ma shooting game, I'll play ma'self.' He spun around in his leather shoes and aimed his gun at a pile of sheep who were dozing on the opposite bank of the stream.

Connie heard the terrifying click of the trigger as he took

aim and threw her hands in the air just as the blast of another gun ripped open the turgid afternoon.

The man stepped out of nowhere. Taking long, confident strides. Like a knight in shining armour, he was tall and rugged and had the most piercing blue eyes she had ever seen. The barrel of his conker-shiny shotgun, pointed at the sky, was smoking. He looked over at Connie. Only fleetingly, but enough to feel something pass between them. Something she didn't have the vocabulary for, but it was as if she had known him of old.

If this man's sudden appearance had startled her, her reaction was nothing compared to the shock it gave Ian and Myra. Whoever this man was, the look he gave them was enough to drain the blood from their faces.

36

Thursday, 30 September 1965

Black Fell Farm, Saddleworth Moor, West Riding of Yorkshire

Out in the copper glow of evening, Ronald returned to the yard to finish up for the day. He sluiced his boots under the outside tap and stood for a minute, water dripping, to listen to a song thrush. He liked to think it was the same bird who came to sing to him each day. The soul of his dead mother. The thought was a comforting one. Not that he would share something as fanciful with his brother. He couldn't let him know there were chinks in his armour. Thomas had enough heart for the both of them.

The child was there, straddling the gate with a curry comb in her hand. Bramble stood, patient and obliging. Hanging her large head in her lap, the mare allowed her forelock to be groomed. Wispy and flyaway, thin with age, the hairs followed the brush in the same way the child's hair did when Thomas brushed it.

'Hello, Ronnie,' she grinned and jumped down. She had taken to following him around the yard. Whenever he turned, there she was. His little shadow. This evening, she was informing him of the names of the clouds, sharing the words learnt from Thomas's book of photographs. The child was persuasive, and Ronald looked up and asked her to identify them for him.

When they went inside, they found Thomas shimmying around the living room, a feather duster in one hand and the vacuum cleaner plugged into the ceiling light socket in the other. He had set something to play on the mahogany gramophone. No doubt inserting a new brass needle from a cup of them, winding it up and choosing records from his stack of seventy-eights in their brown paper covers. Old-fashioned songs their mother had taught them that Ronald claimed to have forgotten.

'Hello, you two.' His brother lifted the stylus when he saw them. The music stopped. 'Tea won't be long.'

On top of the piano sat a vase of pink roses.

'They're pretty.' The child, on tiptoes, pushed her nose to them.

'It's amazing they're still blooming. It seems everything's better since you came here, little Gracie.' Thomas gathered her up in a ball of giggles.

'Ronnie made me a swing.'

'You did?' His brother looked at him in astonishment.

He shrugged. 'It's nowt special. Old tractor tyre. Threw a rope over the bough of a tree up by the stream.'

'It *is* special.' The child pushed between them. 'It's really special.' She seized his brother's hand. 'Come see, Tommy... come see.'

'Later,' Thomas laughed. 'I'll look later. That's kind of you, Ron.'

'It's nowt.'

Ronald turned on the wireless and they listened to the rasped news details, telling them about the ongoing search for the train robber, Ronnie Biggs, who escaped from Wandsworth prison in July. Then the voice of a woman. Hesitant, full of despair, appealing for her missing child... *Someone must know something, seen something... I just want my Kathy home. Please... if there's anyone out there who knows where she is... please...*

Trading nervous looks with his brother, Ronald switched off the wireless.

'Was that Mam?' The child's face paled. 'Is she looking for me? She's not coming to get me, is she? I don't want to go home. Please don't let her take me. You won't, will you?'

Her large eyes were like two wet pools. What were they supposed to say? Ronald didn't know. But Thomas did.

'Don't worry, sweetheart. No one's going to take you anywhere you don't want to go. Poor little mite.' He wrapped her in his arms. 'You're safe with us. There, there, don't upset yourself, poppet.'

Ronald sucked on his bottom lip and turned away. Since meeting Pamela in the Waggon and Horses on Tuesday and again yesterday, at a café in town, he'd been hatching a secret plan he hoped would allow him to return the girl to her family with the least fuss and trauma. *But we're her family too.* The gnawing began again, but he refused to heed it. Shouldering the burden of guilt and anxiety as great as this day in, day out, was taking its toll and the only way they stood a chance of being a legitimate part of the child's life was if they did the right thing now. If his plan was to succeed, he needed to trick his brother and the child, and this made him feel rotten. Unbeknown to his brother – because of Ronald's reluctance to worry him – they were sitting ducks. It was only a matter of time before the child was discovered. If not by that horrible Myra woman and her loathsome boyfriend – who knew exactly who the child was and could turn up at the farm any time – then it would be someone else.

After their meal, Ronald retired to the living room to sit in his armchair. Too distracted to read, he stared out through the window at the moor. Watched the rooks diving into the trees, then breaking away with things in their beaks, their black wings flapping against the shifting sky. To the clattering accompaniment of dishes as Thomas washed up, the child did as she had become accustomed, and pushed her way into Ronald's lap. Usually, he would read her a story, but she didn't come to him with a book tonight. Tonight, she came to him with questions.

'How did you get that mark?'

Ronald felt the inquisitive press of her fingers following the line of proud flesh that snaked down past his eye. Just like her grandmother had done a few evenings ago.

'My father gave it me when I were a lad.'

Thomas had entered the living room and shot him a look that Ronald ignored.

'Did it hurt?' A soft frown.

'Aye, it did rather.' A memory of the belt buckle. The pain when it struck the side of his face. He squeezed his eyes shut for a second. Opened them on the child who was wriggling in his lap.

'My mam gave me this.' She had rolled down a sock that Thomas had knitted her, exposing a three-inch scar on her shin. 'Mam had an argument with Grandad and got all angry. She pushed me off the swings in the park.'

Sudden tears stung his eyes. Moved by her declaration, her acceptance. *This was what all parents did to their children, wasn't it?* her expression seemed to say. This was his daughter she was talking about. And again, the uncomfortable question prodded him: what kind of mother could do that to her child?

What kind of person did it make Connie? *Not someone I'm in any great hurry to meet, that's for sure.*

'I'm so sorry, little one. Such a shame you couldn't have lived with your gran. I bet she wouldn't have left you in the back of a car to go drinking.' The statement was out before Ronald had realised his mistake.

'Cor, how d'you know about that?'

'Aye, Ron?' Thomas had taken up his seat by the fire.

Two pairs of eyes shone out through the diffused lighting of the living room: one trusting, the other suspicious.

'You must have told me.'

'Did I?' The child pulled up her sock.

'Aye.' He dared a look at his brother, relieved to see he was concentrating on his knitting.

Ronald would love to promise the child she could stay and that they would keep her safe. But it wasn't true, and he was telling enough lies to Pamela. Let Thomas tell her she could stay forever. Ronald didn't know what forever meant and didn't think he had the right to promise the future when the future wasn't his to give.

'It's funny.' The child making herself comfy in his lap. 'Because I didn't think you had a daddy.'

'No, why's that?'

'Because not everyone has one. I don't. Why aren't there any photos of him? You've lots of your mam.'

Ronald cast around to confirm what he already knew. 'What an astute little lass you are,' he congratulated her, smoothing her curls.

'Right then, Gracie.' Thomas set aside his knitting. 'Bedtime.'

'Sweet dreams.' Ronald kissed her forehead, and she slid to the floor.

The time before lights out belonged to his brother and the child, wrapped in the comfort of what used to be their mother's bedroom with its soothing light and cosiness. This was a time for stories, for sitting side-by-side on the patchwork quilt Thomas had stitched from their mother's old dresses.

By nine thirty, Ronald was ready for bed. Upstairs, his brother was still reading to the child and he watched them from the doorway in secret. The child was cuddling up to Thomas and the teddy bear. The cat, with its fondant-pink nose, was curled up between them. It was a contented family scene that, instead of soothing him, had him pressing a hand to his chest and feeling the corkscrew that already pierced his heart give another three-quarter turn.

———

A fistful of rain was thrown against his bedroom window. Ronald, waking from a sleep that had barely begun, listened to the volley of weather move over the farmstead. Snug beneath the covers, he pictured it as something with fangs gnashing and crushing everything in its path. He turned heavily onto his side, the bedsprings creaking. The movement released the smell of him. A puff of sweat, the vague vinegary whiff of his feet. And the farm. Something he carried wherever he went. Wide awake in a dark that had always coated like a second skin, he pulled his hands under the blankets and pressed them to his sides, heavy as stones.

Still churned up from seeing that Myra woman and her Scottish boyfriend in the pub with Pamela, he wished he'd decked him there and then. Squashed that ugly smug rat face of his into the drink-sticky carpet. At least he'd got the chance to put the wind up them on the moor yesterday. Frightening them by firing his shotgun when they had been showing off to their friends. Thinking this, an idea occurred to him. Could one of

the other young women with them have been Connie? His
daughter? He turned over again, letting go a groan of desperation at not being able to drift off. His mind, full of twirling
images, spun brightly lit scenarios on a perpetual loop. He had a
daughter that, until two nights ago, he hadn't known existed.
How did this make him feel? Not as thrilled as he should be.
Connie obviously struggled with motherhood. He hadn't
needed Pamela to tell him; he'd seen the evidence himself. And
not just the bruises. It was apparent from the state of the child's
clothes and the way she cowered if you moved too quickly,
fearing she was going to be struck. These were complicated feelings he was dealing with, no wonder he couldn't sleep. Might
his daughter have grown up a better person if he'd been a father
to her? There was no way of knowing, and the question was
futile.

The rain stopped, and the moon slipped its moorings,
poking a white tongue of light through a gap in the curtains and
lighting the room that had remained unchanged since childhood. He glanced at the ceiling, half expecting to see the hangman's noose swinging over him. Something that was never far
away in his mind. Much like his father's grave. Out there in the
blackness with only the ceaseless wind for company. He envis-
aged the cold black rocks above Hollin Brown Knoll and the
slow, still history of them. Ronald could pinpoint the grave
exactly and wondered how much of his father had been
preserved by the peat. One thing he was sure of was that the
gold fob watch would still be there. Nothing would rot that.

Out of the semi-darkness came a rasping sound. Abrasive,
like sandpaper, rubbed over a block of wood. It was coming
from the yard and Ronald, up on his feet, pushed back the
curtains. He looked out at the moon hanging mellow and low,
its pale face silvering the puddles.

And something else.

Another face.

He gasped and, turning back to the room, tugged on his clothes and dashed down the stairs to investigate. When he stepped outside, the only sound was the screech of a barn owl, amplified against the cloth of night. It spooked him, and he reached back inside the kitchen for the torch he kept there for emergencies. He opened the barn door and whistled to his dogs. They hadn't barked; no one had disturbed them. Maybe he'd imagined it, he thought, as he paced around the wet yard. Stabbing the torch beam into the flickering undergrowth triggered a long-buried memory of torchlight around the farm and over the moor when the police searched all night long for his father.

What was that?

Human or animal?

Ronald couldn't be sure, and his sheepdogs had missed it. But something definitely scurried into the trees. He swallowed. Listened to the ancient creep of Saddleworth Moor and waited for confirmation. For whatever it was to show itself again.

Nothing.

Perhaps he had imagined it. Were his dreams spilling into his waking life?

As he breathed into the dangling moments of eerie calm, what the torch claimed next wasn't a dream: a collection of spent cigarette butts littering the tufts of grass and nettles. Ronald and Thomas hadn't smoked cigarettes for years, and he bent to examine them, alarmed how dry and fresh they were. Someone had been here, watching the house.

He stepped inside the barn. Its deep, velvety blackness instantly engulfed him.

'Hello? Is anyone there?' He swung the torchlight around, hunting the recesses and illuminating the shadows before throwing them back to black again.

Satisfied nothing was amiss, Ronald was settling the dogs into their beds, when they began to bark at a tall figure who emerged from the shadows, blocking his exit.

'Ye looking for something, old man? Tucked away down here, ain't ye? Real little pocket in the wilderness. Dinnae suppose ye get many visitors.'

'Christ! You!' The sight of him was nearly enough to stop his heart. Ronald hadn't imagined it. The bastard had been lurking here all the time. 'What are you doing?' There was no sign of the revolver, but he could have hidden it in the folds of his leather coat. *Don't make any sudden moves,* he warned himself.

'Let's just say I'm familiarising ma'self with the place... getting my bearings, so to speak. Ye like what I scratched on your car, did ye?' A chilling laugh.

'Clear off, go on, get out of here. This is private property; I could have you arrested.' Ronald heard the tremor in his voice.

'Arrested? I dinnae think ye want police sniffing around these premises. I'd say ye have something to hide... something tucked away down here that ye shouldnae have. Am I right, Grandad?'

Ronald froze.

Why didn't I fetch the shotgun along with the torch before coming out? Stupid... stupid...

The situation he was in echoed that night all those years ago when his father stood on this very spot, threatening to expose him. Gun or not, could he kill again? Silence this bastard, too?

'Ah, I can see I'm right?' A mordant chuckle. 'So, what secret are ye hiding all the way out here, old man? Maybe I should be the one to call the police for ye? What do ye say?'

37

Friday, 1 October 1965

Underwood Court, Hattersley, North-East Cheshire

There was still no news of Kathy. The appeals Connie had made on the radio and in the newspaper had come to nothing. All she could hope was that her daughter was alive and well and that any day she would walk through the door. It was what she had prayed for at St Francis's. Peaceful amid the subdued light that spilled in through the vast stained-glass windows. Lighting candles and making deals with God; believing only He could help her.

She was on her way home from church now, and it was almost dark by the time she reached Underwood Court with its seven skyscrapers rearing above the huddle of council houses. Each block, with its starkly lit stairwell, was about as welcoming as a cold hearth. She'd run out of cigarettes, and seeing the lights still on in the newsagent's was a relief. Drawn like a moth to a flame, she crossed the tarmac, ignoring the voices that called her name from their darkened doorways. No one had set on them in the street since that night, but she feared it was only a matter of time before they did.

The lift was out of order again and Connie climbed the stairs, listening to the clatter of her heels echo around the concrete stairwell. Huffing and puffing, she reached her floor and found Myra waiting outside the flat.

'Where've you been? Ian's fucked off to Manchester, and Gran's gone to bed. Could do with some company if you're up for it?'

'Yeah, okay,' Connie yawned as she dug through her bag for the key. She thought Myra looked peaky without her make-up.

'Who the hell did this?' Myra pointed to the graffiti on the door. '*Child killer*? Christ, Con. Is that what they're calling you?' A horrified look.

'It's what they're calling Fred.'

'I suppose you've tried scrubbing it off?'

'No point. They'll only scrawl it on again.' Connie unlocked the door, and Myra strode inside. 'Where d'you say Ian's gone to?'

'Manchester. Said he were gonna watch the queers down Central Station.'

'He's always going there. What's so interesting?'

Myra shrugged. 'All I know is I'm to pick him up at eleven. Honestly, Con, he treats me like a flamin' skivvy.'

Connie took a bottle of whisky from the sideboard and poured two large measures you could never buy in a pub.

'You're getting a taste for this.' Myra chinked her glass against hers. 'You used to hate it.'

'I still do. It's the effect I like.'

'It's not fair, him leaving me on my own.' Myra sat on the

settee. 'Where's Fred?' she enquired as she lifted a hand to the rollers under her headscarf.

Connie saw their bedroom door was closed. 'Asleep. He's up so early in the mornings.'

Myra scowled and kicked off her pumps, lighting one of her Embassys without offering Connie one. Sitting side-by-side, the friends talked, drank whisky and smoked, lighting the next cigarette from the last. Connie cuddled the Tiny Tears doll Fred had fixed.

'You're obsessed with that thing. I never remember you cuddling your Kathy like that.' Myra flicked fag ash onto the rug at her feet. 'You're gonna have to live with this, Con. Supposing the kid never comes home? I know you think I'm being hard on you, but you weren't cut out to be a mother. Maybe the kid's found somewhere better.'

Connie was sick of the same conversation. How could Myra understand? She wasn't a mother.

'I should've brought a bottle of wine with me. I prefer wine.' Myra drained her whisky.

'Seem to be managing okay with that.' Connie eyed the precious bottle she relied on to get her through the day.

'This is like old times. You and me, chewing the fat.'

'Yeah, it's nice. Not seen much of you since you took up with Ian. I thought you'd gone off me.'

'Gerroff, you're me best pal.' Myra gave Connie's hand a reassuring squeeze, but the feel of her skin, so cold and dry, robbed the gesture of any reassurance. Myra must have sensed her reticence and pulled back her hand. 'Shit!' A glance at the clock had her extinguishing her cigarette. 'I'm gonna be late collecting him. Fancy coming with me?'

Connie nodded. She didn't like to refuse.

· · ·

They drove through the rainy streets. Beyond the car, everything looked melancholy and murky. The city's night-time suburbs, metrically cut by the repetitious swing of the wind-screen wipers. She watched the rain bounce against the gleaming tarmac, a sudden spray from a low-loader passing on the opposite side hissing against the windscreen. Then, when the rain eased to a drizzle, Myra cut the wipers and swapped their squeaking for the spooky stillness of the virtually traffic-free streets.

'This is where I dropped him off.' Myra flicked the indicator and turned into the car park adjacent to Manchester Central railway station. 'It's where we always meet,' she explained, before cutting the engine.

They waited, but there was no sign of Ian. Connie's head was swimming with the booze and pills she'd popped that day, and the smell of Myra's perfume was suffocating.

'You stay here.' Myra opened the driver's door and the burst of fresh air revived her a little. 'I'm gonna find him.'

Connie watched her walk up the grand set of steps; the self-conscious touch of the rollers under her headscarf when she turned to wave, communicating there was no sign of him.

'What d'you think about Dave Smith?' Myra asked as soon as she was back behind the wheel.

'He's all right,' Connie yawned.

'I hate the fucker. I think him and Ian have got something big planned.'

'Yeah; like what?'

'I dunno, but Ian's been different with me. He has these great long conversations with Dave, really involved. I've been feeling pushed out for ages.'

'D'you think he's going to finish with you?'

'He wouldn't dare.' The look was vehement. 'I know too much.'

Two slow hours passed. Myra, periodically starting the

engine to warm the car when it got too chilly, was growing increasingly angry. Connie, her head lolling, slipping in and out of sleep, wished she'd stayed at home.

'He's here. Quick, Con, get in the back. The seats are up.'

Connie did as she was told and climbed into the rear of the car.

'Where've you been?' Myra demanded when Ian had fumbled his way into the front passenger seat.

'None of ye damn business.' His voice perforated the dark and prickled against Connie's skin. He stank like a wet ashtray.

'You're pissed.'

'So what if I am?'

'You selfish pig. I've been waiting hours. Eleven o'clock, you said.'

'I've been thinking... and I'd say the victim's family's got the right to kill ye. An eye for an eye. A tooth for a tooth. What do ye say, Hessy?' The drink had strengthened his accent.

'Shut up, you stupid bastard.' Myra smacked the steering wheel.

'Aye. The murderer should face the family of the one he's killed.' Slurring, drunk, frothing at the mouth – he looked frightening.

'For God's sake, shut your gob,' Myra warned him again, tilting her head to indicate Connie.

'What the fuck's she daeing here?' Ian demanded, casting a look into the back.

'Never mind about her, I wanna know where you've been?'

'None of ye fuckin' business.' He belched and pummelled the dashboard. His eyes were unnaturally bright and shining through the darkness.

'It's my bloody business when you make me wait half the night in the cold.'

'I've bin watchin' the queers. Bloody worms... bloody shirtlifters. Place is swarming with 'em.'

Connie listened to Ian's fevered rant from the rear seats of the car.

'Nazis had it right, if you ask me. I'd eradicate the fuckin' lot of 'em... I'd dae it with ma bare hands.'

'I dunno why you're so interested in them?' Myra pulled up at a set of traffic lights.

'I dinnae have to explain ma'self to ye.'

'I'm just asking.'

'Nag, nag, bloody nag.'

Myra was furious, speeding down empty roads, then slamming her foot on the brake for no reason.

'What the hell d'ye think ye daeing?' Ian's breath was sour and Connie feared she might be sick. 'I coulda gone through the fuckin' windscreen.'

'Serves you right,' Myra yelled. 'Treating me like I don't exist.'

Ian swung out an arm and struck Myra over the head so hard Connie heard the plastic rollers snap.

Everything went quiet. She didn't dare ask if Myra was all right, fearing Ian would remember she was there and punch her too.

'Quiet out, this time of night, isnae, Hessy?' Ian began laughing and talking normally again, their argument forgotten. 'I like ye driving me places when it's late like this. Nice empty streets, just cruising around.'

'You still haven't told me what you've been doing?' Myra, softer, fed him a smile through the dark.

'Maybe I'll take ye with me next time, Hessy. Would ye like that? Educate ye?' He nodded, calm. His rant over.

'You do spend a lot of time watching those types of men, Ian,' Connie giggled. Relieved the atmosphere had lightened, she wanted to make a little joke of it. 'Myra says you're always watching them. That you find them fascinating.' A bolder laugh. 'Is it 'cos you fancy trying it out for yourself?'

Without warning, he was on her, spinning like a snake from the passenger seat and taking her throat in one hand. Squeezing the life from her.

'Ye fuckin' bitch! Are ye calling me a queer? I'll fuckin' kill ye.' Screaming, his spit flecked her face. 'I will, I'll fuckin' kill ye!'

The emergency stop saved her. Thrown hard against the dashboard, Ian had no choice but to let her go. Connie was thrown forward, too. Coughing and gasping for the breath she thought she would never breathe again; she saw Myra turn to look over her shoulder.

She was smiling.

38

Saturday, 2 October 1965

Ashton-under-Lyne, Lancashire

Ronald had a real dread of roofscapes and streets. He saw the narrow alleyways and brick-walled ginnels as a trap. Used to hills and the expanse of the moor, these terraced houses seemed squalid. The walk from where he parked the truck was gritty and took him along endless pavements under a weary-looking sky. Tall factory chimneys pumping out ochre-coloured smoke flanked the canal, and he peered down over the bridge to where a troupe of children were playing on the muddy banks. They were so sad-eyed and grubby, he couldn't bear to look at them for long and diverted his gaze to watch a paper bag somersault in the breeze. This unexpected beauty amid the shabbiness wasn't something he'd have noticed before the child came into his life.

With thoughts of the child, his mind spun to the skirmish in the barn two nights ago. He could still clearly see that bastard's face lit by the torch, that evil glint in his eye as he stepped backwards out of the barn, jabbing a finger and saying, in that harsh accent of his before disappearing into the darkness, 'I'll get ye, old man, ye can be sure of that. Nae one gets to talk to me the way you did... I'll be back for ye, and there'll be no warning next time.' Ronald shivered a little into the memory of that man and the menace he oozed. But, it was all right, he kept telling himself, if the bastard knew the child was living at the farm, he'd have acted on it by now. Whatever he thought he had on him, whatever secret he was threatening to expose, he was bluffing. Not that it made the situation any less stressful for Ronald. He needed to make Thomas understand it was only a matter of time before the police came knocking. But what if it was too late to take her back? How could they justify their reasons for keeping her this long? What a mess everything was. Stuck in the middle, he despaired of it all.

Ronald yawned as he referred to the list. 'I want to make her birthday the best she's ever had.' His brother's request replayed in his head when he turned the paper over to the diagram of the child's measurements Thomas had drawn on the back.

All this talk of birthdays had got him thinking about his father again. Not that Jacob Cappleman was the kind of man to remember birthdays. It was why Ronald had been so surprised when his father had come home with a velvet-eyed spaniel tucked under his arm on the eve of Thomas's thirteenth – only to discover that he'd won the dog in a card game. Not that Thomas had cared, handing over his raw young heart the moment he clapped eyes on it. A boy or a girl – his only concern. Not that it mattered because in no time at all, blamed for stealing a ham from the kitchen table and taking chickens from the henhouse even when there was clear evidence of a fox, the dog – 'I warned you not to give him a name' – was going. It was cruel in the extreme to come home from school one day to find it gone. Sold to a man down the Bull for a couple of pints of bitter. 'But you gave him to me!' Thomas had cried; his heart breaking. Ronald suspected that the little dog continued to pad through his brother's dreams even now.

When Ronald reached the high street with its scores of shops, he consulted his brother's list again and found the entrance of C&A, where he stood looking at the window display for a long time. A child-size mannequin in a jersey and skirt and a little red anorak with a hood interested him. But red stood out. The descriptions the police had circulated said they were looking for a child in a red coat. But she liked red, didn't she? He'd buy her one. It looked smart and practical. It didn't matter that it wasn't on the list; he was sure Thomas would approve. The shop had dressed another mannequin in a little riding outfit that included a hacking jacket and shiny boots. Perhaps they could buy her a pony? He carried these thoughts in through the revolving door. Only to tell himself off for being swayed by Pamela's revelations and thinking he had a say in the child's life when really he didn't.

Having collected a basket, Ronald located the children's section and wandered up and down aisles where items were folded onto shelves or hanging on rails. The store was full, and the lights dazzled him. The nightmare of noise and business was confusing. He found the red anorak in her size and now all he needed were vests and pants and socks. But where were they? He looked around but there were no sales assistants, so he plucked up the courage to ask a woman he saw hovering by the lift to the menswear department with carrier bags of her own.

'Excuse me? You don't happen to know where children's vests and things are?'

The woman didn't answer straight away. She seemed a little dazed, and he needed to prompt her.

'Oh, yeah,' she said eventually, her dark eyes barely focusing. 'Yeah... they're over there.' She pointed, and he noticed a slight tremor in her hand.

She was younger and prettier than he first realised. There was something oddly familiar about her. He put it down to her long, dark curtain of hair that was like Pamela's when he first knew her.

'Very kind. Thank you.' He smiled and tried to ignore the whiff of booze on her breath.

Ronald found the items he needed and was on his way to the till to pay – his mind curling back to the young woman, for something in her expression had entered his soul – when he saw a delightful coral-pink shift dress with a square neckline and a hem that fell below the knee. He couldn't resist it and knew the child would love this little extra present from him. To go with the dress, he found a pair of white pumps with gold lettering gleaming on the insoles. He was being silly; it wasn't as if she had anywhere to wear them. Not yet, maybe, he reminded himself. Because the girl would be leaving the farm just as soon as he'd worked out a way to make it happen.

Pleased with his purchases, Ronald left the store, looking around one last time for the young woman. She had gone. But not the memory of her. The sense of loneliness and loss she left him with. The stark emptiness in her face under her dark fringe. Odd to be affected by a stranger this way. He wondered what had brought her down so low, but with no way of finding out, he pushed his seemingly unwarranted concerns for her from his mind, reminding himself he had enough troubles of his own.

———

Driving home under a sky as pink as corncockles, he kept an eye out for the turquoise Mini Traveller. Relieved to see no sign of it or the motorbike, he relaxed a little and wound the window down to feel the cool rush of air on his cheeks. Turning into the lane that led to the farm, he spotted the bright orange berries of the rowan trees in the raggle-taggle of hedgerows. The flutter of interested birds. Thomas, a great advocate of free food for the table, who harvested everything and wasted nothing, let the birds take these, claiming no amount of sugar could sweeten them. The blackberries Ronald had watched ripen from green to red to black were in abundance, too. It was only early October, but the mornings were misty, and he'd already identified the chill of autumn, warning of the harsher weather these parts were renowned for, that was never far away. He had always thought the mood of the moor suited the winter – the stunted days when it barely grew light, the seemingly endless dark letting secrets stay secret.

His first view of the farmhouse was the tail of smoke rising from the chimney. At his back, the wind combed the moorland, and the clouds condensed. He pulled up in his usual place and cut the engine, sitting with the window down for a minute or two. Smells of baking wafted out through the kitchen window and he could see Thomas moving about within. As he watched him, Ronald thought about how little his brother had demanded of him over the years. Until the child arrived and changed everything.

Ronald went inside carrying the shopping bags. The doll with its colourless hair, its sleepy eyes lolling behind the cellophane window on the box tucked under his arm. It amazed him that something this ugly could appeal to a little girl.

'For the child,' he stated the obvious when Thomas looked over at him. 'I had to hunt around for it. I hope it's the right one.'

'Aye, that's Flopsy.' His brother, coming over to check, looked flushed and pink and had wine-coloured fruit stains on his apron. 'Oh, she'll love it, Ron. Well done.'

Ronald unpacked his purchases, lining them up on the work surface. He unwrapped the red anorak, the coral-pink dress and the little white shoes with a kind of childish glee. Thomas was peeling and slicing. His recipe book open on the page that said 'Jellies & Jams'. The early autumn winds had shaken the trees in the orchard bare and the kitchen was full of apples and plums. The air was ripe with the tangy smell.

Ronald breathed it in as he removed his jacket and rolled up his shirt sleeves, exposing his well-muscled forearms. The trees that huddled around the house threw a carousel of shadows over the kitchen floor as he watched Thomas heating beeswax to secure the jars of blackberry jam. It was a smell that hurled him back to a day in his childhood. He lifted a hand to touch the ridge of scar tissue on his cheek that purpled with the winter cold. He saw himself as a boy of nine, seated on the draining board, his feet in the sink while his mother bathed his cut knees and hands, the blood on his face.

'You've gone too far this time, Jacob Cappleman,' she had hollered at his father.

'Aye? And what are you gonna do about it, woman?'

Ronald's eyes wandered to the shotgun. He thought of the years of abuse that were to be lived through before he grew strong enough to stand up to the bastard.

'Did you fetch candles, Ronnie?'

His brother's voice brought him back from the unsettling place his memory had led him, and he fished around in the shopping bag.

'Do you like what I've done?' Thomas, eyebrows expectant, had abandoned his jam-making to circle the table he'd laid in readiness for the child's birthday tea. He was glowing with plea-sure and grinning broadly. Ronald could tell the way it looked pleased him. And indeed, it should. Aside from the spangled cloth – something he must have embellished with sequins – it offered a spread of everything from griddle scones to glossy-topped fruit pies decorated with pastry leaves. And as a centre-piece, what must have been the largest cake he had ever seen.

'Looks grand, Tom. Terrific cake. Very pink.' He eyed the high-sided sponge smothered in buttercream icing.

'I found some cochineal.' Thomas pointed to a little bottle with a rusty lid that must have been loitering in the cupboard since their mother was alive.

Ronald was hungry and put his hand out to take a pie.

'Don't you dare!' Thomas swatted him away.

'Go on, Tom. I've had nowt since breakfast.'

'No.' His brother was firm. 'We're to wait 'til we're all together.'

Ronald excused himself and nipped upstairs to change, returning to the kitchen minutes later.

'I meant to say,' Thomas was securing the last jar of jam with its lid, 'we had visitors today.'

'Visitors? Oh, don't tell me it was that flamin' salesman with his brochures again? How many more times? I'm not interested.' Ronald recalled the man's face when he showed him the hay meadows with their diversity of grasses and wildflowers. The way he had looked at him with amused contempt, as if he was some charming but delusional old fool from a bygone age. 'Telling me to spray our pastures to rid them of "weeds" and reseed with modern grass... *modern grass?* You ever heard the like? The idea our farm could be owt more than a productive business was alien to him.'

'He had a point, Ron. You have seen our overdraft?'

'Huh. Idiots like him, they know the price of everything and the value of nowt.'

'It's good enough for our neighbours.'

'I hate it. I hate it when the wind blows it in.' Ronald blamed the use of pesticides on his mother's cancer. Something

Thomas wouldn't consider; preferring to blame their father and the years of stress he put her through. 'Nature's clever; it's building a resistance. You must've noticed they need to spray it more and more?'

'Oh, calm down... getting all hot under the collar. It weren't him, anyway. It were a couple.'

'A couple?' Ronald was still thinking about the salesman.

'Aye. Came asking if we had eggs to sell. I told 'em we only had enough for the farm. It were odd, though.'

'Odd?' He was still only half-listening.

'Well, aye,' Thomas frowned. 'I asked how they found us. They were hardly passing by, were they? We're miles off the beaten track.'

'Hang on, Tom.' Finally registering. 'A couple, you say? How old were they?'

'Young.' A soft chuckle. 'But then everyone looks young to me nowadays.'

'How young?'

'Mid-twenties.'

'What did they look like?' Ronald's skin had shrunk beneath his clothes and he braced himself for the answer.

'She had hair a bit like that Marilyn Monroe, but not as pretty. Bit hard-looking, if you want the truth.' Thomas pulled a face. 'And I think he were a Scot. Not that he said owt much.'

Ronald gulped his shock and pushed a hand up through his hair.

'I'm surprised you didn't pass them in the lane. You must've missed them by minutes.'

'A turquoise car?'

'So you did see them?'

'Not exactly.' Loath to alarm his brother, Ronald didn't elaborate. 'Erm... have you...' he hesitated, suddenly afraid to ask.

'What's the matter, Ron? You've gone all pale.'

'It's probably nowt... but, erm...' He tried to breathe past the frightening thought that had just occurred to him. 'Where's the child, Tom?'

'Gracie?'

'Aye.'

'Isn't she playing in the yard?'

'Not when I drove in. And she weren't in her room, neither.'

39

Ashton-under-Lyne, Lancashire

Somehow it was Kathy's eighth birthday. Connie, having spent most of the last month sprawled on the settee in front of the TV, moodily sipping whisky, did not know where the weeks had gone. She made next to no effort with her appearance, and the only person she bothered with, aside from Fred and her mother, was Myra. Since Kathy disappeared, the weeks had passed in a miserable blur of booze and pills. Time seemed to have paused, yawning off into a future she couldn't imagine. It was already mid-afternoon on a day that had never grown properly light. Not that Connie noticed. Necking the usual whisky straight from the bottle and popping in a Valium before catching the bus to Ashton, she was noticing less and less and found it suited her.

She turned up the collar of her raincoat, left the bus depot and walked to the high street. Connie had arranged to meet Fred later, but first, she wanted to buy Kathy a few things to mark her special day. As if thinking about her daughter at that moment had magicked her up, she spotted one of her mother's leaflets, blown into the gutter. She stooped to pick it up. It was wet from the recent rain and she unfolded it carefully, fearful of ripping it, staring at her daughter's ruined face. It was like looking at a stranger. The image of another mother's child. Connie wanted to feel something, but there was only the usual dead kind of emptiness and she let the leaflet fall from her fingers and continued on her way. She glanced down at the canal. Oil-black and greasy under the rippling reflection of a slate-grey sky. The police had dredged this, and every other waterway. According to Mounsey, they had conducted a fingertip search of the surrounding area, but there was no trace of Kathy. Aside from the doll Myra claimed to have found in the pub car park, her daughter had vanished. But it was better than the alternative, she told herself. Supposing they had found her body; then what? At least if her child was missing, there was still hope.

Within a few paces, her reflection in a newsagent's window blocked her way. Was that really her? She gawped, disbelieving it, and stood frozen to the spot. Ignorant of the space she claimed on the strip of pavement, of the stream of disgruntled shoppers who parted like water around a rock. When did she evolve into this mess? What did Fred see in her? She needed to sort herself out, otherwise she would lose him too. Just as Ian had so savagely said.

Abandoning her reflection, Connie made a beeline for the enormous windows of C&A. A soulless setting of glass and concrete she didn't much like. But Fred did, and he was the one who had to come here each day. Claiming it was a nice clean environment and better than working in that filthy foundry all his life like his father, Fred saw his job at C&A as a step up, and he'd been lucky to get it, given his juvenile conviction. Mr Matthews, the store manager and one of those Christian types who thought everyone deserved a second chance, had taken a real shine to Fred.

She stood looking at the revolving door, and deciding she needed another tablet before venturing inside, opened her bag and dug through its rattling innards. Finding the Valium, she unscrewed the lid of the brown bottle her mother had since willingly given her and gulped one down. Tasting the bitterness on the back of her tongue, she wished she had the guts to take them all and drift off into oblivion.

Finished buying presents for her daughter, the handles of the carrier bags carving into her palms, Connie was about to take the lift to the menswear department when a middle-aged man with a thick mop of dark grey hair stepped up to her.

'Excuse me? You don't happen to know where children's vests and things are?'

Connie couldn't answer him straight away. A little dazed, her hesitancy forced him to ask her again.

'Oh, yeah,' she replied eventually. 'Yeah... they're over there.' She pointed in the direction he needed to go, pleased to have been a help. Up close, there was something familiar about him; she had an odd feeling they had met before.

'Very kind. Thank you.'

He smiled. She thought he looked nice. Ruggedly handsome in his workman boots and corduroy jacket. And pressing the button to summon the lift, it troubled her she couldn't place where she might have seen him. If only she could think straight. Exactly how much had she drunk that day? How many pills had she taken? Connie carried the questions up to the next floor and stopped in front of a mirror fixed to a pillar. Shamed into improving her appearance, she combed her hair and applied a smear of lipstick, a touch of eyeliner. Better, she appraised herself, blotting her mouth. She pulled down the silk scarf she'd tied about her neck to hide the bruises left behind by Brady's fingers that had darkened to an ugly purple necklace around her throat. She had needed to work hard to keep the damage from Fred, certain he'd want to confront Brady but fearing he would come off worse. It was apparent to her the man was mad and, because of it, even more dangerous.

Moving into the menswear section and casting around for Fred, she could only identify the nameless faces of his colleagues. Then she saw him at the exact moment he saw her. He beamed. Did it mean he loved her still? After everything that had happened and all the awful things she'd said? She hoped so.

'Okay,' she mouthed when he held up his hand and spread his fingers to show how long he'd be. She found a chair tucked out of the way and sat down with her shopping, pressing a finger to her temples to squeeze away what remained of her hangover.

'What you been buying?' Fred, suddenly there, bent down to kiss her. He smelled of aftershave and cigarettes.

'A few things for Kathy.'

'Show me.'

She opened the bag that held the birthday cake. Lifted the lid of the box for him to read the name she'd paid the bakery extra to pipe on it. The nurse's play outfit; the Monopoly set; the small electric sewing machine.

'Nice. She's gonna love them.' Fred smiled, his kind eyes going into their creases. She loved him for not saying she had never done this for Kathy when she'd had her. Or that she was nuts and shouldn't be wasting her money; that her daughter wasn't coming home. 'You're not the only one who's been buying presents. I've got one for you.'

'You have?' She felt herself smiling. And because it felt alien, she pushed her fingers to it.

'I'll give it to you later.' He paused at the same mirror

Connie had used and reached into his back pocket for his comb. He ran it through his hair, teasing out the front with his fingers. 'There,' he sighed, when the sultry quiff was complete.

They linked arms and left the store, Fred offering to carry her shopping like the gentleman he was. Out in the street, the day had darkened to the colour of a bruise, not unlike the ones around Connie's neck.

'When we get home, I want us to sit down and have a good long talk.'

'What about?'

'The future.' Fred's leather jacket creaked when he walked.

'Oh, no. You're not dumping me, are you?'

'Look.' He didn't answer. Too busy pointing across the street. 'It's Dave. Dave!' he shouted.

'Don't, Fred. I'm not in mood.'

'Too late, he's seen us.'

And he had. Dave Smith, his thumbs hooked into his black studded belt, sauntered over in his drainpipe jeans. Dave nodded hello to Connie, then fingered Fred's jacket. 'Nice, mate. Must've set you back a few bob?' He seemed edgy, unable to keep still.

'Got it on discount from work. Sort you one, if you want?'

Another nod. 'So, how you doing?' Dave crouched to adjust the six-inch zips at the bottom of his trousers, then bobbed up again. His fidgeting made Connie nervous. 'Not seen you in ages.'

'Considering we're neighbours. You and Maureen keep saying you'll call over but you never do. Plenty of time for Ian, though.' A wry smile. *Was Fred jealous of Dave and Ian's friendship in the same way Myra was?*

'Nice yer face's cleared up.' Dave was obviously avoiding the question.

'Probably be left with a scar.' Fred touched the bridge of his nose and scowled.

'Scars are distinguished.'

'Don't talk rot.' He laughed and bumped Dave's arm. 'Fancy grabbing a quick coffee at Siv's? Like the old days? Been ages since we played the jukebox.' Connie knew Sivori's Café. She used to go there with Myra. Drinking expresso, filling the ashtray. Smearing the small white cups with lipstick. Toe-tapping to Del Shannon's latest hit. It was Myra who taught her to jive. When had they last gone dancing? She couldn't remember.

Dave consulted his watch. 'Not really got time, mate. I'm meeting up with Ian.'

'Again?'

'Aye.' A wide grin. 'He's got some shit going down. Wants me in on it.'

'What shit?' From Fred's tone, Connie could tell he didn't like the sound of that.

'I dunno, do I? The man's a mystery.'

'There's summat not right with that bloke. He's trouble, Dave. You wanna stay away from him.'

'Nah. He's all right when you get to know him. He's been lending me books and stuff. Trying to give me an *education*.' Dave presented the word to them like a package.

'Aye. And I've an idea what kind of books 'n all. Tried to get me to read 'em. Summat about torture and bondage. No thanks. I'd say you're right up his arse. Too far up it to see what a weirdo he is. Lanky streak of piss, thinking he's better than the rest of us. I mean, who wears a V-neck with a shirt and tie? The bloke dresses like your old man.'

Connie said nothing, busy remembering the afternoon she and Fred had laughed about Ian's turn-ups... those last blissful moments before realising Kathy had gone.

'You wanna open your eyes, Dave. All that shite he talks, I can't believe you've fallen for it.'

'Yeah, maybe. But he seems so certain about everything.'

Dave, continuing to shift from foot to foot, looked the most agitated she'd ever seen him. 'I like that in a person.'

'You only think that because he's older than you. Bloody know-it-all.'

'You were all pally-wally with him that day on the moor. What were that all about?'

'The maniac had a gun, didn't he? He were pissed out of his head. Anything could've happened. I were frightened he were gonna shoot one of us.'

When Dave walked away, Connie and Fred talked about him, exchanging concerns about how Dave had fallen right under Brady's spell.

'I'm really worried about him, Con. He's ultra-vulnerable since him and Maureen lost their baby. That bastard's taking advantage. I know he is.'

'I don't like it neither. That man scares me.' She put a hand to her neck.

'He's why I don't like you hanging around with Myra.'

'She's all right when she's not with him. But it's a shame about Dave, he used to be your best mate.'

'It's not that. He's a grown person. It's who he's choosing to spend his time with that bothers me.'

Black Fell Farm, Saddleworth Moor, West Riding of Yorkshire

Ronald had been gripped by a sudden terror for the child's safety. 'Think, Tom. When did you last see her?'

His brother flicked his eyes to the clock before turning to the sink and the washing up that waited for him there. 'Must've been a while.'

'For God's sake, Tom? *Think.*' Ronald tried not to shout.

'Must've been after breakfast.' Splashing noises.

'What? That can't be right; she can't have been out all day?'

'I'm sorry, Ron.' Thomas dried his hands and turned to him. 'I've been rushed off my feet. Sorting the food, the table—'

'But you must have seen her since this morning?' he cut him off.

'I haven't, no. You know what she's like. Off in her own little world half the time.'

Ronald had detected the merest fissure of anxiety in his brother's voice. Was he fearing the same thing he was? How could he? Thomas didn't know the things he knew; Ronald hadn't told him.

'Right, come on. We need to find her. Leave that... we need to go now.' He pulled on his jacket.

'Why are you so flustered, Ron? She can't come to harm round here.' Thomas untied his apron and folded it over the nearest chair.

Ronald swept aside the fly screen, swapped his slippers for boots and charged into the yard.

'Perhaps she were so busy playing, she forgot about her birthday tea.' Thomas trotted after him. 'Gracie... Gracie? Where are you, sweetheart?'

Forgotten her birthday tea? It's all she's gone on about. Ronald tried to tell himself there were loads of places she might be. His brother was right; she'd just lost track of time. These were the only thoughts he allowed himself, as they checked the nooks and crannies around the outbuildings and barn, searching as far as the boundary wall and water trough. It was the farthest Ronald had seen his brother walk for years. Usually, there wasn't the need for him to venture much beyond his chicken coops and roses. Bramble gave them a whinny and wandered to the fence.

'We'll feed you in a minute,' Thomas told her. 'We've to find Gracie first. Might she be with the hens? She loves my hens. Gracie!' he panted; his top lip wet with perspiration. He turned to Ronald, a look of anguish in his eyes. 'Where can she have got to?'

'I tell you what,' Ronald said, fearing Thomas was about to keel over, 'you go back to the house and stay there in case she turns up. I've thought of a few places I can try.'

'Have you? Like where?' Thomas brightened.

'Her swing.'

'Oh, aye. Good idea.'

'And there's that old tree. The one that got blown down

but's still growing. Now, you're not to worry,' Ronald assured him as panic bounced: a rubber ball against the wall of his stomach. 'She's gone off playing and forgotten the time, that's all this is.'

'I hope so, Ron.' Thomas rubbed a hand over his face.

Ronald left his brother behind to follow a path that cut through the lower meadows. Sheep dozing in a pile, soaking up the last snatch of warmth, scattered as he passed by a gap in the hedge. While he hurried along, he thought about how the milestones that portion up the lives of others had not applied to him and Thomas. The roles of father, then grandfather had passed them by. Until the child, it never occurred to Ronald that he'd missed out on something. He found he was bereft of her chatter, and it was strange to feel the lack of her when he could be so awkward around her. He didn't know how to behave with children. Living with only his brother for company had made him selfish and his monotonous work on the farm was not stimulating enough for such a bright little mind. It embarrassed him that he wasn't nearly entertaining enough; that midlife was a place he had come to without realising and because of this, he had forgotten how to play. If indeed he ever knew; his mother used to say that he had been born fully grown.

Jogging one minute, walking the next, determined to stay positive and telling himself the child would be where he thought she was, Ronald evaluated the life he might have lived; the woman he should have married; the house he might have inhabited; the children they might have filled it with. The life that because of his cowardice, his inability to ask for what he wanted, had never materialised.

The sheep had worn the path smooth over the years, and the stones that had worked to the surface felt loose underfoot. He skidded once, then twice, and warned himself to slow down.

It wouldn't help anyone if he turned an ankle, or worse. Late summer butterflies darted and flitted, and the air was heavy with airborne insects. He batted them away as he scrambled down to the stream that was nothing more than a trickle, despite the downpour a night or so ago. He couldn't imagine it full again, but he could see the proof. The high-water line left behind by winter storms. Gripping the hulking branches beached on its bank, he hauled himself up to the cluster of saplings that clung to the rocky sides, their roots exposed to the elements, waiting for the rain and to be covered by the stream again. A bumblebee bobbed between the purple heather and crowberry, and he followed it out to the clearing.

'Gracie... Gracie!' He called the name his brother had given her. The name she answered to. Even though Ronald knew her name was Kathy – a name he never used in a feeble attempt to distance himself from her – now wasn't the time to quibble.

The wind blew across the fields, bending the grass and turning it silver. Some of his sheep looked up as he rushed past. Poised to flee, but they didn't. He climbed a stile and followed a trail that skirted the edge of the moor, passing close enough to his ewes to hear them tugging at the grass. The boughs of the tree where he'd hoped to find the child were empty. As too was the tyre swing he'd tied to the adjacent tree. He stared at it swaying forlornly, listening to the wheezing in his chest. Ronald knew why she wasn't here and he knew who had taken her. He threw a desperate glance at the sky. Saw the sun had set to a red stripe on the horizon. If he was right, and that Myra and her boyfriend had taken her, driven her home to her mother – only one of the awful scenarios that were churning in his head – how long would it be before Pamela found out Ronald had lied? That he'd watched her cry and talk of her distress, all the while knowing the exact whereabouts of her missing granddaughter, but said nothing. She would never forgive him; she wouldn't want anything to do with him again.

A blackbird watched him from a high bough and opened its throat to the last vestiges of the day. Ronald looked up at it, too angst-ridden to appreciate its beauty. With nowhere left to search, he had no choice but to retrace his steps to the farm.

'Oh, Ron. Where is she?' Thomas was pacing the kitchen like a caged animal. His cheeks were wet with tears. 'Where's my little Gracie?'

Ronald wiped the sweat from his brow and looked over at the table set with its fine birthday tea. The big pink cake seemed to stare back at him accusingly. 'She's nowhere.' He wrung his hands.

'I don't know what to do!' Thomas sobbed, his shoulders shaking. 'What are we going to do?'

'Those people who came to the farm – how long were they here?'

'Minutes, Ron. Why?'

'Because I think they might have had something to do with this. Look, Tom, sit down. There's things I need to tell you; things I should've told you before today.'

'What things?' His brother wobbled forward, and Ronald guided him to a chair.

'Sit down, you're breathing all funny, you're worrying me.'

'And you're worrying me. I don't want to bloody well sit down.' His brother flapped his arms around. As ineffectual as the clipped wings of his chickens. 'Just talk to me, tell me what's going on.'

Ronald stood with his back to the room and peered out on the yard. Darkness had gathered over the sky. He needed a moment to build up to the enormity of what he was about to share. To arrange his thoughts into some kind of coherent order before coming clean about the ghastly threats that wicked pair had made; about meeting up with Pamela and learning he had a daughter... that the child was his granddaughter. And that any minute, the police would pull up outside to arrest them both.

'Hang on, what's that?' Ronald pressed his nose to the window. 'Tom, I think I saw something. A light, maybe. Coming from the barn.' He hunted around for his torch but couldn't find it.

'Come on, then. Stop buggering about.' Thomas was spurred into action.

Ronald had never seen him move so fast. He'd been about to say he would go, wanting his brother to take it easy. But Thomas had already stepped outside, calling for the child.

They charged across to the barn and pushed open the large double doors.

'Gracie? Are you in here, sweetheart?'

Nothing. Only the dogs looking up from their beds, bewildered, the whites of their eyes caught in the light leaking from the porch. Owl-light, eerie and ominous, clogged the barn and Ronald struck a match and lit the oil lamp. He swung it around, throwing their shadows, tall as giants, against the walls.

'Is anyone here?'

Again, nothing. Only the shadows that were deep enough to push his hands into.

'Sorry, Tom. I thought I saw something. I must've been mistaken.' Ronald set the lamp down on his workbench and was about to extinguish the flame when he felt the weight of his brother's hand on his sleeve.

'*Shh.*' He held a finger to his lips. 'I heard something.' They held their breath to it. 'There. Did you hear it?' Thomas hissed, flicking his gaze to the rafters. 'Quick! Give me the light.'

Ronald passed him the lamp and followed him to the foot of the ladder that led up to the hayloft.

'Gracie? Is that you?' Thomas pleaded through the gloaming.

Silence, but for the wind moving through the trees, the ewes talking to the last of the lambs as they grazed the perimeters of the farm.

'We won't be cross.'

They waited. Hopeful.

'Come on, Tom. No one's here.' Ronald took his brother's arm to steer him away.

Then Thomas gasped. Jabbed a finger upwards. 'There is, look.'

Ronald did. And what he saw made his heart surge with joy.

'Have they gone yet?' A little head looked down on them from the hayloft, haloed in curls.

'Has who gone, poppet?'

'That man and woman. They give me a bad feeling in my tummy.'

You and me both, Ronald thought, crediting the child with good instinct.

'They're scary. I thought they'd come to hurt me.'

'Ronnie and me wouldn't let anyone hurt you, little one.' Thomas was choked with emotion. 'Come on, come down. You've birthday tea and presents waiting.'

Underwood Court, Hattersley, North-East Cheshire

Darkness fell. There was hope for Connie when there was light in the sky. It was the night-time that was the problem. When it was cold outside, it left her imagining her little girl out in it, and that was when the terror set in. When the faces of those other lost children – drained of colour and looking just as they had in the newspapers – turned on a loop in her mind. What she wanted to do was go out. To roam the streets hunting for Kathy. What stopped her was the fear that if she gave in to this need, she would become like poor Mrs Reade, whose daughter, Pauline, had been missing for over two years. And this frightened Connie. Because by searching for your lost child, it seemed you stopped them from coming home and would never see them again.

She poured herself another tot of whisky and wandered into the kitchen with her glass. Standing in the doorway, she sipped it and stared at the table set for Kathy's birthday tea. The pile of unwrapped presents. The space at the table where her child should be, like an open wound. She could tell Fred thought she was off her head doing this and was grateful to him for not voicing it and confirming the fact.

She glanced at the clock. The day had almost gone. Connie put down her glass and picked up the cake with its eight unlit candles. The name 'Kathy' piped in pink that had bled into the pristine white icing. And steeling herself for the saddest thing she had ever done, she took the few paces necessary to cross the small kitchen and tipped the cake into the bin.

42

Wednesday, 6 October 1965

Black Fell Farm, Saddleworth Moor, West Riding of Yorkshire

The Virginia creeper was a blaze of red against the farmhouse walls. October's gift, his mother used to call it. Ronald lay in bed and listened to the fingers of wind rattling the window frames, pestering to be let inside. He'd been lying awake half the night working out the finer details, and they found him just as the sun came up. After days of wrestling with certain ideas – that because of this reason or that had failed before he even got the chance to carry them out – this was a new fail-safe plan. Inspired. Minimum fuss. They could send the girl's things on later. His priority was to get her out of the house and into the truck. The rest would be easy. Not that his heart told him this. He had grown so very fond of her, but the situation could not go on as it was.

. . .

Joining Thomas and the child in the kitchen as they finished their breakfast, he was sure he could pull it off. Smiling and happy, she was standing in the slanting morning sunlight that slid in through the window. Thomas had brought down their mother's old jewellery box and lifted out the gold locket the brothers had bought her one Christmas. Ronald watched his brother fasten the clasp at the nape of the child's neck while she held up her headful of curls. She was wearing the coral-pink dress and when she saw Ronald, she did a little twirl and giggled into her hands. It was lovely to see because not so long ago there would have been tears, and the idea that he was about to return her to that life was an uncomfortable one.

The child reached up to kiss Thomas, then Ronald. The spontaneous show of affection made Ronald gasp, and he turned away, fearful of catching his brother's eye.

'Let's do your hair all nice, shall we? Can't go on your secret errand with Ronnie looking like that.'

The child's curls had grown longer and, instructing her to sit, Thomas stood behind her, wetting his thumbs on his tongue and catching the stray hairs as he pinned it up at the sides.

'It is a secret, isn't it, Ronnie? A really special one.' She shifted her gaze to his and grinned, saying nothing of his whispered request earlier that morning... *'I'm buying Tommy a birthday cake from the baker's and I need you to help me choose.'*

'Ooo.' His brother rubbed his hands together. 'I can't remember the last time anyone made a fuss for my birthday.'

'Well, it is your fiftieth, Tommy. We should mark it.'

———

'Why so sad, Ronnie?' the child asked, sitting beside him on the truck's front seats, zipped inside her smart red anorak.

'I'm not sad, lass.' He gave her a queasy smile.

Other than this brief exchange, they sat in silence. Stealing sidelong glances, he could tell the child was excited to be playing a part in Thomas's birthday surprise. *A surprise, all right.* Ronald, gripping the steering wheel, felt a little sick. What he had done by duping Thomas into believing he and the child had big plans for his special day had been calculating and sly, and it wasn't hard to imagine what his brother would say when he returned to the farm without her.

Parking in his usual place behind the market, Ronald tried not to think of the trouble he and Thomas were going to be in. Pamela had been in such distress the last time he was with her, he decided enough was enough. Not that he hadn't reached this point before. Sitting with Pamela, holding her hand while she shared her anguish for her missing grandchild had made him feel less than human. Rotten to his core. Leaving her to suffer when he could have eased her torment in the blink of an eye. But, returning to the farm, his resolve always crumbled away. Because no matter how upsetting it was to witness Pamela's suffering, seeing the love between Thomas and the child and the joy that filled their home meant he couldn't bring himself to break his brother's heart by taking the child away from him.

So, what was different about today? Ronald didn't know. He just could not continue to lie to the woman he loved. It didn't matter if she never forgave him, that it would be the end of them – the only likely outcome, he thought, sadly. Regardless of his own deep affection for the child and the cold fact that he was betraying his brother – again – he had to be brave. He had to do the right thing.

Ronald helped the child down from the high front seats of his truck, careful not to let her coat make contact with its muddy sides. They set off. The feel of her little hand in his, trusting him, brought a lump to his throat. He steered her towards the café where he'd agreed to meet Pamela when they were last together. Busy. Anonymous. Not that Pamela had the slightest inkling he was bringing her granddaughter with him today. This was his secret. He hadn't dared share it with anyone.

When they turned the corner into the high street, the roar of the football crowd instantly engulfed them. A chanting, singing swill of men and boys sporting scarves in their team's colours and swigging beer from stubby brown bottles. Trust him to pick a day when there was a mid-week friendly. Not that this crowd looked friendly, moving as one along the pavement. The hot press of them was vaguely menacing, and he scooped the child in his arms, carrying her against the tide. The noise was such that he could barely hear what she was saying as she chatted away, close to his ear, her head and shoulders above the throng.

Until she swung out an arm and pointed to a leaflet fixed to a lamp post. Then he heard her.

'Look, Ronnie. It's a picture of me.'

Afraid someone might recognise her, he didn't stop. With her skull bumping against his collarbone, he weaved through the sea of football fans, wincing under their shouts and shrieks and merry obscurities.

'Aren't we going to get Tommy's cake?' The child didn't miss a trick. She'd noticed they weren't stopping at the bakery.

'Aye, little one. We will. Even though he'll complain at the extravagance, saying he could've baked one himself.' She laughed at this, and he felt the low rumble of it through her chest. 'We'll just wait for this lot to go.'

The football crowd eventually thinned, and with his back to the café doors, the view intermittently extending the length of the high street, they watched the constant flux of lorries, buses and cars. Where was she? Pamela had never been late to meet him before. He was as aware of the coming and going of people as he was of the dwindling time. The child was restless in his arms, itching for something to happen in the same way he was.

'I'm cold, Ronnie.' It had started to drizzle, and a little cough punctuated the child's declaration. The sound evoked a memory of her early days at the farm when she'd been so poorly, they feared she might not survive.

He set her down on the pavement and crouched to pull up her socks and zip her anorak as far as it would go. When he heard a screech of brakes, he sprang upright, spinning to the commotion further up on the opposite side of the street. Then a sound ripped open the air. A motorbike. Tearing open the morning. Snarling down the high street, weaving through traffic. It was a black and chrome Tiger Cub and the rider, clad in crash helmet and goggles, his long black leather coat billowing out behind him like a sail, was someone he recognised. The noise of it rattled the shop windows. Woke babies sleeping in their prams. Then, in an instant, it had passed. Fading to a long, sad drone and he knew Pamela wasn't coming. That she had stood him up.

'Come on, lass.' His heart breaking. 'Let's go and fetch Tommy's cake.'

43

Thursday, 7 October 1965

Underwood Court, Hattersley, North-East Cheshire

Connie had thought it was a police siren that disturbed her, but now she was awake and all was quiet, she supposed she must have dreamt it. She turned over and extricated herself from Fred, whose hand was coiled in her hair, his left leg over hers. She waited, listening for the steady rhythm of his breathing before slipping from under the covers. The rooms of the flat were never truly dark. The streetlamps on the estate saw to that. Crossing quickly to the door, she padded to the bathroom, urinated but didn't flush. Her mood was sour. She wanted oblivion and swallowed a Valium before moving into the living room. Feeling ropy for so long, she couldn't remember a time when her head was clear and her mood bright. Was this how her life was going to be from now on?

When she opened the balcony window, cold air slid under her nightclothes and into the room. The estate below was coming to life as the early morning sun fell across the tarmac. Something had happened. Connie could smell it on the crisp autumnal air and reached for her cigarette packet, only to find she'd smoked the last of them. She dressed and left the flat, purse in hand, to wander over to the newsagent's. Inside the shop, she saw that a group of residents had gathered by the till.

'Have you heard?' someone intercepted her.

'Heard what?'

'Some lad's been killed.'

'Killed? Where?' She had heard a siren, after all.

'Wardle Brook Avenue. There's a load of cops there.'

That's Myra's street – she'll know what's going on. Cigarettes forgotten, Connie hurried out of the shop and through the estate. Reaching Wardle Brook Avenue, she saw that a small throng had congregated around a house that was being cordoned off by police officers. Their squad cars parked on the pavement. Connie stared in disbelief. The house was Myra's.

The next shock was Ian. Limping and lacking his usual cockiness, he emerged from the house handcuffed to a police officer. Then Myra appeared. Slouching along behind him in her shabby tartan pumps. They both looked hollowed out. As if they hadn't been to bed. Myra, her hair a mess and yesterday's make-up smudged, was wearing an old jumper and a skirt with the hem hanging down. Ian was bundled into the back of a squad car and driven away. Myra, who didn't once look up, denying Connie the opportunity to ask what was happening, was taken away in another.

She recognised Mounsey's blue Hillman Minx. What was going on? What was he doing here? No time to ask him, either. His car had sped off before she could reach it. Within seconds, another squad car drew up. An estate car this time. And hunched in the back, to Connie's surprise, were a pale-faced Dave Smith and Maureen.

Saddleworth Moor, West Riding of Yorkshire

Ronald had been to the livestock mart to sell off the last few lambs. With his trailer now empty and rattling behind him, he put his foot down and followed the snake of the A635 as it pushed over the moor. In the driving mirror, lights from the town threw a tangerine belt across the sky and ahead, a shaving of silver, as the sun slipped down over the moor. A thought unfurled. Winter was nearly upon them. This colourless existence would be his life forever, now Pamela was no longer a part of it. Things would go back to the way they were in the years without her. Except that this time it would be worse. Even with the child still living with them, nothing would ever bloom again and he would be trapped in this grey, barren drabness.

The A635 soared, and when it dipped down again, Ronald could see the way ahead was blocked by police vans and TV crews.

What the hell?

He instinctively turned his head to the jutting ridge of the Knoll and to his horror he saw a long line of men moving over the moor, down towards the reservoir. Some with sticks, others with spades. Their dark silhouettes stamped against the dusk.

His heart, a galloping horse he couldn't rein in, caused a momentary lapse in concentration. He lost control of the driving wheel. The truck swerved and there was a terrifying moment when the wheels bounced along the verge. It brought him to his senses. He righted the truck just in time and rammed his foot on the brake and skimmed to a halt. He lurched forward in his seat and the shopping Thomas had asked him to fetch from town slammed against the side of the passenger footwell.

Silence. Save for his laboured breathing and the ticking down of the engine. The smell of rubber stinging the air.

Staccato images of that night came back to him. His father's moving mouth, whatever he said, long forgotten. The final blow. The sickening crack when the butt of the gun hit the base of his skull. Then the dead weight of his father as Ronald dragged him by the scruff of his collar. The smell of the shire horse beside him as they climbed the hill. The sound of the spade slicing through the earth and the hole filling with black peat water. Sweating. Hauling his father's body and kicking it into the grave he'd never been able to convince himself was deep enough. Shovelling in the earth, stamping it down. Then falling to his knees on the ground and collapsing on the grave, exhausted. Sobbing with relief and fear. A fear that had never fully left him.

Ronald dared another look at the row of men marching over the moor. He did not know why they were there, but his gut told him it wasn't for anything good. He was surer than ever his time was almost up. This had always been his fate. For years, he'd been living in the shadow of the noose, and now it was in sharp focus. He was going to hang for murder. He touched his neck. Imagined the death that awaited him as dark thoughts crowded in. In the early years, he used to force himself to stay awake, too frightened to blink, still seeing the congealing blood, the small glistening pieces of brain. Recalling the smell that had filled his nostrils – like nothing he had experienced before or since. But time had passed and the events of that dreadful night had appeared dreamlike, unprovable. But lying beneath the fantasy of safety and stability, like a layer of granite, were other assumptions that in his busy life he had mostly avoided dwelling on. Like what would happen if they found that unmarked grave and the bones of his father. The gold fob watch with its clear inscription.

A loud rapping on the window gave him a start. Ronald turned to the face of a police officer in full uniform and helmet. The man was so close to the glass he could see the web of capillaries across his eyeballs.

The officer tapped the glass again, and Ronald wound down the window.

'Is there anything the matter, sir?'

A few seconds passed before Ronald could answer: his mouth dry, his voice quivering. 'Erm, I just w-wondered w-what was going on?' He waved a hand at the slow-moving band of men in the distance.

'I'm afraid I'm not at liberty to share that kind of information, sir. So, if you'd just move along, please. There's nothing here you need to concern yourself with.'

Underwood Court, Hattersley, North-East Cheshire

The door to the flat clicked open, and Fred strode in, waving a newspaper through the air. 'You're not gonna fuckin' believe this.' Panting, his forehead sweaty, he took off his leather jacket and threw it on the back of a chair. The chair toppled over under the weight.

'Believe what?' Connie rose from the settee. She'd been waiting all day to tell him what she'd seen first thing that morning. By the time she'd returned to the flat, Fred had already left for work.

'That bastard Brady's gone and murdered some bloke.' He righted the chair and swept a jittery hand up through his hair.

'*Murdered?*' she gasped. 'I heard about someone getting killed, b-but murdered? I-I... I thought there must've been some kind of accident. No one said owt about murder. Christ, Fred – and you're saying Ian did it?' She slumped on the settee again. 'I were going to tell you I went round there. I saw the police taking him away. My God, Fred.' She balled her hands into fists. 'I can't believe it. This is... this is terrible.'

'Too right, it's terrible.'

'Who was he?'

'Some lad Brady lured back to the house.'

'Is it in there? Let me see.'

Fred handed her his copy of the *Manchester Evening News*, and she stared open-mouthed at the photograph of Edward Evans. A good-looking youngster with light brown hair and an engaging smile. A fan of Manchester United.

'Poor kid were only seventeen, Con. *Seventeen?*' Fred was pacing the room and wringing his hands. 'How the hell did Brady get hold of him, let alone persuade him back to Wardle Brook? And why? For God's sake, why? A lad like him. What harm could he do to anyone? Let alone fuckin' Brady.'

Connie, alarmed by the quiver in Fred's voice, got up and guided him to the settee, urging him to sit.

'It's senseless, Con. Bloody senseless.'

She poured them both a drink to steady them, pushed a tumbler into Fred's hands and sat down next to him. Plumped the cushion behind his back to make him comfy. It felt good to be looking after him for a change.

'How come you know so much? It's saying bugger all in the paper.'

Fred downed the whisky in one and returned the empty glass to her. 'Dave's dad came to see me at work.' He took off his tie and wound it round his hands, tightening it and slackening it.

'I saw Dave. He were in one of them panda cars outside number sixteen this morning. Maureen were with him.' She gulped a mouthful of whisky, then gave Fred what was left. Encouraged him to finish it. 'What's he got to do with it?'

'Dave were there when it happened. He watched Brady do it.' He took a sip.

'Christ, Fred. Watched him do what?'

'I'm not sure I should tell you. It's horrible, Con. Really horrible.' Fred looked shattered.

'Tell me. You can't not tell me. What happened?'

'Apparently, so Dave's dad said... oh, Connie, it were horrible. Horrible. I told you Brady were fuckin' mad.' Fred was squeezing the glass so tightly, Connie worried he'd break it and slice his hand open.

'Oh, love, you're a bundle of nerves. Honestly, it's all right.' She rubbed his back, wanting to soothe him. 'You can tell me.'

'He bludgeoned him to death, Con.' Fred, still gripping the glass, had begun to shake. 'That fuckin' evil bastard Brady.' He lifted his bloodshot eyes to hers and held her gaze. 'He bludgeoned that lad to death with an axe.'

'What?' A little stale whisky rose in her throat. 'When? When did this happen?'

'Last night. Dave's saying that Brady showed no emotion. That he were dead calm when he were doing it. That there weren't nothing frenzied. It were for no reason... no reason at all. Raining axe blows, he were. The poor lad crawling around their living room carpet screaming for mercy.' Fred put the glass down and shook out a cigarette from her packet. But his hands were trembling too much to make the lighter work. Connie lit it for him and put it between his fingers. 'Dave's in a hell of a state.' He took a good long drag. The nicotine seemed to calm him.

'And Dave saw it all?'

Fred was smoking and nodding.

'That's horrendous.' What Connie was being told was too much to process. 'But why didn't he try to stop him?'

''Cos Brady had a fuckin' axe in his hand.' Fred gave her a look that knocked her back. 'He were shit-scared the bastard were gonna do the same to him.'

'Where's Dave now?' She stared at the cold electric fire, at the two grey filaments, turning her engagement ring round her finger. The modest diamond Fred had handed over almost one month's wages for still felt alien. As did the idea they were to be married.

'Down the station. They're questioning him.'

'I bet they are.'

'He ain't done owt, Con. It's Dave what reported it. It's down to him the police picked Brady up.'

They sat knee to knee. Numb with shock. Fred finished the whisky.

'I don't know what to say. I can't believe it.' But when she put a hand to her neck and remembered Ian's violence that night, she thought: *Yes, I can. I can believe he could kill – the maniac nearly killed me.*

'Dave's saying about him and Maureen spending time with Ian and Myra on the moors. You know, like we did?'

Connie nodded, not that she knew where this was going.

'Yeah, and the thing is, he's saying there could be others...'

'Others? What d'you mean?'

'Dunno. Not for sure. It's summat Dave said Brady told him. Not that the police believe him.'

'And what d'you think?' She was still rubbing Fred's back. It was a relief to see some colour return to his cheeks.

'I believe him. Dave's saying Brady were bragging about them burying bodies on the moor. It's why they've got a load of cops out searching.'

'*Them?* But Myra's not involved.'

'Myra's part of it.' Fred cracked his knuckles.

'Don't be ridiculous.' Connie pulled back her hand. 'She's my friend, I'd have known if she were capable of owt like that.'

'She's involved, Con. Dave were there; he saw her.'

'This has nowt to do with Myra. This is Ian. It's got Ian stamped all over it. I always knew there was something wrong with him.' She put a hand to her neck again. Thought of the bruises she'd hidden from Fred.

'Well, yeah. But not this. You can't have thought him capable of something as bad as this?'

Connie picked up the empty glasses and refilled them. 'Honestly, Fred. Myra can't be involved. For God's sake, I've known her all my life. Dave's father must've got the wrong end of the stick.'

'Myra were involved, Con,' Fred persisted with his claim and ran a thumbnail along a deep groove in the coffee table.

The air stank of spent cigarette smoke and, as if suddenly noticing it, she crossed the room and slid open the balcony doors.

The night air struck her face. Black. Cold. She shivered. The temperature had dropped and she could see the white puff of her breath. And somewhere, down there in the darkness, was Wardle Brook Avenue.

46

Saturday, 9 October 1965

Black Fell Farm, Saddleworth Moor, West Riding of Yorkshire

Ronald let his concerns reel him into their sickening giddiness. Riddled with anxiety, he'd been unable to sleep since he saw the lines of police searching the moor. His aching heart, which he thought beat too irregularly these days, caused light-headedness whenever he stood up too quickly. All symptoms of his crimes. He wondered if he should see a doctor and make a full confession, but he didn't want to hear himself condemned.

He confronted his face in the mirror and found it creased by the pillow. He supposed this was what a man who was on his way to the gallows looked like. Disliking what he saw, he swivelled his head, hoping for a glimpse of the man he had once been. A version of himself from a time before he committed the sin that was to shape his life and his place in it. Something, anything, to lift his mood and allow him to shed the tendrils of the dream he knew he would trail around all day. But there was no solace to be found. All his reflection confirmed was that the older he grew, the more like his father he became. His father – big and tall and too fond of drink; too fond of using his fists or his belt to communicate rather than words – a man as rough as the moor itself, with a full head of hair. A full head of hair he was still in possession of the night Ronald had lowered him into the hole he had carved out of the moor. Jacob Cappleman. Long forgotten by the rest of the world. Lying in his peaty grave. Ronald shouldn't be too hard on himself; he was the one keeping the bastard's memory alive. His penance, he supposed.

At this moment, he glimpsed his father over his shoulder. Felt the draught of ghostly breath on the nape of his neck. He jumped, ice-cold beneath his nightclothes. He remembered experiencing something similar a few nights after he'd killed him. But nothing since. Why was he seeing him again after all these years; had his father come back to gloat at what must surely be Ronald's impending punishment?

For two days he had kept the letter in the pocket of his overalls. Unopened. And each day that passed it grew a little heavier and hotter, so that today, he could almost feel it burning a hole through the material. It had been a fluke to intercept the post that morning. Usually he would have been out on the moor, checking his flock. But he'd slept late after a night full of complicated dreams that still wouldn't leave him alone.

He slipped his hand inside his pocket, fingering the sharp corners of the envelope as he walked. He was afraid to open it. Afraid Pamela had ended things with him.

Clocking up another sleepless night had left him short-tempered and tetchy. He paced about, running on adrenaline, dreading the questions he would inevitably have from his brother if he didn't pull himself together. At least he had his work to occupy him. Even if he wanted to, he couldn't give in to his malaise and mope around the yard all day. There were jobs to be done, and ensuring all was well with his tups would at least give him the valid reason to get on up there and see if the police and those other men with sticks had gone.

He had left the farmhouse as soon as he was dressed and headed out onto the rainy moor without so much as a cup of tea, reckoning the swirling sickness in his stomach would only throw it back up again. Wearing his oilskin coat, his dogs by his side and the Purdey broken over his arm, he cut through the fields and gateways that portioned up his land. His tups were the most valuable stock on the farm and he liked to check on them each day when he had let them loose with the ewes. Heading for the marshy ground where the farm's pastures met the moor, he stopped to breathe in the ancient landscape he had always imagined as a living thing. He climbed up and up through the rain and mist to the plateau and took out the pair of binoculars he had tucked into a pocket. Polished the lenses with the tail of his shirt. The tups stood on the ridge. All heads, shoulders and horns. He counted them up. Nine. It was good to see they were in fine health, with no sign of lameness, no cough.

As he turned, something flashed beyond them in the direction of the road. In the layby and parked along the verge, buses filled with police had lumbered up to the moor, tailed by squad cars and a Black Maria. He could see areas of the moorland had been marked out and the dark line of men he hoped had gone away were there again. But it was worse than this. They were moving closer, with what appeared to be an unwavering determination. To his horror, they had crossed Shiny Brook and had almost reached the lightning tree. The sight of them progressing over the reeds and the heather, their methodical, almost mechanical movements, sent him spiralling into a sudden panic. What the hell were they doing? Why were they here? The spasms he'd been suffering since Thursday gripped his insides like a vice, and he doubled over to vomit. Nothing much to show for his efforts, he had eaten little of substance. The cramps made him heave again and the stinging after-effects were enough to make him cry out. Meg and Bess hunkered down nearby and eyed him warily. Beads of sweat had collected at the corners of his eyes and ran down his face like tears. He brushed them away and wiped his mouth on his handkerchief. Took out his pipe and, turning out of the wind, tried to light it. But the wind was too strong, it kept blowing out his match.

He put his pipe away and looked again at the line of men who were pushing through the driving rain. Their steady marching kept time with his heartbeat as the raucous barking of police dogs carried to him on the wind. Seeking shelter beneath a stand of trees, he lifted the binoculars and watched the row of police in full uniform and helmets. Others had bamboo sticks and hiking boots, their trousers tucked into socks. An unstoppable army that could rip his life apart. Fear had settled into his bones and blew through him like an icy wind. There were definitely more vans today. There were scores of journalists with cameras and recording equipment, too. Whatever was going on, they had stepped up the operation. But what had brought them out in conditions such as these? He'd been keeping an ear on the wireless, scouring the news, but there had still been no mention of Saddleworth Moor.

He licked away rainwater and, whistling for his dogs, moved from the trees and into the full force of the weather, pausing every few steps to monitor the lines of men. The rain was worse now – a cold driving rain these parts were renowned for. Water rolled off his oilskin coat, soaking the legs of his overalls and trickling down inside his boots. Straddling a deep-sided stream, he could do no more here and, feeling impotent, he turned his nose towards home and whatever awaited him there.

———

He kicked off his boots before stumbling inside. A swirling mess of sickness and fear, he couldn't be bothered to remove his overalls and hoped Thomas would not make a fuss. Smells of whatever his brother was cooking turned his stomach. How to tell his brother he was too knotted up in fear to eat? That the net was closing in, and at any moment the police would come to the farm and cart him away.

'They're there again.'

'Who are?'

'Those troops of police I told you about. There's more today and they've come up as far as Shiny Brook.'

Ronald washed his hands and skated in his socks over the flagstones Thomas would have mopped that morning. He couldn't find his slippers and didn't have the strength to look for them. He sat down and gawped at the plate of food his brother put in front of him. Gnawed his bottom lip. Cottage pie, forked over the top, cheese crispy from the oven. Gravy leaking, bubbling out. Mashed spuds, carrots pulled from the garden. He turned his face away from what was usually his favourite meal.

'But that's on our land. Don't they have to ask permission?' his brother asked.

A frazzled Ronald picked up his fork, then set it down with a clatter.

'Aren't you hungry? Not like you, Ron. Are you quite well?' Thomas, frowning, was on to him. 'You're like a cat on a hot tin roof about the place.'

The kettle whistled, adding to the drama.

'Why don't you offer to help with whatever it is?'

'You what?' Ronald was miles away... back on the moor, following those long dark lines of men.

'If you did, they'd have to tell you what they're up to. You know the lay of the moor better than anyone; you could manoeuvre them off our patch if you're worrying they're damaging grazing, upsetting the sheep.'

'I can't get involved, Tom. Whatever it is will just have to run its course. Where's the child?' The fear that Myra woman and her boyfriend could turn up at the farm was never far away.

'I sent her off with a scoop of grain for my hens and carrot peelings for Bramble.' His brother made a pot of tea and set it on the table. 'Has the state you're in got something to do with what you were about to tell me on Gracie's birthday?' Thomas was not letting this go.

'What?' Ronald wasn't listening.

'That day we couldn't find Gracie... you were gearing up to tell me something. Come on, it's obvious something's eating you up.'

'It's nowt to do with that.' *God, if only that were all I had to worry about. This is a hundred times worse.*

'So it's something, then? Do you good to get it off your chest?'

'Leave it, Tom.' Ronald slumped on his arms at the table. Held his breath for his brother's rebuke that thankfully didn't come.

'I know what your problem is. That's where you buried him, weren't it?'

'Him?' Ronald lifted his head.

'You know who. Oh, lord, no wonder you're as jumpy as a bag of frogs.' His brother retied his apron.

'Supposing they did dig him up? What then, Tom?'

'All right, we don't know what they're doing out there, but say they do find a body – how are they going to know who it is? It'll just be bones. Probably not even them after all this time. I bet there's been loads of bodies over the years we know nowt about. Very unforgiving terrain, you know that better than anyone, Ron. Think of those hikers and all those people who might have got lost out there. It'd be a surprise if they didn't find a body, don't you think?'

'Aye,' he nodded. That could probably be true. Except, if they found their father's remains, they would know exactly who it was. That bloody fob watch. He knew it would come back to bite him. 'News, Tom.' Ronald jabbed a finger at the wireless. 'Turn it up, will you?'

'... *the body of a young man has been found in the rear bedroom of a house on a Hattersley estate... the police suspect murder...*'

'Murder? How terrible.' Thomas exclaimed, and Ronald pressed a finger to his lips.

'... *Mrs Ellen Maybury, seventy-six, who has lived there for twelve months with her granddaughter, Myra Hindley...*'

Ronald recognised the name. 'Did they just say "Myra Hindley"?'

'*Shh.*' Thomas's turn to tell him to be quiet.

It was lucky his brother hadn't heard him. Ronald wouldn't be able to tell him how he'd come by the name of that woman without mentioning Pamela. And he didn't want to do that.

'Is that all they're saying?'

'Aye. Only that a man's helping police with enquiries.'

'Nowt about searching the moor?'

Thomas shook his head.

'Well, that's something.'

He stood up. His stomach gripes had eased a little, and he unbuttoned his soggy overalls, letting them slip free of his shoulders. But as he bent to fold them down over his legs and step out of them, his letter slid to the floor. Ronald could only look at it lying there, face-down on the flagstones, as if embarrassed at having been caught out.

Now what?

He cursed his carelessness and willed for what just happened to unhappen.

Ronald held his breath, incapable of moving.

What's the worst that can happen? he asked himself and while he was making his mind up, Thomas reached down to pick it up, his expression clouding.

'Pamela? It can't be. What's going on?'

Ronald couldn't believe his brother had identified the hand-writing so quickly after all this time – but it seemed he had. He had finally been caught out, and now he had nothing to say. The things he'd rehearsed should this moment ever come evaporated like the autumn mist that floated down from the moor.

'So this is where you've been sneaking off to? You've been meeting Pamela?' Thomas dropped the name between them like an unexploded bomb. 'How long have the two of you been back in touch?'

Ronald shrugged. He was frightened of hurting him. As far as he was concerned, his brother hadn't boxed his pain away; he was still suffering.

'I think I always knew the two of you were better suited.' Thomas pulled up a chair and sat down. 'You should've been with her, married her. Had a life with her.'

Ronald thought he must have misheard. 'You what?'

'Oh, Ron. It makes me sad you missed out because you were too afraid to tell me. Aye, it were a shock at the time. Humiliat-ing, her leaving me stood at the altar like an idiot. But, well, a few weeks away with the army, it didn't take me long to realise I'd made a mistake. That I should never have asked her to marry me.' A deep sigh. 'We weren't right, Ronnie. Me and Pam. I didn't miss her half as much as I should have.' He raised his arms then dropped them again. 'I wish you'd just told me. Why didn't you tell me? Think of all the years you and Pam could've had together.'

Ronald was too stunned to respond. *Why aren't you yelling at me? Calling me every name under the sun? I betrayed you in the worst possible way.* It was then he realised just how little he knew of what was going on in his brother's head, despite knowing him all his life.

'Oh, Ronnie.' Thomas pressed his hands together. 'I'm so sorry. We should have had this conversation years ago... say something, Ron.'

'I don't know what to say.' He wobbled forward, then sat down beside his brother. 'And anyway, it hardly matters now.'

'How so?'

'She stood me up. We were supposed to meet the other day. She must've decided she wants nowt to do with me. That'll be what her letter's about.'

'How d'you know? You haven't opened it.'

'I just know, Tom. It was all for nowt in the end. Seems like we both lost her.'

'Ooo, you can be a negative bugger sometimes. Open it, you daft ha'p'orth.' Thomas returned the envelope to him. 'See what she's got to say.'

Ronald took a deep breath and tore open the flap, unfolding the single sheet of paper.

'And?' Thomas was trying to read over his shoulder. 'What does she say?'

'She's in hospital,' Ronald said, his heart in his mouth.

'Hospital? Dear me, is she all right?'

'She says... hang on, let me read it... she says she were in town, all set to meet me like we planned... oh, no... bloody hell... a speeding motorbike knocked her down.' He raised his eyebrows to Thomas, who was breathing hard at his elbow.

'Good lord. And is she all right?' his brother wanted to know.

Ronald referred to Pamela's letter again. 'Cuts and bruises. Two broken ribs, a broken ankle.'

'Ouch. That's dreadful.'

'She's saying she were lucky. That it could have been much worse.'

'Lucky?' Thomas echoed. 'That's Pammy for you. Always upbeat, whatever's the trouble. That's why she'd have been good for you, Ron.'

'She wants me to go and see her.'

'Then you must.'

'Are you sure?'

'Daft bugger.' Thomas grinned. 'Your fear of me minding has stopped you doing enough, wouldn't you say? I can't be any clearer, Ronnie. You have my blessing. You and Pamela. Go for it, man. Oh, Ron, you're bleeding. Look, you've cut yourself.'

'Have I?' He looked down at his hands, turned them over. 'I didn't notice.'

He had been about to ask if he could take the child to see Pamela, but that would have meant explaining that Pamela was her grandmother and he didn't have the energy; that news would have to wait.

'You've got blood on your letter. *Ooo*, you really are a bag of nerves. Come on, I'll bathe it for you.' Thomas steered him to the sink and was just reaching into the cupboard for his first aid box when the kitchen door flew open and there stood the child, the hood of her red anorak pulled over her head, dripping rainwater.

'It's Bramble.' She rushed towards them, her eyes swimming with tears. 'She won't get up. Something's not right, Ronnie. You've to come and see to her. Quick! You've to come, quick!' She tugged at his sleeve.

The cut forgotten, Ronald refastened his overalls, pulled on his boots and followed her out into the rain. He tipped his gaze to the gathering dusk and a pair of geese who were circling above. Prayed it wasn't bad news.

They crossed to the barn and found Bramble lying down, her large head hanging. The child crouched beside her, held her hands to the mare's muzzle.

'She don't huff no more, Ronnie.' Her face full of woe. 'And her warm's all gone.'

'That's because she's not there anymore, little one.'

'Not there?' A soft frown. 'But where's she gone? I don't understand.'

'She's died, child.' He put an arm around her. 'But you're not to be sad. Bramble had a good long life. She were very old. It were her time, that's all. It's what happens with people and animals when they get old.'

'So, only the old die, do they, Ronnie?' The child looked up at him from beneath her hood, her brown eyes communicating a wide expectant look as she struggled to swallow things that were too big to understand. 'Not children? Children don't ever die?'

47

Sunday, 10 October 1965

Underwood Court, Hattersley, North-East Cheshire

Connie, home from visiting her mother in hospital, found Fred standing at the sink peeling potatoes.

'How's your mam bearing up?'

'She's all right. Bones will mend. She loved the flowers, told me to thank you.'

'Least I could do.'

'I think it were the shock of it more than owt. Mam were convinced that motorbike came at her deliberately.'

'And he didn't bloody stop. That's hit and run, that is.' Fred dried his hands. 'Have the police been to see her?'

'Yeah, and she says she's tried giving them a description of the bike, but she doesn't remember much. There's a couple of witnesses, so you never know, they might catch the bastard.' Connie unbuttoned her raincoat. 'Mam's not going to be able to manage on her own when she comes out, though.'

'She can't come here, Con. What I mean is, there's hardly room, is there?'

'Don't worry. That weren't ever going to happen. Last place on earth she'd come. No, d'you remember me telling you about that old boyfriend of hers? Mam reckons she's going to go and stay with him, that he wants to look after her.'

'Cosy,' Fred grinned, then his grin slid away. 'You seen the state of Dave and Maureen's door? Covered in graffiti again. Council were only here this morning, scrubbing it off.'

'Their turn now, poor buggers.' Connie pegged up her coat and swapped her heels for slippers.

'Police won't leave Dave alone. They're trying to pin it on him.'

'Well, if they think he's got something to do with it...' She stepped up behind him, wrapping her arms around his waist.

'He ain't. It were all Ian and Myra.'

'I've told you, Fred. She wouldn't be involved in this. It's nowt to do with her.' Connie let her arms fall away and stepped back. Pressing her spine to the fridge, she felt its mechanical innards vibrate against her own.

'She's involved, Connie. He's not right in the head. But her... you wanna talk to Dave. She's worse. She's human, she's got feelings. Not that the cops can see it. They've let her go.'

'Let her go?'

'They've charged Brady with the murder of that Evans lad and that's just the start.' Fred returned to the potatoes. 'But, yeah, they've let her go.'

'See, I told you she had nowt to do with it.' Connie stuffed her feet back inside her shoes and put on her raincoat.

'Where you going? Tea'll be ready in a minute.'

'I'm going to see Myra. I want her to tell me to my face that what Dave's saying is true.'

'You're going now?' He dropped the knife in the sink with a clatter.

'Yeah. I want answers, Fred. I won't be long.' She tied the belt of her raincoat around her middle and left the flat.

It was chilly out and Connie, rubbing her arms through her sleeves to warm up, lit another cigarette from the butt of her first. She smoked it hastily as she nipped along the empty streets, the static hum of pylons that towered over Hattersley crackling with electricity.

When she reached Wardle Brook Avenue, she found there was a uniformed officer standing guard outside. Connie stopped and stared into the front garden of number sixteen. At her back, the evening sunlight splintered the street. She saw that along with Ian's motorbike, the Mini Traveller was missing, too. The space below the wall that ran the length of the short terrace was empty and Connie's mind replayed the image of Myra vaulting the white picket fence the night she came to tell them Kathy was missing. She gasped at the memory.

'Everything all right, miss?' It was Mr Braithwaite, Myra and Ian's neighbour. He was putting out his rubbish.

'Yes. Sorry. I'm looking for Myra?'

'She's staying with friends. The street behind this one.'

'Oh, right.' Connie finished her cigarette and squashed it under her heel. 'Thank you.'

She heeded Mr Braithwaite's directions, and found a female police officer guarding the door this time. Connie, smartly dressed from visiting her mother, walked straight past her as if she was meant to be there.

'Is Myra here?'

'Who wants to know?' A red-haired woman, hostile, barred her way.

'It's all right, Florrie. This is Connie Openshaw. Myra's old school friend,' Granny Maybury intercepted. 'She's just through in the kitchen, love. She'll be glad to see a friendly face.'

'Thanks.' Connie squeezed her hand; the old woman looked done in.

'Would you like a cuppa?' the redhead offered.

'That'd be nice,' she nodded.

'Will you make one for Myra too?' Granny Maybury asked. 'Poor lamb's had nowt all day.'

Connie nodded and stepped into the kitchen where she found a dishevelled Myra standing with her back to the door, gazing out on the garden, her arms folded over her chest.

Connie coughed into her hand. 'Hi, Myra. I just wanted to see how you're doing?'

She didn't get an answer and, staring at Myra's hair, saw it was flat against the back of her head as if she'd just got up. Connie made a pot of tea and poured it into a pair of bone china cups. She put a couple of biscuits on the saucers, and handed one to Myra.

'Myra?'

She turned. Dressed in a floral frock and saggy cardigan, her friend looked exhausted.

'I've poured you a tea.'

Myra took it, her expression blank. After a couple of sips, she put the cup and saucer down again and turned back to the window.

'Myra? What's going on? What's all this about Ian?'

'They've taken the car,' Myra spoke at last. Her voice croaky, in need of an oiling.

'The car; what car?'

'My car. They're doing forensic tests. I'm having to get the bloody bus everywhere.'

What was she moaning about the car for? Connie wanted to know who this lad Edward Evans was, and why Ian had been charged with his murder. But when she opened her mouth to speak, Myra gave her such a black look, she swallowed her questions.

'Are you staying here? Can't you go home?' Connie asked instead.

'Not allowed. Supposed to be staying with me mam, but I can't stand it.'

'Where are you going to go?' A horrible moment passed between them when she thought Myra was going to ask if she could stay with her and Fred.

'Aunty Kath's.' Myra's dog trotted in. His claws ticky-ticky-ticky against the linoleum. She reached down and scooped him up like a baby, kissing his head. 'They won't let Ian out.'

'Well, I don't suppose they will if he's been charged for murdering that lad.'

'It weren't Ian.' Myra, suddenly fierce. 'It were that fuckin' Dave Smith.'

'Dave?' Connie put her cup and saucer down and gawped at her. If Myra was saying this, then it had to be true. 'Maureen's Dave?' she asked, wanting her to clarify.

'Yeah. The bastard went and grassed to police it were me and Ian. It's not fair. They won't let me even see Ian, and until they do, I'm sayin' nowt.'

'The police want to speak to you? Why'd they want to do that?'

''Cos it happened in our house.'

'The murder?' Fred had told her all this, but Connie wanted to hear Myra's side of things.

'Yeah. Me and Ian helped Dave to clean up the mess. And this is how the fucker thanks us.' Myra cuddled Puppet close to her face, breathed into his coat. 'Ian didn't do it. I didn't do it...' her protestations muffled.

Connie followed Myra, who was still carrying her dog, into the living room where the redhead and Granny Maybury sat staring into the empty hearth.

'I'm frightened, Con. Police have found Ian's notebook and our photo album. They've started searching the moor.'

'What are they doing that for?' Connie pretended this was news to her.

At that moment, a young man in a suit and tie barged into the house. He scanned around. 'Are you Ian Brady's girlfriend?' he quizzed Myra.

'I am, yeah.' Myra eyed him and put her dog on the floor beside her grandmother's feet.

'The name's Clive Entwistle.'

'From the police?'

'*Manchester Evening News*.'

At this, Myra flew at him, yelling and screaming. 'Get the hell out... go on, clear off. Bastard vultures.'

'What d'you say about the police saying your boyfriend is linked to the disappearances of—' the journalist, unperturbed, consulted his notebook. 'With the disappearances of Lesley Ann Downey, John Kilbride, Keith Bennett, Pauline Reade and—'

'Get out! Get out!' Myra was frothing at the mouth. 'Them's got nowt to do with my Ian.'

'Ah.' The man stood his ground. 'So you're not denying you've heard of Pauline Reade and John Kilbride? Because your boyfriend, Ian, he's been boasting about there being other murders.'

Myra seized hold of him and shoved him out the door, slamming it in his face so hard it made the glass panel rattle in its frame.

'You won't be able to shut the police up.' The journalist shouted through the letterbox. 'They're joining forces. Manchester's got hold of this now... and this volcano's going to blow.'

48

Saturday, 16 October 1965

Black Fell Farm, Saddleworth Moor, West Riding of Yorkshire

Ronald stepped into his brother's garden, a patch of ground claimed from the wild and sheltering between a pair of drystone walls. There was peace to be found there, a place under his brother's care where weak things grew. With Thomas's permission and secateurs at the ready, he leant in to press his nose to the last of the roses. Breathing in their subtle bouquet, the softness of their vermilion petals made his eyes prick with tears. Why the tender things in life were so much harder to deal with than injury, he didn't know. Clipping the best three, he snagged a finger on a thorn and watched a bubble of blood bloom like a ruby.

Seconds later, the three red roses and a greaseproof parcel of cakes Thomas had made on the seat beside him, Ronald was positioned behind the wheel of the truck. Wearing his best trousers and corduroy jacket, he was as conscious of his heartbeat as he was of the blustery afternoon going on beyond the windscreen. He should be excited about seeing Pamela again. She was improving each day and the hospital expected to discharge her soon. But his head was too full of dreams of sunken pools in the peat that he needed to slosh through, the mist coiling around him. In the dream, he would traipse around until he found a white, withered stick poking up out of the ground, nudging it with the toe of his boot, knowing there was something lurking underneath. Under the stinking bog water. And it was about to be discovered, and there was nothing he could do to prevent it.

Bumping along over the potholes, he wound down the window. Sniffed autumn's melancholy breath. The swallows and house martins were long gone and any blackberries that were still gripping the bramble-filled hedgerows had begun to grow their furry mildewed coats in readiness for winter. It made him think of the pear and apple windfalls, bird-pecked and maggot-holed, that his brother had left to rot in the grass that would continue to grow long after the dark, sunless days set in.

When he reached the bottom of the track, he turned left to join the A635. Saw how the moor was washed in a strange blue shadow. Ronald thought of all the jobs that still needed to be done before the winter set in, but the best days of the year were behind him, and the thought made him sad. Speeding along with the accompanying thump, thump of windscreen wipers now the rain had begun in earnest, Ronald lit his pipe in the hope a smoke would steady his nerves. He shook out the match and threw it out of the window.

A twist in the tarmac, and even though he had been half-expecting to see it, it was no less of a shock: the snarl of police vehicles, the blue flashing lights. More than he had ever seen in one place. Alarming enough, but when he reached the layby with its views of the moor sloping down to Greenfield Reservoir, there they were again, searching out by the rain-blackened

rocks of Hollin Brown Knoll. Hadn't they explored it thor-
oughly enough already? The sight of these bands of police officers and volunteers made Ronald's insides cartwheel with
dread. There were lines and lines of them, moving slowly,
picking over every inch of the moor. Pushing their sticks of
bamboo into the peat and sniffing the ends, or so he supposed,
for any whiff of putrefaction. A grisly job and one that, each day
it continued, threatened him.

He slowed to a crawl for a group of what he suspected were
sensation-seekers, waiting for them to cross from one side of the
open moorland to the other.

'Christ, they've brought a bloody picnic with them.' He
groaned at the sight of a hamper, thermoses. This was morbid
curiosity gone mad. What was the matter with people? All they
needed was an ice cream van and a mobile chippy.

The news reports on the wireless weren't wrong: public
interest in this case was running high. The road was teeming
with journalists, too. Men and women spilling out of vans to
stand around in the rain with cameras at the ready. They
weren't a surprise; the press had been there from the start, but
now they were in their hundreds. International ones, too, he
could tell by the names emblazoned on the sides of their vans.

He pushed his foot to the brake and slowed further, grazing
alongside a man gripping a clipboard with papers flapping in
the wind. Grey-faced, unshaven, close enough to touch. Ronald
supposed he was one of those plain-clothed detectives he'd
heard about and was careful not to make eye contact.

Then a shout went up, followed by a flurry of urgent voices.
Enough to make him swerve and pull in on the opposite verge.
A sudden blaze of flashbulbs and a burst of activity from the
crew of journalists was followed by shouting. He swung around
in his driving seat and saw that a tent had been erected. Army
green and billowing in the wind. Uniformed officers standing
guard.

What's that for? Have they found something... someone? Have they found my father's bones?

What Ronald saw next nearly stopped his heart. He couldn't believe his eyes and blinked, then blinked again. But there was no mistaking it.

A crew of police officers bearing a stretcher with something wrapped in black polythene.

Underwood Court, Hattersley, North-East Cheshire

The estate was dark, save for the orange glow of streetlights. Connie, hands in pockets, crossed the tarmac with its puddles of rainwater. She was on her way home from visiting her mother in hospital, her head still full of Myra and the upsetting accusations the hack from the *Manchester Evening News* had fired at her last week... 'What d'you say about the police thinking your boyfriend is linked to the disappearances of Lesley Ann Downey, John Kilbride, Keith Bennett, Pauline Reade...' Why react with such vehemence if she knew nothing of which he spoke? Was it because Myra knew Ian had something to do with them?

Where was Kathy in all this? Had that journalist been about to add her name to the list, before Myra threw him out? DCI Mounsey thought their cases were linked, didn't he?

An image of Pauline Reade's mother flashed into her mind. That poor broken woman. Connie shook the terrible thought from her mind. Determined it couldn't be true. There was no way Ian could be mixed up with whatever had happened to Pauline. He was a gangly, long-legged weirdo, who wore old-fashioned suits and thought he was superior to everyone else, but he wasn't a child killer.

But he was a killer. And that poor lad, Edward Evans, wasn't much older than a child.

Hang on.

What was she thinking? Didn't Myra say it was Dave Smith who did the killing?

Connie pressed a weary hand to her head. She didn't know what to think or who to believe. All she knew was that along with the other vile and hurtful things Ian had said to her, it was his strange kind of threat in the Waggon and Horses the day Kathy vanished that she couldn't shake off... 'What if ye went back to the car and she wasnae there?'

When Connie let herself inside the flat, Fred was waiting up for her.

'Where the hell have you been?'

'You know where I've been; I went to see Mam.' She kicked off her shoes and pegged up her coat.

'I'm sorry, love.' Fred was beside her, taking her hand. 'I've been worried, that's all.'

'No need. I had to wait an age for the bus.'

'Come and sit down in here.'

'Sit down? Why, what's the matter?'

'Best you do, come on.'

'Fred? Tell me. Why are you acting all weird?'

'We've had the police here, Con.'

'You what?' she yawned.

'I really think you better come and sit down. I'll pour you a drink.'

'What do the cops want now?'

'Have some of that first.' He handed her a glass of whisky. 'Listen, love. They've... erm,' he hesitated, rubbed his hands together. 'They've found a body up on the moor.'

Connie froze; the glass halfway to her lips. 'A body! What d'you mean? What body? Whose body?' She put down the glass and pressed a hand to her quickening heart.

'They dunno, Con. But they want you to come and take a look. You know, just in case. They have to be sure, don't they? But you know—' he took a deep breath, 'it won't be Kathy. It won't be her.'

She sat on the settee. Dropped her head into her hands. She had that shooting pain in her arm again.

'Connie?' Fred reached for her through the dim light of the living room. 'Connie?'

She couldn't move, couldn't speak. Fighting for breath, the sound when it came, was a raw, base animal sound. A sound that frightened the man in her life, there being nowhere to run and hide from it. Nowhere to shelve his emotions and detach himself in ways he usually might.

Black Fell Farm, Saddleworth Moor, West Riding of Yorkshire

'They've found human remains on the moor, Ron. Announced it on the news. You just missed it.'

This was Thomas's shocking greeting when Ronald, back from seeing Pamela, stepped inside the house. His brother was wearing what he called his 'Dunkirk Look' beneath his thatch of snow-white hair.

The declaration, coming without warning, made the ground shift beneath his feet. This was it. He had always known this moment was coming. And now it had.

'It's him, isn't it?' Ronald slumped against the wall. 'They've found him.' He rubbed his hands over his face in a gesture of despair. 'I saw it on my drive to the hospital. They'd put a tent up and were carrying something on a stretcher. Oh, Christ, Tom, I'm bloody done for. I am. I'm bloody done for. What am I going to do?'

'It's not him. For God's sake, pull yourself together, man.

Like I said to you before, there'd be nowt left of that monster after all these years. No, Ronnie. Somehow it's worse than that.'

'Worse? How could it be worse?'

'It's body of a little girl.'

'You what? No?' Ronald sat down on a kitchen chair. 'A little girl?'

'Dreadful, isn't it?' Thomas sighed, his eyes shining with tears.

'You didn't let the child hear it, did you?'

'Don't be stupid. I made sure she were out of earshot.'

'Are they saying who the little girl is?' Ronald felt bad that he was relieved. He was disgusted with himself. His selfishness had reached a new all-time low.

'No, nowt like that. I suppose they're waiting until her poor family's identified her.'

————

It had been raining since teatime. Not drizzling or spitting, but streaming over the bow-walled farmhouse in heavy, grey slanting slices. Ronald and Thomas watched it sluice the night-blackened window panes.

'God alive,' they complained in unison.

Their evening meal over – what little Ronald had eaten of it – they had moved from the kitchen into the living room.

'Nippy tonight.' His brother rubbed his plump palms together and placed another log on the fire.

Ronald's nerves were shot. He had never been in such turmoil. It was a struggle to process the unfolding horror they were being drip-fed on the news. He didn't think it could be worse than the killing of that teenage lad, Edward Evans, but it seemed it was. The police, having found a little girl's body, were looking for more children that had been buried on the moor.

The name of the perpetrator had meant nothing to him until Pamela told him it was the man who threatened her in the Waggon and Horses. That he was Myra Hindley's boyfriend. Ronald now knew that the bastard who'd held a gun to his head – and turned up to harass him on the farm – was called Ian Brady and that his despicable crimes were why the moor was being searched. A strange irony then, that this Brady continued to be a threat to Ronald, even though he was locked in a police cell, charged with murder.

Listening to the wind push its lopsided weight against the house, he watched the fire sputtering in the grate, the occasional puff of smoke being blown back down the chimney and into the room.

'Best let it go out, Tom,' he advised when his brother lifted himself out of his armchair to place another log on the dying flames.

The rain gurgled along the guttering and Ronald worried the roof slates wouldn't hold. He pictured the farm's waterlogged pastures opening out onto the moor. He yawned and thought of his bed. How good it would feel to slip between the cool cotton sheets and hand himself over to sleep. But he wouldn't turn in yet. If he went to bed, he would only lie awake, plagued by his fears again. It was nice sitting here. Thomas was playing the piano and he was enjoying listening to the child singing along. Often, coming in from the fields, Ronald would find them together like this. It brought happy memories of when their mother had played for Thomas to sing. Ronald could still picture his brother standing there in his short trousers, his voice as sweet and faultless as birdsong in the same way this child's was now.

Ronald must have fallen asleep, and he woke with a jolt in the armchair. Opening his eyes, he blinked, disorientated, panicking a little. But he could see nothing was amiss. Thomas was still playing the piano, and the child was singing. All was well. His mouth was stale from sleep and his legs inside his trousers were cold. He must have been sleeping for some time because the room was chilly and the fire had gone out. He was about to go to the kitchen to fetch a glass of water when the cosy glow of the living room was abruptly exchanged for the searing glare of vehicle headlamps. It burst in on them: startling, dazzling; flooding the space from floor to ceiling. Then came the unmistakable thud of a car door and the music stopped.

'What the hell?' Ronald sprang to his feet and strode to the window. The violence of the storm meant they hadn't heard the warning rattle of the cattle grid as they usually might. 'Quick, Tom! Quick! Hide the child.'

Thomas snapped the lid of the piano shut and ushered her up the stairs. 'Nowt to fret about, sweetheart,' he whispered. 'We'll just see off whoever this is. It won't take a minute. Stay in your room for us, there's a good lass. Try not to make any noise.'

Bang-bang-bang-bang.

The sudden and forceful pounding on the front door had them jerk their heads to it in alarm. The cat skidded over the carpet and bolted away.

Bang-bang-bang-bang.

'I don't know what to do?' Ronald was frightened.

More banging... insistent... louder.

'You'd better answer it.' Thomas grimaced; a fist shoved against his mouth.

'Christ, Tom. Supposing it's the police?'

Bang-bang-bang-bang.

'Ron, just get it. Before whoever it is kicks the door down.'

Still dithering with one hand poised on the bolt, Ronald could feel his pulse hammering in his neck.

'I can't. Supposing they've found him? Or... or they've come for child?' he hissed, remembering that Brady bastard's warning in the barn that night. 'Supposing someone's seen the child and told them she's here?'

'For God's sake, Ron. Just answer the bloody door,' Thomas yelled at him through the confusion.

Black Fell Farm, Saddleworth Moor, West Riding of Yorkshire

Ronald drew the bolt across and flung open the door. Was forced back by a gust of wind and the clattering rain. The sight of two men in overcoats and trilbies filling the porch whipped the air from his lungs.

'Good evening, sir.' One of them flashed a warrant card and spoke over the gushing sounds of the guttering that could barely cope with the rainwater. 'This is Detective Chief Inspector Mounsey and I'm Detective Constable Baines. Sorry to disturb but we wondered if we might come in? We've a few questions.'

The dread Ronald had been lugging about for days squeezed tighter around his heart. He was at breaking point and, fearful of making eye contact with the plain-clothed detectives, of giving himself away, he looked over their shoulders, through the dark and the rain to a strange land where a cold wind from years gone by still raged. Echoes of things long past rang in his ears as he tried to refocus on the brace of detectives. He shivered. This was it. They were here to tell him his father's remains had been found, and from the state of the skull, they could tell that someone had bashed his brains out.

'Questions?' he said eventually, stepping aside to let them in. 'Um, well, aye.'

As the senior of the two men entered, he produced a clip-board from under his sopping coat and Ronald noticed the brooding mugshots of two people he recognised. The seconds passed in expectant silence while he waited for someone to speak. The only sound was the plopping of rainwater hitting the flagstones.

It was Thomas who saved the day, striding between them, offering refreshments and a generous smile.

'Please, gentlemen,' he talked over the sudden rush of water as he filled the kettle, 'do sit down and have a warm-up by the stove. A terrible night to be out and about, I'm sure.'

'Very kind of you, Mr...?' the one Ronald thought had been introduced as DCI Mounsey wanted to know.

'I'm Thomas Cappleman.' He tapped his chest. 'This is my brother, Ronald.'

'And you own this farm?' The men each dragged out a chair and sat down at the table. They undid the buttons of their coats but didn't remove them.

'Aye, that's right. It's just the two of us now.'

Ronald sat down with the detectives and watched the younger of the two lick the end of his pencil and scribble something on his notepad.

'Very good. As I said, we're sorry to disturb but as you probably already know we've men out searching the moor.'

'Aye, we've seen. I've been saying to Ron that he should volunteer. No one knows the lay of the moor better than our Ronald.'

He must have made a noise because the pencil-holding detective lifted his head and eyed him quizzically. 'Aye, I'd be happy to help.'

'Very kind, Mr Cappleman.' Inspector Mounsey raised the palm of his hand. 'But we've plenty of volunteers for the moment.'

The kettle came to the boil and sang between them. Clattering sounds followed, as Thomas busied himself in cupboards, digging out their best china and a plate of biscuits that he set down on the table, inviting the detectives to help themselves.

'We would like to know if you've seen any recent activity up on the moor? Anything suspicious, or out of the ordinary?' Mounsey placed the clipboard on the table between the teacups. 'If either of you have seen this couple.' He tapped the faces that had been captured in the black-and-white photographs.

Thomas, holding the teapot by the scruff of its cosy, leant in for a look. 'That's them,' he gasped, putting the pot down heavily enough to rattle the cups on their saucers. 'That's the couple who turned up here asking if we sold eggs.'

The detectives exchanged glances. 'When was this?'

'I can tell you exactly. It's easy,' Thomas replied, looking pleased with himself, as if he was answering questions in a quiz and was to be marked on it afterwards. 'It were Gracie's birthday. Oh.' He realised his mistake and closed his mouth, looking at Ronald to help him.

'May we ask who Gracie is?' The younger man took a biscuit. Filled the silence with his crunching.

'Aye. She's erm... she's our granddaughter. Well, she's *my* granddaughter; Thomas is her great-uncle. Aren't you, Tom?' Ronald encouraged him with his eyes.

'Aye. Oh, aye. That's right.'

'So, the date, if you have it, Mr Cappleman?'

Ronald wasn't sure who the question was for so he let Thomas answer.

'October second. Early afternoon. I remember it plain. Ronald were in town, weren't you, Ronnie?'

He nodded, obedient, his hands gripping his thin knees beneath the table top.

'They just turned up in the yard. They had a blue car. Well, more turquoise. A kind of minivan with them wooden panels. I thought it were odd, truth be told.'

'Odd?' Mounsey bounced back the word.

'Aye. We aren't exactly accessible. You'd have to know we were here.'

'Are you saying you think they turned up under false pretences?'

'I think I can help you out there, inspector,' Ronald interjected. 'I know these two. What I mean is, I'm familiar with them. I've been seeing them up on the moor regular. Same spot, or thereabouts.'

'You have?' Thomas was the one who was surprised; the detectives, sipping their tea and munching biscuits, barely looked up. 'You never said owt.'

'No idea why they like it so much. Only ever seen the odd hiker before. But these two aren't hikers. They was always togged out for a night on the town. He's always taking photos. Photos of her and their dogs.'

'Why didn't you tell me?' Thomas glared at him.

'I did tell you. When I brought the lambs home.'

'You never said it were same ones who came to the house.'

'Tom? Can we do this later?' He cast an anxious glance at the two detectives. 'I never said owt because I didn't want to worry you.'

'Why would seeing them worry your brother, Mr Cappleman?' Mounsey brushed crumbs from his tie.

'Because, erm...'

'It's perfectly fine, sir,' the inspector assured him, sensing his reluctance. 'They can't trouble you now.'

'Never be bothering anyone again with what we're about to

charge 'em with.' The other, too flippant for his senior colleague, was given a stern look of disapproval.

'I stumbled on them one day when they had a revolver. Him —' Ronald jabbed a finger at the printed face of his nemesis. 'He were shooting bottles. Frightening my sheep. And, well, I tried reasoning with them but they... they turned the gun on me. Made me beg for my life. I thought they were going to kill me. She—' he tapped the woman's face this time, his finger ends grazing those pitiless grey eyes that still haunted his dreams, 'she were goading him to do it. Saying they could bury my body on the moor and no one would know.'

'Ronnie? I can't believe you never said owt about this.' Thomas plonked down on a chair, put his head in his hands.

'Can I ask when this incident occurred, sir?'

'Aye. Early September. Fourth, I think it were.' Ronald knew perfectly well when it was. It was the day the child arrived at the farm. But unlike his brother, he wasn't about to give that information away. 'Sort of stuck in my mind. It's not every day you get a gun put to your head.'

'I should think it did stick in your mind, sir.' Mounsey put down his teacup. 'Didn't you think you should've reported this at the time?'

'I'm wishing I had now,' Ronald said, still gripping his knees. 'But when you're living as remote as we are, I were fearful of reprisals. The likes of them, they could just turn up here and what protection would I have? *We* have?' He swung out an arm to include his brother. 'But if there were a chance it could've saved that poor lad... That poor Edward Evans. 'Cos it's them that's done it, isn't it? And they've murdered others, I heard. Little kiddies.' He stared at the set of ugly mugshots: stark, chilling, black-eyed. Was repulsed by them and what he knew of them. 'I could tell they were evil. They had it written all over them.' The room fell silent for a moment until Ronald broke it. 'There's something else I need to tell you.'

'Go on, Mr Cappleman,' Mounsey encouraged, clearly sensing there was more to this. 'Like we say, neither of them can harm you now.'

'They shot two of our ewes. I found one dead, the other dragging her guts around behind her... I had to put her out of her misery.'

'I'm very sorry to hear this, sir. You writing this down, Baines?'

'I am, boss.' The pencil-holding hand, frantically scribbling, needed to turn to a new page.

'It weren't no great surprise when Tom told me they'd driven here. They made threats, see. Saying they knew where I lived and something about burning the barn down.'

'They did what?' Thomas yelped.

'I found something out there. On the moor. Same day I had that altercation with them.' Ronald ignored the looks his brother was giving him; he would explain everything to Thomas once these men had gone. 'Strange, it were. I found it where I've seen them picnicking. It were a girl's shoe. A dancing shoe.'

A rumble of heightened interest from the detectives. 'You don't still happen to have it, do you, sir?'

Ronald nodded. 'Aye. I don't know why, but I kept it. It's in the barn.'

'Do you think you'd be able to show us where you found it?'

At this moment, there was a creak of floorboards from the room above. Ronald felt Thomas stiffen in the chair beside him. Heard his breathing change.

'Anyone else living here?' DCI Mounsey tilted his head to the ceiling.

'No. Just us.' The lie burned in his mouth.

This was met with a sceptical-looking nod from the inspector. 'Would you mind if I used your bathroom?' Mounsey had risen to his feet.

'The WC is outside, I'm afraid. Not much in the way of

mod cons here.' Thomas was on to him. Like Ronald, he could tell the detective didn't need to use their facilities; it was just an excuse to have a snoop around.

'Is that so? Right, well. Much obliged to you, gentlemen.' Mounsey rubbed his hands together and edged towards the door. 'If you'd be so kind as to locate that shoe, Mr Cappleman. Then we'll be on our way.'

52

Sunday, 17 October 1965

Underwood Court, Hattersley, North-East Cheshire

Condensation fogged the glass of the balcony doors. The morning was bitterly cold. Connie stood outside, smoking her first cigarette of the day. Fred had made her toast and tea and called her inside, even though she'd told him she couldn't eat. Despite the Valium and glug of whisky she'd had first thing, she still felt as if she'd been wired to the electricity pylons that loomed over the estate.

'Come in out of the cold, Con,' Fred coaxed her. 'They're here, we'd best get going.'

Her face, when she saw it reflected in the glass doors, was a shock – creased and puckered, her skin thin and papery-looking, her thick black fringe flat to her forehead. She swore she'd aged ten years overnight.

Two police officers filled the living room, their heads bowed, waiting until she had organised herself. Fred had put both bars of the electric fire on, but she still felt cold. It was as if the freezing autumn morning had reached down and iced over her insides. She knew what they were here for. She was to accompany them to the mortuary. To see if the girl's body they had found on Saddleworth Moor was her Kathy.

'I need the loo,' she told them before rushing from the room.

The police officers hadn't spoken to her since Fred let them in and their silence agitated her further.

She locked herself inside the bathroom and stood at the basin, gripping the porcelain. It was cold beneath her fingers and she looked down at her hands, at the whites of her knuckles. These were the hands that were always too quick to punish her poor, dead daughter. And now the hope she'd clung to of having the chance to make amends, to be a better mother, had been smashed to smithereens.

'Come on, miss, we need to be going.' The voice on the other side of the door was firm, but not unkind.

She didn't move. Couldn't move. Could she really go through with this? She ran the tap and splashed her face with water, gasping in shock.

'Connie, love?' She heard Fred's voice now, and gentle tapping. 'I'll be there, right by your side. You won't have to do this on your own. But love—' She felt his hesitation. 'Everyone's waiting, yeah?'

'Can't you leave me alone for one bloody minute? I need a minute. One minute.' She grabbed a towel, pressing its slightly musty smell to her wet face. Stale like her, she thought, squeezing her eyes tight shut. When she opened them, she threw the towel down and slid the bolt across. Fred stood on the other side of the door, his eyes large and questioning. He looked small next to the pair of hefty police officers. He looked as afraid as she was. He kissed her cheek and took her hand, leading her out of the flat towards the lift, with the police officers following.

'There's a load of press out there, so be careful,' one officer warned. His broad body clad in its black uniform, screening them from the car park and the estate beyond.

Fred put on his sunglasses, and she did the same.

'They're here for that Dave Smith, not for you. But we don't want to be hanging around.'

They were herded towards the waiting patrol car, moving like zombies, steered by someone else's hand. A wave of noise hit them like a wall. Then a rush of cameras, microphones, flashbulbs.

The patrol car smelled of soap and aftershave, and Connie sat back, watching the town skim by. She felt sick. The air was hot; the heaters were on full. She would have liked to ask them to open a window but couldn't form the words.

'You all right, Con?' Fred enfolded her hand in his.

'I'm scared. I'm not sure I can do this.'

Fred could not accompany her to the mortuary because he was not a blood relative, and it was an Inspector Chaddock who stood by her side as she identified the clothing.

He warned Connie. Asked her to prepare herself. They showed her the tartan skirt, the pink cardigan, a string of white plastic beads.

She shook her head. 'No, these aren't Kathy's.'

She was led down one corridor, then another, the smell of rubber and formaldehyde in her nostrils. The room Chaddock showed her inside was colder than outside and goosebumps prickled her arms. A green sheet covered the little body from stomach to feet. They had drawn it up to hide the right-hand side of her torso and face. A beautiful little girl. She looked to be asleep. Connie winced when she saw the swelling around the child's lips. It was as if she had bitten down hard on them.

The child lay so silently. Kathy had always been a quiet girl,

but the silence of this transcended anything Connie had experienced. This was the absolute silence of death. But this wasn't
Kathy. She was someone else's little girl. And Connie dropped
to her knees, sobbing into her hands, out of relief but also pity
for the poor mother whose child this was.

53

Monday, 25 October 1965

Underwood Court, Hattersley, North-East Cheshire

Connie stirred at last. She had not gone to bed last night and, after taking a tranquillizer, had dozed on the settee for most of the afternoon. Now it was evening, and she gathered her dressing gown around her and made her way through the dark-ened living room to the bathroom, where she ran a basin of tepid water and gave herself a perfunctory wash and swallowed another Valium. This done, she went back to the living room and lit up a fag. Smoking it, she looked down on the car park and saw it was still swarming with reporters who were trying to get to Dave and Maureen, their lenses trained on the Smiths' balcony and the main door downstairs.

Since the news broke, Connie had sensed a change around the estate. The fear that anyone's child could have been snatched from streets that were once safe to play unwatched and unsupervised was palpable. No kids had been playing today, she'd noticed, even though those who had made these once safe places dangerous were themselves in custody and could do no more harm. But Connie doubted that this neighbourhood, or indeed any neighbourhood, where children had been free to play, would ever feel safe again. Forever sullied, an innocence lost.

A copy of the *Daily Mirror* Fred had brought home was on the coffee table. The story had gone nationwide... worldwide. Myra and Ian were notorious, their faces suddenly claimed as public property and sent into orbit. Since the bodies of Lesley Ann Downey and then John Kilbride had been found, Connie's fear for her child's safety had intensified. Were they about to find Kathy on Saddleworth Moor, too? No one would talk to her. She'd been telephoning the police station but was told that DCI Joe Mounsey was in Manchester and was too busy to come to the phone. They weren't nasty; they were just doing their job. Assuring her they would be in touch if there was any news. Telling her not to worry, that the press was making it out to be worse than it was to sell newspapers. Connie knew the police were making light of it. That it was as bad as the tabloids were saying. What was wrong with them? How could it be worse than the murder of children?

What was a struggle to accept was that Myra was as guilty as Ian. That, along with him, she had been charged with the murders of Lesley Ann Downey and John Kilbride, and as an accessory to the murder of Edward Evans. Connie felt a fool. Duped by a person she'd known all her life. It left her feeling sad, bereft. She knew she should, but she couldn't turn off her emotions as if they were a tap. She missed her friend, the person she'd believed Myra Hindley to be. How could she trust anyone again? Was anyone who they claimed? There had to have been clues she missed, but what they were, she did not know.

Carrying this thought, along with a smouldering cigarette, she went into Kathy's bedroom and, without turning on the light, pulled out the shoebox she kept under the bed. She emptied the contents over the pink candlewick bedspread. There were photographs of her and Myra, one of Myra holding Kathy when she was a baby, taken at the same time as the one in a frame on the sideboard. With the curtains open and the street-lights leaking in, it was just bright enough to see Myra's smiling face.

'How can you be responsible for such horrific crimes?'

Talking to herself, trying to work it out, she shouted into the gloom, furious with herself for failing to find a way through it all. Why had there been no mention of her daughter? The last time she spoke to Mounsey he said he feared Kathy might be one of Myra and Ian's victims – in the same way that Manchester Police suspected Pauline Reade and Keith Bennett were also their victims – especially as Connie had found Kathy's doll in the glove box of Myra's car. But until they confessed, or the police found her body, no one could be sure.

If only she could get to Myra. Talk to her. Make her tell her what she'd done. They used to tell each other everything when they were kids, but the distance that had grown between them, especially after Myra met Ian Brady, had widened like the universe. A recollection of her school friend's hooded grey eyes and the coldness she often found there. Another of the time Myra had smiled when Ian seized Connie by the throat and nearly strangled the life out of her. She blinked them away, refusing to give her doubts the chance to form. Myra was capable of love and kindness. She had shown it to friends, to family. But she could also be cruel, she reminded herself. Look how she'd behaved when Kathy first went missing. The heartless comments, her lack of sympathy... the fact she could kick a pigeon to death. But killing pigeons and saying unkind things didn't mean you were capable of the sadistic murder of children. Nothing made sense. The crimes Myra and Ian were being accused of were impossible to understand. But this was as it should be. If such atrocities could be understood, then it meant they could be explained... and if they could be explained, then they could be explained away. And that would be wrong. But there was another fact in all this that bothered her, and it was that Myra and Ian looked no different to the rest of society. They had their likes and dislikes, their strengths and weaknesses like everyone else. But, Connie supposed, shivering a little, what set those two apart were the choices they made. And their first choice had been each other.

'Connie?' Fred came to find her, a cup of tea in hand. 'Are you okay? Your eyes look all funny. Are you still taking them tablets?'

She turned away from him. 'Don't start, Fred. I've told you; until they find Kathy and bring her home, I can't cope without them.'

'I'm worried about you, that's all.'

'I'd be more of a worry to you if I didn't have them, trust me. I'd have bloody killed myself by now.' She gathered the photographs together and closed the lid of the box. 'D'you think Dave knows more than he's telling?'

'He's helping the police all he can.'

'Yeah? Then why's no one saying owt about Kathy? I know she's mixed up in this somewhere, Fred. I know it.'

'Without Dave, those murdering scumbags would still be doing it. He's not a villain, Con, he's a hero. They could just as easily have killed him.'

'Hero?' she snapped. 'Don't give me that. Get him to tell you what they did to Kathy. To Pauline and little Keith Bennett. Are they on the moors too?'

'It's Ian that needs to start bloody talking. Bastard's saying nowt.'

'Tell them to put a spider in his cell.'

'And take that bloody dog off Myra – Dave says she's in it up to her neck, but she ain't saying owt neither.'

'She's my friend, Fred.' Connie knotted the cord on her dressing gown. 'I've known her since I were a baby.'

A small nod. 'But police have got photos. They've got a tape of that little girl, crying and pleading for her mammy... begging for mercy. Myra's voice is on it, Con.' He took her by the shoulders, looked her in the eye. 'A little girl being asked to do unspeakable things for a man by a woman. That Brady bastard and your fuckin' friend Myra tortured and killed her.'

'It don't mean it were Myra's voice on that thing. It could've been anyone. The police could've got it wrong.'

She remembered the tape-recording machine Myra said she'd bought Ian for Christmas. Was that what they used to record what they did to those poor little children? Did they tape what they did to Kathy? No wonder Ian went berserk when she nearly stepped into his darkroom. He must have been hiding incriminating photographs in there.

Connie gave Fred a kiss and wandered back with him to the living room. She looked out of the balcony window in time to see Maureen and Dave getting out of a police car looking like American movie stars in dark sunglasses and winter coats. The journalists she'd seen lurking outside converged, elbowing and jostling. Dave and Maureen were caught in the frenzied eye of a public storm.

'They're back. I've got to talk to him, I've got to ask him about Kathy.'

'Leave it, Con, they've suffered enough.'

'No, I won't. Why do the police talk like he's a murderer? He bloody well knows and I'm going to get it out of him.'

'Dave's a good bloke, you've got him wrong. Myra and Ian are only sayin' what they're sayin' to lessen their sentences. Taking revenge for him grassing them up.'

'But Myra said Dave were involved. That he killed Edward Evans. She wouldn't say that if it weren't true.'

'You just don't get it, do you? Myra's evil, Connie. She's fooled us all.' Fred sucked on his roll-up. 'You can't trust a damn thing that witch says. She's involved, Con. As well as that tape recording, they've found evidence in some suitcases of theirs in left luggage at Manchester Central.'

'The railway station?' Connie thought of that night with Myra. Sitting in the car, waiting for Ian. The night he nearly throttled her.

When she looked back at Fred, he was staring down at his pointy shoes. 'You don't think they took Kathy, do you?' he spoke at last. 'They left the Waggon and Horses before us that day, didn't they? And Myra were the one who said she found Kathy's doll, don't forget. What were that all about? Her saying she didn't recognise it. Huh, I never believed her.'

Connie said nothing. The cogs of her mind turning, straining under the weight of her thoughts. Fred wasn't telling her anything new. She was about to speak when he added, 'I know you don't wanna think that about Myra. I know she's your friend, but Kathy knew her, didn't she? She'd have gone to her easily, trusted her. It's why she were useful to Brady; she lured those kiddies in... probably held 'em down for him when they were frantic with fear and trying to wriggle free...'

'Shut up! Shut up!' Connie shrieked and put her hands over her ears. 'I can't do this no more, Fred. I can't! I can't!'

The atmosphere inside the flat was stifling. When Fred went to bed, Connie sat on her own in the dark. Half an hour ticked by in the silence before she got to her feet and pulled on her skirt and buttoned her cardigan over her nightdress. She pushed her bare feet into her shoes and secured a scarf over her hair.

She had to get out. She needed some air. In those early

weeks when Kathy first disappeared, she would sometimes do this: roam the estate with the stray cats and dogs. Pounding the darkened streets until she gave herself blisters. Fred was right; her daughter would have willingly gone with Myra. She pressed a hand to her churning insides. Whoever Myra was, or Connie thought she was, had long gone. Replaced by some evil-doer with a leaden heart.

Connie summoned the lift that was working for a change and, waiting for it, she heard shouting coming from inside the flat opposite. Maureen and Dave were arguing again. Then Maureen appeared, slamming the door of her flat behind her.

'Are you all right, Mo?' It wasn't the question she had wanted to ask, but seeing the woman's lank, unwashed hair, her crumpled clothes, she changed her mind. Maureen, jittery, her nails bitten to the quick, looked way older than her nineteen years. Fred was right; they had suffered enough. Connie worried for Maureen and her unborn baby. The insurmountable stress she was living under couldn't be doing her any good.

'Hello, Connie.'

'I see it's your turn now.' She pointed to the graffiti on Maureen's door. The words, 'Hindley bitch', scrawled in red. She didn't get an answer, and Connie wished she hadn't mentioned it. 'Where are you going?'

'Got to ring Mam. If she'll speak to me. She's sayin' me and Dave have thrown Myra to the wolves.'

'By speaking the truth?'

A feeble nod.

'They saying owt about my Kathy?'

Maureen shook her head. 'Not sayin' much. Apart from trying to pin it on Dave.'

Emerging on the ground floor and momentarily trapped with the sharp tang of urine, they walked out into the estate together. It seemed as if the press had gone home for the night, but a woman Connie didn't recognise, loitering around the entrance to Underwood Court, charged over and spat at Maureen.

'You evil Hindley bitch. I hope when you have your baby it gets killed and buried on moor like those other kiddies.'

'You ignorant cow,' Connie shouted as she shielded Maureen, who was no bigger than a teenage girl. 'This has nowt to do with Maureen. It's not her fault she's Myra's sister... it's not her fault Myra's done what she's done.'

'Bah, don't give me that. She's that monster's sister, ain't she? They've the same evil blood.' The eyes were indignant, ablaze with hate. 'If it were up to me, I'd hang the flamin' lot of 'em.' The woman stomped away.

As Maureen wiped the spittle off her coat, her nose had begun to bleed and Connie, noticing this, dug around in her pockets and passed her a handkerchief with an apology about it not being clean.

'Thanks for being such a good mate.' Maureen hugged her. At this show of friendship, Connie's eyes filled with tears. 'Me and Dave don't have any mates left.'

'You can't let that sister of yours ruin your life, too. This isn't your fault, Mo. They're only having a go at you and Dave because they can't get at Myra and Ian. God, people are such vicious bastards.' She cast around for the woman who'd abused Maureen, fearful she could be waiting in the wings to have another go. 'They were the same with me and Fred. Any excuse, and your sister's given it to them in spades.'

Once she had seen Maureen safely inside the phone box and checked she didn't want her to hang around, Connie left her to it.

The night was clear and salted with stars. She looked up to where a full round moon hung in the night sky. She wandered, aimless, with no idea where she was heading. Then, as if she had been pulled towards it by an invisible thread, she found herself in Wardle Brook Avenue. Staring at the front door of number sixteen.

The house lay in pitch darkness. Each and every window was smashed and the curtains billowed in the wind that, whispering down from the moor, blew through its still and silent rooms.

54

Tuesday, 26 October 1965

Black Fell Farm, Saddleworth Moor, West Riding of Yorkshire

Cold water droplets dripped down inside Ronald's collar as he descended the hill to the farm through the rain. He was within reach of the yard and was about to open the gate when the call of a curlew made him look up. Following the arc of sound: haunting, hollow, he held his breath to it until the wind reclaimed it. A pair of them, flapping over the sky. He'd not seen curlews for a while. There were certainly fewer around than when he was a boy, and the sight of them cheered him more than he already was.

Whistling as he removed his oilskins and boots, he strode into the kitchen and found his brother chopping carrots, potatoes and onions that he'd pulled from his vegetable patch that morning.

'Mm, something smells good.' Ronald licked his lips.

'Tom's making us a... a nice hearty meal.' The child, seated at the end of the table with her doll and her colouring pad and crayons, tiptoed over the words his brother must have given her. 'It's for when Gran comes.'

'That's right, sweetheart. Thanks to the super stewing steak our Ronnie fetched from the butcher.' Thomas dried his hands on his apron and turned to face him. 'So, erm,' he wavered as if frightened of the answer, 'you been able to show 'em where you found that shoe?'

'Aye. No problem.' Ronald nodded, wiping a drop of rain-water from his chin. 'It seems as if they're having to call off the search. Think the weather's beaten them.'

'Really? That's a relief.'

'It is, aye.' He smiled and wandered over to the child. 'You've been busy, lass.'

'Oh, she has. Show Ronnie what you've made your gran.'

'I've done this... and this.' The child put a hand to the page of her colouring book and turned it for him to see.

'Clever girl.' Ronald ruffled her curls and made a show of admiring the rainbow colours and the word 'WELCOME' written in neat letters over the semicircle. 'She'll love them.'

'What time are you fetching her?'

'I'll just smarten myself up, then I'll be off.'

'Everything's ready here. I've made up a bed downstairs.'

'You've worked hard. Place is gleaming.' Ronald looked around him, appreciating the newly blackened stove, the freshly mopped floor.

'It's been many a moon since Pamela were in this house.' Thomas had returned to his chopping.

'Well, she'll be convalescing for a good while. We'll get her up on her feet, and then who knows, with any luck, she might want to stay longer.'

'You've certainly got my blessing, Ron. I hope you've told her that?'

''Course, I have, Tom.' He smiled again. 'If she thought

there'd be any awkwardness, I'd never have persuaded her to come.'

'I doubt she'll notice much has changed.'

'Aye, but for the fact her granddaughter's living here.'

'You decided what we're going to do? It's going to be one hell of a surprise.'

'I think shock would be closer to the truth.'

'You can tell her it were all my doing.' Thomas glanced at the child. 'Say that I were the one who wouldn't give her up.'

'I couldn't do that, Tom. Look, it's just something we'll have to get through. Let's just pray we can make her understand.' *Not that I fully understand it myself.* 'Hopefully, the relief of Kathy being with us and seeing she's safe and happy will be enough. But if it's not, then we'll cross that bridge when we have to.'

A sudden banging on the front door severed their conversation. The brothers looked at one another.

'Who's that?'

'No idea. But you'd better nip upstairs with the child, Tom. Stay with her, I'll see to whoever this is.'

More banging.

'All right. All right.' Ronald, about to open up, had spotted the crayons and drawing pad. The child had taken her doll. 'Tom? Tom?' he hissed, beckoning his brother. 'Quick! Take her colouring stuff with you.'

He waited until Thomas and the child had disappeared upstairs before opening the door. It wasn't all that much of a surprise to see – because of the vast numbers of them that had been swarming the moors for the past month – the two uniformed police officers standing in the porch.

'Mr Cappleman?' asked the burlier and older of the two, grim authority etched on his hard face.

'Aye.'

Ronald didn't hear the words the officer spoke next; they

were merely muffled sounds on his periphery. His attention was drawn to the other younger officer, or more specifically, to what he was holding in his gloved open palm.

He recognised it at once. Although it no longer shone gold, but was now darkly smeared, its chain knotted with mud. Ronald knew for certain, if only by the fact that these police officers were standing at his door, that the inscription on the inside casing was untainted and fully legible despite it having been buried for more than twenty-four years on the slowly rotting body of his father.

55

THREE YEARS LATER

Saturday, 19 October 1968

Hathersage Road, Rusholme, Manchester

The autumn sunshine broke through the wadding of cloud. It splintered the windscreen and made Ronald blink.

'Would you credit it?' Pamela licked a finger and turned the pages of her newspaper. 'There's some toff bloke, some lord or other... he's trying to get Myra released from prison.'

'*Released?*' Ronald touched the knot of his tie and frowned. 'Surely not?'

'It's what it says here. Not that I'm surprised, she were always good at hoodwinking people. She did it to our Connie enough... bloody evil bitch. Oops, sorry, Kathy. You didn't hear your naughty gran saying bad words, did you?'

'No, Gran.' Kathy, on the truck's back seats, was engrossed in the copy of *Bunty* Ronald had bought her.

'You just can't believe some people. The fool's claiming she's changed, found God again, apparently. Bet he wouldn't be saying that if she'd murdered one of *his* kiddies. Flamin' do-gooders.' Pamela folded the newspaper away into her handbag.

'Whoever it is wants to talk to the victims' parents – there'll never be an end to suffering for them. Pauleen Reade and that little Keith Bennett... they won't even tell them where their bodies are buried.'

'They haven't even admitted to killing them,' Pamela added. 'Even though everyone knows they did.'

'Exactly. And imagine what it's like for their families to hear someone's trying to get that monster parole? Never mind the families of Edward Evans, Lesley Ann Downey and John Kilbride. It's disgusting.' Ronald changed down a gear to accommodate the sharp bend into town. 'Hell of a shame the death penalty had just been repealed. There wouldn't be any question of her getting out. Pair of them would have had their just desserts.'

'Oh, I know,' Pamela sighed. 'And to think how frightened we were that our Kathy were another of their victims.'

'What was I? Another of their what?' Kathy chirruped from the back seats again.

'Nowt for your little ears, madam.'

'All right, Gran.' Kathy was happy to return to her comic and the story of the four Marys.

'Oh, Ron, I don't think I'll ever forget the relief of finding her safe with you and Tommy.'

'I don't think I'll ever forget it, neither.' A dry chuckle. 'I were dreading what you'd do. You and Connie. It were astonishing that Kathy ended up coming to the farm in the first place, but then the situation just snowballed out of control. You know what Tom can be like? He were that taken with her. I did try, loads of times, to get him to give her up. I were desperate to do the right thing. It were awful, Pam, I were torn between you and Tom. Honestly, I still feel bad about it.'

'I know you do, Ronnie.' Pamela put a reassuring hand on

his thigh. 'It were a terrible few weeks, thinking something bad had happened to her. But when I found her looking so well and settled up at your farm, it just took all the recriminations away.'

'You were ever so good about it.' Ronald slid his gaze to hers for a heartbeat, then returned his concentration to the road. 'I still can't believe how understanding you were.'

'I could see the dilemma you were in, Ron. Rock and a hard place, I'd say. But Kathy were so happy. I hardly recognised her; she were like a different child and she made it perfectly clear to me she didn't want to go home to her mam, so that must've made things even harder for you. And, well, she were your granddaughter, too. Strange, though, and I've often thought it, but if she hadn't gone missing, you and me would never have met. I hadn't been to Ashton for years, and wouldn't have gone that day had I not been handing out leaflets.'

'The whole thing were a fluke, Pam. From the moment Kathy got into the back of that van with those lambs... Police were none too happy, though, were they?' Ronald pulled a face, remembering the trouble.

'No, they weren't. It were a close call whether they were going to charge you and Tommy. But me and Connie, we didn't want that.'

'We were lucky you were both so understanding. Honestly, Pam, I really were expecting some kind of reprisal. But it were so difficult... worse, you know, the longer time went on.'

'No need to fret about it no more, Ronnie. All's well that ends well.' Pamela squeezed his leg.

'Aye. And it has all ended well, hasn't it?' Ronald smiled as he pressed his foot to the brake and indicated left into St Mary's Hospital car park.

———

'Eight pound, two ounces. A real little heavyweight.'

'You're telling me, I was the one who give birth.' Connie, propped up on two blue hospital pillows, beamed with joy at the little gurgling bundle in her arms.

'My baby brother.' Kathy, brimming with excitement, sat on the bed and wriggled up next to her mother.

'He is, darling. And have you decided on a name for him yet?'

'What? I can choose what we call him?' More wriggling.

'You can do owt you want, my little princess.' Connie leant sideways and kissed the top of her daughter's head, smelling the Vosene-clean scent of her hair.

'I'm gonna look after him. I promise I will. Can I take him to school with me, Mam? Show him off to all me friends?'

Pamela and Ronald laughed at this.

'He's a bit little at moment, Kathy. Perhaps when he's bigger?' Fred, the proud father, was seated in a chair beside Connie's bed.

'Tommy sends his love. He baked you these, 'cos Pam told him you were partial.' Ronald showed Connie the greaseproof parcel of Eccles cakes, then handed them to Fred to put down on the bedside cabinet.

'That's so kind. Thank him for me, won't you?' Connie beaming. 'Oh, Kathy, I bet you're having fun up at the farm with Gran and Grandad, aren't you?'

'I love Tommy's cooking best.'

'I bet.'

'We're going to see elephants now, aren't we, Grandad?'

'Are you? You're going all the way to Belle Vue now? Isn't it a bit late?'

'No, we've plenty of time, lass.'

'What time is it, anyway? I don't even know what day it is, never mind the time since I had this little one.' Connie rocked her baby son in her arms.

Since being with Pamela, Ronald always dressed smartly

REBECCA GRIFFITHS

when he was away from the farm, and he dipped a hand into the pocket of his suit and pulled out the gold fob watch. Shiny now and a real testament to Swiss engineering in that it never lost a second. It had been kind of the police to return it to him after finding it on the moor. It must have detached itself from its host – the tweed waistcoat perishing under the peat after nearly a quarter of a century – and worked its way to the surface.

'Aye, we've plenty of time.' Ronald gave Kathy a wink. 'We've all the time in the world.'

A LETTER FROM REBECCA

Thank you for reading *The Hidden Child*, I do hope you enjoyed it as much as I enjoyed writing it. If you would like to be kept up to date with my latest releases, just sign up at the following link. Your email address will never be shared and you can unsubscribe at any time.

www.bookouture.com/rebecca-griffiths

I have to say that I really love hearing from readers, it is one of the most pleasurable and rewarding parts about writing for me. So please do get in touch either through Facebook or Twitter and let me know how this book made you feel and what you thought of the characters.

If you did enjoy *The Hidden Child*, I would be grateful if you could find the time to give it a rating and leave a short review. You wouldn't believe how much this helps to spread the word about a book and encourages others to pick it up and read it.

Thank you and happy reading!

Rebecca x

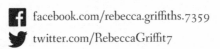

facebook.com/rebecca.griffiths.7359
twitter.com/RebeccaGriffit7

ACKNOWLEDGEMENTS

Special thanks must go to my lovely agent Broo Doherty for her guidance and enthusiasm. There are so many people at Bookouture for whose knowledge and dedication I am grateful too, particularly Laura Deacon, my wonderful editor, for her expertise and valuable advice, Noelle Holten and Kim Nash for promoting and marketing my books, Alexandra Holmes for ensuring the smooth running of the publication, and Alba Proko for managing the terrific audio production.

Thanks must also go to my trusty reader. The top book blogger and reviewer, Jo Robertson and her fabulous blog site: mychestnutreadingtree.wordpress.com.

But most of all my thanks must go to my husband, Steven, for his indomitable belief, love and creative inspiration.

Made in United States
Orlando, FL
15 June 2022

18834359R00214